Barely Home
Back to the Hills

By

Adam Lawler

Barely Home
Back to the Hills

ByAdam Lawler

Copyright 2015 by Adam Lawler
Published by Adam Lawler
West Jefferson North Carolina

Cover Design by Paula Knorr

4

Acknowledgements

Although an author can develop a story and characters, no writer can compose a 100,000-word novel without a little help from his friends. As such, I want to take a few lines and thank some of the people instrumental in making *Barely Home: Back to the Hills* a reality.

First, I want to thank Phyllis Efford. Phyllis took hours of her time and used her professional skills to pour over page after page of manuscript, correcting typos, misspellings, improper punctuation and many other errors that I missed as I read through the rough draft. Phyllis, thank you for taking the time to teach me things that I either did not learn in English class or forgot many years ago.

I also want to thank my beta readers, Cynthia Lawler, and Judy Harris. These women were brave enough to read the unfinished, unedited manuscript of this novel and offer their critique of it, making observations and suggestions that led to its final outcome. Thank you, ladies, for all of your support.

I also want to thank all the readers of the first novel in this series, *Barely Retired*, who encouraged me and provided feedback on my first serious attempt at writing a novel. I am especially thankful for those of you who shared the book on social media and left reviews on various websites, without your help and encouragement, Carter and Connie Sykes would have never gained an audience, and there would have been no need to continue to tell their story.

Finally, I want to thank my wife, Karen Lawler. Besides being my first beta reader, Karen has the toughest job of anyone involved in this project; she has to live with me on a daily basis. I have been known to be a bit obsessive-compulsive about my writing, sometimes being unable to separate the world and characters of my imagination from those of reality. Karen puts up with me when I neglect her in order to work on the book, and supports me even when I ruin a special evening together because I can't talk about anything besides a scene in the story. Thank you, Babydoll, for loving me despite my faults, and for understanding my need to tell this story. Your support makes the whole process possible.

Preface

Barely Home: Back to the Hills is a work of fiction. The plot and all the characters are products of my imagination. Any resemblance to any person, living or dead, or any event, past, present, or future, is purely coincidental.

That said, every writer's imagination is influenced by events and people he encounters. It is often true, truth is stranger than fiction. In places where real people or events form the basis of a character or scene in *Barely Home*, I took great care to assure the created characters or events varied significantly from those in real life that spawned the idea in my mind.

When dealing with small towns, many writers of fiction choose to give the towns fictitious names. I did this in *Barely Retired*, setting the story in the fanciful town of Herbsville, South Carolina, a place you won't find on a map. There are several good reasons for doing so. However, for *Barely Home* I chose to place the action in real towns. I did this for a number of reasons, perhaps the most important being that in *Barely Retired*, I established that Carter Sykes was a native of Haysi, Virginia. Therefore, in deciding to write a sequel about him coming back home, I had to have him and Connie return to Haysi in order to keep the two stories aligned.

While I did use real place names, I made every effort to assure I did not use real names of businesses or streets, except for the major highways in the area. There were, however, a couple of places where using actual locations necessitated that I use real names of organizations and agencies. Perhaps the most notable is the use of the Dickenson County Sheriff's Department as the main law enforcement agency. Since every county has a Sheriff's Department, and the story is set in Dickenson County, it would be silly to give the department any other name. As such, the Dickenson County Sheriff's Department became a corporate character in the story, as did a couple of other governmental and quasi-governmental agencies.

Because of the role the Dickenson County Sheriff's Department plays in the story, I want to take a few lines to make sure the reader understands that the Dickenson County Sheriff's Department portrayed in this story is also fictitious. It is my sincere belief that the real-life Dickenson County Sheriff's Department is truly a professional organization, and the men and women who make it up are fine, upstanding citizens and law enforcement officers. Nothing in this novel should be seen as inferring anything to the contrary about the real-life heroes who put their lives on the line each day to keep the community safe.

One

The old timers in Upper East Tennessee said it was the coldest winter they had ever seen. By Thanksgiving, temperatures settled into a below normal pattern. By Christmas, a succession of arctic fronts kept the Volunteer State plunged into the deep freeze. The new year started with two new record lows, and Kingsport, Tennessee, saw the calendar reach its second week before the ambient air temperature finally climbed above the freezing mark.

People could not say that Mother Nature had not given them fair warning. As winter approached, scientific meteorologists kept babbling about things like El Nino, La Nina, and the Trans-Atlantic something another, and how they pointed to this being a mild winter. In the meantime, prognosticators who used more traditional, time-proven methods to predict the weather kept commenting about how every sign they saw pointed to a tough winter. Most of the wooly worms they saw were solid black, the fall's corn shucks were unusually thick, and squirrels seemed to be hoarding acorns like they suffered from an obsessive-compulsive disorder. Some even pointed out that nearly every morning in August saw fog as thick as pea soup. Even the *Old Farmer's Almanac* had called for a rough winter.

For a while, Carter Sykes enjoyed the cold, and the white stuff that came along with it. While none of the snowfalls were exceptionally deep, they gave him a chance to put the four-wheel drive system of his dark blue, HEMI powered Ram 2500 to work. He threw a chain in the bed, and on more than one occasion, he and his wife, Connie, pulled motorists who had slid into a ditch or simply got stuck in a snowdrift, to safety. Carter imagined his Ram liked the work, and felt that, somehow, the truck gained a satisfaction out of helping people who got themselves into trouble. When he would start mumbling such nonsense, Connie would tell him he was crazy, that trucks were inanimate objects and didn't have feelings of pride. But Carter simply patted the Ram on its fender, above the headlight, and told it he knew better and that he was proud of the work it performed. He reminded the truck that it was HIS truck, and not to listen to Connie's disbelief. He reasoned that since he had spent thirty years serving the residents of Kingsport, he knew his truck got satisfaction in doing the same.

But by the end of January, even Carter Sykes was tired of the cold. A six-inch snow forced him and Connie to cancel a trip they planned to take. The plan was to take their Coachmen fifth wheel and join up with their friends Gil and Mary Ann for a mid-winter getaway to South Florida. Connie, in particular, was looking forward to spending lots of time at Haulover Beach, where she and Mary Ann could once again feel the warm rays of the sun caress their naked bodies and provide them with all-over tans, while they each sipped on a frozen tropical concoction. Gil promised he and Carter would hook up with one of his old Navy buddies and spend a day aboard his old pal's charter boat, fishing off the Florida coast.

Carter was ready for some fishing. He promised himself when he retired, he and Connie would spend more time at the coast in their Coachmen. He planned to spend many summer days on the water with a pole in one hand and an ice-cold beer in the other. But the events of last summer prevented them from taking their usual beach trips. On their first adventure as a retired couple, they stumbled across a murder while visiting the Utopia Sun Club, a nudist park in eastern South Carolina. The discovery of the murder, and the local sheriff's need for their help in solving it, put an end to those plans, at least for last year. Not that Carter was complaining. Both he and Connie thoroughly enjoyed the adventure of their first visit to a nudist camp. And solving the murder of the resort's general manager, Doug Westlake, turned out to be more action-packed than any case he ever worked while a detective with the Kingsport Police Department. It was a thrill to have Connie as his crime-solving partner, and she impressed him with her instincts and resourcefulness. Working the Westlake case allowed him to see a part of her that had escaped him over their thirty plus years together. He knew he loved her before that trip, but he loved her even more now.

One thing Carter missed this winter was playing with his dog, Thor. Carter and Connie were never able to have children, but over the last few years, Thor became as close to a grandchild as they would ever know. Carter loved that dog—loved watching the big, goofy lab mix run through the snow, trying to catch flakes on his tongue as they fell, or simply rolling around in the powder, like it felt good against his fur. He laughed when Thor would run into the house and head straight for Connie's lap, to her chagrin plopping his wet body right on top of her. She would act upset, and in the heat of the moment she probably was, but Carter knew she loved that dog and the way he doted over her. In fact, it was his love for Connie that cost Thor his life. During the Westlake case, Thor was murdered trying to protect her when the two of them were kidnapped.

10

Today, however, Carter was sick of the cold and the snow. He stared out his living room window, looking alternately at the gray sky and the thermometer, wishing for blue skies and rising mercury. He was ready to go somewhere, anywhere. He was ready for a new adventure. He and Connie hadn't retired to stay home and grow old together. They retired to travel, to have new experiences together. He liked to quote Gene Roddenberry; they wanted to explore strange new worlds, to seek out new life and new civilizations. They wanted to boldly go where no retired couple had gone before. The coldest winter of their lives wasn't helping them fulfill their quest.

TWO

The weather pattern that brought the cold winter to Upper East Tennessee finally shifted, allowing spring to thrust its way into the Tri Cities. The arrival of short sleeve weather seemed to trigger a primal instinct within both Carter and Connie to begin planning their next trip in the Coachmen. On the official first day of spring, Connie, pen and pad in hand, sat Carter down at the kitchen table to begin planning their next adventure. Her goal was to leave right after dropping their Federal income tax return in the mail, a reward for completing a despicable chore. Connie was glad Tennessee didn't have an income tax; filling out her and Carter's Federal return was bad enough.

Looking across the table at each other, neither of them had to speak for each of them to understand that this trip would not be to a nudist park. They had thoroughly enjoyed their time at Utopia, but even running around naked as jaybirds in the warm sun had its limits. Something inside each of them whispered that they would someday return to a nudist place, but this time their trip would be a more conventional one.

"We could always head to Morehead," Carter suggested, referring to Morehead City, North Carolina, one of their favorite vacation spots. Carter and Connie had spent many vacations at Morehead City, with Carter fishing from the surf, the pier, and a local charter, while Connie enjoyed the beach and the local flavor of both the Bogue Banks and the Beaufort waterfront.

"I don't know, sweetie. mid-April can still be cool down there. If we're going to make a beach trip, I want to do it when I know it'll be warm. I want to lay on the beach, read a book, and work on a tan on at least most of my body. I think I'd rather save Morehead for summer."

"Well, give me some ideas, then. Gatlinburg? Nashville? Branson?"

"Why don't we stay close to home for our first trip of the year? It'll give us a chance to work out any kinks the cold weather may have caused in the Coachmen. I'm sure we'll have a longer trip later."

"Yeah, it would be nice not to have to make such a long drive," he paused. "I can't believe I'm actually saying that. I must be getting old."

"You know," Connie thought aloud, "I've been wanting to spend a little time with our parents. They're not getting any younger."

"But you know I can only handle so much time around your dad. Hell, I'm fifty-four years old and he still looks at me as that dirt-poor college kid I was when we first started dating."

"I still look at you like you're that young, sexy college kid too, sweetie," Connie said seductively, reaching across the table and touching Carter's hand.

Carter grinned. "You're even prettier than that high class girl I fell in love with."

"Hey, I wasn't high class." She always objected when he referred to her as with that term.

"You had an indoor toilet. You're last name might as well have been Rockefeller," Carter said, reminding her that even though they grew up only one county apart, economically they were raised in different worlds.

"Why don't we take a couple of weeks or so and go visit both our parents?" Connie tried to get the conversation back on track. "I've got it. We can spend a week at the Breaks and visit your family, then spend another week at Natural Tunnel State Park and visit mine. We won't be imposing on anyone, since we'll have our camper. You'll even have a place to hide from dad."

Carter rubbed hand across his face as he often did when contemplating. He liked the Breaks. It was only ten miles from Haysi, Virginia, where he grew up and his mother still lived. He knew he would enjoy that trip. He was also okay with Natural Tunnel. They had stayed there a couple of times for weekend getaways over the years. It was a quick, easy drive to Connie's hometown of Big Stone Gap, Virginia. "That might not be an idea," he said. "Natural Tunnel might be far enough from your dad that we can actually get along."

"I'll tell him you said that." She smiled at him and patted his hand. He may be seventy-five, but he can still kick your ass."

"He probably can. He's that stubborn."

Connie reached up and gave Carter a playful slap across the temple. "It sounds like a good plan to me, sweetie."

"It actually sounds pretty good to me, too. We can even visit Clinch Valley and take a walk down memory lane. Wouldn't you like to visit the spot where we fist kissed?"

She smiled at him. "And the spot that we first...," her eyes met his, flashes of their first time making love with each other flashing across their thoughts. After a few seconds, Connie's thoughts returned to the present.

"It's UVA–Wise now. I think they tore down that dorm where I first seduced you,"

"Just standing on that spot would bring goose bumps." An evil grin crossed Carter's face. "It might even cause something else."

"I'll call mom and see which week works best for her and dad. Then we can decide if we want to go to the Breaks to see your mom before or after that."

"Sounds good to me babe," Carter said, raising his glass in a toast. "Another decision accomplished. Here's to our next trip."

Connie touched her glass to his. "On the road again," she sang.

****

The next day, Connie called her mother to discuss their plans with her. Violet and Hal Brown had arranged to make a trip to the Kentucky Derby May first through the seventh. After some discussion, Connie and her mom determined it was best for Carter and Connie to visit after they returned from Churchill Downs. That worked well for Connie. She and Carter could spend a week, maybe a little longer, in the Breaks, and then migrate to Natural Tunnel, leaving them a short drive back to Kingsport when their visiting tour was complete.

"It will be good to see you again, honey. It seems like it's been so long since your short visit over Christmas," Violet Brown said.

"Yes mother, it has been. I think Carter's looking forward to seeing you, too."

"I'm sure he is." There was sarcasm in Violet's voice. "You know how well he and your father get along," she laughed.

"Well, they'll both have to promise to be on good behavior while we're visiting. I think they can take each other for short periods of time. We'll be staying in the Coachmen at Natural Tunnel, so they'll have breaks from each other."

"You're not going to stay with us? I figured since you don't have that dog anymore, you'd stay here."

Connie didn't immediately respond to her mother. She thought of her dog, Thor, the black lab mix who was killed last year. Tears came to her eyes as she thought of her beloved pet. Her mom and dad would never let Thor come inside their house, and Carter was not about to leave him outside, a fenced yard or not. The tension over Thor had kept Carter from

15

spending the night at Connie's parent's house for several years. "His name was Thor, mother, and no, this is an RV trip for us. We are going to spend time with both you and dad and with Carter's mother. Being gone for so long, it's just easier for us in the RV."

"I can see why you don't want to stay with Carter's mother in that old shack, but I don't understand why y'all want to spend the night in that camper when we have so much room here. Don't y'all get tired of camping out like a couple of gypsies?"

Connie took a deep breath, letting the sound of silence voice her displeasure with her mother's statement. "Mom, Carter's mother may not have a big fancy house, but that place has been in his family for generations. She wouldn't be happy any other place. And that camper has more amenities than our house does. It's got a fridge, microwave, TV, everything we can ask for. Carter even has his ham radio station set up in the living room."

"Does he still play with that CB stuff?" Violet paused for a moment. "I swear, Connie, y'all will have to grow up someday."

Connie had been down this road with her parents many times before. She knew she was fighting a losing battle, that she and Carter could never do good enough in their eyes. She decided to move the conversation forward. "So, we'll be in to see you on the 8th or 9th then, ok? We're going to be up for about a week, so book some girl time for me and you."

"That sounds great to me, honey. I'm looking forward to seeing you. I'll make some shopping plans for us girls. I love you, Connie."

Connie knew despite their differences in lifestyle, her mother really did love her. And she loved both her mom and her father. She knew if she ever needed them, they would be there for her. "I love you, too, mom. Give dad my love, okay?"

"I will, honey. He'll be so glad to see you. Bye- bye."

"Bye, mother," Connie said, as she hit the end button on her phone.

****

That afternoon, Carter made a similar call to his mother. "Mom, how are you doing?"

"Hi, son. I'm making it, I guess. My arthritis hurts a lot nowadays, but I'm okay. Wish I had someone here to take care of a few things for me."

Carter knew where she was going with this line of conversation. Not long after he and Connie graduated from college and moved to Kingsport, she started hinting that he should move back to the old homeplace. Carter knew she realized there was nothing for them in Haysi, besides her, but she looked at every conversation the two of them had as an opportunity to plant another seed, hoping someday, one would take root and grow, bringing her son back home. Carter knew she was proud of him, proud of Connie, and proud of the life they had made. But he realized, like most parents, she wanted her son to come home. It was something Carter vowed never to do.

"Well, mom, I'm not moving back home, but Connie and I are planning on coming up and spending a week or so at the Breaks next month. We want to spend a lot of time with you, if that's okay."

"Of course it's okay, son. You're always welcome here. I'll make sure your old room is ready for you."

"No, mom. We're going to bring the Coachmen and stay in it at the Breaks." He paused for a moment, but before she had a chance to respond, decided to change the subject. "How's everybody?"

"Did I tell you Andy just lost his job a couple of months ago?"

"Andy lost his job? Carter said with a puzzled look on his face, a picture of his goofy brother-in-law entering his mind. "What happened? I thought things were going good for him and Tanya now. Wasn't he working over at Lowes in Grundy?"

"He was. I'll let him tell you about it when you get up here."

"I can't wait to hear this one," Carter said with a chuckle. He knew the pranks Andy Calhoun had pulled over the years, and something told him this one was a good one. "It'll be good to spend some time with you, mom."

"It'll be good to see you too, son. And I'm looking forward to seeing Connie, too. I always did like her. You know, she's my favorite daughter-in-law. She never was too uppity, despite her raisin'."

Carter's mom always made a point of telling him Connie was her favorite daughter-in-law, despite the fact that Connie was her only daughter-in-law. "She's a good one, mom. I'm lucky to have her, so I guess I'll keep her." He had talked to his mother thousands of times over the years and knew, unless he wanted to get into a deep conversation about all the gossip in Haysi, it was time to get off the phone. "Take care of yourself, Mom. I'll see you in about a month or so, okay?"

"Come on up as soon as you can. I've got a few things I need your help with. Family things."

Carter rolled his eyes, knowing she would want to talk about him and Connie moving back into the homeplace. He decided this phone call wasn't the time for that conversation. "I'll try, Mom. I love you."

"I love you too, son. See you soon. Bye."

Carter ended the call and stuck the phone back in his pocket. He thought back to his mother living in the old house all by herself, with flooring from the sixties and a coal furnace for heat. Or worse yet, her living there with his brother, who Carter was sure would take advantage of her. He and Connie had all but begged her to come live with them in Kingsport several times over the past couple of years, but she always refused. He told her if she didn't want to stay in their house, she could find a place that she could afford on her Social Security and be close to them. He tried reasoning that he'd be close by to help with things she needed. But he knew Haysi was her home, and like most mountain folk, she felt a kindred with the steep, rugged hills. She had made it perfectly clear she was going to stay in that old house until her dying day, warning him he better never do anything against her wishes. 'At least she has family around,' he rationalized, but he always knew she would be better off somewhere more modern. When all was said and done, it was her life, and she was entitled to live it on her own terms. That was, after all, all he had ever asked of her.

****

For nearly a month, Carter spent time prepping the Coachmen for their upcoming trip. He drained the pink antifreeze from the fifth wheel's water lines, hot water heater, and tanks, and made sure there were no leaks. He used the compressor to pump the tires back up to their normal pressure. He checked the lights, both inside and out, the electrical system, the Tarheel antenna, and the TV antenna. He checked the slides, the awing, and the jacks, performing maintenance wherever he deemed necessary, whether the manual called for it or not.

On this trip, Carter paid special attention to the camper's TV antenna. Neither he nor Connie watched a lot of TV; but for Carter, watching broadcast television from the Breaks was more about beating the cable and satellite companies than it was about the shows themselves. As a boy, he was furious he couldn't watch shows the kids in town could, because the cable company wouldn't run lines to his house. For Carter, refusing to pay for television was his way of getting even, especially when he could find ways to pick up the programs for free.

The day before tax day, Carter announced the Coachmen fit for the season, and departed for the Dodge dealership to have the Ram serviced. He returned to find Connie at her desk, leaned back in her chair, staring at her computer screen. "Taking a break, babe?" he asked her.

She smiled at him. "Nope, I'm done with these damn things," she announced, picking a set of papers off her printer and holding them up for his inspection, knowing he'd never look at them. "I'll tell you what, taxes and retirement are a pain in the ass."

Carter laughed. "Not when you have a sexy woman to take care of them for you." He walked over and gave her a hug, and received a slap on the rear end for his comment.

"I'd make you go mail them if I hadn't already e-filed them."

"How'd we do?"

"Not bad," she said, and then a grin appeared on her face. "I claimed the dollar we each got for income from the Westlake case."

"You did what?"

"I claimed the dollar we each made from the Westlake case." She paused. "Then I deducted all the expenses from that case."

Carter thought for a moment, proud of his wife's ingenuity. "Even that god damn haircut, I hope," he muttered.

"Even that haircut, sweetie," she chuckled. "But it did look pretty good on Marty Calloway."

Carter thought back to last summer's Westlake case and their undercover episode as Marty and Debbie Calloway, wealthy coal mine operators. "Hey, at least I did get a wealthy man's tax deductions for a change."

"Hey Marty, I wouldn't let you down," Connie joked. "I know you didn't like spending all that money."

"I never said I minded being a multi-millionaire mine operator. I'm just glad to get some of the money we spent acting like one off our taxes."

"I did like the way those designer underwear looked on you, too," she teased.

"I liked the way you took them off of me," Carter laughed, thinking back to their adventure with the Carolina Couples, a swingers club they infiltrated while solving the case. "And what that led to."

Connie slapped his rear again. "Pervert."

****

The next day, taxes completed, Carter and Connie got an early start, pulling out of their driveway about seven, planning to stop at Shoney's in Abingdon, Virginia, to take advantage of the all-you-can-eat breakfast buffet. Connie had worked hard over the winter to make Carter eat better, but relented to his request for a day to splurge on eggs, sausage, bacon, gravy, and biscuits. Truth be known, she enjoyed eating cholesterol dripping food every now and then herself, just not everyday like Carter did.

An hour after leaving Abingdon, the Ram succeeded in pulling the Coachmen over Dante Mountain and through the old, run-down coal camp town of Trammell, Virginia. Connie thought the producers of *The Hunger Games* should have used Trammell as the backdrop for District 12, the impoverished home of Katniss Everdeen. Nearly another hour, and what seemed like thousands of curves, passed before they reached the entrance of the Breaks Interstate Park, a beautiful park built around a magnificent gorge on the Virginia-Kentucky border. While in the park, Connie was never quite sure which state she was in, and always claimed to be in the one that best suited her needs.

The afternoon was cool, even by mid–April standards in central Appalachia, with a drizzle falling, adding dreariness to the day. The Sykeses donned their rain jackets and went to work setting up for their two week stay. Carter unhooked the fifth wheel from the Ram and lowered the stabilizer jacks. Connie hooked up the power and slid out the slides, providing ample living space for the two of them. Carter hooked up the sewer; Connie was a tough girl, but there were some things she just wasn't going to do. Like a well-oiled team, they had the Coachmen set up in a tick over an hour.

"A chicken wrap okay for lunch, sweetie?" Connie asked, opening the fridge.

"How 'bout we go to Fred's for some hillbilly fried chicken?" Carter looked at her and smiled at the thought of the nearly forgotten taste as he reached over his head and turned the handle to raise the TV antenna.

"I don't think so, dear." She laid the wrap fixins on the covered stovetop. "A wrap will do you just fine after that big breakfast." She glanced at him turning the antenna's handle. "Think you'll pick up anything here this time."

"I think so. Being up high, I hope to get the Charleston and Huntington stations. We'll see here in a minute." As he finished raising the antenna, he

20

turned toward her. "Please tell me you've got some mayonnaise for those wraps."

"After all that junk you ate this morning? You're lucky to be getting anything."

Within minutes, the propane furnace was heating up the camper, and Carter and Connie were sitting in the living room, eating chicken wraps and watching Kentucky PBS on TV. "Can we get anything else?" Connie asked.

"Got a CW channel out of Portsmouth coming in, but Maury's on right now. I think Springer is coming on next. I can turn it there if you want."

"I'll take PBS, thanks. What time is your mom expecting us?"

"She said supper would be at six. I figure we can leave about four-thirty and give her a hand, if that's okay."

"That's fine. This drizzle is making me sleepy. You know what they say; this rain is only good for two things."

"Yeah, sleep and ham radio," Carter laughed as he hit the power button on his Icom 7000 radio. "And I'm not sleepy right now."

Connie shook her head. "Sometimes, I like Marty Calloway better. I can't imagine him saying that," she feigned disgust as she turned toward the three steps leading to the bedroom. "I'm going to take a nap while you tell the world you're out in your camper."

"I might just join you in a little bit," he said, raising his eyebrows seductively.

"I wouldn't count of it. This chickie's going to take a nap. Have fun playing ham radio," she said, looking back over her shoulder, giving him a smile.

****

The Ram slowly rolled down the potholed, one-lane, dirt road leading to the house where Carter Sykes spent most of his teenage years. It always amazed him how close the houses along this road were to each other; his childhood memories tricked him into believing they were farther apart than they actually were. He recognized each one; no one had built a house on this road in forty years. Carter knew everyone in the holler; many of them were cousins he had grown up with, played with, and got into trouble with when he was a kid. Many had taken over the properties from their parents or grandparents who had passed away. Every now and then, when his mother would start bugging him about moving home, he thought he might like to build a nice house and move back here, but each time he drove down this road, he told himself he would never subject his wife, or his Chrysler TC by Maserati, to the punishment of the holler.

After what seemed like endless bouncing around the cab of the three-quarter ton truck, they finally rounded the last curve and, at the end of the holler, the Sykes homeplace came into view. Carter's great grandpa Sykes built the house in the twenties, moving the family out of a nearby coal camp. As a youth, Carter's dad helped build the shed in the backyard. After Carter's father was murdered, and with nowhere else left to go, his mother moved the twelve-year-old Carter and his younger siblings in with his grandparents. When it was built, the white, wood-sided house was average-sized for the region, but over the years, it had seen a couple of additions. The house showed its age; it was now in need of a lot of maintenance and more than a few repairs. The paint was dirty, faded, even peeling in places. The chimney was covered in soot from years of providing the exhaust for the coal furnace. Despite it being late April, the yard had not yet been mowed, and looked more like an early season hayfield than a lawn. Carter knew his younger brother had recently moved back in with his mother, but wasn't surprised he wasn't lifting a hand to help with anything around the house, not even something as simple as mowing the grass.

Carter parked the truck in an empty, sparsely graveled spot beside the house and took a deep breath. For the life of him, he couldn't understand what kept his mother here. He wanted to try once again to talk her into moving to Kingsport. But there was something inside Sylvie Sykes that kept her here, like a serf tied to the land. He and Connie sat silently in the Ram, each collecting their thoughts, before getting out and walking, hand in hand, to the front porch.

"Carter! How's my son?" Sylvie Sykes exclaimed as she pushed open the screen door and rushed out to greet them. The thin, almost frail-looking lady, barely five feet tall, her face showing most of the seventy-five years she had lived in these mountains, wrapped her arms around Carter as he opened his to reciprocate. Connie looked at the mother and son, realizing the strength this small woman possessed was one of the traits in her husband she loved most.

"I'm fine, Mom, how are you?" Carter said, stepping back to take a closer look at his mother. "You look as beautiful as ever."

"Don't bullshit your mama, son, I look as old as these hills." Her attention turned to Connie, who stood a step behind Carter. "And how's my favorite daughter-in-law doing?"

"I m doing well, Mother. Just trying to keep your little boy in line. You know how hard that can be."

"But Carter's always been a good boy. He went off to college and married a fine girl like you."

"Maybe, but I can't get him to eat right. Maybe you should have a talk with him."

"What's he eating? Oh wait, I know. Hardees biscuits and hillbilly fried chicken."

"That's all I hear from him."

Sylvie shook her finger at Carter.

"What? I like what I like, Mom. I can't help it if everything I like is bad for me."

"Listen to your wife, Carter. She is a nurse, and I'm hereby putting her in charge of your eating habits."

Connie smiled at Sylvie's admonishment to her husband. "You hear that don't you Carter??

"Where's Ben?" Carter asked, not really caring where his brother was, just wanting to change the subject. It had been five years since he had seen him, and as far as Carter was concerned, another five years could go by. Ben had a myriad of issues that dwarfed his eating habits, so Carter decided to pull out his trump.

"He's inside watching TV. He's staying with me for a little while."

"Yeah, Tanya told me. What happened to that girl he was staying with over in Vansant?"

"That ended about a month ago and he moved back in here until he can get on his feet again. Life's been hard for him."

Carter sighed, then emphasized each word as he spoke. "Mom, he's fifty years old now. It's time he grew up." He turned his head, gazing around the yard that desperately needed mowing. "Could he not at least lift a finger to do something around here?"

He will, Carter, he will. He's just got to get his life back together again. Prison isn't a pretty place. I'm sure you know that."

"Yeah, I've put a lot of men in there," Carter mumbled. "A lot of men just like Ben, men who deserved to be there."

Sylvie ignored his statement, but didn't try to change the subject, creating a tense silence.

Connie finally spoke, breaking the tension. "Let's go in and let me help with supper." She opened the screen door.

Carter took her cue. "Yeah, mom, have you got some of your baked possum fixed up for me?" he asked with a chuckle.

"I made you some 'possum meatloaf this time, honey. I didn't want you to get bored with the same thing all the time." The three of them laughed as Carter and Connie followed Sylvie into the house.

Ben was sitting on the old, floral print couch watching a rerun of *Duck Dynasty* on the forty-two-inch flatscreen television. Carter nodded toward his brother, said hello, but avoided a long conversation by following the Sykes women into the kitchen. As they went to work on dinner, his mind drifted back to his childhood, when the family struggled to watch any kind of snowy signal on an old, nineteen-inch, black and white TV. It took the smell of his mother's meatloaf to bring him back to reality.

"All right, meatloaf," Carter said with childlike enthusiasm.

"Mashed potatoes, peas, fried squash, and cornbread too," Sylvie said, knowing Carter would be pleased with her menu.

"He's all yours now, mom," Connie chuckled, thinking back to the dinner she fixed for Carter last summer to convince him to take on their undercover adventure. She decided this was a good time to let the mother and son have a few minutes alone. Besides, it would give her a chance to see if there was any common ground between Carter and Ben. "I'm going to see what Ben's up to."

Connie turned and walked into the living room. She said hello, and sat on the chair across from Ben, who was engrossed in what she called the "duck guys." At first glance, or even after knowing them a long time, one would never imagine Ben and Carter had the same parentage. Ben was about three inches shorter than Carter, about six inches rounder, and looked about ten years older. What hair he had left was gray, and he wore a scraggly beard that matched it. Connie knew the past thirty plus years of drug use, failed relationships, and the couple of stints in the pen had taken its toll on him. Had he not been Carter's brother she would never have as much as spoken to him. But he was her brother-in-law, and she was determined to be nice.

"What's going on, Ben?" she asked.

"Not much Connie. How's things been going for you and Cart the Fart in the big city?"

Connie grimaced at the name Ben had given Carter back in their childhood, when the boys shared a room together. "We're doing great. I'm trying to keep Carter occupied."

Ben smiled a smile that, despite his missing teeth, let Connie know his mind was in the gutter, but he knew better than to speak what he thought. "He ain't never been one to take it easy."

"What's going on with you? Any job? Any girl?"

"Janet and me broke up about a month ago. She wanted me to get a job down at the pizza place in Haysi. Hell, I've got bigger plans than tossing pizza dough. She told me to take the job or hit the road, so here I am."

"What kind of plans?" Connie asked, wondering what kind of trouble Ben was getting himself into this time.

A couple of guys in Clinchco are making some business plans. I don't want to say too much. I don't want to get mom's hopes up, you know."

"I understand," Connie said, electing not to push him for any more details. She had a pretty good idea those details would involve drugs. "You heard anything from Andy?"

"Yeah, he's picking Tanya up and bringing her and the kids down for dinner. I bet that's them right there," Ben said, leaning to his left and looking out the window at the Chevy Lumina APV coming down the road. "Wait 'til he tells you about getting fired from Lowes. Funniest shit I've ever heard. Hey Fart, Andy, Tanya, and the kids are here," he yelled toward the kitchen.

****

There wasn't an empty chair to be found at Sylvie Sykes' supper table. Sylvie, Carter, Connie, and Ben, were joined by Carter's sister Tanya, her husband Andy Calhoun, and their children Brett, Crystal, and Dylan. The surface of the table was filled with Sylvie's home cooking; meatloaf, real mashed potatoes, made from real potatoes, not flakes from a box, green peas that came from last year's garden, and coleslaw made with a recipe passed down from Carter's great-grandmother. On the center of the table was a covered basket containing hot homemade biscuits, sitting beside a dish holding a block of real butter. Carter was content to sit back and listen to the buzz of conversation going on around him, much of which dealt with the children and how their ball teams were faring on the field. His mouth was engaged in its favorite activity, devouring his mother's home cooking. He was intent on clearing his plate; he knew the ladies wouldn't allow him to dive into the German chocolate cake until he did. Taking the last bite of his buttered biscuit, he looked at his mother. "Mom, if I lived around here, I'd weigh three hundred pounds."

"Now that would be a pretty sight," his younger sister Tanya laughed at the vision of a Carter as big around as he was tall. Tanya was in her mid-forties, with wavy, bleached blonde hair that touched her shoulders. Her face was pretty, but the abundance of makeup made it clear that she was not giving in to the aging process without a fight. She and Andy hadn't married until she was in her late twenties; giving her teenage children when most women she had grown up with were busy tending their grandchildren.

Carter sat back, wiped his mouth with a paper towel, walked to the counter, and cut himself a piece of cake that was bigger than Connie would normally allow. He sat back down, caught her glance at his plate, chose to ignore it, and looked at Andy. "So, what happened at Lowes? I've been told I have to hear this story." Ben chuckled without looking up from his plate.

"Let's just say I got into a little trouble," Andy answered, hoping against hope the subject would go away.

"Huh-uh. Let me tell you what this lame-brain idiot did," Tanya spoke up, the indignance in her tone unmistakable. He and his dumb-ass buddies were working the hoot owl, setting up all the displays and stocking the lawn and garden center for the spring season. That damn George Musick had snuck in a twelve pack and a couple of them got to drinking, including Andrew here." Carter and Connie both chuckled at the use of Andy's formal name, knowing Tanya's anger still ran deep. "Well, one of them got the stupid-ass idea to take a picture of one of them nekkid in one of the lounge chairs they just set up on display." Everyone, including Sylvie, chucked at the image in their minds "Well, it seems George's son, Jeremy, got 'hold of the camera. Now Jeremy is a big time computer whiz, and in a couple of days, he had hacked into the lowes.com website and replaced the picture of that particular lounge chair with the one of lame-brain over here laying there nekkid, smiling, holding up a Bud Light and exposing his tallywacker; on Lowe's national website, mind you. To make things worse, Lowe's Chief Financial Officer's preacher was the one who discovered the pic of my naked husband's ass on the internet while he was shopping for lawn furniture."

"My ass was not on the internet, it was in the chair," Andy tried to defend himself, eliciting laughter from Brett and Dylan.

"Anyway, we're trying to get by on what I make at the nursing home until this Playgirl model here can find something else to do."

"Andy, if you wanted to be naked that bad, you could've gone to one of those nudist places," Carter couldn't resist the comment. A second later, he felt a pain in his shin as Connie's shoe hit his leg under the table. He looked over to see the frown on her face.

"That's alright," Andy said with a grin. "Me and Eric have a plan. A BIG plan. We're going to be rolling in money by the end of the year. I'll let you in on the ground floor if you want. Come on up tomorrow and I'll show you."

"We can't wait to see this one," Connie laughed. She, and everyone at the table, including the children, knew Andy was always dreaming of a get rich quick scheme. He had tried Amway, Herbalife, even got into a couple of pyramid schemes over the years.

"I'm telling you, it's going to be big, real big. Carter, I'm serious, you might want to get in on this one. I'll give you the full demonstration tomorrow."

"I can't wait," said Carter trying unsuccessfully to hold back his laughter.

"I got some homemade apple pie over here if anybody wants some," said Sylvie.

Crystal and Dylan yelped in delight at the mention of apple pie. Carter leaned back and rubbed his overfilled belly, "I can't turn down one piece."

"Connie, you want a piece?" the elder Sykes lady asked.

"I may take one back to the Coachmen, Mom. I'm stuffed. But I'll help you clean up if everyone's done with dinner."

"Thanks, honey," Sylvie said, scooping a piece of pie on Crystal's plate.

After finishing dessert, he and the rest of the family moved to the living room, where Carter, Ben, and Tanya had spent much of their time growing up. For the next couple of hours they talked; first about their family, especially what the kids were into, then about work. The conversation eventually turned to friends they grew up with.

"I saw Teresa the other day," Tanya finally said.

"Oh yeah," Carter said, trying to act nonchalant, but the interest in his voice unmistakable. "How's she doing?"

"Looked like she was doing great. She told me to tell you hello."

From the corner of his eye, Carter glanced at Connie, looking for any reaction to the mention of Teresa. If there was any, he couldn't tell it.

A few minutes later, the Calhoun's piled into the van and drove up the dirt road, with the kids waving out the back glass. Carter, Connie, and Sylvie stood on the porch, waving back.

"Are they going to be ok?" Carter asked his mother.

"I'm sure they will be. You know Andy; he's actually a pretty good guy. Sometimes, he just does things he shouldn't do. Nothing really bad, just dumb stuff. He'll find some work somewhere, he always does. He's just getting too old to go back into the mines again. Tanya's hoping he can find something with a natural gas company, but those jobs are tough to get."

"All I know is I want to see this big project he's working on. You know it's hilarious if Andy Calhoun is involved with it"

THREE

After years of camping in the Coachmen, Carter's morning routine was set in stone. The required bathroom visit, a stop at the fridge for a can of diet Dr Pepper, and a trip to his recliner, where he booted up his laptop and pushed the power button on his Icom 7000 ham radio. He leaned back while the electronics came to life, sipping on his soda, and then proceeded to use his radio to check his email via his Winlink account. After the digital dance was complete, he tuned to a ham radio RV single-sideband net on forty meters, then to the morning Tennessee Navy-Marine Corps MARS net.

Even though he used a headset, Carter's stirrings woke Connie. She rose, put on a robe, and made her morning coffee in the two-cup coffee maker she kept in the camper. Years ago, when they first started camping, she would take the time to make a big breakfast—sausage or bacon, eggs, biscuits and gravy, the works. But as the novelty of camping wore off and RVing became a normal part of their life, she and Carter began to eat more like they did at home, which meant cereal for breakfast. This morning, Special K Red Berries provided their morning nourishment. Connie poured herself a bowl and filled it with skim milk.

After Carter finished his radio obligations, he walked to the kitchen, poured his bowl of Special K, added the milk, and joined Connie at the table. "What do you want to do today?" he asked.

"I don't know; we're in your territory here, Cart the Fart," she laughed.

Carter's face contorted, showing his disdain for the nickname. "Ok, Benjamin," he replied. "I thought maybe we'd ride over to Andy and Tanya's to see the big plan he's working on. Knowing Andy, it's got to be, how can I put this, 'interesting.'"

"I'm kind of interested in his big plan, too," Connie replied. "It's got be a hoot. Besides, he did offer to let you in on the ground floor. If nothing else, it might be the tax break we'll need next year."

"We're retired, you know. We don't need tax breaks; we need our money. I'll call and see if he minds us stopping in for a few minutes."

"He won't mind. He always wants people to see his..." Connie paused for a second, looking for diplomatic words, "...what did Tanya call it, his lame-brained ideas?"

"I'll call anyway. I guess we better get a shower and get dressed before we head out."

"Yeah, I guess we will have to get dressed, won't we?" Connie said with disappointment in her voice. "I'd rather go like this." She opened her robe, exposing the nakedness beneath it to her husband.

Carter laughed. "Somehow, I don't think Andy would mind too much if you showed up at his house looking like that."

"Yeah, but with Andy, I think I might mind," Connie said. "I think I'll throw on some clothes. Something conservative."

****

Within forty-five minutes, Carter and Connie had showered, dressed, and were in the Ram, leaving the Breaks Interstate Park. Carter drove, maneuvering down curvy and hilly highway 80 a little faster than normal; and for Carter, normal was a little faster than most people were comfortable with. It had been a while since he had been on the roads where he learned to drive, and he was having fun tossing Connie around the cab of the truck. It reminded him of younger days, back when they were dating. Carter would bring Connie home to meet his family in his old Dodge Dart, taking the curves too fast, trying to impress her with his driving skills. Little did he know Connie fell in love with him despite his driving like a fool, not because of it. Today, Connie was still not impressed when her husband tried to be Kevin Harvick. As they entered Haysi and traffic forced him to slow to normal driving speeds, Connie's heart rate slowed a few beats, but she knew its rhythm was still erratic.

After turning down a couple of small, one-lane side streets, they found the street Andy and Tanya lived on. Although the streets now had different names, Carter recognized the neighborhood. Back in elementary school, he had a friend who lived here. His mind flashed back to his childhood, to the many wiffle ball and football games he played in his friend's yard. The houses now seemed so close together, and the yards, most around a quarter acre, seemed so small. Yet for a group of pre-teen kids, they made perfect ball fields. Since school was in session, the yards were quiet now, but Carter imagined they would be filled with children playing outside later in the afternoon.

At the end of the street was the house Andy and Tanya had bought a couple of years ago. The thousand square foot, white, wood-framed house sat on a quarter acre lot, but being at the end of the street, it had a more open feel than the houses surrounding it. There was a metal swing set in the side yard, and a homebuilt doghouse sat beside the house; although their Heinz 57, named Roscoe, rarely went in it. The short gravel driveway showed signs of needing a dose of Roundup, as weeds were popping up in the middle. The paint on the house looked good; Carter figured the previous owners put a coat on before listing it on the market.

Carter parked the Ram beside the crimson Ford Taurus in the driveway and he and Connie jumped out of the truck. Their noses were immediately greeted with a pungent odor that filled the air. While the noxious smell was not exactly the same, it reminded Carter of driving past chicken farms on hot summer nights. Connie's head tilted back, putting her nose in the air as it wrinkled up at the same time. She had the odd feeling of not wanting to smell the odor, but at the same time wanting to figure out what it was. "What the heck is that?" she asked.

"With Andy, I'm afraid to ask," Carter replied, as he too curiously sniffed the foul smell. "I'd bet it has something to do with the big project he was talking about."

Connie shook her head. "I don't doubt it. What was the phrase Tanya used, lame-brain?"

"I think that was it," Carter said, as they walked to the door. Carter knocked, but there was no answer. "I bet he's around back," he speculated. He turned, as he had done many times as a police detective, and led the way around the house, quickly making his way into the backyard. Connie followed close behind, afraid of, but yet curious, as to what they might find.

Coming around the back corner of the house, they saw a small green outbuilding with the door open. He heard the voices of two men coming from inside, and recognized one of them as Andy's. The smell increased in intensity, but oddly, it wasn't as revolting as it was when they stood in the front yard. Carter looked at Connie, slowed his pace, and they stepped toward the building. "What in the hell are y'all doing in there?" Carter yelled out as they approached the open door.

"Carter," Andy yelled as he jumped out of the door, meeting them at the shed's entrance. "I'm glad you made it. Eric is here and we're working on the big project I was telling you about. I'd invite you in, but I don't think you want to see it in its current form."

"I don't want to smell it in its current form, either," said Connie. "But it appears I don't have a whole lot of choice."

"Sorry about that. It's one of the drawbacks of the cooking process. But it sure does make a fine finished product." A short, skinny, balding man jumped out of the shed and shut the door behind him. "Hey, you remember Eric O'Quinn, don't you Cart? He was a year ahead of Tanya in school."

"Hello, Eric," Carter said. He barely recognized the man. The last time he saw him was the summer after he graduated from college. Eric was still in elementary school, probably sixth or seventh grade, and had a full head of brown hair parted on the wrong side. He looked back at Andy. "What the hell are you guys doing in there?"

"Hey, man, this is it," Andy announced with pride in his voice. "This is the end of all our money problems. You're getting a whiff of the final development of Clean Pig, the world's first bacon soap."

"What kind of soap?" Connie's jaw dropped open, her eyes widened, and her hands fell to her thighs.

"Clean Pig bacon soap," Andy replied, his face beaming. "What is better than the smell of fresh, fried bacon filling the house first thing in the morning? Now, just imagine taking a bath and having that smell on you all day long. What man wouldn't want that? And what woman, wanting to attract a man, wouldn't take a long bath with it, rubbing it all over her body, especially those special places. Hell, I'd be all over Tanya in a heartbeat if she smelled like fresh cooked bacon. I bet you'd jump Connie's bones too, Cart."

Carter didn't respond, not really knowing what to say. Silence filled the yard until Eric spoke, filling the void.

"Besides, they're already making bacon toothpaste; I saw it on Amazon. Once the soap is perfected, and we're really close, then we'll start working on bacon shampoo. Everybody will want to be a Clean Pig," he laughed. "And we'll reap the rewards."

"Oh my God," Connie said softly. Her expression hadn't changed.

"Hoping to have this on eBay and Amazon by the first of June," Andy informed them. "Hey, Carter, it's not too late to get in on the ground floor of this. We're going to need some capital to get some inventory ready. We need to buy some custom designed boxes and bottles to fill the first orders. I'm thinking something like a Piggly Wiggly pig face on it. I figure we'll need about ten grand to get this pig clean." He laughed at his play on words. "You guys want in?"

Carter was looking for words, but he couldn't seem to find the ones to describe his thoughts. It took a few moments, but he finally came across the excuse he always fell back on when a car salesman would ask him to buy.

"I'll have to talk to Cons about it. We never invest without discussing it with each other. It's the secret of a long marriage."

"What do you say, Cons? I'd rather have family profiting with me, getting rich with me, than to take a loan at the bank and be in bed with them. I never liked that son of a bitch Jimmy Stanley down there, anyway. I never trusted a man who wore a suit and tie on a ninety degree day."

Connie's eyes found Carter's and gave him a look that let him know he'd pay for this later. "I'm not sure the world is ready for bacon soap yet, Andy," she said softly, trying to diplomatically squirm her way out of the mess Carter had skillfully placed in her lap.

"Hey, maybe you can take this idea on *Shark Tank*," Carter said, trying to redeem himself by stepping to his wife's rescue. "Mark Cuban might be a player on this one. I bet a bacon after shave would really get him going." He paused, as if seriously pondering an idea. "The Dallas Mavericks could wear it during their games. That smell would surely distract Kobe and the Lakers."

"Bacon after shave? Hmm. That's genius, man," Eric chimed in. "I've got it, Old Pig. What do you think, Andy?"

"I love it, dude! We could even do gift sets for Christmas. A little bar of Clean Pig soap, a small bottle of, let's see, Hairy Pig shampoo, and a little bottle of Old Pig after-shave. I can hear the commercial now, 'Be a total pig, with a Clean Pig gift set.'"

"Oh my God," Connie said again, looking at the ground as she shook her head in disbelief.

"Think about it, Cart. If you'll invest and get involved, I bet we can get this thing to market by Father's Day. What better gift for dad than a Clean Pig gift set?"

"It's a shame you can't have it ready by Mother's Day," Connie said with a grin, knowing her comment would prompt them to work Carter even harder for investment funds.

"That would be pushing it, Cons. But Cart, if you'll jump into this thing with both feet, we can give Father's Day a shot. I think we can do it. Come on, let's go inside. I need a pop anyway," Andy said, walking away from the outbuilding and toward a small, wooden deck that guarded the back door of the house. Carter and Connie followed him inside. Eric locked the shed and came in a couple of minutes later.

"So that's the big project, huh?" Carter asked.

"Yep. Tanya's not real excited about it yet. She's not a big dreamer like me. But she will be once the orders, and the money, start rolling in."

"She'll probably be more excited if y'all outgrow that outbuilding and get that smell out of her backyard," Connie said under her breath.

"Yeah, it does draw every dog and cat in the neighborhood," Andy admitted with a tone that said he was almost proud of it.

Trying to turn the conversation away from Clean Pig soap, Carter asked, "How's mom doing? How's her health?"

"She's okay. You know her, she's a tough old bird. Tanya talks to her on the phone almost every day. Sylvie stops by here every Saturday when she comes to town to do her 'trading', as she calls it. All in all, she's doing pretty good for a woman in her seventies."

"I'm glad y'all are keeping an eye on her. I've tried to talk her into coming to Kingsport, but she won't hear of it."

"She keeps thinking you and Connie will move back into the old homeplace now that you're retired. She keeps saying that land is meant to be the home of a Sykes."

"I guess that will have to be Ben," said Carter. "'Cause there ain't no way, no way in hell, I'm moving back to this area. I've been gone twice as many years as I lived here. I built my life in Kingsport, my home's there now. I plan to keep it that way."

"She ain't turning that house over to Ben, Carter. She knows how Ben is. She says you're the next Sykes in line. Says she doesn't want every drug dealer in Dickenson County rummaging through that house."

"With Ben, I can see her point. What about you and Tanya? Y'all ever thought of moving in with her? Might be good for everybody."

"We've got this place here, man. It ain't much, but it's ours. And I hate to say it, but I don't want your mom cramping our style. We ain't that old, if you know what I mean."

Carter thought back to his and Connie's recent activities at the Carolina Couples event in Charlotte. "No, y'all ain't that old yet." He thought of Andy going at it with his sister like a couple of teenagers, and decided this conversation needed a new direction. The rumble in his stomach provided him the opportunity. "Hey, y'all want a bite of lunch? Let's go down to Fred's and I'll get us some fried chicken and hillbilly fried tateers. What do you say?"

"You don't have to ask twice, my man." Andy turned to Eric. "You in for some chicken and taters from Fred's, dude?"

"Damn straight. I ain't never turned down chicken and taters from Fred's. You're just trying to impress us, ain't you, Carter? Hoping for a better deal on your Clean Pig investment. I see how you city boys work, man. You'll probably get a receipt and take it off your taxes, too. Smart, dude."

"Y'all know my husband—suave, sophisticated, and a big spender," Connie said, sarcastically.

Carter led the four of them out the front door and to the Ram, where he opened the door to let Andy and Eric into the back seat. "You forgot to lock the house," Carter reminded Andy.

"It'll be ok. This is Haysi."

"You locked that shed, but you're not going to lock the house?" Connie questioned.

"Of course. If someone stole the secret to Clean Pig, our whole future would be gone." Andy explained. "We can't let that happen, can we?"

Carter shook his head as he jumped into the Ram, put it in reverse, and backed out of the short driveway.

****

For nearly an hour, they sat on an old picnic table outside of Fred's, a glorified convenience store at the edge of Haysi. Fred's would have been like any other convenience store in America except for its famous hillbilly fried chicken and taters. They also carried an assortment of subs, coleslaw, and macaroni or potato based dishes for the takeout crowd. For those wanting to eat on site, three weather-beaten picnic tables next to the front of the building provided the accommodations.

After finishing their chicken and taters, Andy and Eric decided to walk back to the house, freeing Carter and Connie to drive to his mother's and spend some more time with her, this time without the whole family around. Carter's work as a detective had always taken precedence over everything else in his life, including spending time with his family. Now that he was retired, he was bound and determined to give some of that time back to the ones he loved.

"Are you sure you haven't thought of moving back up here, Carter?" Connie asked as they drove up the dirt road toward the old house. "If your mother won't leave, we could come here and take care of her."

"Connie, don't tell me she's getting to you. First off, my home's in Kingsport now. It has been for a long time. Quite honestly, I don't think I could get used to living here again. Back home, in Kingsport, if I want something, I'm less than five minutes from Food City, five minutes from Walmart, or fifteen minutes from the mall; God forbid I have to go there ever again, but I can if I want to. Here, it's almost forty-five minutes to get to a real grocery store with over four aisles, and Walmart's over an hour away." He paused for a moment, collecting his thoughts. "Yeah, I've thought about it, I'd be lying if I said it never crossed my mind. But I'm not a back-to-the-lander. I don't think I'd ever be happy living back here in these hills. That's one of the things I thought was so strange about the Westlakes' move, remember? How could they leave a town like Greenville, South Carolina, for a podunk little town like Herbsville? It just didn't make sense to me. Us moving back to Haysi wouldn't make any sense either. Besides, I don't think I could do it to you. You don't really know how things are around here, Cons. Hell, everybody in town knows what you had for supper by the smell of your farts."

Connie laughed. "That's why half this town smells like spoiled Chicken and taters, then. Quite frankly, I think I could handle it okay, sweetie. I'm sure I'd miss the conveniences of Kingsport, but I'd get used to it. These little towns have personality, something the bigger towns with the big-box stores are missing. Something tells me I'd get along just fine in Haysi. I could probably stay busy volunteering at the local clinic or something."

"Of course, you could take off through the woods naked," Carter said with a smile. "No fences to have to put up, no neighbors to worry about, unless old man Rose was out hunting squirrels. We could even put in a little nude beach down at the creek."

Connie raised her eyebrows. "You're getting my attention, now. You still haven't put that fence up around our backyard yet. Look, we're here," she said as the house came into sight. "This dirt road ain't so bad when your mind's occupied."

"Tell that to the TC," Carter mumbled, backing the Ram into its parking spot.

For the next couple of hours, Sylvie, Carter, and Connie sat in rockers on the front porch of the Sykes homeplace, talking about family members whose names, much less faces, Carter could barely remember. The stories his mother told about them were interesting, and Carter tried to envision how life was for his aunts, uncles, and cousins who still lived in the area. His Aunt Mae passed away over the winter; his cousin Jessica just gave birth to her third child, and his cousin Alf and wife Barbie recently arrived back from taping their third episode of *Springer*. Best Carter could remember, everything seemed about normal for his family.

36

The ringing of the phone seemed to give all of them a break from the conversation. Sylvie went inside to answer it.

"One thing about it, being at the end of this holler, I can just use the bathroom off the porch if I want," Carter laughed.

"Carter Sykes, this house does have a bathroom now."

"I know, babe. I helped put it in, remember? But I've peed off this porch a many a time in my life," he said with a chuckle.

"Carrrteerrrrr."

Sylvie's frantic voice from inside the house startled them. They both got up and rushed into the living room, finding Sylvie sitting on the couch with the phone to her ear, all color drained from her face. "It's Crystal. She just got home from school and found Andy laying in the backyard, hurt bad. She says he's bleeding pretty bad from his ear."

"Tell her to hold on, Mom. We're on our way. We'll call 911 from the truck."

FOUR

Once again, Connie was being thrown around in the cab of the Ram, but this time she didn't care. She focused on making the 911 call, but it was two miles up the road before she was able to get the number dialed on the touchscreen of her phone. She finally got through and gave them Andy and Tanya's address, knowing she and Carter would arrive before either the cops or the rescue squad she requested.

Carter manually kept the Ram in a lower gear than normal, allowing him to access more desirable points in the HEMI's horsepower and torque curves to power out of the sharp curves and down the short straights. After a hair-raising twenty-minute drive that only took twelve, they skidded to a stop beside the Taurus sitting in the drive. Without turning off the flashers, Carter and Connie both sprinted toward the front door. "Crystal, Crystal, where are you?" Carter yelled.

"Around back, Uncle Carter. Daddy's hurt bad," the girl called back.

Connie was first off the porch and raced to the back yard. Thirty years of nursing didn't fully prepare her for what she saw. Andy was lying on the ground, on his back, blood pouring from his nose, and coming from his ears. His right side, from his head to his legs, was battered. He was not moving, and his breathing was very shallow. Crystal was on her knees on her father's left side, frantic. She dabbed a cloth to his nose, trying to stop the bleeding, but the helpless feeling showed on her face as the tears streamed down her cheeks. Connie did a baseball slide on the other side of Andy and quickly put her index and middle fingers to the side of his neck. "I've got a pulse," she announced.

"How is he, Cons?" Carter asked, standing over her, catching his breath.

"Not good. He's unconscious. Probably a good thing, because he's been beat up pretty bad." She looked at Crystal and calmly, but forcefully ordered, "Crystal, get me some damp cloths—washcloths, towels, anything you can find, hurry." She turned her attention to Carter. "Carter, call 911 back and tell them to get that ambulance here yesterday, and ask them to go ahead and dispatch Wings, he's going to need an airlift. I'll do what I can until they arrive."

Crystal and Carter followed Connie's directions as she began attending to Andy. First, she cleared his airway, making sure Andy's shallow breaths actually got air to his lungs. When Crystal returned with the cloths, she went to work trying to stop the bleeding, wiping the blood from his nose and his ears. When Carter finished his call, she asked, without looking up, "ETA?"

"Ten minutes on the ambulance, about twenty on Wings."

"Get on your knees, behind his head," she ordered. When Carter got into position, she took his hands and placed them on each side of Andy's head, just below the ear. She held his fingers straight down his neck, in line with the spine. "Hold him just like this. Keep firm, steady pressure. Don't let him move. I don't want any more damage to his neck."

"Roger," Carter said, acknowledging he understood her instructions.

With the neck stabilized as well as available equipment would allow, Connie went back to work making sure the airway was clear and trying to slow the bleeding. She asked Crystal if Tanya had been notified, and when the sobbing girl shook her head, she told her to go inside, call her mom at work and tell her to get home immediately. She again checked the pulse, the airway, worked on the bleeding, and surveyed the damage to Andy's right side. Her trained eye didn't need x-rays to diagnose a lot of the damage. Andy's arm was broken in several places, and his collarbone and shoulder were both severely damaged. The shattered ribcage worried Connie even more; she hoped the lungs and organs the ribs protected were not damaged. But her biggest concern was his head. It appeared a blunt object had struck Andy on the side of the head, explaining the blood from the nose and ears. She was unable to determine the damage to the brain; that would have to wait until he got to the hospital.

The volunteer rescue squad arrived and took over the job of attending to the victim, getting vitals and using their equipment to better stabilize him. After carefully putting him on a stretcher, they loaded him into the ambulance now sitting in the backyard. As the paramedic closed the back door, they heard the Wings chopper fly overhead. "Good thing you had them call Wings," the EMT told Connie, rushing toward the driver's door. "We're going to need every second."

"Where will you load him?" Carter asked.

"Sandlick," he said, referring to the town's elementary school.

"We'll follow you," Connie replied. "Take him to Holston Valley; I was a nurse there."

"I'll let them know." The paramedic closed his door, dropped the shifter into drive, and eased out of the backyard, being careful not to become stuck in the soft ground. Connie and Carter ran for the cab of the Ram and followed the ambulance to the school.

The drive to Sandlick Elementary took five minutes, and in another five, the paramedics and the Wings crew had the patient transferred to the helicopter. They secured both doors and the pilot guided the machine into the air, en route to the hospital in Kingsport.

Carter turned on the Ram's ham radio, pushed a couple of buttons, and spun its large tuning knob until he found the frequency Wings would use to communicate with Holston Valley Regional Medical Center. Both Carter and Connie could sense the urgency in the EMT's otherwise professional voice as he described the situation to the doctors, and the same urgency from the doctors as they gave the crew their orders over the airwaves.

Pulling behind Tanya's van in the driveway, they heard a paramedic call out "Code Four, I have a Code Four" across the radio. Tears filled Carter's eyes as he repeatedly beat on the steering wheel with his left fist. Andy Calhoun's heart had stopped beating.

Tanya and Crystal came running from the house to the driver's door of the truck. "Carter, what's going on? Crystal said something about Andy…"

Carter held up his hand to silence her as he listened to the traffic on the radio. The EMTs had a pulse again. A minute later, they lost it again.

"Oh my God," Tanya cried out. "Carter?"

Fifteen seconds later, the pulse was back. "He's fighting, sis; pray for him. All we can do now is pray." Carter instructed. A minute later, the EMT announced they had again lost the pulse. They were two minutes from the hospital.

"Daddy!" Crystal screamed.

"They'll keep working on him. It's not over yet," Connie said.

But Carter knew better. He knew what two minutes without oxygen to the brain meant. Even if they did get his heart started again, Andy's brain would be damaged. The radio remained quiet, and Carter, using all the skills he developed over his police career, pulled himself together enough to talk. "Crystal found him in the backyard. He was beaten pretty bad. Connie did all she could until the paramedics arrived…," he paused, his voice failing him.

"Wings is taking him to Holston Valley right now, Tanya," Connie took over, telling the new widow the truth, but not everything she too, knew was inevitable. "I know people there, and I can get more information."

"Is he going to be okay?" Tanya asked.

"I don't know for sure," Connie said, realizing the statement was more lie than hope. "Let's all go inside." Carter reached over and turned off the radio, not wanting Tanya to hear any more radio traffic, or the silence that indicated no change in her husband's condition.

Twenty minutes later, Connie called Holston Valley and got the expected report. Andy Calhoun died in transport and the paramedics and doctors were unable to revive him a third time. Connie hung up the phone. No amount of experience or training would ever prepare her for this moment. She sat on the couch with Tanya, took her hands, and gave her the news that her husband was gone. Tanya screamed a primal "NO!" that could be heard up and down every holler in Dickenson County. She buried her head on her sister-in-law's shoulder. Carter went to Crystal to comfort her, but he knew from his own experience of losing his father forty years earlier, there was little he could do to console his niece. She just lost her daddy, and he knew all the time in the world would never completely heal that wound.

Even in the sorrow and pain, Carter recognized the déjà vu of the moment. Sitting there holding Crystal, he felt like his grandfather, who held him decades earlier, as he cried for his murdered father. Carter knew from experience this moment would change Crystal's life forever. That day forty years earlier had changed his; it made him want to be a detective.

After Sylvie arrived, Carter undertook the task of calling Andy's parents to inform them of their son's untimely death. Informing a parent of the loss of their child, no matter the age, was one of the most difficult things Carter had to do as a police officer. He was glad it was a job he didn't have to perform often. This call was especially difficult, since he had known the Calhouns since he was a child. He asked Andy's father if he would notify the rest of the Calhoun family, and he said he would. Carter was relieved; he wasn't sure he could handle calling Andy's sisters, one of whom he had a crush on in eighth grade.

Tanya asked Carter to pick up Brett and Dylan from baseball practice, and he obliged. At the ball field, he asked the boys to walk to the left field fence with him, where he broke the news of their father's passing. As Carter had done forty years earlier, the boys broke down in tears. There were no screams, no yells, just tears of loss, tears of pain, muffled by boys trying exhibit a strength that men three times their age couldn't muster. The three of them knelt in front of the Johnson Chevrolet sign that hung on the chain link fence, Carter with an arm around each of the boys. The three of them cried softly together for nearly a half-hour before walking across the outfield grass, the infield dirt, and through the gravel parking lot to the Ram.

FIVE

Before pulling into the drive, Carter noticed the brown Ford Explorer displaying the logo of the Dickenson County Sheriff's Department. "This ought to be interesting," he mumbled under his breath.

"What, Uncle Carter?" Dylan asked, in a soft, grief-filled voice.

"I'm just talking to myself, Dylan." You and Brett go on in and take care of your mother while I talk to the police, okay?"

"Okay, Uncle Carter," the boys said, almost in unison. Carter parked the Ram in the small front yard, allowing plenty of room for the police SUV. He heard two men talking around back, so he walked around the house, toward the voices. Rounding the corner, he saw two uniformed deputies leaning against the Clean Pig shed, one smoking a cigarette. From what he could hear, they appeared to be in conversation about nothing in particular.

A smirk crossed Carter's face. "Good evening, officers," he said, extending his hand as he approached.

"Good evening." The older of the two spoke first. Out of habit, Carter sized him up—about six feet, two-twenty-five, decent muscle tone for a smoker in his early forties. This cop would never be on the SWAT team, but he didn't appear to fit the profile of an overweight southern deputy. "What have y'all found back here?"

"And just who are you?" the younger cop, a short, skinny man, in his late twenties, who reminded Carter of Barney Fife, asked in a high pitched voice.

"I'm Carter Sykes, Kingsport...," Carter caught himself, "...uh, brother of the widow." After having spent three decades perfecting the phrase, he found it hard not to say "Carter Sykes, Kingsport Police Department," even after nearly a year of retirement.

"We're not seeing a lot back here," the older deputy said. "The state boys will be here in the morning to go over this place a little better, but there ain't a lot to be found."

Carter had heard these lines before. He remembered Sheriff Tedder's comments back in Herbsville, South Carolina, right after Thor discovered Doug Westlake's body in the woods. But even more vivid in Carter Sykes' memory were similar words coming from the mouth of a similarly dressed

45

deputy forty years earlier, discussing the findings in Carter's own father's murder case.

"There are always clues to find." Carter insisted, his tone changing, a bit of defiance, a bit of exasperation creeping into his voice. "We just have to be smart enough to find them."

"And just who the hell gave you a badge and made you Columbo?" the Barney Fife look-a-like asked with an attitude.

Carter bit his lip and counted to five as he gently shook his head. "Shit, not another damn Columbo watcher," he said under his breath, referring back to Sheriff Ralph Tedder associating him with the famous sleuth throughout the Westlake investigation. "I'm Carter Sykes, the brother of the widow. And I happen to know a thing or two about murder investigations."

"Sykes? I know that name." The older cop thought for a moment. "Yeah, Carter Sykes, the guy from Haysi who became a detective in Kingsport. Didn't I hear something about you being a private detective now? Let's see, didn't you solve a murder in a nudist colony last year?"

"No, I'm not a private detective, but yes, we caught the killer." Carter smiled, taking pride in being able to say those words. "Now, what's back here that we can discover?"

"Not a lot, really," said the first cop. "We haven't seen anything that could possibly be the murder weapon. No unusual tire tracks around front, and the ambulance's tracks messed up anything that could have been in the back. The tall grass makes it hard to see anything small that could have fell to the ground; maybe the state boys will find something tomorrow."

"Okay, then, let me ask it this way; what's not here? What's missing that you would expect to see?"

"Hmm, good question." The officer thought for a moment. "There's no sign of a struggle. No murder weapon, nothing really out of place. A little odd for a beating like that guy took."

"Okay, since the murder apparently took place in the back yard, and there's no sign of struggle, we can assume the victim knew the killer. No sign of struggle also shows that the vic didn't expect there to be trouble, at least trouble of the magnitude of murder. Let's look at this yard; it's the second half of April and it hasn't been mowed yet. That's a sign of a man who had something on his mind besides his domestic duties, wouldn't you say? What could that have been?" Carter tapped his knuckles on the wall of the shed. "What's in here? That might give us something else to go on."

"Don't know yet, we haven't looked," Barney Fife spoke up. "It's locked."

"Locked? You haven't looked in the shed yet?" Carter asked with amazement. "Why not?"

"We didn't see how it had anything to do with the murder. The man was killed out here, on the ground, remember?" Fife said, in a tone that implied "dumb ass" at the end of the comment.

Carter lowered his gaze and shook his head. "I see law enforcement hasn't advanced in Dickenson County since I left," he muttered, purposefully loud enough to be heard, then looked at Fife. "Boys, let's look in the shed. Is it really locked?"

"I don't know." Fife's tone was less cocky.

"Let's check it. Y'all got any gloves? A handkerchief? Anything so we don't mess up prints?"

"In the Explorer," the older deputy said.

"Then please go fetch each of us a pair so we can take a closer look around."

While the deputy retrieved the gloves, Carter backed up to the edge of the yard, trying to get a better look at the big picture. The house was at the end of the street. It backed up to the woods, and with leaves beginning to appear, there was little to view beyond the yard. Carter knew this made it unlikely a neighbor saw anything, but he hoped one would have at least heard something—an argument, a scream, anything that could be valuable in piecing together the events of the murder. "If Andy had that damn bacon soap thing going, I know no one smelled anything," he thought. "I found the body on the other side of the yard," Carter said aloud, almost as if explaining his thoughts to himself instead of speaking to the remaining deputy. "What was it doing over there? If Andy had walked up to meet someone entering the yard, wouldn't he be over here? Looks like he was trying to get away. I hope there's some skin or DNA under the vic's fingernails, but I doubt it; looks like he was running, not fighting."

Barney Fife returned with a box of latex gloves. "Put these on, boys," Carter commanded, as he had done so many times in his law enforcement career. "Let's look in that shed."

The three men walked to the door of the shed, which faced the far side of the yard. "Why is the door to this shed facing in such an odd direction?" Carter asked. "Wouldn't it make more sense to have it facing the house, or at least the side where everyone approaches from?"

"That is an odd way to set it in here," the older cop agreed. "Almost like someone didn't want anyone to see what was inside."

Carter snapped his left glove in place and approached the door. He turned the handle and it opened. "Did you guys unlock this thing?" he asked.

"Haven't touched it," the older cop admitted.

He swung the door wide, wanting to get a wide-angle sense of the shed. He shook his head, stepped forward, and looked both ways through the doorway into the nearly empty outbuilding. There was an old, empty paint can along the wall, two cheap wooden chairs pushed to the edges of an eight-foot long folding table, which was sitting against the back wall. Otherwise, the shed was empty.

"That was a waste," Fife's voice trumpeted. "There ain't a goddamn thing in here."

"What did I ask you earlier?" Carter asked, without even looking at the deputy.

"Uh, I don't know?"

"I asked you, 'what's not here?' remember? Now, there's a lot that's not here, we just have to figure out what it is."

"How in the hell are you going to find what's not there?" the other cop asked.

"By asking questions," Carter replied. "Who's the lead detective on this case?

The deputy looked to the back porch. "Here he comes now."

****

When Cecil Vanover came out the back door of the Calhoun house to gather the deputies, Carter Sykes was the first person he saw. "Aw, shit," Carter read his lips, as the same two words crossed his own mind.

'I should have known,' Carter thought. Vanover was, after all, the top detective for the Dickenson County Sheriff's Department, and of course he'd want to be here; a murder didn't occur every day in his jurisdiction.

The history between the two detectives predated their law enforcement careers. During their senior year in high school, Vanover was a monster on the mound for the Clintwood High School baseball team. His fastball topped out in the low 90s, and most scouts agreed, with some strength training and proper coaching, it would consistently hit the upper 90s when he matured. His curveball was wicked, buckling the knees of nearly every batter he faced, including the college players who accompanied the scouts on their recruiting visits. During his senior year in the Lonesome Pine District, he went 8–1, with an earned run average measured in fractions of a run. He had already committed to play for East Tennessee State University, but the White Sox were also scouting him as a possible mid-round draft pick.

The game was the last of the regular season, the annual showdown between Dickenson County rivals Haysi and Clintwood. Bottom of the seventh, Clintwood up 1-0, with Vanover pitching a two hitter. The pitcher was tiring, but the coach stuck with his ace for the final inning, trusting him to get the last three outs. He walked the first batter of the inning on five pitches, but recovered to strike out the next. The third hitter saw a get-me-over fastball and laid down a sacrifice bunt that the third basemen flung into the right field bleachers, leaving runners on second and third. Number 33, Carter Sykes, stepped to the plate, tapped the bat against his cleats, and dug in.

It was one of those unexplainable statistical oddities that happens in sports, but for some reason Carter, a mediocre ballplayer at best, had Vanover's number, hitting over .500 against him. Clintwood's coach came to the mound, instructing the pitcher to walk him, but Cecil convinced him he could get Sykes out. Vanover's first pitch was a curveball just off the outside corner. Somehow, Carter was able to check his swing. With the second, the hurler provided a little chin music, sending Carter's backside to the dirt getting out of the way. With a 2–0 count, Carter knew the next pitch would be a strike and the weary Vanover provided an eighty-five mile per hour fastball right down Broadway. Carter unloaded, sending the ball to the right-center field gap, all the way to the fence. The runners on base trotted home, and Carter wound up on third, mobbed by his teammates. It would be Cecil's only loss of the season, and the crowning achievement of Carter Sykes' athletic career.

Cecil Vanover got even that summer, however. At the Independence Day festival at John Flannigan Dam, Carter, trying to earn some money for college, picked up a few hours of work with the Army Corps of Engineers. Cecil also attended the festival, not to work, but to celebrate the signing of his contract with the White Sox and his impending departure to join their rookie league team. While at the festival, he met Teresa Robinson, a pretty girl who just graduated from Haysi High. That day, they began a torrid romance. They dated for two years, and got married the winter after Cecil

49

was promoted to AA, just before a rotator cuff injury ended his professional baseball career. The odd thing about their meeting was Teresa Robinson came to that festival to pick up her boyfriend, Carter Sykes, whom she left, forcing him to hitchhike home that evening.

"Carter Sykes, I hate we have to reacquaint under these circumstances," Vanover said professionally, holding out his hand. "I'm sorry about Andy."

"Hello, Cecil," Carter returned the greeting. "What do you know so far?"

"Not a lot, really. There's little physical evidence out here. Tanya says she can't think of anyone who would want to hurt Andy, much less kill him. He was a big clown; everyone liked him. That picture on the Lowes website, that was classic Andy Calhoun. Everybody in the county knows about it." He grinned as he paused to collect his thoughts. "Hell, Carter, quite frankly, you know as much as I do right now. We're still gathering evidence."

"There's some odd things out here, Cecil. Lots of missing things."

"Carter, let us do our job. Hell, I know you were a damn good detective, but you're too close to this to start poking around. This ain't no nudist colony in South Carolina; this is your home, your family. Let us do our job. When we get the State Police assisting us and get their findings back, we'll put together what happened here."

"Just like they did with my dad's case?" Carter asked defiantly.

"That's not fair, Carter, and you damn well know it. I wasn't working that case. We were what, twelve years old, playing little league baseball, when that went down. Let us do our job. That's all I'm asking, man."

"No offense to you personally, Cecil, but I've seen the law at work around here. As my wife told me last summer, 'if you want something done right...,'" he took a deep breath, measuring his words. "I want this case done right."

"Carter, take my advice and stay the hell out of the way. It will make things easier for everybody."

Cecil knew enough about the reputation of Carter Sykes to know he was wasting his breath. For Carter's part, he wasn't going to waste any more of his arguing about being involved in the investigation. "Whatever you say, Cecil, just find the son of a bitch who did this. And keep me posted."

"Carter, I mean it, man. Stay the hell out and let us do our job."

Carter smiled. "Cecil, quit worrying about me. Just find the sorry motherfucker who killed my sister's husband."

"We will," Vanover promised, trying unsuccessfully to mask his frustration.

Carter walked into the back door of the house and sat down beside his widowed sister. "What did Cecil ask you, Tanya?"

"Basic stuff, I guess," she answered through subdued sobs. "If Andy had any enemies, if he had been threatened lately, if he recently had any fights with anyone, if he owed anyone any money; you know, those types of things. I kept telling him no, I didn't know of anyone who would want to hurt Andy." She began to cry again. "Carter, I can't handle this."

He took her hands in his and stared straight into her eyes. "You have to handle this, Tanya. You've got three guys over here who are counting on you to handle it. Mom handled it, remember? The difference this time is I'm here. I'm going to get the son of a bitch who did this. This won't end the same way as daddy's death, I promise you."

Tanya looked up at Carter with tears streaming down her cheeks. "Promise me not to let this end up like daddy?"

"I promise, sis. I promise. I just need to know one thing right now. Focus for me. What did Andy and Eric have in that shed? What were they doing out there?"

She wiped her eyes with the back of her hand. "I'm not real sure. He hadn't worked in a couple of months now. He said he was working on his crazy pig soap thing during the day, and I believed him. Hell, it's all I could smell when I came home." She chuckled through her sobs, grabbed a new Kleenex, and blew her nose. "But I really don't know what he was doing during the day."

"Was he hanging out with any new people? Any strange faces come to the door?"

"I can't really think of any. Nights were pretty much normal around here. You know, a lot of our time in the evening was spent with the kids and their baseball and softball. I was actually looking forward to the season being over and things settling down a bit."

"Was Andy involved with the kids and their ball games?"

"I reckon. He never was a sports fan, you know that. I think the kids get the baseball thing from you. But since he lost his job, he'd take them to practice and to the games and pick them up. It seemed like he enjoyed it. It gave him something to do, hang out at the ballfield and be a dad."

"Ok, sis, that's enough for now. If you think of anything strange, no matter how small it seems, let me know, okay?"

"I will, Carter. Thanks for picking up the boys this evening."

"It was my pleasure, sis." Carter scooted over and gave his baby sister a big hug. Without saying another word, he got up and went into the kitchen.

****

The ride back to the Breaks was a long, slow drive up a winding mountain road. Carter didn't throw Connie around the cab this time. His mind focused on the fact that his sister's husband was dead, and, of all the people on the planet, Cecil Vanover was heading up the murder investigation. 'What could be worse?' Carter thought. As often happened, a voice in his head answered, 'Well, you could not be here. Haven't you learned yet, you're usually where you're supposed to be? Do you really think it's an accident?'

Carter often wondered where that voice came from. It always seemed to be full of wisdom, even if he didn't understand it at the time. His spiritual experience during Connie's kidnapping, along with her revelation that she had a similar episode, made Carter wonder whether there was something more to this God stuff than he had ever considered, more than what most humans ever considered. He always wrote off religion as make-believe, but at times he wondered whether there could possibly be some force, or someone, working in his life? He didn't know, and right now he didn't want to expend the energy to ponder it. There were more pressing matters on his plate, things he actually expected to get resolved in his lifetime.

"Nickel for your thoughts, sweetie," Connie finally spoke.

"Nothing, really. I guess I'm just thinking about what has happened today."

"What part of it?"

"The murder. The fact that Cecil Vanover is the lead investigator. The fact that we're here when it happened."

"Where do we go from here?"

He looked over at her. "We?"

"Yes, we," Connie said. "We are *McMillan and Wife* now, remember? I know you, you're not going to stand back and let someone else work

Andy's case. Especially not Cecil Vanover. What happened between the two of you, anyway? Didn't he and Teresa start dating after you two broke up? Something tells me I haven't heard the whole story."

"It was a long time ago," Carter dodged the question. "As far as I know, Cecil's as good a cop as there is in these parts. I hope the state will send some decent techs down to go over the crime scene. Those deputies were worthless."

"What time do you think the State Police will be there?"

"I'd guess eight-thirty or nine. They'll be coming from Abingdon, and I don't expect them to leave too early," Carter said, as he made the left turn into the Breaks.

"You are going to be there when they arrive, aren't you?"

He nodded. "I plan on it."

"Good. I'll be there with you. I'll help Tanya with the kids. I really like Crystal. Sometimes I wish we had tried to have a child one more time."

"Sometimes…" he paused, reflecting on the voice he had just heard in his head, "…things happen for a reason."

"Carter Sykes, sometimes, you almost sound religious."

"Connie Sykes, bite your tongue," he chuckled as he turned down the road leading to the campground. "Since you said that, I think I'll pour me a strong drink before going to bed."

"Sounds like a plan, pour me one, too. Please. It might help us get to sleep," she said, giving him a soft, loving smile.

"You know I can't turn down that smile, babe. One strong one, coming right up."

SIX

Carter pulled the Ram into the Calhoun driveway at eight o'clock the next morning. He was not surprised that he beat the State Police to the scene. "I'll bet they stopped for some coffee and donuts," he told Connie.

"Carter, try to play nice," she chastised him as she opened her door.

"I am playing nice," he said. "I didn't say what I really thought."

Connie shut the door and went inside the house to check on the family. Carter settled into the three-quarter ton truck's leather seat and pushed a button on the steering wheel to make a call using the bluetooth connection between his truck and phone. He always preferred hearing the telephone conversation coming from the Ram's ten speaker sound system rather than the phone's tiny speaker.

"Tony Ward."

Carter was glad to hear his former partner's voice on the other end. "At least there's a cop somewhere in this time zone working right now."

"Man, let me tell you, old habits die hard. We used to have this slave-driving detective around here. A real son of a bitch, you know the type. Expected us to be in a half-hour early and stay a half-hour late. Made us work weekends if necessary. I was glad to see his ass retire. But I can't break his habit of coming in early."

Carter laughed. "Yeah, yeah, I hear you. How are things?"

"Things are good, but I know you. This ain't no social call. Whatcha need, man?"

"I wish it was, Tony. You'll probably see something come across your screen this morning about Andy Calhoun. A murder case being handled by Dickenson County."

"Yeah, I see it right here." Tony read his monitor. "Oh shit, man, that's your brother-in-law?"

"Yeah, Cons and I found him nearly beat to death in his backyard yesterday afternoon. Connie had the foresight to have him flown to Holston Valley. He died in flight. I'm going to need all the info you can get me on this one."

"Who's heading up the case?"

"One guess."

"Aw, shit, man. Don't tell me it's Cecil Vanover?"

"Yep."

"You've got to be kidding me, man. The Cecil Vanover? The one who stole your girlfriend in high school?"

"The one I cracked that game winning triple off of in high school, that's the one."

"I bet he still hasn't got over that hit yet?

"Me neither." Tony could hear the smile in Carter's voice.

"I figured you would have hugged his neck and thanked him by now. If he hadn't stole that girlfriend from you, you may never had met Cons. I don't know that girl, but you got the good end of that one, man."

"Someone's always putting me in the right place," Carter said, reminding himself as much as telling Tony.

"Don't worry, man, I'll keep you in the loop. You got Internet service this time, or are you at another nudist colony."

Carter laughed. "No, I expect I'll be here at Tanya's most of the day. She's got wifi here. The State Police should be here as soon as they finish their stop at Dunkin Donuts. Just zap me what you find. I'll let you know if I need more."

"Consider it done, man. And Carter, this time be a bit more careful. I don't want to see you or Cons getting kidnapped again," Tony warned, purposefully keeping the terror of the Westlake case fresh in Carter's mind.

"I'm always careful. I appreciate it, Tones."

"Just let me know what you need on this one, man. Someone hurting your family makes it personal for me, too."

"Thanks, man. Hey, I see a Charger rolling into the driveway. Damn, it can't be the state boys; it's only eight-fifteen. I'll be in touch." Carter hung up the phone with his steering wheel control. "One helluva partner," he thought. "Notice how you always have the right people around you," the voice answered him back. For a moment, Carter stared blankly out the window before giving his head a short shake to clear the thought.

He looked in his rearview mirror and noticed the car had state plates on the front, confirming his hunch that the State Police's CSI team had arrived. Carter jumped out of the Ram and walked to the driver's door of the sedan as the man behind the wheel crawled out. "Carter Sykes," he introduced himself with his hand out. "I'm a retired detective from Kingsport and the brother of the widow."

"Good morning, Mr. Sykes. I'm Tom Monroe and this is my partner, Keith Johnson," the officer said, motioning toward the man accompanying him. "We're here to go over the crime scene. Can you show us where it is?"

Before answering, Carter took a second to size up the men. Monroe was in his late thirties, about six feet, two hundred pounds, muscular, wearing a dark-blue collared pullover shirt and gray slacks. He wore his photo ID on his belt. Johnson was in his mid-twenties, about six-two, very slender, not skinny, but built more like a Tour de France cyclist. He had sandy hair and wore a shirt that matched his partner's, but chose to complement it with tan slacks and wore his ID on a lanyard around his neck. Carter assumed he was a recent college graduate, and Southwest Virginia was his first post. He noticed neither man wore a wedding ring. "Follow me, gentlemen. I'll show you the crime scene," Carter said, as he turned and led them toward the back yard. The men followed, until he stopped just past the outbuilding. "My niece found her father back here, and called us right after she found him. My wife, a retired nurse, administered first aid until the rescue squad arrived."

"So the vic was alive when you found him?" Monroe asked.

"Yes, but badly beaten. Completely unresponsive," Carter explained.

"Where did you find the body?"

Carter took six steps until he saw a faint bloodstain still on the grass. "He was on his back, right about here," he said, motioning with his hands to indicate how the body was lying on the ground.

Monroe squatted and looked at the blood stains. "Anything else been disturbed?" he asked.

Carter raised his eyebrows as he realized Monroe had picked up on the faint trace of blood. "The deputies went over the scene, but I don't think they touched much. The ambulance was in the backyard, so you'll see its tracks. The only thing I've done is open the door to the shed, with gloves on, of course. It appears to have been cleared out."

"Burglary?" asked Johnson.

"I'm not sure yet. I don't know what was in there. I talked to my sister and she said she didn't know either. Apparently, Andy and his friend, Eric O'Quinn, were working on a special project our here."

Monroe's ears perked up. "Special project? You were a detective, you know what that usually means."

"Yeah, my first thought, too. But according to Andy, it seems he and Eric were working on a special recipe for..." Carter paused for a moment, thinking of what he was about to say. "I know it sounds crazy, but you have to know my brother-in-law. They were working on a recipe for bacon scented soap."

"What?" Johnson asked. "Bacon soap? You've got to be kidding."

"Like I said, you've got to know Andy. They were working on it when I came over yesterday, but I never saw inside the shed. I just know it stunk like hell." His mind flashed back to the odor. "You know, it did kind of smell like burnt bacon."

Monroe shook his head. "I can only imagine. This case would be a lot simpler if it was meth."

"I thought of that," Carter said. "I still haven't ruled drugs out yet. But right now, I don't have any evidence to lead me down that path. No one has said anything about Andy being involved in drugs."

"I understand," said Monroe. "Why don't you go inside and see if your sister or her kids have any more info on this bacon soap project. We'll go over this place with a fine tooth comb. We'll dust the shed for prints, and test to see if there's any residue."

Johnson chuckled, "Who knows, maybe we'll uncover this bacon soap formula." He put on his gloves, walked over to the shed, and opened the door, then stepped back. "God damn!" he yelled out. "What the hell was in here?" he asked, shaking his head and backing away another step. "It smells like chicken shit in here."

Carter grinned. "I told you, bacon scented soap. You have to admit, there's a tinge of burnt bacon odor. Don't you think it'll take the country by storm?"

"That doesn't smell like bacon to me." Johnson shook his head again. "I've heard it all, now. Smells like they still had some work to do on it. I think I'll stick with Irish Spring."

"You should have smelled it yesterday morning," Carter added. "It was all over the neighborhood."

"That solves the case," Johnson announced. "The neighbors ganged up on him and killed him. Hell, I'd kill one of my neighbors if they got the 'hood smelling like that."

"Okay, guys, we've got a crime scene to go over here," Monroe interrupted. He looked at Carter. "Give us some room to do our job. Talk to your family and ask them if they can remember anything about what was in this shed. It might help us reconstruct what happened."

This wasn't Carter's first rodeo; he knew when he was being politely pushed out of the way, and he didn't like it. However, he was a detective, not a crime scene investigator. He was smart enough to realize he would be of little help to the State Police as they combed the tall grass, dusted for prints, and took samples from the shed in their effort to uncover evidence. All he wanted was the results of their work. Even though he didn't particularly like it, he felt by cooperating with them now, he might have a better chance of persuading them to cooperate with him with later.

Carter was also aware that at some point he needed to sit down with each family member and see if they knew of anything that might give someone cause to murder Andy. Anything at all. He really wanted to know what was in that shed, Perhaps Tanya had remembered something. Or maybe one of the kids had been in there with their dad and could provide an insight as to its contents. This was the perfect time to question them and try to find out what was so important in that shed that someone beat Andy to death and then cleaned it out.

Then Carter's thought changed directions. Did he have it backwards? Was this simply a burglary gone wrong? Was someone cleaning out the shed when Andy spooked them? It was a possibility. Instead of watching other cops work, Carter knew he needed to play on his strengths, one of which was asking question.

"Let me know if you find anything," he requested. "This vic is my kin."

"We'll let you know if we need you for anything," Monroe replied, only half hearing Carter's request. "Let us know if you learn anything."

Carter didn't have to analyze the response, he knew the investigator's carefully phrased words meant getting information from them would be difficult at best.

****

Inside the house, Tanya was drinking the morning's third cup of coffee. She looked as if she had aged ten years in the past twenty-four hours. Yesterday's makeup was smeared over her face, her hair had not been brushed, and the bags under her eyes came from both her tears and her lack of sleep. She had on a blue gown and wore a matching lightweight faux-satin robe, loosely tied at the waist.

The three Calhoun children sat at the kitchen table, finishing the Cap'n Crunch cereal Brett had poured for them a few minutes earlier. Connie enlisted Crystal's help to wash the accumulation of dishes that sat dirty in the sink from both breakfast and from dinner the night before. She directed the boys to tidy up a bit for the guests she knew would soon begin arriving as word of the family's loss spread around town.

"Babe," Carter said as he came into the house, "why don't you help Tanya get a shower and get cleaned up a little. The kids and I will clean up in here."

Connie turned to Tanya. "Come on, girl, let's get you a shower." She gently took Tanya's elbow in her hand, wrapped her arm around her waist, and led her toward the bathroom. "People are going to be coming over this morning and we need to make you look presentable."

Without saying a word, Tanya put down her half-empty coffee mug and followed Connie's lead to the bathroom. Carter moved beside Crystal at the sink and began washing dishes. The girl grabbed a towel and began to dry.

"Crystal, can I ask you a couple of important questions while we work?"

"I guess so, Uncle Carter."

Carter thought for a second, choosing his words carefully, not wanting to lead her into answers he wanted to hear. "When you found your dad, what exactly did you see? Walk me through what happened when you got home."

The young lady started to sob as she spoke. "He was just laying there. I knew he was hurt, I could see the blood on his face. I hollered at him, 'Daddy, Daddy,' but he didn't move. I ran to him; I could tell he was breathing, but he wasn't moving. That's when I ran in here and called Mamaw."

"When you got home, did you see anybody here? Maybe someone hiding?"

Crystal thought for a second. "No."

"Did you see a car leaving the house?"

Crystal shook her head. "No."

"How about before you got home, while you were on the bus? Did you see anyone who could have been coming from the house?"

"The only thing I saw was an old, green truck."

"What kind of truck, Crystal?"

"I don't know." Her frustration at not remembering the details caused the tears to return. "All I know was it was green."

"Was it a full size truck or a compact truck?" He paused, realizing the pre-teen girl might not understand automotive jargon. "Was it a big or little truck?"

"It was a big truck. Not quite as big as yours, but it was bigger than Mamaw's."

"Was it an old truck?"

"I think it was pretty old."

"Think, now, did you notice anything else about it?"

Crystal's hands quit drying dishes as she concentrated on the memory. "The paint on the hood was faded pretty bad. I think it had some rust on it."

"Do you remember how many people were in the truck?"

"No, I'm not sure."

"That's fine, honey, you're helping a lot." He placed a couple more rinsed dishes in the drainer. "Now, do you remember if the bed of the truck was empty or carrying anything?"

Again Crystal thought. "It was full of stuff. I don't know what, but it was full."

"Good job," Carter encouraged her, putting his left arm around her shoulder and pulling her toward him. "Is there anyone else who may have seen that truck?"

"Molly Senter might have. She was sitting with me when it went by."

"Molly Senter? Is her daddy Stuart Senter?"

"Yes."

"Good, I remember Stuart. Do you think Molly will talk to us if we need to ask her some questions?

"I guess so, she's a nice girl," Crystal said, as she dried a bowl and placed it in the cabinet.

As Carter and Crystal finished the last of the dishes, Connie emerged from the house's only bathroom, leaving Tanya, dressed in a simple white blouse and jeans, to fix her hair, and put on her makeup. When Carter hugged his wife, the unspoken vibe he picked up told him his sister was not handling the situation as well as they hoped. He walked to the bathroom door and leaned against the doorframe. "You ok, sis?"

"Do I look okay, Carter?" she snapped at him. "Hell, no, I ain't okay. My husband was just killed, I've got three kids to raise, and I've got a shitty-ass job to try to do it on. I might never be okay again." She laid her brush down and faced Carter. He noticed a new tear beginning to run down her cheek "I really did love him, you know. Sometimes he did crazy shit, but that's one of the things I loved about him." She lifted her eyes and a chuckle joined her tear. "With Andy, there was never a dull moment."

Unfortunately, Carter was no stranger to upset widows. As a detective, he was forced to ask many grieving women questions they really didn't want to answer. He just wasn't used to his sister being one of them. He took a deep breath, giving them both a moment to settle down, and then began to ask her the questions he knew the police would ask her again over the next couple of days. "Sis, I need to ask you a few questions. First, what did y'all have in that shed?"

Tanya gave him a puzzled look. "To be honest, I have no idea. All I know is that for the last month or so, Andy and Eric had a terrible stink coming out of it. He said something about some new soap. I figured it was another of his lame-brained get-rich-quick schemes. You know Andy, he always had a crazy idea to get rich. It was his shed, so I just let him do what he wanted out there. As bad as that smell was, I wouldn't dare go in there. As crazy as his dreams were, I never wanted to be the wife who caused him to quit dreaming."

"Are you sure they had something in it? Could the shed have been empty?"

"No, I know it had stuff in it. Andy and Eric messed around in there all the time. Sometimes Ben would come over and help them. I thought it was good for Andy and Ben to spend a little time together. It was good to have some kin around again. You know, Ben had been in jail, and you, well, you never came around anymore."

Carter took the jab at his absence, but didn't flinch. "So Ben and Eric should know what was in that shed?"

"I'd think so. Just ask them."

"Don't worry, I will. I promise you, I will get to the bottom of this. I'll find out who killed Andy."

"I know you will, Carter. One thing I know about you, when you set your mind to something, you usually finish it."

When Connie came back to the bathroom door, Carter instinctively put his arm around her and pulled her close. He knew all too well, especially after last summer's events, it could easily be either him or Connie in Tanya's place right now. How many times had he been in real danger of losing his life with the Kingsport Police Department? He knew if Connie had only known, she would have made him leave the force years ago. Even so, the memory of Connie's kidnapping nine months earlier loomed large in his mind. Connie must have read his thoughts, because she, too, pulled him tighter.

In some kind of silent code that only a man and a woman who have been lovers for over three decades can master, Connie knew Carter had pulled something from his conversations with Tanya and Crystal that he wanted to think about. With one last squeeze, she let him go, knowing it was her turn to reassume Tanya's care. Carter walked out the back door and stood on the small deck, looking out toward the crime scene unit going over the yard and shed. Their actions were not his focus, though. His thoughts centered on the shed, and the contents, which were no longer there. What did Andy and Eric have in that shed that was so important that Eric made sure it was locked? What was so important that whoever killed Andy took the time to remove it? Who was driving the old, faded, loaded, green truck Crystal saw leaving the neighborhood? Was it carrying the contents of the shed? And what was Ben, of all people, doing with Andy and Eric in there? Carter knew in any investigation, especially a murder investigation, there was very little left to coincidence. Carter knew in his heart all these pieces were tied together like the Gordian knot. He simply had to figure out a way to untie it. Or, if he couldn't unravel it, like Alexander the Great, he would have to think out of the box to get it apart. "Whatever I have to do," he thought, "the end justifies the means."

His moment of introspection complete, Carter stepped off the back porch. "Y'all find anything interesting?" he asked.

"Nothing obvious," Monroe replied. "We pulled a few prints we want to take back and run for matches. Don't know if that will turn up anything; they may just be family and friends. We also found a couple of small fluid samples we want to take back to the lab and analyze. We're not quite sure what they are yet. They could be drugs, they could be the secret to bacon soap. I'm hoping we'll know more this evening or tomorrow."

"Can you guys keep me informed of your findings?" Carter asked.

"We really prefer not to give out too much information to family members..."

Carter interrupted. "I'm not an ordinary family member." He looked at Johnson. "I was a detective longer than you boys have been alive. Let's be honest, here. I know how law enforcement works in these parts. If you think I'm going to sit back and watch this case get bungled up..." He paused. He was going to say, "like my father's case," but knew such a statement was a sure way to get kicked out of the loop. He didn't like keeping his mouth shut, but, if he was anything, he was pragmatic. He knew there was a time to put his personal thoughts on hold and stick to the facts. So he opted to focus his frustration on an easier law enforcement target. "...by some local cop with a degree from the community college; that's not going to happen. I'm asking you, out of respect for the time I've served in law enforcement, to keep me informed. Otherwise, I'm going to have to waste my time sneaking around and digging up all the shit you're finding. I don't want to do that, and you guys don't want me sneaking around behind your backs."

"Tell you what, Sykes. I'll give you all the information I can, but you have to share anything you find with us. Deal?" Monroe stuck out his hand.

Carter knew before his hand went out to meet Monroe's, there was no deal here. He knew he would get nothing from these guys that he couldn't find in the Bristol *Herald Courier* tomorrow morning. He was a cagey old vet; he realized this was simply a ploy to get him to provide them whatever information he found on his own. "Deal," Carter said, the fingers of his left hand crossed and a smile of deceit appeared on his face. He reached in his pocket. "Here's my card. Call me or email me with anything you find."

"Most definitely." Monroe smiled back.

Carter recognized it as the same smile he was giving. "They're young, but these boys are a little more refined than they were forty years ago," Carter thought. "But they still can't outdo the old master."

SEVEN

The Breaks Stop, better known to the locals as Fred's, was Haysi's hot spot for lunch. Featuring what they called hillbilly fried chicken and taters, lots of mayonnaise based salads, and pre-made subs, it was the mortal enemy of a retired nurse trying to keep her husband on a semi-healthy diet, especially when the husband was named Carter Sykes. There were better eating places in Haysi, but Fred's was less than a mile away from the Calhouns' house and Carter swore he could smell the chicken and taters from the front porch.

Lunch provided Carter and Connie the opportunity to get out of the house, stretch their legs, and get a few minutes of freedom from the visitors who began streaming in about ten o'clock. Carter, especially, needed the break. The visitation to the family's home became as much a reunion as anything else, and many of these people Carter hadn't seen since leaving for college. Once they finished with their hugs and attempts to comfort Tanya and the children, they were more enthralled with telling Connie about the things he did as a kid, especially the things Carter found embarrassing, than they were about anything else. In a way, the tales served to ease the family's pain, at least temporarily, reminding them of their youth, and taking their minds off their current troubles and back to a happier time.

Carter also used the walk to fill Connie in on the case and share with her the questions that were floating around in his head. As with most of his cases over the past couple of years, including the Westlake murder they solved together, it gave him a chance to vocalize his thoughts, to put them into words, and allowed him to make better sense of the situation. Connie was now quite adept at playing devil's advocate, offering solutions with varying degrees of plausibility for the detective's consideration, forcing him to look at possibilities he hadn't yet considered. In a real sense, she was taking over the role of his partner, since he no longer had Tony to turn to for a new idea or for a different point of view.

As they approached Fred's, the smell of hillbilly fried chicken and taters drove Carter over the edge. Even Connie's objections to the grease and fat filled foods were not going to stop him from having the calorie-laden lunch a second straight day. Connie found a small turkey breast sub and a small container of coleslaw in the cooler, rationalizing that even if it wasn't the healthiest lunch on earth, it was the best thing she was going to find in the convenience store. They each grabbed a diet soda, Carter paid at the checkout counter, and they sat on one of the picnic tables out front that served as the dining room.

"I swear, Carter Sykes, one of these days, you're going to look like Chris Christie," she chided him.

"Not as long as you work it off of me, babe," he said smiling at her, He was proud of his comeback and hoped the topic of sex would earn him a reprieve from the discussion of food.

"Trust me, sweetie, you no longer have the stamina to work off all those calories." Her face beamed with the confidence that her reply would put him in his place.

Carter knew better than to reply. One thing about Connie, she held her own when it came to talking about sex. She always won these little tit-for-tat battles of words between them. He knew the longer he drug out this line of conversation, the worse it would get for him. "Hey, I am drinking a diet soda pop," he defended himself. "I promise I'll do better tomorrow," he pleaded. "I promise, tomorrow, I'll eat lunch somewhere else."

"I know you'll do better tomorrow, I'm picking the lunch stop," she informed him. A look of satisfaction crossed her face.

"I guess I better eat up today, then." He picked up a drumstick and took an exaggerated bite, doing his best Henry VIII impersonation as his moans of culinary pleasure reached into the parking lot.

Although Haysi was Carter's hometown, he recognized very few of the faces he saw walk in and out of the store. He was sure very few recognized him, either. He had left the small town nestled in a valley in the Appalachian coalfields nearly thirty-five years earlier in order to attend college at what was then Clinch Valley College, a small branch of the University of Virginia, located in Wise. While Wise was not that far from Haysi, a recession, a gas crisis, and a severe lack of funds kept Carter from coming home very often during his college years. Instead, he picked up a part time job at a gas station near the college campus. It was at that gas station he first filled up the tank of another student at Clinch Valley, a pretty, preppy sophomore with auburn colored hair named Connie Brown.

Carter came back to Haysi the summer after his freshman year, getting a job running the campground office at the Breaks, where he first met RVers and fell in love with the idea of towing his home behind his vehicle.. Staying at home allowed him to save some money, but his Dodge Dart kept highways 83 and 23 hot going back to Wise to meet up with his college friends whenever he had the opportunity. Over the course of the summer, it became clear to Carter he had grown apart from his high school friends, most of whom were trying to get jobs in the area's coal mines, where wages and benefits were excellent, but the work was hard and dangerous. A week before dorms opened, Carter packed his things and went back to Wise, couch surfing with a couple of guys who had an apartment in town, and was able to reclaim the job at the gas station the owner had promised to keep for him until he returned from summer break. As much as he enjoyed the RVs, he enjoyed working with cars after studying all day even more. He especially liked filling up the tanks of the girls, and Connie Brown quickly became his favorite customer.

"Carter Sykes, you old son of a bitch, is that you?" The deep, accented voice jarred Carter from his daydream and he looked to see the man it came from. "What the hell brings you back to Haysi?"

He stared up into the bearded face of the giant who stood in front of him. The man looked familiar and the voice reminded him of someone from his past, but the six foot, six inch frame gave his identity away. "The only mother in Haysi who is that big is Junior Rasnick," Carter said. He looked the man over, noting he had added a beard and probably a hundred pounds over the years. "We were just up visiting until Andy was murdered. Now it looks like we have a case to work on."

"Hey, man, I'm sorry to hear about Andy. It's a damn shame. How's Tanya and the kids taking it?"

"Not good, Junior, not good at all. To be honest, none of us are. Cons and I were just with him yesterday morning. We ate lunch right here at this picnic table with him before it happened. I keep thinking, maybe if we had driven him home."

"Cart, you can't beat yourself up over it, man. Do the cops have any leads yet?"

"Not yet. We'll get the son of a bitch though. Trust me. I won't rest until the cocksucker's on death row."

"If anyone can do it, you can, that's for sure." Junior turned his attention to Connie. "I didn't know that you had such a gorgeous daughter."

"Junior, this is my wife, Connie. Connie, this is Junior Rasnick. Junior was the line on our football team in high school, and I do mean the line. He was also the frontcourt of our basketball team. There was a reason I didn't play football or basketball in high school. His name was Junior Rasnick, and I would have had to practice against him every day. I may not have been a great athlete, but I wasn't dumb, either. At least in baseball, ninety feet separated me from him."

67

Connie put her fingers to her temple and flipped back her auburn hair. "Hello, Junior," she said with a smile. "It's good to meet a man who intimidated Carter. I haven't found too many of them."

"Ma'am." Junior tipped his ball cap, revealing a severally receding hairline. "Carter, I can't believe you haven't brought this beautiful lady around and showed her off. Every guy in Haysi would be jealous."

"And risk her meeting some SOB like you or Silas Witt?" He looked at Connie. "Hell no, son. This one here is worth keeping."

"We ain't as bad as that Cecil Vanover," Junior blurted out before realizing Carter may not have relayed to Connie the story of Cecil stealing Teresa from him. "Sorry, man. I didn't mean to bring up that subject."

"Don't worry, man, I ran into Vanover yesterday. He's the lead detective on Andy's case."

"Ah shit, man. That sucks."

"Yeah," said Carter, with a moan in his voice. "But hey, that shit between us went down a long time ago. We're both professionals now. We'll get through it." Carter looked toward the road, collecting his thoughts. "In the end, Vanover did me a huge favor." Carter reached over and took Connie's hand, holding it gingerly in his.

"I should say so," Junior said with a smile directed at Connie. "Looks like you came out pretty good in the deal, Cart."

"What are you doing these days?" Carter asked, thankful for the opportunity to change the subject.

"Still driving a goddamn coal truck." He looked back at his rig across the parking lot. "Times are tough, though. Obama's killed coal. I'm only getting in about three days a week; I guess I'm lucky to get that. I'm hoping to hang on another ten years and get out."

"You working union?" Carter asked.

"Hell no, son. Things have changed since you left. There ain't many union jobs left 'round here. There's a few, but most operators are so sporadic now, they'd rather shut down than go union. Most of the drivers, hell, most of the miners, are non-union nowdays. Pay's better if you go non-union. They'll pay a little better not to have to put up with all the union bullshit."

"Yeah, but what about the benefits? Best I remember, the union had a helluva health and retirement plan."

"We've got health insurance, but it ain't as good as union insurance, for sure. Not much of a retirement plan, but with the extra pay, I've been able to put back a little bit. I may be an old country boy, but I ain't stupid, you know."

"I'm glad to hear that, man. Hey, are you still married to Patti? How is she?"

"Nah, man. She took off about fifteen years ago. She found out I was banging some bitch over in Elkhorn City." He looked over at Connie. "Sorry ma'am, sometimes I just say things like they pop in my head." He looked back at Carter. "She got the double-wide we put up at her parents' place, so I put a trailer up at dad's; I don't need a lot for just me."

"Are you married? Seeing anybody? Anybody I know?"

"I date a few women around here, but nothing serious. I've always liked a little variety, if you know what I mean. I'm too damn old for anything serious. Hell, I ain't letting no bitch get what I've worked my whole life for. I did that once, It ain't happening again." He looked over at Connie. "Sorry ma'am."

"Sounds like you're happy though," Carter said.

"It's been one helluva ride, man, and I ain't slowed down yet. Everybody tells me it's going to catch up with me some day. It probably will, but it's going to have to run pretty goddamn fast." He laughed. "Cart, I hate to run, man, but I've got a load of coal I've got to get to the tipple. It sure is good seeing you again." Junior turned to Connie. "And it's great to meet your beautiful wife. I don't know where you found her, but if I had a woman that looked like her, I might settle down, too. Y'all take care now, okay?"

"I'll probably be in town for a couple of weeks, maybe we'll run into each other again. Maybe get together and have a beer."

"Sounds good. I'll see you guys later." Junior tipped his hat to Connie, then turned to walk away.

"Nice to meet you, Junior," Connie yelled after him.

Junior stopped and looked back. "My pleasure, ma'am." He shook his head, and his eyes met Carter's. "Carter Sykes, you sly dog." He smiled, stuck up the thumb of his left hand, then turned and walked to his coal truck.

"Seems like quite a character," Connie said, a broad smile across her face.

"He always was in high school. He was the one guy you didn't want to piss off, that's for sure. I guess I was lucky; I was always able to stay on his good side. I think his parents and my parents used to be friends, that's probably why; I don't really remember. If Junior Rasnick had your back, things were good. If Junior didn't like you, you were screwed. It was just the way things were."

"I'm glad you were on Junior's good side, then." Connie rubbed his forearm. "I wouldn't want my sweetie getting beat up by a boy named Junior," she giggled.

Connie tossed their trash and she and Carter walked hand in hand, back down the street toward his sister's house. On the way, Carter insisted they stop at a store Carter referred to as the dime store. Here, he picked up a few pieces of poster board and a package of colored markers.

"Crime board?" Connie asked.

"Yeah, a crime board. I want to lay out the evidence on it, get a visual of the situation. I want to look at everything at once, and see if it will help us see what is going on; see if anything connects. I'll set it up in the Coachmen so it will keep our attention."

"That's a great idea. That way I can look at it whenever I want to, too."

"I can sure use your eyes on this case, babe. You've been known to find things that I don't see."

"I was trained by the best detective around." She smiled at her husband. "You know, maybe that's what you ought to do in your retirement, teach a class at the community college."

"Then I'd end up responsible for some flunky like Cecil Vanover getting a job as a detective. I'm not sure I want that responsibility."

"Yeah, but you might find a good one, a protégé, so to speak. Then you would be proud."

"You've got a point there, babe. Who knows, 'Professor Sykes'? Mom would be proud of me then."

"Your mom is proud of you now. You know that." She put her arm around Carter's waist and laid her head on his shoulder as they walked down the street. If it had been thirty-five years earlier, they would have been high school sweethearts. Now they were a retired couple, still in love.

EIGHT

That afternoon, a steady stream of friends, family, and neighbors made their way to Tanya's house, offering their sympathy for the loss of her husband. Most brought food; so much food that Carter envisioned a platoon of Marines stopping in for dinner and there being leftovers. Looking at the selection, it was clear Fred's hillbilly fried chicken and taters, macaroni salad, and slaw were community favorites. The table was also filled with homemade cakes, pies, and other desserts supplied by the ladies of Haysi.

While the women gathered in the small house, Carter stayed on the porch, speaking with, and listening to, folks who had finished passing their condolences to Tanya and the children, as well as those who could no longer resist the urge to light up a cigarette. Carter knew he needed to use this time wisely, and complaining about cigarette smoke in a town like Haysi wasn't the way to win friends and influence people. He needed to listen closely to the various conversations around him, and learn as much as he could about what others knew, or claimed to know, about Andy: what he was into, who he hung out with, what kind of man people in town perceived him to be. And maybe just as importantly, what kind of rumors were floating around about Andy Calhoun. Experience taught him that those rumors, while rarely entirely true, often were the smoke that would lead to the fire.

Carter hadn't mentioned it to anyone yet, not even Connie, but, especially after the Westlake case, he considered the possibility that Andy could have had another woman. Andy had the opportunity, since he wasn't working during the day. And he was a decent enough looking guy, with a great sense of humor that could easily attract a lady who felt lonely and neglected. While Carter knew it was rather obvious this crime was committed by a man—women didn't typically kill their victims by beating them —the murderer could easily be a jealous husband who decided the best Andy was a dead Andy. Tanya didn't seem to think so, but Carter figured if Andy were having a fling, someone in this small town would let the cat out of the bag, hopefully sooner rather than later. If they disclosed their secret on this porch, Carter wanted to hear it.

More people recognized Carter than he expected. Most of them were older distant family members or high school classmates who had lived in Haysi their entire lives. Carter had long ago tucked most of these memories deep into his subconscious, never expecting to need them again. When he left town, he put Haysi in his rearview mirror and only looked back to visit his mother or his sister and her family, and he didn't visit them all that much.

He tried to make small talk with the visitors, but, even in his hometown, he felt naked without Connie beside him. He could always count on her, her great looks and her outgoing personality, to be the center of conversation. "Oh, Carter, you need to bring this beautiful woman around a lot more," people would say. But he knew right now her place was inside the house with the women, politely marshalling the crowd so they didn't overwhelm his newly widowed sister. On the porch, he was their focus, something he wasn't comfortable with, but something he knew Tanya needed him to do. His goal was to turn each conversation away from him and Connie, and back to Andy. He did it with varying degrees of success; some people were eager to discuss the deceased, while others only wanted to find out about the kid who left so long ago.

Everything he did hear about his brother-in-law told of a man with a never-ending sense of humor, who, however silly some of his pranks were, people in the community liked. They told stories of Andy being a dreamer, not a provider, but of a man who loved his family very much. Carter thought back to Andy's excitement over Clean Pig the morning before his death and understood their comments. No one mentioned the possibility of another woman; and when Carter tried to hint around about the possibility, there was universal denial that he would ever have done such a thing.

When Jimmy Stanley, the longtime manager of First Miner's Bank and Trust, Haysi's only financial institution, stopped on the porch, Carter recognized his opportunity to steal an insight into an area of Andy and Tanya's life he had yet to delve, their finances. He assumed after Andy's firing from Lowes, things had been tough on them. He also knew if there was anything that rivaled drugs and sex as a cause for murder, it was money. In a town the size of Haysi, the town's only banker tended to have a good understanding of everyone's financial situation, and if Carter's vague memory of Stanley was accurate at all, he figured the bank's chief executive had already refreshed himself on the Calhoun's situation, at least as far as it concerned his bank. "All I need to do is get him to open up," Carter thought.

"Well, here's someone I've never had the opportunity to loan money to. Hello, Carter Sykes. Sorry to hear about Andy," Stanley said, offering Carter his hand. Carter took note that the banker was the only person he had seen that day who wore a tie, much less a three-piece suit. Carter reminded

72

himself he never trusted a man in a three-piece suit, especially one who made you think he was doing you a favor.

"Thanks, Mr. Stanley. You know I can't afford to borrow money; I'm an old, retired cop now. It's hard to pay back a loan on a fixed income."

"We make loans to retirees all the time, Carter. Retired government employees and coal miners, they're some of our best customers. If you need something and those big boys in Kingsport won't work with you, come on down to First Miner's and see ol' Jimmy. We make things happen."

Carter recognized the bank's longtime slogan and was impressed that Stanley found a way to seamlessly fit it into a conversation. "I'll keep that in mind," he said, knowing he wouldn't. "Come over here just a minute, Mr. Stanley, I need to ask you a couple of questions. " Carter grabbed the banker by the elbow and led him off the porch to the front of the Ram. "You know I'm a detective," Carter started, realizing the statement was a small fib, since he was, in fact, retired, "and you know I'll be looking into Andy and Tanya's financials for clues in his murder investigation." He hated to use the word clues, but knew lay people ate it up. "How are they doing financially?"

"Well, I'm not supposed to say anything, but since you're a detective, and will probably get a warrant anyway..." The banker paused and gave a slight head nod. "Things could be better. Since Andy lost his job, they got a couple of payments behind on the house. Last month they caught things up, but you and I both know when the house payment starts getting behind, things are rough. Quite honestly, I don't see how they're doing it on what Tanya makes. I took a look at her direct deposits this morning. I couldn't feed three dogs on her income, much less raise three kids."

Carter smiled, glad to see his instincts were still good and the banker had indeed reviewed the Calhouns' financials. "I've wondered that myself, Jimmy," purposefully shifting to his first name to indicate their new partnership in solving the murder. "You say the house payment is okay now? I just want to make sure, just in case they might need any help. Don't want to see the kids without a place to live. You know how poor we grew up. Do they have any money in savings?"

Stanley put his hand over his moustache and thought for a moment. "Now that you mentioned it, Carla, my secretary, told me Andy opened up a savings account a couple of months ago. I remember it because I was surprised. I knew he still didn't have a job, and wondered how he got the money to both catch up his house payments and to open a savings account. I'm not sure how much he deposited, I assumed it wasn't much. But I do know Tanya's name wasn't on the account. Don't worry though, we'll make it easy for her to access it if she needs to. That's one of the benefits of banking with your hometown bank." A smile beamed across his face. "We don't hide behind some big-city lawyer; we take care of our people."

"Anyway you could check and let me know how much was in that account? It might give me some insight into who killed him."

"Carter, I may have said enough already. Are you officially working on the investigation? I heard Cecil Vanover was handling it personally. I sure don't want to step on the shoes of the next sheriff."

"He is, but being a detective is like being a banker, Jimmy. Once you get it in your blood, you never get out, at least not completely. I'm just trying to help move things along. Cecil knows I'll be asking some questions." Carter unleashed a smile of his own, proud that his statement, while deceptive, wasn't an untruth.

"I understand. Give me a call tomorrow and I'll see what I can tell you. Here's my card." Stanley reached inside his shirt pocket and produced a business card. "Keep this handy for when you need that next loan, too."

"Thanks, Jimmy, I appreciate it. You never know when Connie may decide she's ready for a new fifth-wheel."

"You never know, she may decide she wants a class A diesel pusher this time. Just let me know, Carter. We've got some great rates right now." He put his arm around Carter's shoulder. "Remember, we make things happen."

****

Once back at Breaks, Carter began transforming the living room of the Coachmen into the headquarters of a murder investigation. He took one of the poster boards, laid it on the dinette table, uncapped a marker, and began to jot down some notes.

"What are you doing, sweetie?" Connie asked, putting her arms around his waist.

"I'm starting a crime board," Carter informed her. "It will allow us to stand back and take a look at what is going on, to see everything at once. It may allow us to see how two things fit together that we can't see in our mind alone. For example, my first question is, 'Why did Eric lock the shed?' He took a black marker and wrote, "Why did Eric lock shed?" Then I want to know why it was unlocked when we found Andy's body. He wrote "Shed Unlocked" on the board underneath the first question.

"And why was the shed empty when you and the deputies went inside?" Connie added.

"Exactly." Carter wrote "Shed Empty" on the next line.

"Perhaps you should make that 'Shed Cleaned Out,'" Connie suggested. I don't think Eric went to the trouble to lock an empty shed. We know something was in there, we smelled it earlier in the day."

"Good point." Beside "Shed empty," he added the words "Cleaned out."

"What else do we know?" Carter asked. "We know the body was on the wrong side of the yard." He started a new column, writing the words "Wrong side of yard." "Now let's see, from my conversation with Jimmy Stanley there appear to be some financial irregularities. The words "Financial Inconsistencies" formed the top line of a third column, with "Two House Payments Behind" and "New Savings Account—No Tanya," underneath.

"How'd you find out about the finances?" Connie asked.

"I asked Andy and Tanya's banker." Carter informed her. "Sometimes detective work is as easy as asking questions."

"What does it mean?"

"I don't know yet. There could be a simple answer for it. Maybe he got a loam from one of his relatives. Or maybe he sold a gun or something to get the money. But if I was a betting man, I'd bet these financial issues will shed some light onto his murder. We'll have to do a little digging to find out."

Carter picked up the poster board and looked for a place to put it. He wanted a place where it would be out of the way, but, at the same time, be in plain view. His eyes fell on the couch, located in the camper's living room slide-out. His first instinct was not to use the couch, remembering it was Thor's bed. But Thor would not be using the sofa for a bed anymore. A tear came to his eye as he leaned the board against the cushion and stepped back to take a look.

Next, Carter got another piece of poster board and began constructing a timeline. He started with Andy losing his job, added the opening of the bank account, noted that he and Connie met Andy and Eric yesterday morning and finished with Andy's death during transport yesterday afternoon. He left plenty of room on both ends of this line to add things of relevance as they became known. He moved the timeline to the couch and placed it beside the first board.

"Now, let's make a board for all the information we know we need. What information do we need to find out that we don't have on the first board?"

"Forensics," Connie quickly answered. "Was there a struggle? Did Andy have any DNA underneath his fingernails?"

"Good," Carter encouraged as he wrote. "I want to know about the faded green truck. It may be nothing, but Crystal saw a loaded one leaving the neighborhood when she was coming home from school."

Connie stared at the boards on the couch. "Hey, where is Eric, anyway? I don't remember seeing him stop by the house today. Did you see him?"

Carter stopped writing and turned toward Connie, his brow wrinkled with thought. "No, I haven't seen him since lunch, yesterday." He scribbled "Eric?" on the third board.

"Maybe forensics can give us the murder weapon," Connie said, and Carter wrote "Murder Weapon?" on the board.

"What about another woman?" Connie asked.

Carter was a little surprised his wife asked that question. "If there was one, nobody seems to know about it. And that's hard to imagine in a town this size. Unless I find something to lead me to believe otherwise, I'm going to leave it off of here, at least for now.

"Is that it?" she asked.

Carter took the final board to the couch. "I think so, at least for now. Hopefully we can add to them as the case builds. But I think our work is done for tonight."

"Well, if we're off duty now, do you want a drink, sweetie?"

"If you're making, sure, babe. I thought I'd check my email before I go to bed."

"Rum and Coke okay?"

"Do we have whiskey instead? If it's not too much trouble."

"Coming right up," she said with a smile.

Carter sat in his recliner, opened the laptop, and pushed the power button. He reached over and turned on the new cellular modem. When it finished coming to life, Carter was pleased to see that, even at the Breaks, he did have a decent 3G signal. It wouldn't be blazing fast, but it was plenty for what he needed. He brought up his Yahoo! account as Connie handed him his drink. "Thanks, babe," he said, taking it from her and raising the plastic glass to his lips.

"You're welcome. If you're going to get on that computer, I'm going to relax with a little TV, okay?"

"It won't bother me. You'll probably only get PBS from Kentucky. Or maybe some religious broadcast."

"That's fine, anything to help me wind down. Who knows, maybe I'll learn something. Or maybe I'll get saved." She flipped on the TV. Carter could tell she was flipping through the channels as his inbox appeared on the screen.

In his inbox, he found a couple dozen emails, some spam, some from his radio nets, and some from people giving their condolences about Andy's death. Carter checked ten boxes and hit the delete button to do a mass delete of emails he knew he'd never read. A few more appeared on the screen, and he began clicking to delete them as well. He stopped and did a double take when he saw a Facebook notification informing him he had a new message from Teresa Robinson Vanover. Carter frowned. Teresa wasn't on his Facebook friends list. Connie would die if she found out his old high school girlfriend was contacting him, even if just to express her sympathy. Why was she messaging him? He decided it was better not to know and checked the box to delete the email. He placed a checkmark beside a couple other messages he wanted to get rid of. Then he stopped, looked back at the notification from Teresa, unclicked it, and deleted the rest. He looked at Connie, sitting in her recliner, feet up, watching a PBS show on Neanderthals. He stared back at his screen and felt his heart race as he clicked on the message from Teresa to open it.

****

Carter Sykes, it's been a long time. This is Teresa Vanover, but I guess you'll remember me as Teresa Robinson. Cecil told me you were in town, and I thought I'd say hello and tell you how sorry I am to hear about Andy. I really didn't know him very well; I've lost touch with a lot of Haysi people since we built up here on Caney Ridge a couple of years ago. I would love to get together with you and try to catch up and reminisce about old times. I'll take a half day off tomorrow if you want to get together for lunch. You do eat, right? Anywhere but Fred's is fine with me. I can't believe there are guys who actually think getting that garbage is a date, ugh. Anyway, it would be great to see you. Please message me back and let me know when and where to meet you.... Teresa

****

Carter reread the private message, then looked back over at Connie, who seemed captivated by the Neanderthals. He wondered if she had any idea what he was doing; if she could tell his heart was pounding and his palms were sweating. He took a long drink of his whiskey, leaned back in his recliner and moved the arrow to the link that took him to Teresa's Facebook page. He studied her page, noting all the pictures she had posted of herself and her many different looks. "What would Connie think of you checking out Teresa's Facebook page, much less you having lunch with your old high school girlfriend?" that internal voice asked him. "She probably wouldn't like it," it answered for him.

"But it's not like you've got any sinister motives," another voice, a sweet sounding voice that he knew was bad but he liked to hear, jumped in. "Why shouldn't you meet an old friend for lunch? Ain't you just a little curious about what she's like now?"

"Because it's not right by Connie. Besides, if she finds out, it will hurt her," the first voice, the one Carter knew made sense, replied. But this time, it was fainter than before.

"She'll never know, and what she don't know won't hurt her," the second voice said, this time bolder and more confident. Carter stared at his computer screen for a moment, looked back over at Connie, then hit the reply button and told Teresa Vanover to meet him at The Pizza Parlor tomorrow at noon. He glanced at Connie one more time, seeing she was still captivated by the Neanderthals, and a tinge of guilt swept over him. He closed his eyes as he moved his arrow over the send button and pressed the touchpad.

NINE

At nine the next morning, Carter, Connie, Tanya, and her kids were sitting in the Ram, in the parking lot of the Russell Fork Funeral Home. Andy and Tanya had not made their final arrangements ahead of time, so it fell to Tanya to take care of Andy's. Dealing with the business of burial was the part of the bereavement process Carter despised the most. He felt it was wrong that two days after her husband was murdered, Tanya faced a several thousand dollar decision for a family that was already stretched financially. Tanya asked Carter, the always-calculating member of the family, to come along to make sure cool heads prevailed.

Carter looked over his shoulder at his little sister. "I'm not here to dictate to you, sis, but whatever you do, don't make a rash decision based on emotion," he told Tanya. "Make sure you make a decision that is best for you and the kids. That's what Andy would really want."

"I know, Carter. I just need your advice. You're always so good at these things."

Carter pursed his lips together, not liking the pressure that statement put on him. He climbed out of the cab, and, as the rest of the clan exited the truck, saw Sylvie Sykes' red, two-wheel drive Dodge Dakota Club Cab make the turn into the parking lot. She pulled to a stop on the left of the Ram, and the kids ran to give their grandmother a hug. After the adults greeted her, they all walked tepidly up the concrete walkway that split the small, freshly cut front lawn, to the entrance of the brick funeral home. Carter pulled open and held the right of the double doors, allowing Tanya, followed by Crystal, Dylan, Brett, Sylvie, and Connie to enter before he stepped in behind them, blinking his eyes, trying to get accustomed to the reduced light in the foyer. Within seconds, a tall, slender man, immaculately trimmed, wearing a freshly pressed, off the rack, black coat and tie, stepped out of an office to greet the family.

"Hello Tanya, how are you holding up?" the man gently asked, using both of his hands to gently cradle her right one.

"Hello, Wayne. I'm okay, considering. I think you know my mother and my children." She glanced at the kids. "Do you remember my brother, Carter?"

Everyone's eyes turned to Carter and Connie. "I only know of the legend," Wayne Mitchell said, holding out his hand. I think you were about ten years ahead of me in school. I've heard the stories, though. Especially the one about your romp through town after the track meet."

Carter took Wayne's hand and grinned at the veiled reference to the winning streak the Haysi High School boys track team made through town many years ago. "He's pretty good," he thought. "The man knows how to flatter." But besides the flattery, there were other things about the funeral director that put Carter more at ease than he expected; the way he softly held Tanya's hand, the way he firmly shook Carter's, his easy, non-pressuring tone of voice. First impressions told Carter that Wayne Mitchell really did care about his clients, that he didn't run one of those chain funeral services that were more interested in the bottom line than the family's well being. Carter understood Mitchell was a businessman and a salesman; he knew he would make the pitch for the more expensive items. But Carter's first impression told him, in the end, Mitchell would understand the plight of a family which had just lost their husband and father, and not put undue emotional pressure on them. "The legend scares me," Carter said with a smile. "I don't know if I can live up to it."

"It shouldn't. Most everything I've heard is good."

"I'm glad. I just hope it's not too good." Carter turned toward his wife. "This is my wife, Connie." Carter noticed that, even in a situation like this, even after all the years they had been together, he still beamed with pride when he said those words.

"My pleasure, ma'am." Mitchell smiled at her, gently shaking her hand.

"Thank you, Mr. Mitchell," she replied with a subdued smile of her own.

Mitchell led the family through a room that resembled a sanctuary in a Southern Baptist church. Carter looked up at the wall behind the podium, expecting to see the previous week's attendance and offering statistics posted along the wall, but he only saw a simple cross hanging there. Coming to another double door, Mitchell held the right side open, leading them into a room with approximately ten caskets sitting on stands, each with a sign showing its name and price. "Take a few minutes and pick out a casket," Mitchell instructed. "I'll be back in a few minutes to see if you have any questions and we'll go over the details."

"Thank you, Mr. Mitchell," Carter said softly, as the funeral director left the room.

Carter glanced around the room at the signs on the coffins. "Holy shit," he thought to himself, noticing the Presidential casket with a price tag north of ten grand. "Who in the hell would pay that for a box to be buried six feet under the ground in for eternity? It ain't like anyone will ever see it again. Whatever happened to the simple pine box?" He blinked his eyes and did a subtle headshake to clear his head. "This is the time to be frugal, but not to come across as cheap," he reminded himself.

Tanya gravitated toward a light brown casket in the four thousand dollar price range, and the children gathered around her. They liked the designs on this one, thinking it matched Andy best. Carter moved toward one that was rather plain, dark brown, and a couple thousand dollars less expensive. "This one is nice," he said, stressing the nice, and not the cheap.

Tanya frowned. "That's just not Andy," she said. "This one fits him better. It's not gaudy, but it represents the dream he was always talking about."

Carter took a deep breath. "Sis, do you and the kids really want to pay for his dream?"

Up until that point, Sylvie, the matriarch of the Sykes family, had been unusually quiet, watching the interaction between her children. Her silence made her voice that much more authoritative when she did speak. She looked at Carter. "We're not putting that casket in our cemetery. We'll get the one Tanya and the children want."

"But Mom, nobody will ever see it again," Carter pleaded. "Nobody will ever know…"

Sylvie's hand gesture cut Carter off. "I'll know. And, it's going in the cemetery where your father is buried. And where I will be." She turned her attention to her daughter. "Tanya, which one do you want?"

Tanya looked around for a minute, and migrated toward a coffin in between the "if money was no object" one she was considering and the cheaper one Carter recommended. She looked at her children to see if there were any signs of disappointment. She didn't detect any. "This one here will do fine, mom. I think Andy would be pleased with it."

The children nodded their agreement.

"You sure?" Sylvie asked. "It's your call, Tanya."

She again looked at her children. "I'm sure, Mom."

"Then that's the one we'll get," Sylvie said decisively. Carter recognized her tone, and knew the discussion was over. He nodded his approval, knowing it was futile to do otherwise.

Mitchell re-entered the room and they all moved to his office, where they sat down and went over various aspects of the burial. The director offered them the thickest gauge vault available, but Carter stood firm on getting the thinnest, even when Tanya attempted to compromise by suggesting they go with a middle-of-the-road grade. Since Andy had no family needing to travel more than a couple of hours to get to Haysi, they agreed to hold the service as quickly as possible. Setting the viewing between four and five the next evening, with the service, then the burial, to follow. They all agreed to make the Sykes family cemetery, a small piece of land on an east-facing ridge, set aside by Carter's grandparents, as Andy's final resting place. There, he would join Carter's father and his grandparents, and await the rest of the Sykes family. They worked out the pallbearers, preacher, and other aspects of the service. Carter asked about the total cost, Mitchell punched a few buttons on his adding machine, and estimated everything would run about five thousand dollars, give, or take, if the family took care of digging the grave. Carter thought it was ridiculous to spend that much money to bury someone, but he had already said his peace, and knew it best to hold his thoughts. At least he felt comfortable that Wayne Mitchel had simply presented them with their options and let them decide what was best for their family, without putting undue pressure on them. "There are advantages to living in a small town," Carter thought.

****

Back at Tanya's, Carter decided it was time to work on finding the person responsible for Andy's death. He reached in his wallet and took out the card of the State Police investigator, Tom Monroe, retrieved his phone from his pocket, and dialed the number. "Monroe," the voice came across the smartphone's earpiece.

"Tom, Carter Sykes, Andy Calhoun's brother-in-law. Have you got a minute?"

"I can take one," Monroe replied. "What can I do for you?

"I'm hoping you have uncovered some information about the Calhoun case.

"Yeah, the Haysi case." Monroe paused. Carter expected to hear the investigator flipping through papers, looking for his notes. But instead, he heard keys on a keyboard tapping. "Not a whole lot to tell you, Mr. Sykes. I was hoping you had something for us."

"Did you find anything in the shed?"

"Not really. Someone wiped it down pretty good."

"What about on the body? Any skin or DNA under Andy's fingernails? Any idea on what the murder weapon was?"

"Mr. Sykes, as a former detective, you know the procedure. If you want any information about this case, you really need to go through the local sheriff's department. They are the ones heading up the investigation. The State Police are just assisting. The investigator there is…" he paused and Carter heard more keyboard clicks.

"Cecil Vanover," Carter's tone didn't mask his disappointment in Monroe's shun. "I know him well. Unfortunately, I have a pretty good idea exactly how much cooperation I'll get from Cecil."

"Yeah, Vanover, that's it. Check with him; he's the contact person. Any information released has to come from him."

"You got anything you can give me, anything at all?"

"Sykes, I hear you were a damn good cop, but I have to follow protocol. Unless you can get yourself named lead investigator, I'll have to tell you to go ask Vanover. He's the man in charge."

Carter took a deep breath, but it didn't calm him down. He realized he wasn't going to get any help from the Virginia State Police, so he figured he might as well get some satisfaction from this call; let them know he wasn't going away. "Monroe, after spending over half my life serving as a detective, a fellow officer of the law, the fucking answer I get is go ask that son of a bitch Vanover? Quite frankly, that sucks, man. Sucks out loud. Have it your way, but know this, I ain't going away. Trust me, I'm the best damn detective on this case, and I didn't get that way without having ways to get the info I need."

"Mr. Sykes, that's the only information I'm authorized to pass out at this time. Anything else has to come through the sheriff's department. It seems you know Detective Vanover; give him a call," Monroe politely repeated. "If you do find anything out, let me know. If we work together, it might help us solve this case."

"Work together?" Carter nearly screamed in the phone. "How about you working with me a little bit here?" Carter shook his head. "Thanks for your time, Monroe." He punched a button on the touchscreen and ended the call. This was one time he wished he had an old-fashioned desk phone with a handset he could slam into the cradle, both to release his tension and to allow Monroe to hear his frustration on the other end. He looked at the phone in his hand as if it was Monroe himself, and shook his head. He took a deep breath before using an app he downloaded when he was on the Kingsport PD to look up the number of the Dickenson County Sheriff's

Department. He touched the display one time to dial it, and waited while the phone rang.

"Sheriff's Department, Vance," the voice on the other end said after the fourth ring.

"Cecil Vanover, please," Carter said.

"Can I tell him who's calling?"

Carter hesitated, wanting to say, 'His worst nightmare,' which he figured wasn't too far from the truth. "Carter Sykes," he finally answered.

"Just a moment, Mr. Sykes."

Carter waited on the line, listening to WDIC, the local radio station the sheriff's department played for people on hold. After a couple of minutes, the country music finally stopped and Carter heard Cecil's voice. "You have reached the voicemail of Cecil Vanover. Please leave a message at the beep and I'll get back with you." Carter heard the beep.

"Cecil, Carter Sykes." He was struggling to keep a professional tone. "I just want to find out if you have the forensics report on the Calhoun case? Give me a call as quickly as you can. The number's 423-555-3829. Thanks." Carter hung up the phone. "I know when a son of a bitch is dodging me," he said under his breath. "That's all right; I've got other ways of dealing with these peckerwood rednecks." Carter didn't need to look up the next number he called; it was number 2 on his speed dial list, right after Connie's. The phone rang.

"Ward."

"Tony, Carter, what's up?"

"Ass deep in crime, you know the routine, man. Bad guys won't quit. Hell, they won't even take a vacation."

"Yeah, I know," Carter laughed.

"Hey, that rookie the chief hired to replace you, he ain't half bad. Bringing in some new ideas. I think he's going to straighten us old farts out."

"I hope so," Carter chuckled. Somebody needs to do something with you sons of bitches." Both men laughed. "Hey, I need a favor."

"Your brother-in-law's case?"

"Yeah. I'm getting shut out on this one. Can't get any info from anybody—locals, state police, hell, I don't even think the FBI would help. Is there any way you can stick your nose out there and see what you can find? Forensic report, anything would be helpful."

"I told you, whatever you need on this one, man. Technically, it's not in our jurisdiction, but since the body ended up here, and probably died in my airspace, I've got a little leeway. But I'm curious, the VSP wouldn't give you any info? I talked to some guy, named after a president I think, who was asking questions about you. I told him to help you any way he could, that you were the best detective in Tennessee. They way he talked, I thought he'd keep you in the loop."

"He cut me off quick. Almost like someone ordered him to. Anyway, I've been through these administrative gauntlets before. Thanks for helping me out, Tones. You know I'll owe you one."

"Big fuckin' deal," Tony said. "How many is that you owe me now? I've lost count, man."

"Hey, I didn't get that twenty-five-year-old blonde at the swinger's club last year," Carter reminded him."

"No, but you did get that fifty-year-old beauty you're married to. I think you ought to owe me for that."

"Whatever. Don't forget, you've got Suzie. She ain't half bad herself."

"True, bro, true. All right, we'll call it even. Let me see what I can find out. I'll call you this afternoon."

"Sounds good, Tones. I'll talk to you later." Carter hung up his phone and looked at the time on the phone's display. Eleven-thirty. "Shit," he said, remembering his lunch appointment. He walked inside to find Connie.

"Cons, I've got to meet a guy downtown," Carter said when he found Connie and Tanya. He walked over to her and gave her a kiss on the cheek. "I think I'll just walk, you're always saying I need the exercise. I'll be back in a couple of hours."

Connie stared at him with a puzzled look. "Ok, sweetie. You want me to come with you?"

"No, no, babe, I'll be fine. I think Tanya can use you here."

"Ok, then. See you this afternoon."

"See ya', babe. I'll be back." He took a couple of steps toward the front door.

Connie stood up. "Wait a minute, I'm not letting you leave like that, sweetie." She walked to her husband and put her arms around his waist. "I love you." She gave him a kiss that let him know she meant it.

"I love you, too, Cons. I'll be back in a little bit." Carter turned and walked out the door. "What the hell are you doing, Sykes?" he asked himself as he walked down the one lane street. "That is the best woman you could ever dream of having. What is your problem? You are lower than a worm," the voice told him. Carter knew it was right. But he kept walking.

****

Fifteen minutes later, Carter walked through the front door of The Pizza Parlor. The Pizza Place, as the locals called it, would never be accused of being five-star, but, in a town much too small for a Pizza Hut, this locally owned eatery filled the gap between a decent place to eat and no place to eat at all. The waitress, a lady in her late forties, who introduced herself as Vanessa, greeted him at the door, led Carter to a table with a good view of the front parking lot, and handed him a menu. She looked familiar to Carter, but he couldn't quite place her. He glanced over the menu; pizza, subs, and a few house specialties were the main choices, along with a few appetizers and a couple of house salads. After a moment, Carter laid the menu down, thinking it safer to let Teresa pick the dish when, no, if, she showed up.

"What can I get you to drink, honey?" Vanessa asked.

Carter made a face. He never liked other women calling him honey. Or sweetheart. Or any other term of endearment. "Do you have diet Dr Pepper?"

"I'm sorry, honey; all we've got is diet Coke."

"That will be fine," Carter replied and the waitress left to get his drink.

At fifteen minutes after twelve, Carter watched as a silver, nearly new BMW X5 pulled into the parking lot. "That's a lot of car for Haysi," he thought. When the door opened, a well-dressed woman with a medium build, sporting L'Oreal black hair, and wearing designer sunglasses got out. She sashayed across the lot and through the glass door, removed her sunglasses, and looked around.

"Hello, Teresa," the waitress greeted her. "What brings you to Haysi today?"

Teresa's eyes caught Carter sitting in the back. "I think I see the man who's bringing me to town, Vanessa," she said, nodding at Carter. I'll be dining with that handsome gentleman over there."

Vanessa turned to look at Carter and whispered, "I know that man from somewhere. Who is he?"

"That, my dear, is none other than Carter Eugene Sykes."

"THE Carter Sykes?" Vanessa asked with hushed excitement. The one you used to date?" She took another, longer look. "He still looks pretty damn good."

"That would be the one. But that was a long time ago. We're just meeting here for some lunch and to catch up while he's in town."

"Teresa Vanover, if I know you, and I do, you'll be having more than just a sub for lunch." Both women smiled at the comment. "Come on, I'll walk you over to his table."

The women walked to the back booth, where Vanessa stepped aside, allowing Teresa to stand beside the table.

"I'll be damned; it is you, Carter."

Carter stood. "Is that you, Teresa? God, it's been a long time," he said, sticking out his hand.

Teresa took his hand, and pulled him into an embrace he was not ready for, one that made him a bit uncomfortable. "It's me, Carter, can't you tell?" Teresa said, breaking the hug and spinning around so he could get a 360-degree view. It didn't take him long to notice that the years had brought a few surgical enhancements to her already nice body.

"I was expecting a brunette," he said, avoiding the fact he also expected a woman with smaller breasts, who looked to be over thirty-five.

"I decided I'd be jet black this month," she laughed. "Who knows what I'll be next month. I may decide I want to have more fun again," she winked. "Damn, Carter, it's nice to see you." Her eyes covered him from head to toe. "You're looking good. Retirement seems to be treating you well."

Carter wondered how she knew he was retired, and then dismissed the notion, realizing news travels fast in a small town like Haysi. "Let's sit down," he said, extending his arm as she slid into the booth. He slid in on the other side after she was seated. "I'm enjoying retirement immensely," he said. "You know, all kinds of boring stuff to do." His mouth couldn't help but form a little grin, since his retirement had been anything but boring.

The waitress asked for their order. Teresa ordered one of the house salads and an unsweetened iced tea, along with a pack of the pink stuff. Carter, glad she didn't want to share a pizza, ordered a Philly Cheesesteak sub and asked for a refill of his diet Coke.

"Boring ain't what I hear. News gets around in these parts, honey, even about a man who's been gone for, what, thirty-five years now. You'll always be a part of Haysi, Carter. I hear you've been solving murder cases in nudist colonies and swingers clubs," she said with a chuckle.

Carter figured Cecil must have picked up on the case through police channels. He tried to hide his discomfort talking to his former girlfriend about nudists and swingers with a laugh. "Well, they don't call 'em nudist colonies, but yes, we did solve a murder in a nudist park last year."

"I wish something exciting like that would happen around here. This is Dickenson County; the most exciting thing that happens here is a high school football game. And if your kids are grown, who cares."

"How many kids did you and Cecil have?"

"I've got two," she replied. "A boy and a girl."

Carter caught the evasion in her reply, using the pronoun "I" instead of "we." Was she saying Cecil had fathered kids by another woman or was she implying her children were not her husband's? He decided this was a conversation, not an interrogation, and it was best not to pursue his curiosity. "Where are they now?" he asked.

"Matt's in Roanoke, working for a technology company. Millie, bless her soul, married a guy from Clintwood and lives in Foxtown. She's an RN at the hospital. I so hoped she'd find her way out of this place."

"Sounds like they've done great. How are you doing, Teresa?"

Teresa took a deep breath, then sipped on her drink. "You know, I'm loving every minute of being married to the big baseball star, Cecil Vanover. What else could a woman ask for, right? Big man at Clintwood High. Professional ballplayer. Top detective with the sheriff's department. Hell, he'll be sheriff when Hamilton retires this fall. It just doesn't get any better than this."

"Are you happy?" Carter asked, already knowing the answer from her sarcastic statement. Something inside him just wanted to hear her say she wasn't.

"Some days," she said, ending her sarcasm. "I don't reckon it's a bad life, at least not for a girl from Haysi. It's just not what I imagined when I married a man who signed a pro contract and appeared destined for the majors. Shit happens, rotator cuffs tear. Like I said, it's not bad. It could be worse. I could be a coal miner's wife, living in some trailer up Tarpon."

"What are you doing now? Working anywhere?" asked Carter.

"I'm working at the clerk's office, where I've been the past fifteen years. Cecil got me the job there after Millie started school. He said we could use the money, and I wanted out of the house. It's not bad; it's just not where I expected to be at this point in my life."

"It could be worse, you know. You did date me, remember? My wife doesn't drive a Beemer."

"That I did," she said, a smile crossing her face. "If I'd had any sense, I'd probably still be with you, Carter," she admitted. "You were smart. You got the hell out of here. That was my goal, too, to get out of these damn hills. I just didn't see you leaving this little town. I thought your mama would keep you on that homeplace of y'all's forever."

"I didn't go far. Kingsport's just a couple hours away."

"Kingsport is a world away from Haysi," she reminded him.

He didn't say anything for a moment, considering her remark. Although Haysi and Kingsport were separated by less than one hundred air miles, she was right. Kingsport, Tennessee, and Haysi, Virginia, were, in many ways, a million miles apart. After all the years of being away, he couldn't imagine still living here. "I couldn't fathom having to drive twenty miles to visit a real grocery store or over an hour to pick up something at Walmart. But no matter where you are, you're who you are," he said. "No place should define you."

"I don't know, Carter. I think, to a large degree, where we live makes us who we are. I think I'm defined by Dickenson County, like it or not. I think I always will be. And honestly, I don't much like it."

The waitress brought their food and refilled their drinks. Carter was glad for a needed break in the conversation. While part of him was glad Teresa's life hadn't quite turned out as she hoped, he was getting more information than he wanted in a casual reunion over lunch. For the first time in his life, he thought he owed Cecil Vanover a big thank you—a thank you for stealing Teresa Robinson away from him, a thank you for freeing him from this high maintenance, color of the month woman. He now saw her not as the lovely girl he knew in high school, but as a woman whose main concern is what is in it for her. He owed Cecil a thank you for opening the door for the best thing to ever happen to him, Connie Brown. Thinking of Cecil Vanover, Carter finally asked her, "How's Cecil?"

"Fine, I guess. What little I see of him. If it's not work, it's something. God only knows what. Some case he's working on. Some business deal he's messed up in. Some twenty something he's screwing, I'm sure. I'm not really complaining. It keeps him away from me. I don't have to hear about the world of the great Cecil Vanover. Lets me do what I want to do," she said with a wink.

"Sounds … interesting," he said, choosing his words carefully.

Teresa picked a pickle out of her salad and seductively slid it into her mouth. "Ever think about rekindling old flames, Carter?"

Carter's attention left his sub and he looked at the gorgeous woman sitting across the table. "Teresa, we never really did anything to rekindle. We dated for nearly a year, but I was too shy, remember?"

"I remember, all right. I wanted you, I really wanted to make it with you, Carter. I thought you were so cute. I would have screwed your brains out if you would have given me half the chance." She stopped, looked him in the eye, searching for his reaction. Deciding she had broached the subject, she continued. "You know, it's not too late to see what might have been." She swallowed her pickle and smiled.

"Teresa, I'm flattered, really, I am. But I'm married. Happily married. To the most wonderful lady in the world. There is no way I would ever do anything that would hurt her, or our relationship. Quite honestly, I can't imagine my life without Connie."

The smile left Teresa's face. "You know, I've always wanted to hear a man say that about me. I don't guess I ever will. Your wife is one lucky woman, Carter Sykes."

Carter's attention was so focused on the conversation, and Teresa's proposal, he hadn't paid attention to what else was going on around him. He was shocked to hear Crystal's voice yell at him from the take-out counter, "Hi Uncle Carter." Carter looked up and saw his niece holding two pizza boxes and Connie paying the cashier.

"Shit," Carter said under his breath.

TEN

The walk back to his sister's house was the longest walk of Carter Sykes' life. Connie hadn't said a word; she simply stared him straight in the eye, the anger blazing across her face when she saw him sitting in the booth with his old high school flame. After what seemed like an eternity, she broke the gaze and told Crystal, "Come on, let's get out of here," turned, and walked out the door. They got into the Ram, and the sound of burning rubber caused Carter to cringe as his truck sped out of the parking lot. He offered his apologies to Teresa, paid the bill, and left immediately. His pace was fast; somehow he hoped to catch his justifiably angry wife and explain the incident away. Finally realizing he wasn't going to catch the Hemi-powered Ram, his steps slowed. As he approached the house, he didn't see the truck in the driveway, so he decided to walk a bit further to settle his thoughts. A half hour later, he finally climbed the steps to Tanya's porch, tail tucked between his legs. He opened the front door, not quite sure what to expect, but knowing it wouldn't be good.

"You sorry son of a bitch," Tanya screamed at him as he walked into the living room.

"What?" Carter asked, feigning innocence.

"Don't 'what' me. How dare you sneak behind Connie's back and meet that slut, Teresa Vanover. You ought to be ashamed, Carter Sykes. For the first time in my life, I'm ashamed to be your sister."

"Wait a minute, now. First off, I didn't know Teresa was the way she is when I agreed to meet her. Second, it was a casual meeting in a public place, in broad daylight. And third..."

"Third, hell, Carter. You snuck behind Connie's back to meet another woman. Not just another woman, your old girlfriend, plain and simple. There ain't nothing else to say about it. You're a skunk; you stink."

Carter hung his head. He could argue. He could plead his case. But he knew his sister was right. He was a skunk. Meeting Teresa without first telling Connie was wrong. He knew it. He also knew pleading his case made him look worse. He understood battling his sister wasn't the biggest problem he faced. He would, at some point, have to plead his case to Connie. "Where's Cons?" he asked.

"I don't know. She dropped off Crystal and the pizza, told me what she saw, and took off out of here like a bat out of hell. If I was her, I would have made a beeline to the nearest divorce lawyer to file the papers. If it were me, I'd take you for everything you've got." She stared at him. "I don't know why you wanted to meet that Teresa Vanover. She ain't nothing but a two bit slut."

"I realize that now." Carter said, her proposition ringing in his ears. "But sis, I really didn't know that when I agreed to meet her. Really, I didn't know. I hadn't talked to her in years, not since our high school reunion. She found me on Facebook, sent me a message, and asked if I'd meet her for lunch. I didn't tell Cons because I didn't want her to get jealous."

"How'd that work out for you?" she asked.

Carter sighed. "Apparently, not as well as I'd hoped. I guess I need to try to find her." He turned around, walked out on the porch, and dialed Connie's phone. It dropped to voicemail, meaning either she had no service, which was possible in Haysi, or she wasn't answering his call, which was also a definite possibility. Carter couldn't be sure which. He thought he'd give her time to cool down, hoping she would come back soon.

He looked out across the small front yard, and noticed Andy's Ford Taurus sitting in the drive. If he couldn't talk to Connie, he could use the time to work on the case. He went back inside. "Sis, do you mind if I take Andy's car over to Clintwood? I've got a few questions I want to ask at the sheriff's department."

"You sure you ain't going over there to meet that tramp, Teresa Vanover, again? I ain't going to be no part of that."

"No, I promise. I'm hoping to catch up with her husband. He's not returning my calls, and I want to find out what he's learned about the forensics. I'll put gas in it, I promise."

"Yeah, go ahead and take it. That car's an old piece of shit, so try to drive sensible, okay? Keys should be in it; Andy never took them out. He said nobody would ever steal that thing. He was probably right."

"Thanks. I just want to see what they've found out, or at least what they'll tell me. I'll be back in a couple hours or so."

Getting into the car, he realized his sister was right, this car had seen better days. The cloth seats were torn, the dash cracked, the driver's side door panel was falling off. He turned the key and the dash came to life, showing over two hundred twenty thousand miles on the odometer. "I hope this thing actually runs," he thought as he turned the switch one more click to activate the starter. The car's engine started, but it sounded like it was on life support. Keeping one foot on the brake and one foot goosing the gas pedal, he dropped the shifter into reverse and felt the transmission jerk the whole car. He backed out of the driveway, hearing the squeal of the brakes as he stopped. "This will be an adventure," he thought, as he put the car into drive and began the trip to the county seat.

****

Pulling into the parking lot behind the sheriff's office, Carter saw an empty spot with a sign that read, "Reserved for Sheriff Bob Hamilton." "Damn," Carter thought. He figured talking to the sheriff was his best chance to get the information he wanted. He noticed another reserved space, this one with a Ford F350 dually King Ranch, complete with Powerstoke badging, and bearing the vanity plate VANOVR45 parked in it. "A Beemer and a King Ranch dually diesel?" Carter said to himself. "Maybe I should have come back here to work after college." Three spots over, Carter found an empty, unreserved parking place and pulled the smoking Taurus into it.

Walking through the back door of the jail, Carter could hear noise coming from the area housing the department's lone prisoner. The old jail was built in the 1930s, probably by the WPA, and showed the wear of its years. "At least my office was better," he muttered, taking in the surroundings as he walked down a long hallway. At the end of the corridor, he startled the middle-aged deputy, who doubled as the dispatcher, sitting at the front desk. "Excuse me, I'm looking for Cecil Vanover."

The deputy closed whatever webpage he was viewing on his computer and spun his chair to face Carter. He wanted to ask how Carter got back there, but decided it was better to skip that question as long as the answer didn't cause him any trouble. "He should be in his office, second door on the left," he said, pointing back down the hall.

"Thanks," Carter turned and retraced his footsteps as if he belonged there. He looked in the doorway of the second office he came to and saw Cecil, sitting at his desk, his attention focused on a stock market page displayed on his monitor. "How's the market today?" Carter asked, as he stepped into the room without knocking.

When he heard Carter's voice, Vanover turned his attention toward the door, but made no move to close the webpage.. "Sykes, how'd you get back here?"

"I know my way around a police station, even one built before my dad was born," Carter laughed, trying to be cool. He snuck a peek a Cecil's screen and considered asking the detective what the hell he was doing watching the stock market instead of trying to catch Andy's killer. Instead, he checked himself, deciding confrontation was not the best way to get the information he wanted. As hard as it was, he put on his best smile and his friendliest voice. "I was in town and thought I'd stop in and see what you've found out on Andy's case." He decided the statement wasn't quite a lie: he was, in fact, in town, and he was stopping by.

Cecil squirmed in his chair. "Not much, really. My deputies canvassed the neighborhood, but nobody saw anything. I'm expecting the ME's report in the morning; I'm hoping it will have something in there to go on. We're keeping an ear on the street, hoping someone will start bragging. I'm still waiting for the state boys to give me their findings; they can be a bit slow, you know that."

Carter kept his smile, not faking it anymore. He always liked catching a man in a lie, and he knew Cecil already had Monroe's initial report. He was surprised the state cop hadn't warned the local detective that Carter was asking questions, but felt it best not to look a gift horse in the mouth. "You don't have any info from state?" he asked, giving Cecil one last chance at truth.

"Haven't heard from them. You know how slow those state boys are. Some things never change, Carter. They sure haven't sped up around here."

"Hmm, I was hoping for a little information." Carter took a longer glance at the financial page displayed on Vanover's screen. "You'd think with all this technology, things would have sped up some. I see y'all do get instant market updates."

Cecil smiled, not seeming to care that Carter had caught him researching stocks. "Got to keep up with investments. I make more from the market than I ever dreamed of making solving crimes."

Carter couldn't stop the frown from forming on his face. He couldn't understand how any detective could be more concerned with Intel's stock price than solving a murder case. It took him a moment to regroup. "You'll let me know when you find something?"

"Sure will, partner. I've got your number right here," Vanover said, pointing at a post-it note Carter couldn't read from halfway across the room. "You'll be the first call I make."

Carter hated it when someone called him "partner." People only use the term in a condescending manner, especially when they were staring them in the eye and telling them lies. Once again, Carter bit his lip and chose not to confront, not wanting to risk the possibility of getting information later, regardless of how much he wanted the personal satisfaction of blasting Vanover right now. "Thanks, Cecil, I appreciate it." He turned, started to walk off, sending Cecil reaching for his mouse, then stopped. "By the way, nice King Ranch."

This time, Cecil didn't bother to take his hand off the mouse. "Oh, thanks. Tree and I are going to our place at Hilton Head in a couple of weeks, and I wanted something to carry more than her car will haul. This truck was on the lot at the Ford place in Wise, and I said, 'What the hell,' and picked it up. Pretty sweet ride."

"I'll bet it is. Personally, I never wanted a diesel, too noisy. That's why I have a Hemi. Call me when you get something on the case." Carter walked away, slapping the doorframe as he started back down the hall and out the back door. Once in the parking lot, he stopped and stared at Vanover's Ford. "A Beemer, a King Ranch, and a place at Hilton Head?" he thought aloud. "Like he said, the stock market must be more profitable than solving murders."

Crawling back into the Taurus, Carter felt a tinge of embarrassment and jealousy. Here he was, getting into a five hundred dollar ride, while his high school competitor had a seventy thousand dollar luxury truck sitting in his reserved parking place three spots away. Carter shook his head. "I didn't have anything in high school when I cracked that triple to the fence. I didn't have a damn thing when I won the heart of Connie Brown. I sure don't need anything now to solve this case, in spite of Cecil Vanover," he thought, as he turned the key and heard the sick sound of the Taurus' V6 engine. "I just need this piece of shit to get me back to Haysi."

****

Driving back to Haysi, Carter began the process of developing an action plan for his personal investigation into Andy's death. First order of business was to learn more about the people in Andy's life. He needed to see if anyone new had come on the scene recently, any oddities that might cause suspicion. He would check his brother-in-law's entire list of associates to see if any of them raised a red flag. Carter knew the quickest way to get started was to go through Andy's cell phone contacts, his email list, and his Facebook friends. By the time he arrived at Tanya's, he had a plan in his head.

"Sis, have you got Andy's cell phone?" Carter asked as he walked into the house.

"Actually, I do," Tanya replied. "A few minutes ago, one of the deputies brought it over with the rest of the things Andy had in his pocket."

"A few minutes ago?" Carter thought aloud, then looked at his sister. "Mind if I take a look at it?"

"I don't reckon. I laid it back here on Andy's dresser. You think there might be something important on it?" She asked as she walked into the bedroom. She returned a few seconds later and handed it to him.

Carter opened up the outdated flip phone and studied it a few minutes, trying to remember how to turn it on. Finally succeeding, he sat down on the couch and thumbed through the menus on the screen. A puzzled look came across his face.

"How long had he had this phone, sis?"

"Three or four years now, I guess. Why?"

"Did he have any other phones? A newer phone, perhaps?"

"No, not that I know of. Our contract ended a couple of years ago, and we decided we'd just keep the phoned we had instead of going into another contract. What's wrong?"

"Did he keep contacts in his phone?"

"Sure, everybody does. He always got a kick out of using that voice thingy to make a call. He said it made him feel like Scotty on *Star Trek*, talking to that computer." She laughed. "He even had his boss at Lowes stored as Asshole. He'd pick up that phone and say, 'Call Asshole.' Then the phone would say 'Calling Asshole', then his boss would answer. Brett and Dylan always got a kick out of that."

Carter didn't acknowledge the humor. He put the phone in his left hand and curled the pointer finger of his right hand around his upper lip, in deep thought.

"What's going on, Carter?" Tanya asked.

"The phone's been wiped clean," he said softly. There's nothing on it. No contacts, no missed calls, no dialed calls, no nothing. It's wiped totally clean."

"What's going on? Why would someone wipe it out?" Tanya asked.

"There must have been something on this phone that someone didn't want us to see. But what? And maybe more importantly, who cleaned it? And why?" He paused for a second. "Mind if I hang on to this phone this afternoon?"

"No, do what you need to with it."

"Is there a computer that Andy used to get on the Internet? Can I take a look at it? I want to go through it and try to find everyone he contacted."

"Sure, it's in the bedroom, come on back."

They walked into the overly crowded bedroom. In the far corner sat a small desk with a monitor, keyboard, mouse, and printer on it. Carter planned his route, and then weaved his way through the obstacles that cluttered the floor. He sat down at the keyboard, wiggled the mouse, and the screen came to life, showing the Calhoun's desktop.

"What did Andy use for email?" Carter asked.

"I'm not sure," Tanya said, clearing a chair and sitting behind his right shoulder.

"Well, here's an Outlook Express icon, let's give it a try." Carter clicked on the icon and the program appeared on the screen. He clicked the address book, but there were only a few entries. He checked the inbox and found it empty. The sent items box contained very little, and the files it did have were old. The deleted items box showed mostly deleted spam. Carter shook his head. "That would have been too easy."

"What now?"

"Let's look at his bookmarks, see what Internet based service he used for email. Most people have their computer remember their password; let's hope Andy did, too."

Carter clicked on favorites in the toolbar and saw Yahoo! and Google among them. Being a Yahoo! man himself, Carter tried it first. He clicked on mail, but it asked him for his user name and password. "It looks like he rarely used Yahoo! Let's try gmail." He brought up the Google page and went to gmail. In a second, the screen filled with Andy Calhoun's email account. "Bingo!"

Carter's first stop was the contact list. Of the seventy-five names listed, Carter only knew a couple, but Tanya was able to identify about three-quarters of the rest. That left the ones, identified with only a letter, A–F, that neither of them recognized. Carter checked the email address associated with each these contacts, only to discover they were web based addresses, and their prefixes, such as "xkf325" provided no clues as to the identities of their owner. "Any idea who these could be?" he asked his sister without looking away from the screen.

"No. I ain't got a clue."

Carter frowned, intertwined his fingers, and rested his thumbs on his lips. After a moment, his hands returned to the keyboard and mouse, checking the inbox, sent items, and trash. All of these folders were empty. "Who the hell cleans out these folders?" he mumbled. After checking a couple more folders without finding anything, he reached into his pocket and pulled out his smartphone. "Well, we'll get a little help from our friends," he said, as he began typing the email.

****

Tony, Carter here. I need a little help man. I found these email addresses on Andy's computer; they are only identified by a letter, and Tanya doesn't recognize them. Let me know what you find.

Also, a deputy brought his cell phone to Tanya today and it was wiped clean— no contacts, no call history. See what you can find out about the number … 276.555.8251. Thanks.

Carter
****

Carter added the email addresses to the bottom of the email and pressed the send button. "Tony will get us all the info he can get about these addresses." He put his hands back to his mouth. "Sis, is this the computer where Andy accessed his Facebook account?"

"As far as I know," she answered. "Carter, I really didn't keep tabs on his computer activity."

"I'm going to pull up his Facebook account. Let's take a look at what he's been up to on social media. You wouldn't bring me a diet Dr Pepper, would you?"

"All I've got is diet Mountain Dew."

"That'll be fine," he said, making a face at the computer screen to express his disappointment without letting it show in the tone of his voice. As Tanya stepped away, he pulled up Facebook on the computer and was glad Andy stayed logged in to his page. He was looking at Andy's timeline when Tanya returned and handed him his drink. "Sit down here and let's see what he's been up to."

"I kind of feel dirty doing this," she said, sitting back down behind Carter.

"It's what detectives do," Carter said. "We search through everything, hoping to find something. Anything important. We're especially looking for something odd, out of place. You need to let me know if you see anything that doesn't make sense to you. Anything at all. It may not be important by itself, but combine it with something else, it may break this case."

"Like those email contacts?"

"Exactly like those contacts."

Together, Carter and Tanya read Andy's timeline for the past four months, finding Andy wasn't as comical online as he was in real life. His posts seemed strangely serious, concise, and to the point. Next, Carter and Tanya went through his photos, his notifications, his likes, and his groups. Finally, they went through his about page. Looking at a blank Family and Relationships page, Carter frowned and shook his head. "Something's not right here."

"I don't see anything odd," Tanya said, staring at the screen.

"It's not what you see, it's what we don't see that's odd. If you look at him on Facebook, Andy has no family. Where are you? Where are the kids?" He clicked back on the photos and they began to scan them again. "Everyone posts pics of their wife and kids on Facebook. Andy has none of you guys. No mention of you guys in his timeline, no mention of things you did together, nothing. For the past couple of months his posts appear to be measured. This online Andy Calhoun ain't nothing like the real life Andy Calhoun." Carter clicked on the Family and Relationships page. "Look here. No spouse, no relatives, nobody important to him. I know he had you listed as his wife six months ago, and I know he had pics of the whole family at Christmas; Connie mentioned seeing them on her newsfeed. Carter clicked the About button again. Look, he's got his hometown listed. He's even listed that he used to work at Lowes. But everyone he cares for is gone, vanished. That's odd."

"What do you think it means?"

"I'm not a hundred percent sure. It could mean he had another woman in his life and wanted to hide you guys from her, but I doubt it. If he were having an affair, his mistress would probably already know about his family. He would most likely overcompensate and post more about his family, trying to keep up appearances. Besides, despite looking for one, I'm finding no evidence of another woman. No, this is almost like Andy was trying to hide you and the kids from someone. He didn't want somebody to know there was anyone important to him. Almost as if he was trying to protect y'all. But hide you from who? And why? Why would a man hide his wife and kids?"

"Are you sure, Carter? Do you really think Andy might be involved in something that would put us in danger?"

"No, I'm not sure, but it's as good a theory as I have right now. He was obviously involved in something. Let's see who else remained on his friend list."

Again, Carter clicked on Andy's list of Facebook friends. Most of them Tanya knew, and they didn't waste time looking into them. Most of the ones she didn't know appeared to be people he worked with at Lowes, but Carter jotted them all down for further research. Toward the bottom of the list, Tanya found a couple of names she didn't recognize.

"Bill Williams. I don't know him. And I have no idea who this Ken Rosenthal is."

Carter clicked on their names. Bill was an administrative law judge in Roanoke. Ken listed his employment as pharmacist in Pikeville. "How'd Andy know these guys?"

Tanya shook her head. "I have no idea, never heard of them before."

Carter jotted them down and proceeded scrolling through the final few people on Andy's friends list. Suddenly, Tanya saw a name that caught both her and Carter's attention—Teresa Robinson Vanover.

"What the hell is he doing with that slut as his friend?" she blurted out.

"Well, they're not that far apart in age. They did go to the same high school."

"Yeah, but he didn't like her. You don't know what she is into, do you Carter?"

"Well, no, not really. I told you, I hadn't even spoken to her in five years before this afternoon."

Tanya looked her brother in the eye. "Now I don't know this for a fact, but rumor has it there's some pretty wild parties up on Caney Ridge."

"What do you mean by 'wild'? Drinking? Drugs?"

"You know what I mean. Stuff like drugs, wife-swapping, all kinds of crazy shit."

Carter's ears perked up. "Wife-swapping? You mean Teresa and Cecil are swingers?"

"I don't know for sure. God knows I ain't been to no party up there. But rumor has it that's what's going on. About once a month, there's a bigwig party at their house. People come in from all over—Abingdon, Bristol, Kentucky, even Bluefield. Mine operators, politicians, big names. I hear that the Number Nine Club is their meeting point."

"What's the Number Nine Club?" Carter asked.

"You have been gone a long time. About ten years ago, someone from out of town bought several houses up a dead end street in Clinchco. He tore a couple of the older houses down and made them into a parking lot. The biggest house, he renovated into a bar and somehow got the county to give him a liquor permit. He hired a band, put in a dance floor, and started serving snacks and booze. Before long, it was attracting some of the wealthiest people in the area. Then, about five years ago, it mysteriously burned down. They said it was an electrical fire from all the music equipment, but some said a bunch of religious people burned down that den of iniquity. Others said the owner torched it for the insurance. Anyways, he took the insurance money and built a high-class nightclub. Every Friday and Saturday night, the place is packed with all kinds of high priced cars—Mercedes, Porsches, BMWs, you name it. Rumor has it there is more served there than just beer and whiskey."

"I take that as drugs?"

"Yeah, 'bout anything you want. But this ain't no Hideout. This is big time. You've got to have some big money to get in there."

"Hmm, sounds like a place Cons and I need to check out."

"Carter Sykes, don't you dare even think of taking your sweet little wife up there. Your whole family will disown you."

Carter thought back to his and Connie's undercover trip to the Carolina Couples event last summer. If Tanya only knew what kind of show his sweet little wife put on in Charlotte. "I'm not talking about a pleasure trip, Tanya. I'm talking about an undercover trip. You know, trying to get information. We would be trying to see who's there and what's going on. See if there's any connection to Andy's death."

"Andy couldn't get enough money for the cover charge to that place. How do you think it fits into Andy's murder?"

"I don't know yet. But the only way to find out is to get inside." He thought back to Charlotte. "It's what we cops do."

"Carter, you're a cop, but you better not get Connie hurt."

Carter smiled. "I won't let nothing happen to Connie. But trust me, sis, Connie is a big girl. She can take care of herself just fine." He paused for a moment to refocus on the case. "Drugs, sex, and money; sis, you've given me the perfect recipe for murder. If this turns out to be a dead end, we've

101

wasted a few bucks. If there's anything to it, we have to follow it. With Andy's addition of a couple of high-end friends, we have to see where it leads.

ELEVEN

Carter knew where there was smoke, there was fire, so he felt sure there was something to the rumors about Teresa and Cecil. He was well aware that sex, drugs, and big money was a perfect recipe for murder. He didn't know how Andy fit into all this, though. He had tried, but had not yet found evidence of Andy being involved in any kind of sexual misconduct. He had considered that Andy could be involved in drugs, but so far nothing had surfaced to fuel the theory. The disappearance of Andy's entire family from his Facebook page, the recent addition of Teresa Vanover and a couple of big money men as friends, and the mysterious email addresses were the only real clue he had at this point. He realized he had no choice but to follow them and see if the led anywhere.

But Carter knew he couldn't pull off getting inside the Number Nine Club alone. He needed his new partner, his beautiful wife Connie, to help him become a member of the inner circle. They needed to become a part of the Mountain Empire's rich and famous. To get her help, he had to find her. She was mad as hell at him, and Carter realized, as much as he tried to rationalize his actions, she had every right to be. Somehow, he had to find her and make things right. He had to get his partner back. Somehow, he had to find Connie.

He pulled out his phone and dialed her number, but once again, it dropped to voicemail. "Damn, she's pissed," he muttered. "Where in the hell is she?" He looked at Tanya. "Sis, this is getting serious. Look, I know Connie's mad, I know she has every right to be, and I know you sympathize with her. But I need to find her. No games now. If you have any idea where in the world she might be, please let me know."

Tanya could see the sincerity on her brother's face, and decided it was a good idea to cooperate with him. "I'm really not sure, Carter. She tore out of here pretty mad."

"Well, you're a woman. Any ideas where she might have gone?" he asked.

"Well, if I were guessing, I'd say she went to Mom's."

"Mom's? How do you figure that?"

"It's a girl thing, you'd never understand. Every time Andy and I would fight, where did I go? Mom's. The fact that she can run to YOUR

103

mother for support will just make it all that much sweeter for her. Want me to call mom and find out if I'm right? I'm curious now."

"No, I can call Mom myself," he said, pulling up her contact in his phone and dialing. "Mom," he said, then moved his phone in front of his face and stared at it. "Damn, she hung up on me."

"I told you to let me call. Connie's there, then. Told her everything, too. Now all the Sykes women are pissed at you."

"Great. That's all I need right now. Next thing you know, Crystal will let me have it too."

"When she finds out you hurt her Aunt Connie, you're damn right she will."

Carter redialed the phone. This time it rang five times before his mother picked up. "What do you want, Carter Sykes? You worthless piece of shit," she slurred the words into her handset.

"Mom, have you been drinking?" Carter asked.

"I'm trying to help Connie get over your sorry ass. I don't know how I ever gave birth to someone like you. I told Connie she could stay with me as long as she needs to."

"Mom, can I talk to Connie, please?"

"No," she screamed into the phone. "You don't deserve her. You don't deserve a good girl like Connie." The effects of alcohol were evident in her altered speech.

"I know, Mom, I've always told myself that. But I really need her right now. Can I talk to her, please?"

"You should have thought of that before you screwed around with that no good Teresa Vanover. Connie." Carter could hear his mother talking to his wife. He imagined them sitting in the living room, Sylvie in her recliner and Connie on the couch. "Do you want to talk to that sorry ass husband of yours?"

"Hell, no." Carter could hear his intoxicated wife in the background. "I don't ever want to talk to him again. Tell him if he wants that woman so much, he can have her."

"Mom, is Connie drunk, too?"

"It eases the pain of your sin. The pain you caused." Carter could swear he heard tears in her voice.

"Shit," Carter said under his breath, then gathered himself. "Ok, Mom, just tell her I love her, okay?"

"You tell her yourself."

"I will, Mom, if you'll let her talk with me."

"She ain't never going to talk to you again."

"Ok, Mom. Tell Connie I love her. I love you, too. Bye." Carter hung up his phone and walked into the kitchen doorway. "Can you believe it; they're sitting over there drunk together? Drunk as skunks."

"Yeah, I could have told you that. You don't know how many times Mom and I got drunk when Andy would pull some lame-brained stunt. Last time was when he got fired from Lowes." A slight smile crossed her face. "That one was a humdinger."

"Will you take me over there, please? I need to talk to Connie, if I can get her sober enough. I'm going to need her help on Andy's case."

"The big detective Carter is going to need his little wife's help?"

Carter signed. "Yes, I'll need Connie's help. We're a team now, kind of like *McMillan and Wife*. Come on,"

"What's in it for me?"

Carter thought for a moment. He knew what she really wanted to know, but he always dodged her questions. He figured if he was going to play the card, this was the time. "I'll tell you about last summer's case."

"Oh, you've been holding this back; this ought to be good."

"You've got to promise not to tell Mom."

"I promise, but I want details. Let's go." Tanya grabbed her purse and keys and they walked to the minivan.

Carter spoke slowly and deliberately as Tanya drove. He drug things out enough so he only got to the part where Thor found the dead body at the nudist park before they turned up the road leading toward the homeplace.

"This is good stuff," Tanya said, laughing for the first time in two days. "Wait until I tell Mom you've been to a nudist colony."

"You promised."

"Yeah, but this is too good. I can't wait to see the look on her face when she hears you were running around naked."

"I'll tell her you're making it up."

"She won't believe you, not after what you've just done."

He knew fighting this battle with his sister was useless. He might as well try to gain something. "At least wait until I'm out of town, then."

"Okay, I'll wait until you're gone," she agreed, still laughing.

Carter got out of the minivan and walked along the path to the porch. Sylvie's dog, a border collie mix, growled at him as he stepped up. "You mad at me, too, Sadie. I guess every Sykes woman on the planet, even the dog, is mad at me today." He kept his eye on her as he walked to the front door. He didn't knock; just opened the door and walked into the living room. His imagination had been correct; his mother was in her recliner, with Connie on the couch, feet up, leaning against the arm, glass in her hand.

"What the hell do you want?" Connie's voice slurred.

"I've come to tell you I love you, babe. And that I'm sorry."

"You've got a funny way of showing it, sneaking around with that Teresa Robinson, uh, Vanover, whatever the hell her name is."

"I'm sorry, babe. I was wrong. But I need you. I need your help." He waited, giving the words time to sink in.. "I need your help on Andy's case. We are *McMillan and Wife*, right? Remember, Rock and Susan?"

"Who the hell's Rock and Susan?" Sylvie asked.

Connie didn't say anything for a moment, letting his words make their way through the alcohol-induced fog in her mind. "You ain't no Rock. Rock would never cheat on Susan."

"Who the hell's Rock?" Sylvie asked again.

"Honey, I didn't cheat on you. It was lunch, nothing more. I'll give you all the details back at the Coachmen. I'll tell you everything that happened. I promise."

"You'll tell me everything," she demanded. "Every last sordid detail."

"There are no sordid details, babe." Then he remembered that Teresa had propositioned him. His thoughts switched from trying to get his wife to go with him to Teresa's attempt to lure him into bed. He realized she hadn't been very shy in offering herself to him, even though they hadn't seen each other, except for two high school reunions, in thirty-five years. "Another sign that this swinger thing has legs," he thought.

Refocusing his attention on Connie, he decided playing on needing her help was working, and was his best shot at get her to cooperate. "Cons, I really do need your help with this one. This is a case I don't think I can solve without you."

Her glazed eyes looked at her mother-in-law. "He needs me, Sylvie."

"They always do, honey. And we always end up taking them back, don't we? No matter how sorry their ass is."

Connie didn't say anything at first. Even in her inebriated state, she realized it had been a long time since she and Carter had a big fight. Little ones, like the spat before she was kidnapped, yes; but not a big one like this. If that little argument led to such trouble, how much worse would a knock-down, drag-out be? "I guess we do, Sylvie. They need us, you know. We have to take them back. I'll make him pay, though, I promise you that." She glared at Carter. "You know you'll pay."

"That's it girl, you make him pay for his wicked ways," Sylvie cheered her on.

Carter moved to the end of the couch and started rubbing Connie's sock covered feet. "I know I'll pay, babe. But I'll do anything to show you I love you." He looked at her glass. "What have you two been drinking?"

"Nothing you'll find in that liquor store, that's for sure," his mother laughed. "Your daddy knew where to go when he wanted the good stuff. Don't think I didn't learn, too. I know where half the stills are in this county," she said proudly. "I keep me a stash just for times like this."

"Somehow, I don't doubt that, Mom," Carter said, shaking his head. "Cons, can we go back to the camper now, please? I've, I mean we've, got some work to do to solve this case. Tomorrow's going to be a long day."

Connie sat silently. Carter waited on her, knowing it was her turn to talk. If he spoke before she did, he lost. He looked at her for what seemed an eternity until she finally spoke. "I guess. But I'm still pissed as hell at you."

"I know, babe. And I don't blame you for being mad. But I do love you and I need you, more than anything." He reached for her sneakers and started to put them on her feet.

"I can put those on myself," she said, grabbing the shoe from his hand. Awkwardly, she slipped her shoes on, glad she didn't have to tie them. Carter helped her to her feet, and she leaned on him for support. He helped her out of the house, off the porch, and up the path leading to the Ram. Tanya, having stayed to see the outcome, walked to the truck to help Carter get Connie into the cab. Carter looked his sister in the eye. "You just remember your promise," he reminded.

"Oh, trust me, I won't say anything tonight. I want to make sure Mom remembers everything about it when I tell her."

"Oh, boy," Carter said, as he opened the door for Connie and he and Tanya helped her make the big step into the four-wheel drive, three quarter ton truck. Even in this precarious situation, he couldn't keep himself from sneaking a feel of his wife's rear as she swung herself into the seat. Tanya shut her door as he walked around and got in the driver's side. As he turned the key, she smiled at him and said, "I felt that."

"I could never resist you, babe."

"You better not ever try. But you better resist every other goddamn woman on this whole planet."

Carter knew, even if she was drunk, she meant what she said. "Thirty-one years ago I promised I would, babe. I meant it then and I mean it now." He reached over and grabbed her hand. "You're such a sexy drunk. I love you."

"I'm still pissed.""I know, but I still love you." He cranked the truck, put it in gear, and started down the dirt road. He pushed the radio's power button; it was on their favorite SiriusXM station. Theory of a Deadman's "Bad Girlfriend" blared from the Ram's speakers. Carter turned it down to a more comfortable level. He wondered whether the song was indicative of his wife in her current state or his old high school flame in hers. Probably a little bit of both, he decided, as he guided the midnight blue Ram 2500 towards the Breaks.

TWELVE

Once back at the Breaks, Carter undertook the task of getting Connie inside the Coachmen. The moonshine had dulled any sense of reality, and, after ten minutes of trying to coax her inside, he threw her over his shoulder and carried her, kicking and screaming, into the fifth wheel. Getting her up the camper's three steps and setting her on the foot of the bed, he turned down the covers, took off her clothes, placed her so her head was on the pillow, and covered her up. After giving her a kiss on the cheek and whispering he was sorry and loved her, he walked into the kitchen and, looking for something to calm his nerves, mixed himself a drink. He sat down in his recliner, turned on his ham radio, and checked into the Tennessee Sideband Net on 75 meters.

After the net ended, and with his glass containing only shrunken ice cubes, he looked at the poster boards sitting on the couch. He grabbed a marker and added "A–F Email Addresses" to his notes. After reading over them again he added, "Friends with Teresa Vanover?" He stepped back and pondered the boards a third time, then added "Swingers?" beside Teresa's name and put the marker down. He wondered if he was more interested in his high school flame's sexual habits or in how her alleged promiscuity might actually pertain to the case. Taking a seat in his recliner, a pair of questions hit him, "What was Cecil Vanover doing with a King Ranch diesel? And how did he afford it on a Dickenson County detective's salary?" He wasn't quite sure why he thought these questions needed to go on the boards, but they had nagged at him all day. Maybe he was simply jealous that he didn't have a Bighorn Cummins diesel to pull the Coachmen, or that Connie wasn't driving a European import. Maybe Cecil was just a stock market genius; after all, he was studying the market instead of working on solving crimes. But something in his gut told him it didn't add up. He retrieved a red marker and wrote, "BMW and King Ranch?" on the right side of the third board.

Next, Carter opened his laptop, started the boot up process, and walked into the kitchen. In the freezer, he couldn't find any of his usual fat laden foods. Connie had only packed microwaveable bags of steamable vegetables in her effort to clean up his diet. "I knew I should have stopped at Fred's on the way home," he muttered to himself. After a minute of moving frozen bags of food around, he placed a bag of roasted potatoes and field peas in the microwave, set the timer for ten minutes, and pushed start.

He refreshed his drink and sat in the recliner with his laptop to check his email.

The only wifi at the Breaks was at the Visitor's Center, so Carter grinned when he got his 3G connection for his mifi service from a tower in Kentucky. After not having any Internet last summer in rural South Carolina, he decided a mifi device, along with a data plan, was a good investment if he and Connie were going to camp in rural areas. He could have used ham radio for email, but didn't want to depend on Tony for his basic Internet needs. With the mifi, he could do all the research he wanted, right from his easy chair.

An email from Tony confirmed Carter's suspicions that the A–F email addresses were tied to Internet-based, virtually untraceable, email services. There was no way to obtain the identity of their owners, at least not by conventional, legal means. His partner also passed along some information from the coroner's report. The cause of death was blunt force wounds the ME noted were "consistent with those produced by a baseball bat." The report stated nearly all the impact areas were on the right side of Andy's body. There was only one blow to the head, and it was the one that caused the bleeding in the brain that led to Andy's unconsciousness and, eventually, to his death. Tony noted there was nothing unusual under Andy's fingernails, except for what appeared to be some strange soap residue that didn't match anything in the database. There was no bruising of the hands to indicate Andy put up any resistance.

Carter leaned back in his recliner, trying to get a possible scenario to play in his mind. "Someone Andy knew came to the backyard. Andy didn't feel threatened, at least not initially. Once the attack started. Andy stumbled across the yard, the attacker chasing with a baseball bat. He beat Andy, then cleaned everything out of the shed, loaded it in an old, green truck, and left." Carter frowned. "What the hell was in that shed?" he asked himself. "It had to be more than some bacon scented soap." For a moment, Carter had a mental image of corporate thugs from Proctor and Gamble walking into Andy's backyard and killing him for the secret to Clean Pig. He shook off the thought, and a new one appeared. As far as he was aware, the only three people who knew the contents of the shed were Andy, Eric O'Quinn and the killer. Carter didn't know who the killer was, but he did know Eric O'Quinn. Or did he? What if there was no third person? Was it possible that Eric and Andy had actually stumbled onto something big with their bacon soap idea? Was it even remotely possible that Eric got greedy and wanted the entire Clean Pig empire to himself? Intrigued, Carter reached into his pocket and pulled out his phone.

After getting Eric's number from Tanya, he gave Andy's friend a call, only to have the phone dump to voicemail. He left a message, and then used an online phone directory to check for a landline number. There wasn't one, but the listing did give him an address, which Carter jotted on the notepad lying beside the radio he used to copy morse code.

Carter had heard the microwave beep ten minutes ago, but had forgotten about his potatoes and peas. He walked to the kitchen, pulled the bag from the microwave, placed the contents in a plastic bowl, and reheated them for one minute. He ate his light dinner, cleaned his dishes, and checked on Connie, who was snug and sound asleep under her blanket. With twilight approaching, he decided to ride his bicycle to the view of the gorge that made the Breaks so special.

After three miles on his Trek hybrid, he arrived at the overlook of one of the deepest gorges in eastern America. Walking down the short trail to the observation deck, he noted the rugged beauty of the area he grew up in, a beauty he never really appreciated when he was young. Leaves filled the branches of the trees in the valley, but on the ridges, the foliage had not reached maturity, leaving the rugged peaks exposed to his eyes. He sat down and observed the landscape as the light began to fade, seeing images only visible under such conditions, and wondering how much of it was the mountains playing tricks with his mind.

In a matter of minutes, the outing began to have its desired effect and his mind began to wander from the case. It turned to the people of his hometown and to their economic plight. "Why is there such poverty in an area this beautiful?" he wondered. He recalled the poverty he witnessed in other beautiful places he and Connie had visited—the locals in the Caribbean, the inhabitants of the Brazilian rain forest, the natives of the American Southwest. He theorized a lack of economic prosperity must be the price people pay for living in places filled with wonder, places they love so dearly they will never leave, no matter the cost.

But, especially in central Appalachia, it just didn't seem right. Hand in hand with all the natural beauty and the poverty was a wealth of natural resources, resources that long ago were exploited by those from outside the region. Most of the coal barons cared little for the region's environment or its inhabitants' well being. They wanted the wealth of its minerals, and were willing to use any means necessary to acquire it. Over the years, legal measures such as the broad form deed assured that most local residents would never reap the rewards of the minerals underneath the land they cherished. In many cases, the scars of strip mining destroyed the homes their ancestors had built. When the locals finally earned a respectable wage

111

for their work, mechanization cut the number of workers needed, leaving many unskilled and unemployed.

The rugged terrain made building decent roads both difficult and expensive, and the lack of highways, as well as the lack of infrastructure and education, kept businesses away. Carter thought of his native Dickenson County, a county that, in the twenty-first century, still did not have one mile of four-lane road. From his involvement in ham radio, Carter knew that the entire EM87 maidenhead grid square, which encompassed a large part of the coalfields, didn't have one inch of interstate highway. Despite all the region's beauty and natural resources, General Motors, Ford, or Honda were never going to build plants in this region. AT&T, Verizon, or Amazon were not going to open huge customer service centers. Poverty seemed to be a never-ending cycle for central Appalachia's people.

Carter heard the train approaching in the valley a quarter-mile below and waited for it to rumble down the track that ran along the river at the bottom of the gorge. The impending darkness allowed him to see the light in the distance, and then the cars, loaded with black rocks that would never get the opportunity to become diamonds, rolled past in what seemed like a never-ending stream. Carter could only imagine the wealth that was in that one train alone, and knew many similar trains rolled across that same track each day. He realized long ago someone was getting rich off that coal; it just wasn't the people of Appalachia who reaped the rewards of the earth.

The thoughts of money and poverty played in Carter's mind as he walked to his bike and pedaled his Trek back to the campground. The thoughts of the region's riches, both mineral and aesthetic, made him realize one thing: he hadn't yet found the money trail in Andy's murder case. He recalled Tony reminding him during the Westlake investigation to follow the money trail. Did Andy's murder have a money trail to it? If it did, it hadn't turned up yet. Walking back into the Coachmen, he flipped the light switch and walked to the poster boards on the couch. Underneath the last entry he had made, he placed the words "Money Trail?", and recapped the marker.

****

Carter wasn't a coffee drinker, but when he woke up, he brewed a pot in the small, two-cup, Mr. Coffee coffee maker just for Connie before he began his morning routine. When he looked up from his radio, he was surprised to see his wife walking into the kitchen, her dark purple robe wrapped tightly around her. She poured herself a cup of java and opened the refrigerator.. He smiled at her, she mouthed, "Thank you," and he took the headphones off his ears. "I hope you like the coffee, babe. I did the best I could."

She finished adding her favorite creamer. "I'm sure it's fine. Thanks."

"You feeling okay?" You and Mom tied on a good one yesterday."

Connie took a moment to assess her situation. "Actually, I'm not feeling too bad," she said, realizing by all rights she should have awakened with a raging hangover. The reason for her and Sylvie's party came to mind. "We wouldn't have tied one on if it hadn't been for you. What were you thinking, no obviously your weren't thinking what were you doing, sneaking out with your old girlfriend?"

Carter hung his head. He expected the question, and while he hoped Connie wouldn't ask, he had prepared his plan of attack. "I didn't really think anything about it," he lied. "I guess Cecil told her I was in the area. She sent me a message through Facebook, and I guess I was curious. I hadn't even spoken to her since our twenty-fifth high school reunion."

"Well, did you settle your curiosity?"

"Yes," he paused briefly, "and no. I have decided I owe Cecil Vanover a huge 'thank you' next time I see him. Being married to her must be pure hell."

"She didn't look so bad to me," Connie said, letting him know she, too, was checking out his old flame.

"I guess not, not if you like plastic, silicone, Botox, and L'Oreal," he laughed. "Me, I like my woman to be a natural beauty. That's why I love you, babe."

Connie chuckled. "Nice try, bub. Keep it up, though; you might win me back by the end of the year." She looked over at the poster boards leaning against the back of the couch. "What's new with these?"

Carter told her about the strange email addresses in Andy's contact list, the phone that was wiped clean, that Tanya and the kids were gone from his Facebook page, and about being stonewalled at every turn when he asked for information on the case. He mentioned Teresa being on Andy's Facebook friends list, and the rumors floating around about her and Cecil. After a pause, he admitted, "And I guess I'm just jealous over them having a hundred and thirty grand in vehicles. I remember how hard we worked to get the TC."

"A hundred and thirty grand in vehicles? What are they driving?"

"A Beemer X5 and a King Ranch with a Powerstoke. Both current model year."

"That's odd." Connie said, and then let her memory drift. "I remember at the high school reunion, both of them couldn't quit talking about the TC, going on and on about it being a Maserati. What was it they were driving back then?"

Carter laughed. "Teresa was driving a Pontiac Aztek, one of the butt-ugliest cars ever built. Cecil was so mad at her for buying that car."

"Oh, yeah. That's it, an Aztek. I remember her saying, 'I earned the damn money, I'll drive whatever the hell I want.'"

"Well, she's still working at an office job for the county. How do you buy BMW's top SUV on twenty-two grand a year?"

"And afford knockout hooters, too?"

"Were they really knockout hooters?" Carter asked, trying to hide his smile. Connie grabbed a cushion off the couch, took a step forward, and swung it, hitting him in his upper right arm. Suddenly, Carter's face turned to stone, serious as a heart attack. "Do that again," he commanded.

Connie paused, trying to read Carter's sudden change in temperament. "Do what again?"

"Hit me with that cushion. Like you did just then."

A frown of confusion crossed Connie's face, but she had seen similar changes in Carter before. She knew something had clicked in the mind of her detective husband. "All right, here goes," she said as she reared back and swung the pillow, once again pounding Carter's right arm.

"You're left-handed."

"Always have been," she said, curiosity getting the best of her. "You know that."

"Tony's email about the coroner's report said it appeared Andy's injuries were consistent with blows from a blunt force object, like a baseball bat. He said the injuries were almost all on the right side of his body, including the one to his head that caused his death.

"Yeah, I remember noticing that when we first saw him in the backyard. So what?"

"Let's reenact this. I'm Andy. That cushion is a ball bat. I know you and you walk up to me carrying it. We have an argument, you raise the bat..." Connie followed his directions, raising the cushion like a Louisville Slugger, "...and boom, you hit Andy with it. Where's the bruising?"

She swung the cushion, once again hitting Carter's right arm. "On his right side," she answered.

"Now give me the bat," Carter said, reaching for the cushion. Connie let him take it; anxious to see where he was going with this. I walk up to you and, pow, I pop you with it. Where did I hit you?"

"On my left side. But you're right-handed."

"Exactly. Andy's killer was left-handed," Carter proclaimed. "That narrows our search down to only ten percent of the population."

"But what if Andy was turned away from him?" Connie asked. "Then the wounds would be on his left side."

"Someone having the balls to attack a man in his own backyard, in bold daylight, would want the vic to know who was beating him. This wasn't a sneak attack from behind. The small amount of bruising on the left side could have happened when Andy turned around and tried to run. But trust me, a killer with this mindset, this killer, would have stood in front of Andy and pounded away. He would have wanted Andy to know who it was. Whoever did this was left-handed, there's no doubt in my mind."

"Maybe I should hit you with a cushion more often, sweetie," Connie laughed. "It seems like I knocked some sense into you."

Carter didn't notice his wife call him "sweetie" for the first time since their fight; he moved to the poster boards, uncapped a marker, and added the words "Killer was left-handed" to the one on the far left. He stepped back and read the boards. It doesn't tell us anything right now, but…"

"When the first piece fits, they'll all fall into place," Connie finished the sentence she had heard her husband say so often.

"You've learned fast, babe."

"Only because I have a master teacher," she said as she laid her arms over his shoulders and surprised him with a quick kiss.

"I like that better than getting hit with a cushion," he whispered in her ear and returned her kiss with one that lingered.

"Remember that before you sneak off with an old girlfriend again." She smiled before leaning forward, parting her lips and tasting those of her husband.

"I have no idea who you're talking about," he purred when the kiss ended. "There's only one woman in the world for me."

"You better remember that, buster."

Their passion built into a succession of kisses. Carter pulled Connie close to him and tugged the belt on her robe until it loosened, letting him know she was naked underneath. She didn't protest as he ran his hands down the V in the front, exposing her breasts to his eyes. Softly, his hands caressed each one, tweaking her nipples. "Umm," he sighed, lowering his mouth to her neck.

"Oh, yes." Connie's head tilted back. Carter raised his head and looked her in the eyes. "Feels like makeup sex to me."

A seductive smile formed across her face. Her hands took the hem of Carter's t-shirt and lifted the faded garment over his head. "I love makeup sex."

Carter raised his arms to allow Connie to lift the shirt over his head, letting it fall to the floor. He gently pulled on her belt, opening the robe completely, and pulled her against him, their bodies melding together, their hearts beating rapidly in rhythm. She wrapped her arms around his waist, placed her thumbs between the waistband of his sleep shorts and his skin, and began to lower them over his hips. She slid her hands along the waistband to his sides and helped the fabric clear his erection as it fell to his ankles.

"The neighbors might see in," he protested, glancing at the window with partially open blinds.

"People have seen you naked before, sweetie," she teased, "Here, I'll share my robe," she whispered, pulling him against her again and wrapping her robe around both of them. Again they kissed deeply, Connie moaning as she felt Carter's manhood against the soft skin of her stomach.

"Makeup sex," they both whispered simultaneously as their lips separated. They giggled and Carter squeezed her tightly before letting go. He took her hand and led her toward the bedroom, stepping aside to allow her to ascend the stairs first. He slid the purple robe from her shoulders, nibbling on her neck as it fell to the edge of the bed. Carter knew her sensitive spots well, and gently sucked on her neck, nibbled softly on her shoulder, then moved his attention to her right breast, applying a small amount of suction as he swirled his tongue slowly around her nipple. A long, low moan escaped his occupied lips as she reached with her left hand and slowly began to stroke him, scratching his testicles with her fingernails at the bottom of each stroke. Carter squatted slightly, wrapped his arms tightly around her waist, lifted her off the floor, and laid her in the unmade bed. He leaned down and kissed his wife on her stomach, circling her navel as he moved down her body. His lips eased their way down her right thigh to her knee, then patiently worked their way back up her left leg, giving each inch a nibble before healing it with a kiss. Just before he reached his ultimate destination, he lifted his eyes to meet hers. "I love you, babe."

116

"I love you, too, sweetie," she whispered, then moaned as her husband found the spot he was looking for. Slowly, he worked his magic on her, and she moved her hips ever so slightly to help him pinpoint the perfect location.

"Please, Carter, I need you."

Carter stood up, hooked his forearms around her thighs, and pulled her back to the edge of their bed. Holding her legs in the air, he placed himself against her and slowly entered the promised land. She moaned, but he refused to increase the pace, each of them enjoying the mounting tension. Finally, Carter stopped thrusting and began to rock Connie's body back and forth, slowly at first, then faster and harder. When he could no longer force his hips to stay steady, he released her legs and put his hands on the bed beside her shoulders. In seconds, they simultaneously reached their peak, and Carter fell on the bed next to his wife.

It took a few minutes, but they eventually found the strength to wiggle their way to the pillows. Connie put her head on her husband's chest and felt the rhythm of his breathing. She remembered how close they came to losing each other last summer when she was kidnapped and her captor was trying to lure Carter in for the kill. They survived that experience, partly because of their survival skills, but mainly due to their love for each other. As she felt Carter's breathing, she was convinced some divine force meant for them to be together. She wasn't ready to go so far as to call that force God, but she truly felt destined to be with this man. "There is no way I'm letting some two bit hussy get between me and the man I love," she thought.

"Penny for your thoughts, babe," Carter whispered.

"Just thinking of us, sweetie. Of how we love each other—how we're meant to be together."

"And we always will be, babe. No one, nothing, will ever change that."

He pulled her body tight against his and she threw her arm across his chest, using the momentum to roll herself on top of him. Looking deep into his eyes, she sternly told him, "You better make sure of that, mister. I like makeup sex too much."

****

For Carter, after visiting a nudist park, the bathhouse was the worst part of being at a conventional campground. At Utopia, he and Connie

117

could go into the same bathhouse, shower in stalls right beside each other, and talk as they dried off and got ready for the day. When they left the shower room, it didn't make any difference if they were still damp; with no clothes clinging to their skin, their naked bodies would soon dry naturally in the fresh, outdoor air.

At the Breaks, as in most all campgrounds, the bathhouse was segregated by sex. The men's showers were on one side of the cinder block building, while the women's were on the other. It seemed lonely getting out of the shower. There was no one to talk to, even though his life partner was just on the other side of the wall. Putting on clothes in the sticky, humid building was awkward; there was no way to fully dry with a towel, so his clothes stuck to him as he struggled to pull them on. It would take another thirty minutes standing outside in the light breeze blowing across the ridge before Carter Sykes would feel completely dry again.

"What's the game plan today?" Connie asked as she approached the camper.

Carter hung up his phone and took a swig from the morning's third can of diet Dr Pepper. "I'm not sure. I need to find out what was in that shed. Problem is, the only person I know who knows what was in there is Eric O'Quinn, and he's not answering his phone."

"Want to run by his house?" she asked.

"I guess I'll have to. And, you ain't going to like this. I want to run by and take a look at Cecil and Teresa's house on Caney Ridge."

"You're right, I don't like it. Why in the hell do you want to go up there?"

"Remember how I told you about the rumors about them?"

"The wild parties? Yeah, I remember."

"And about the Beemer and King Ranch?"

"Yeah, so?"

"I'm curious about what kind of house they have. I'm thinking back to Doug and Maggie Westlake. They hosted swingers' parties in their home, but they had a half million dollar house in Greenville, South Carolina. I'm wondering what kind of house Cecil and Teresa have. Is their house big enough and fancy enough to host these parties?"

"Are we talking a drive-by, or are you planning to stop in for brunch?"

"Just a drive-by. I can get the address off the Internet."

"I guess I can live with a drive-by, as long as I'm with you, kemo sabe."

"Don't worry, babe. I've learned my lesson." A smile crossed his face. "And the makeup sex will make sure it sticks in my head."

"I do have a purpose in all my plans, you know," she said seductively, then reached up and kissed him on the cheek.

"I like the way you carry them out. As much as I'd love to see what else you have planned, we need to get moving. Want a pop for the road?" he asked, as he walked into the camper.

"A pop? I haven't heard you call a soda a pop in years."

"Hmm, I guess it's just part of being back here, of coming back to the hills. That's what everybody calls 'em around here."

Connie frowned. "I know. I just thought I'd trained that out of you."

Minutes later, Carter was driving the Ram back down highway 80, and Connie was once again hanging on for dear life. She didn't loosen her grip on the door handle until they pulled into the gravel drive of Eric's small trailer. Carter smiled when he saw the Chevy Cavalier still sitting in the driveway. He followed Connie up the steps to the porch. He knocked on the front door, but received no answer. Carter checked the doorknob to find it locked. "Shit," he said, then looked at Connie with an sinful grin. "You hear something inside? Sounds like someone's calling for help to me."

"Wait, let me listen," she said, picking up on where he was going with his question. "Yeah, sounds like a moan. I thought I heard someone cry out 'help me.'"

"I thought so, too. I guess we better check it out."

"Want me to call the police?" she asked.

Carter already had his card out, easily picking the lock on the door of the forty-year-old manufactured home. "No, you're a nurse. If he's sick or hurt, I'll need you to take care of him. Come on." He pushed the door open wide. "Anybody home?" he called out.

Silence.

Methodically, they searched the trailer, calling Eric's name, but no one was there. Standing in the kitchen, hands on his hips, Carter looked at Connie. "We've checked his house and I've called his phone multiple times with no luck. Go ahead, concerned citizen, and make that call."

Connie dialed 911, knowing it wasn't a true emergency, but rationalizing 911 was easier than looking up the regular number with the 3G on her smartphone. She explained the situation to the dispatcher. For the next fifteen minutes, they alternated between snooping around the outside of the trailer and sitting on the porch steps. Finally, a Haysi town cop showed up. Carter stuck to their story that both of them thought they heard someone in the house. "Must have been a cat or some old water pipes," he reasoned, knowing it didn't make any sense, but hoping the man wearing the badge wouldn't think too much about it. They followed the officer inside, and had another look around. The policeman walked down the hall and into the bedroom, while Carter and Connie glanced around the living room, looking for anything suspicious or out of place. The policeman moved to the bathroom while the Sykeses hit the kitchen. Carter opened the fridge and checked the cabinets above the stove for any clues as to where Eric might be. "It doesn't look like anyone's been here in a couple of days," Carter said as he looked in the trashcan under the sink. "This piece of bread in the trash is gross and starting to mold."

The officer walked back down the hallway just as Carter pulled the trashcan from under the sink and stooped to see what else might be hiding under there. Using the counter to help raise himself, he looked back at the town cop and calmly and professionally said, "Let's get out of here. Call the meth unit. Now."

THIRTEEN

It took two hours for the Virginia State Police to deploy their meth squad to Haysi. It took half that time for them to clear the house and complete their investigation. The small amount of methamphetamine Carter discovered under the kitchen sink was the only drugs, legal or illegal, they found in the house. There was no meth lab, no larger stash, no pot, cocaine, or heroin anywhere on the property. It could have been that Eric was simply an occasional user of the illicit drug, and behind the trashcan was his storage place. But Carter's suspicious mind refused to believe that. The phrase of the week again rose above his brain's noise level. "Where there's smoke, there's fire," he thought. Andy Calhoun, arguably Eric's best friend, was dead, and now drugs were found in Eric's house. And it appeared Eric was missing; no one had heard from him in two days. "Plenty of smoke," Carter mumbled. "Another item to add to the board once we get back to the Coachmen."

Carter looked at his watch to make sure he and Connie had time for the drive-by of the Vanover house on Caney Ridge before they needed to get ready for Andy's funeral that evening. He insisted, despite Connie's objections, that they grab some lunch to go at Fred's. After all, the only other restaurant in Haysi to eat was The Pizza Parlor, and he was smart enough to avoid that place at all cost. After a brief discussion, Connie finally submitted, but insisted her husband settle for a pre-made sub with no mayo, literally tearing him away from the fried chicken and taters counter.

They stopped at the 4-way gas station/convenience store, where Carter entered the Vanovers' address into his GPS before ascending the narrow, winding road leading to the ridgeline that overlooks Clintwood and Coeburn on one side, and the valley that contains the small, coal camp towns of McClure, Nora, and Trammel on the other. This time, Carter eased the Ram along the road, not only looking for the Vanovers' home, but studying the ridge, dreaming about how much he would enjoy working ham radio from the top.

The diversity of the houses along the ridge caught Connie's attention. A beautiful, nicely landscaped, quarter-million-dollar house was sitting beside an older, twelve-foot wide mobile home without underpinning. There were many older, wood-sided houses along the ridge, some were well maintained, some needed to be condemned. Trailers and double-wides were shoehorned in beside many of these homes, obviously the best housing choice for the landowners' children. Her mind echoed Carter's thoughts of the previous night about the economic disparity of the regions inhabitants. In most places, one had to change neighborhoods, boroughs, or sides of town to notice the difference. In the coalfields of Appalachia, one only had to look at the house next door.

Carter and Connie didn't need the GPS to tell them they were approaching the Vanovers' place; they saw it a half mile away. It was a house Connie imagined Marty and Debbie Calloway lived in. Carter slowed the Ram a quarter-mile from the hilltop mansion, measuring it from afar. All Connie could say was, "Oh my God," just before the GPS told them they had reached their destination.

Surrounded by a huge yard leading to dense woods on three sides, the house had a neatly manicured, nearly one acre front lawn, split on the left by a two lane concrete driveway, leading to a connected two car garage with a mother-in-law apartment above it. Carter's mind laughed at the thought of Teresa's mother living there, giving Cecil hell every time he turned around. The house itself was two stories; Carter guessed five or six bedrooms, with a covered, concrete front deck with columns straight from a Roman estate. From where the tree line began, the backyard looked to be nearly as big as the front, but they couldn't see back there from the road; the eight-foot-tall hedge prevented anyone's eyes from gaining access.

"This is a million dollar home," Connie exclaimed softly, her eyes wide open as they crept by. "How in the world? I thought you said his baseball career fizzled out in double A?"

"I guess they do better in double A than I thought," Carter replied. Best I remember though, he was a mid-round draft pick, seems like the fifteenth round or something, so there wouldn't have been a signing bonus. This money didn't come from baseball. And it sure as hell didn't come from being a detective in the sheriff's department and an office worker for the county clerk's office."

"Where did this come from, then?" Connie wondered aloud.

"I don't know for sure, but we'll find out. One thing I do know, though. I know they have a place on this ridge big enough, and private enough, to host whatever kind of party they want."

"Yeah, they could put on one hell of a swingers' party," Connie said. "And we've not even seen the backyard yet." Her mind raced with thoughts, but she didn't take her eyes off the mansion. "Don't you dare ask me to go to a swingers' party with your old girlfriend. Makeup sex ain't that good."

"Don't worry, babe, it ain't going to happen. I took you to one swingers' party and that was enough for my lifetime. Besides, the TC is our official car of swinging, and it's back in Kingsport." He chuckled as he thought of the Maserati built convertible. "The Ram, with my badge airbrushed on the back, just doesn't fit in at those events."

"Apparently Cecil Vanover's truck does."

"Hmm," was Carter's only reply. He allowed himself one more long stare at the house, then punched the gas pedal and the Hemi engine, which had been idling along as they gazed at the ridge top mansion, came to life, taking them off the ridge and down the curvy road to highway 72 and the small community of Darwin. Connie hung on while Carter wasted no time, once again driving too fast on the narrow mountain road. Even as the road straightened out a bit, she remained quiet, each of their minds racing with the same thought: "How could the Vanovers afford such a place?" Carter's mind went one step further: How could he begin thinking about researching to discover how a couple working county jobs could afford such a place.

***

Carter and Connie arrived at Tanya's right at four o'clock to take the Calhoun family to the funeral of their husband and father. Since neither Andy nor Tanya were churchgoers, she agreed to his parents' request to hold the service at their church, the Backbone Ridge Old Regular Baptist Church, in the community where Andy was raised. The name Backbone Ridge referenced the shape of the ridgeline on which the community was located, which early explorers said resembled a human backbone.

Carter, Brett, and Dylan wore slacks and button up shirts, but no neckties. The ladies wore conservative black dresses, Connie borrowing one from Sylvie, as she hadn't packed anything appropriate for a funeral. Out of respect for Old Regular Baptist tradition, none of the women wore makeup, and the only jewelry anyone wore was Carter and Connie's wedding rings. Tanya and Sylvie crammed in the back seat with the boys, while Carter and Connie slid Crystal up front between them. Carter reached over and rubbed his niece on the top of the head, letting her know he was glad to be there for his family during this tough time. His heart melted at the smile he received in return.

He took his time on the narrow, crooked, mountain road leading to the small, cinderblock church built in the 1940s. Before this building was constructed, Backbone Ridge had been part of the traveling circuit ministry

123

of Brother Eugene Sykes, no relation to Carter, and later, Brother Jonathan Sluss. Before moving into their current building, the church met the second Sunday of each month in the house of Brother Tiberius Turner, whose home was chosen because he had a spacious barn if attendance at the service got too large for the house. When Brother Sluss passed away, the church came under the ministry of Brother Ernest McCoy from Pike County, Kentucky, and they built the current building. The congregation added indoor bathrooms around the turn of the century. More than sixty years after it was erected, the old building still served the spiritual needs of the small mountain community.

Carter parked in the gravel parking lot and the family walked toward the building. Once on the concrete sidewalk, they were met by Andy's parents, Bennie and Joan Calhoun, and his older brother, Larry. Together, the family walked into the church for their private time with the deceased. In typical Old Regular style, the church was sparsely decorated; the family walked over the unpainted concrete floor, between a dozen rows of plain, wooden pews with no hymnals in the back. Carter looked up at the back wall, expecting to see the typical Baptist offering and attendance register, but found only a simple cross hanging there. In front of the crucifix stood a podium that served as the pulpit, also adorned with a basic cross. The Sykes and Calhoun families gathered around the casket, which sat in front of the pulpit, surrounded by a plethora of flowers donated by members of the community.

Andy's body lay in the casket, wearing the green polo shirt Tanya picked out for him, saying he just wouldn't be comfortable wearing a necktie for eternity. The mortician had promised to do his best to make the body and face look natural, but evidence of the beating that led to his death was still apparent. Seeing the damage, Tanya turned away in tears and buried her head in Carter's shoulder. When she regained some composure, Carter walked to the funeral director and asked for a closed casket service.

As the casket was being closed, Carter held up his hand, indicating he wanted a moment with the body. Wayne Mitchell stopped, allowing Carter some time with his brother-in-law. Connie took a step back from his side, well aware of the ritual her husband was going through. Carter stood in front of the casket alone, looking at Andy, and made the same promise he made to Doug Westlake and so many other victims whose murders he investigated over the past thirty years. He promised Andy he would find his killer and bring him to justice. It was a promise Carter never took lightly, but it had even more meaning this time; he was dealing with kin. He knew personally the pain each member of his family felt losing their loved one at the hands of what Carter could only fathom was an evil murderer.

The voice that often rose up inside Carter spoke silently to him. "It is your duty to give your family closure."

"I know," Carter answered back without speaking. "But this is hard. This isn't some stranger; this is my family. Is there no one else?"

"You'll have help," the voice assured. "But this is your task."

Carter nodded his head. The funeral director took it to mean he was done, and moved to close the casket. Carter did not object, but the nod hadn't been to the funeral director; the nod had been to the voice inside of him, telling it he understood.

After their private time, the family sat on the front row of pews. For the next hour, residents of the Haysi area, through tears and hugs, offered their condolences to the family. Each person stopped at the closed casket to offer their last respects to the body inside before moving back outside the church for a smoke and to await the start of service. As six o'clock approached, the gathering moved back into the block building, and Brother Vernon Braswell took his position behind the podium. Tanya looked down at Carter and whispered through her tears, "Where's Eric? Has anyone seen Eric O'Quinn?"

Carter looked at Brett and asked, "Have you see him anywhere?" The teenager shook his head and Carter excused himself and stepped outside. He asked a couple of men finishing their last cigarette if they had seen Andy's friend. They knew Eric and were surprised he wasn't at the church. One of them commented on how close Andy and Eric had been, especially the last year or so. "They were more like brothers than friends," he noted. Carter nodded, and as Brother Braswell began to speak, he returned to his seat, glancing at Tanya and shaking his head.

The mountain church had no nursery, and one baby was fussing as Brother Braswell spoke in a powerful voice that fit his day job as a high school history teacher. He began slowly, talking about Andy's parents and relayed a story of Andy as a teenager. After a couple of minutes he stopped, looked down at the podium, and opened his Bible to an unmarked page. He stared at the passage for a moment, raised his eyes to the ceiling as if asking for help, then began to read. "And when Paul had gathered a bundle of sticks, and laid them on the fire, there came a viper out of the heat, and fastened on his hand. And when the barbarians saw the venomous beast hang on his hand, they said among themselves, No doubt this man is a murderer, whom, though he hath escaped the sea, yet vengeance suffered not to live."

There was a slight stir among those gathered. Many Old Regular preachers simply turned to a random page in the bible and drew their sermon from that passage, feeling inspired by the Holy Spirit. But this time, it seemed even Brother Braswell was confused as to where the Spirit was leading him with this verse. After the briefest of pauses, he continued. "And he shook off the beast into the fire, and felt no harm." His voice began to get louder and his tempo increased. "Howbeit they looked where he should have swollen, uh, or fallen down dead suddenly, uh, but after they had looked a great while, uh, and saw no harm come to him, uh, they changed their minds, uh, and said he was a god, uh."

Several men in the church shouted "Amen," and "Praise glory," and Brother Braswell was on a roll now. Believers would say the preacher was "in the Spirit" his entire demeanor changed, as if someone else was speaking through him, and the cadence and volume of his voice took another step up. "But I say to you, uh, Paul was not no god, uh, but he served a God, uh, a God that knew exactly what he was doing, uh, and who delivered Brother Paul even from the clutches of death by a viper, uh."

The sound of several members of the congregation yelling "Amen" and other praises rang through the little block sanctuary and Brother Braswell continued. "God had a great plan, uh, and in his own time, uh, and in his own way, uh, many were healed and many were saved, uh."

More amens filled the room, allowing Brother Braswell to catch his breath, gather himself, and return to the tone and tempo in which he began the sermon, "I don't know why God has allowed this family to go through this terrible tragedy, but he has a plan, something we do not see or understand. And just as it looked like Brother Paul was surely dead, God brought a good no one could have imagined out of it. Something tells me, God will bring good out of this tragedy."

In most of his sermons, Brother Braswell usually built back up to a second, then a third crescendo, but tonight, there was only one. He called out a line from a song, almost as if reading it from a hymnal, and the congregation sang the same words. Again, Braswell called out almost in a chant, the next line, and again, the crowd sang it. This went on for five minutes until the song was finished. Once the song was complete, Brother Braswell asked if anyone needed to receive the Lord, and waited patiently for a response.

Carter never liked a church invitation. He always felt uncomfortable, as if he should do something, but he wasn't quite sure what. So he sat in the wooden pew, trying to make sense of Braswell's message. "God will bring good out of this tragedy" kept ringing in his head. "But there was no good in my father's death," he thought. "How will good come from Andy's?"

"Trust me," the voice said, then disappeared.

****

After helping load the coffin into the hearse, Carter drove the family to his old homeplace and up the hill to the land his grandfather had designated to be the Sykes family cemetery, where Andy Calhoun would join Carter's grandparents and his father in internment. After Braswell spoke a few more words, he dismissed the few who came to the gravesite. Without hesitation, he walked straight for Carter.

"You're Carter Sykes, right?"

"Yes, sir." He gripped Connie's hand. "And this is my wife, Connie."

"I want you to know, I have never preached a funeral from Acts twenty-eight. I've never heard a funeral preached from it. But when I opened up my Bible, there it was, right in front of me. Out of obedience to the Lord, I began to read that passage of scripture, still not knowing what God was doing. Then I saw you. I couldn't take my eyes off you. You had a serpent wrapped around you, trying to get its fangs into you. Carter, I don't know what it means, but you are Paul. Your family has been shipwrecked. The serpent is going to fasten itself to you. All the barbarians will think you are dead. But fear not. The Lord delivers those he has called."

Carter looked at Connie, who was staring intently at the preacher. "What do you mean?" she asked. "I know it's figurative, but what is the serpent?"

"That's all I know, ma'am. That's all the Lord has shown me. I tell you out of obedience to Him. If you'll excuse me, I have done what was asked of me. I do have to work tomorrow."

"Of course, Reverend, thank you," Carter said, stepping aside so Brother Braswell could pass by. He looked at Connie, shrugged his shoulders, and walked toward the Ram.

FOURTEEN

The next morning Carter knew it was time to roll up his sleeves and go to work. By eight, he had updated the board to reflect the meth they found in Eric's house. He called the Haysi Police Department to confirm Eric hadn't been located overnight, and then added his disappearance to the first board.

Stepping back and looking at his notes, Carter began to ponder Cecil and Teresa's rise to riches. So far, there was no evidence to indicate anything besides honest, if not always ethical, gain. After all, Carter did catch Vanover paying more attention to Wall Street than to Main Street. "But there is too much smoke," he kept telling himself. He wanted to find out more about how they came to own a mansion, luxury vehicles, and places at the beach. It wasn't part of his murder investigation, but something in Carter's gut told him there was more going on here than met the eye. He sat in the recliner, eyed the crime board, and sipped on a can of diet Dr Pepper.

Suddenly it came to him; he wasn't a cop anymore. He could proceed on this case any way he felt. He wasn't constrained by the legal system. He was now a private citizen, not bound to uphold suspects' constitutional rights. The information he found wasn't subject to defense attorney scrutiny as to how it was discovered. He didn't have to answer to a police chief as to why he was looking into an angle. He only had to answer to himself. He was pondering the possibilities as Connie poured her coffee and sat beside him in her recliner. "Murder on your mind, sweetie?" she asked.

Carter's thoughts jumped back to the moment. "Of course. I'm just trying to figure out which bases to cover first. Too many things are pulling me in too many different directions in this case."

"You know, you've got a partner. Put her to work."

Carter looked at his wife. She was right. She was smart, quick on her feet, and got along great with everybody. For years he bounced ideas off her and found her instincts to be better than most, sometimes better than his own. She had been as good as any cop he ever worked with during the Westlake case. He knew she would be more help than trying to convince some local deputy to become a double agent to help him, and he knew he could trust her. Like him, she was not bound by police protocol. He could send her on any assignment, because she was just as much a cop as he was these days. "You're right, babe. It's time you do some investigating on your own."

"Yes, sir," she said, saluting him. "Tell me what you need."

Carter laughed. "This ain't the Marine Corps, babe, it's a private investigation. You don't need to salute." A seductive smile crossed his face. "Of course, you can come over here and kiss your superior officer if you want."

"Superior officer?" she questioned. "You know damn good and well, Carter Sykes, who the superior officer in this relationship is. And don't you ever forget it."

"Yes, ma'am," he said, standing up and snapping to attention, this time his hand raised in salute.

"That's better," she chuckled, then walked over to him, threw her arms over his shoulders and kissed him gently on the lips. "Now that all that's straight, what do I need to do?"

"There's two things we need to do. First, I need to get with the Haysi police chief and see if he will be any more cooperative than the sheriff's department or the state. We may need some resources he can provide. Secondly, I want to see if there is any connection between Cecil and Teresa's wealth and the murder."

Connie's ears perked up. "You know something?"

"No, just a gut feeling. You know me, anytime things don't line up, I become suspicious. That the Vanovers are now wealthy and Andy is now dead may have nothing to do with each other, but … well, let's just say, I'm curious."

"Not jealous?"

"What would I be jealous about?"

"Well, let's face facts, Teresa's a pretty hot woman. And she was your old girlfriend. If I remember the story right, Cecil did steal her from you. And now they're rich, and he's in line to become sheriff this fall. Could it be you're letting your old high school competition get the best of you?"

"Yep, and him stealing her freed me up to find you, babe. There is nothing about Teresa Vanover that remotely interests me." He thought for a split second. "Except for those big plastic boobs." A smile crossed his face.

Connie knew her husband was toying with her. She hit him in the shoulder and stepped back a step and spread her arms. "Buster, there's a lot more here than plastic boobs."

Carter nodded his head in affirmation. "Umm, you've got that right."

"Men!" Connie exclaimed. "I'll go to Clintwood and see what I can find out about Cecil and Teresa. You stay here and play with your police buddies."

Carter called Tanya to confirm he could use Andy's Taurus. A half hour later, they were in the Ram, riding too fast back down the treacherous road to Haysi. Arriving at Tanya's, they finalized their plans, and Connie jumped in the big truck's driver's seat. Using the power controls, she adjusted it to fit her body and moved the steering wheel and mirrors. "Want to kiss your partner goodbye?" she asked.

"I'm glad I never heard Tony say that," he chuckled as he put his head through the window to meet her lips.

"Yeah, me too, sweetie. See you this afternoon." She dropped the Ram into reverse and backed it out of the drive.

Carter walked inside, got the keys from Tanya, and walked back to the old car. He grimaced as the sick engine came to a semblance of life, and drove to the police station to meet with the police chief. He walked into the office, and waited on the medium-built, dark-haired, mid–50s uniformed cop behind the desk to hang up from his phone call before introducing himself. "Officer Roland?" Carter read the man's nametag. "Carter Sykes." He stuck out his hand.

The officer, a couple of inches taller than Carter, rose from behind the desk. "That's Chief Roland," he corrected, reaching his right hand forward and grabbing Carter's with a firm handshake. "My officer tells me you're the man who discovered meth in my town?"

"Yeah, that's me, Methman," Carter chuckled. "As I'm sure you know by now, I'm a former detective with the Kingsport PD, and I need to do a little snooping around on my brother-in-law, Andy Calhoun's, murder case. I could really use a cop I can trust. Back at O'Quinn's house, your officer didn't try to pull authority on me. He simply did his job. That tells me you run a professional operation; one that values justice more than pride."

Roland was a small town cop, but he could recognize an attempt at flattery when he saw it. "No, I just happen to know who the people in my town are, Sykes. I know who your mama is, your sister, and your scumbag brother. I made a call to your former partner, what was his name...," he looked at a paper on his desk, "Ward, Tony Ward, and he told me to watch out for an SOB like you. Told me if I wasn't careful, that you and that pretty little wife of yours would end up solving this damn murder. By the way, where is that pretty little wife of yours? I caught a glimpse of her at the funeral; I could have swore I've seen her somewhere before."

"I've got her on special assignment this morning," Carter chuckled. "I doubt you know her, though; she's not from Dickenson County."

"Neither am I," Roland announced. "I came here twenty years ago from Big Stone. Thought it would be a short-term gig. I ended up meeting a lady, fell in love, and stayed. Happens that way sometimes."

"Well, maybe you do know her then; she's from Big Stone, too. She was Connie Brown before we got married."

"Connie Brown? The Connie Brown? Majorette in the band? Dated that sorry piece of shit Donnie Johnson. That Connie Brown?"

"That would be the one. She finally got smart in college and dumped that dumbass. I didn't wait around; I nabbed her as quick as I could."

"Well, I'm glad, because that motherfucker didn't deserve a girl like her. He didn't deserve any decent girl. I guess that's why no one ever married his ass."

"Sounds like you haven't lost any love for him either."

"Let me tell you about it. I had a '70 Road Runner, sweet car—383 commando, 4 speed, nice. The son of a bitch got drunk, took it for a drive without my permission, and totaled it. His rich daddy hired a big lawyer from Bristol and got him out of it. His insurance didn't even have to pay. I was young, I didn't have collision, so I didn't get a goddamn dime out of that car. I've been waiting for the day his ass shows up in Haysi." He turned his head and looked over his shoulder. "I've got a cell I'll make sure that asshole spends a night or two in."

Carter grinned. "Sounds to me like we can be friends, Roland."

"Anybody who hates that son of a bitch is a friend of mine." Roland raised his right hand and Carter met it in a high five.

As much as Carter enjoyed bashing Connie's old boyfriend, he knew it was time to get to business. "Here's what I need. I need some info. Do you have any idea what Andy had in that shed behind his house?"

"No, but whatever it was, it stunk like hell," Roland said. "I'd walk around town and smell that shit. I asked him one time what he was doing, and he told me some cockamamie story about some bacon-scented soap. What was it he called it?"

"Clean Pig. He told the same story. He tried to get me to invest in it."

"Yeah, that's it, Clean Pig. I laughed my ass off. No one really complained about the smell, so I didn't bother him anymore about it; Andy was always a dreamer. I certainly didn't want to squash a man's dreams, no matter how crazy they sounded to me."

"I understand. When we found Andy, the shed was wiped clean. Whoever killed him wanted whatever was in it."

"I can't believe someone wanted a shed full of anything that smelled like that shit. You don't reckon he was on to something, do you?"

"Nah, I considered it, but I don't think so. The only person I know of who knew what was really in there was Eric O'Quinn. And now he's missing."

Roland looked through the papers on his desk. "You sure? I don't have a missing person's report on him."

"Nobody's seen him since Andy died. He wasn't at the funeral. I'd say he's missing."

"And you found meth in his house," reminded Roland. "My guess is, he's either Andy's killer, and took off with the secret to the Clean Pig fortune, or he met a fate similar to Andy's."

"Where can I find out more about drugs here in Haysi? Where do the dealers and users hang out?"

"I wish I could tell you there wasn't any, but that would be a lie. I run a two-man force in a town that can barely pay its bills. I don't have much of a budget; last year I had to choose between a retired State Police cruiser and keeping my only officer." He pointed toward the front door. As you can see, I'm still driving that piece of shit out there. Brandon has a wife and two kids to feed, I couldn't put him on the street. The sheriff's office is supposed to handle drug enforcement in this county, but 'supposed to' is the operative phrase. The two big drug places around here are the Haysi Hideout, where the lowlifes hang out, shoot pool, and drink beer, and the Number Nine Club, where the big shots, the untouchables, party. Honestly, I'm glad the Number Nine Club is out of my jurisdiction, I'd be all over those rich-ass bastards."

"Big shots like Cecil Vanover?" Carter blurted out without thinking.

"Exactly like Cecil Vanover," confirmed Roland.

****

Arriving in Clintwood, Connie Sykes parked the Ram on Main Street right after she entered the town. Her goal was to talk to people, as many as possible, and see what she could find out about Cecil and Teresa Vanover.

133

She dressed conservatively, wearing a light blue blouse, dark, loose fitting jeans; she had left her below-the-shoulder auburn hair loose, and she carried a small purse over her shoulder. She smiled at everyone she passed, speaking to those who seemed friendly, stopping and talking with those who were inclined to talk to a stranger. She started with small talk, trying to lead into a conversation about things in town, especially those involving the sheriff's department. Maybe it was just her, but to Connie, it seemed each time she mentioned law enforcement or Cecil Vanover, the person excused himself. Having walked through downtown and back through a small shopping center, she had yet to get a conversation started that revealed any meaningful information. Her frustration mounted as she neared the library, where she saw a young, early twenties lady coming out of the door. She was struggling to carry several books, some small ones Connie assumed were for her children and a couple of larger books that appeared to be novels. She had a baby boy in her arms and a two-year-old girl in tow. Connie kicked her walk into a jog, and grabbed the little girl just as she broke free from her mother's grasp and started for the street.

"Thank you so much," the young lady said. "I thought I could make it to the car. This one's getting strong." She nodded her blonde head at the girl whose hand Connie now held.

"No problem, glad I was walking by to help. I'm Connie."

"Ashley," she said. "Ashley Mullins."

"Good to meet you, Ashley. It's great to see a mother at the library with her children."

"I want 'em to learn. I want 'em to have opportunities I didn't get. When Ruthanne was born, I made my life about her. They have a nice children's book program here, and we've been coming for about a year now." She looked at her son. "I read to David now, too. They tell me it's good for me to read to him, no matter what it is." She glanced at the copy of *Catching Fire* she was holding. "I doubt he understands it, but they tell me it's good for him to hear me read. He's eight months, he'll be in the program next fall."

"That is wonderful. It takes dedication to be a good mom."

"I'm lucky, I married a good man. Josh got a job in the mines right out of high school, making good money. Most of the girls getting out of school weren't that lucky. They either got married to some guy who quickly tires of them and looked for something younger, or they got knocked up by some man ten years older than they are, who offered them some drugs as bait, trying to feel young again. Josh is a good one. He don't blow money, drink, or use drugs like so many guys around here. We save a lot; someday we're going to have a better life."

The mention of drugs piqued Connie's interest. "I'm so glad to hear that, Ashley. Do you have time for a cup of coffee?" Her mind raced, quickly concocting a story to entice the lady to talk. "You see, I'm studying the lives of young Appalachian women, and I would love to hear more of your story. My treat."

Connie smiled, proud of her story and her quick thinking. No, it wasn't true, but she was, after all, on another undercover mission. She reasoned it was no more a lie than being Debbie Calloway last summer.

Ashley looked at her watch. "Sure, I've got time. It'll keep me from having to spend all morning with my parents. I promised I'd take dad to the doctor, but his appointment ain't until two."

"Great. Here, let me help you." Connie took the books and held Ruthanne while Ashley buckled David into the car seat, then waited while the young mother buckled her daughter into the seat on the other side of her Dodge Nitro. "Where's a good place for coffee?"

"There's the Pancake House or the Bluebird Café."

"Are either of them locally owned?" Connie asked, preferring to patronize a local eatery rather than a chain restaurant.

"Bluebird's local; it's right downtown. Come on, I'll drive."

Connie walked around and got in the passenger seat. "My husband would love your car," Connie remarked.

"Oh, yeah? Why's that?"

"It's a Dodge," Connie laughed. "That's about all it takes for Carter."

Ashley smiled. "'Nuff said. Josh is the same way. He wanted a SRT4 so bad when we got this one. Luckily, we couldn't find one, so he had to settle for this. I'm happy with it. But Josh, he's always looking for a hot rod. If he's got one downfall, cars is it."

Connie laughed as Ashley started the car and pulled into traffic. "Let me tell you about Carter. Years ago, when we were still fairly young, he just had to have a Chrysler TC by Maserati. We didn't have any kids, and I couldn't talk him out of it. I hated that car for years, but we've still got it, and I've still got him, so I don't guess it was too bad."

Ashley laughed as she parallel parked in front of the Bluebird Cafe. "Boys and their toys."

Connie chuckled, went to the backseat, and unbuckled David while Ashley got Ruthanne. Carrying the baby carrier, Connie wondered if this is what it would have been like to have been a mother. Even though she had long ago come to terms with not being able to have children, times like this made her consider all she and Carter had lost by not having a family. She blinked her eyes twice to try to regain her focus on the task at hand and led Ashley into the diner.

Sitting at a booth with a window, the ladies each ordered a coffee, and Ashley ordered a child's apple juice for Ruthanne. "You mentioned drugs a few minutes ago," Connie restarted the conversation. "I'm curious, how bad of a problem are drugs around here?"

"It's bad," Ashley confirmed. "I hear it used to be pot, which ain't too bad, I don't reckon. Then coke got to be big. Now, it seems the big thing is meth, meth and prescription drugs. Meth is easy to get. Easy for even the little guys to cook. Prescription drugs are easy, too. There's always a doctor who will write a prescription as long as Medicaid will pay for the office visit. And if the doctors write it, the drug stores are happy to fill it. The kids, they fall into two classes. They're either looking for money or they're looking for a release, a way out. Without education or good jobs, drugs are the easy way to get both."

"Do you know a lot people using?"

"Yeah, unfortunately. A lot of the girls I went to school with are. The government check comes in, the drug dealer shows up—it's a regular routine. Once the fix from the government check is gone, they start trying to sell their food stamps. I've had girls I went to school with offer to sell me their WIC vouchers they get for their kids for twenty cents on the dollar. I bought 'em a few times, not realizing why they was selling them so cheap, or what they was doing with the money. Josh had a fit. He explained to me what was going on, that those girls were starving their babies to feed their habit. It was a great deal for me, but that money was going straight into the hands of a drug dealer. I just couldn't do it anymore."

"I used to be a nurse," Connie confided, "and I saw these young girls and their babies in the ER. It wasn't pretty. You and Josh did the right thing by not buying their food stamps."

"But it's a double edged sword, Connie. Those girls will get their fix somehow. For a lot of them, their only source of income is between their legs. I've seen it happen too many times. They start off not wanting to, but they need the high too much. After a few times, it becomes old hat for them. Anybody, anywhere for a fix."

"How did you avoid it?" Connie asked, sincerely wanting to know.

"I got lucky. Me and Josh dated in high school. He was a good boy, with good parents. He was set to go to college when the recession hit. His daddy lost his job, and needed him to work. Josh was smart, and one of the mine bosses recognized it and snatched him right up. We got married, and both of us stayed clean. I've always thought, if it hadn't been for Josh, I'd probably be just like those other girls."

"Somehow, I think you're different," Connie said. "You're taking care of your kids, making sacrifices to make sure they have a future. It takes a special person to do that."

Ashley blushed, "Thanks, Connie, I appreciate that. I try."

"Why don't the cops clean this drug mess up?"

"Clean it up? They're the problem. Most of the cops around here are in it up to their necks."

"The cops?" Connie asked. "They're dirty?"

"Yeah, the cops are filthy dirty. Some of them are dealing, some of them's just on the take. Either way, drugs are on the open market here in these parts."

"Are you sure?"

"As long as you deal with the right people, a kid's got a better chance getting busted trying to buy a six pack than meth."

"And if you deal with the wrong people?"

"If you buy from the wrong people, you'll be lucky if you ever make it to prison."

Connie felt a tingle ride up her spine. "Any idea who is in charge of this drug ring around here? Just us talking."

Ashley hesitates, and Connie realizes she was still a stranger to this girl, and here she was, trying to get her to drop names. "I'm not for sure," Ashley answered, not quite a lie, but not the whole truth. "I don't think Sheriff Hamilton is involved. Daddy says he just wants to retire. It's his last year, you know. But I hear it goes pretty high up."

The waitress refilled their coffees and Connie asked her to bring them an order of chili fries to share. In the back, someone dropped a plate, and the noise woke David. He began crying and Ashley looked at her watch. "It's time for him to eat." She reached in her diaper bag, grabbed a blanket, and threw it over her shoulder. Connie unbuckled the baby from his seat and handed him across the table to his mother. Ashley slid him under the blanket, and in a few seconds he was nursing.

137

"That's amazing," said Connie, her attention focused on the mother and son. "You did that with such ease and grace."

"Its part of being a mom," Ashley said with a smile. "By the time I got to him, I was pretty good at it."

Again, a pang of regret went through Connie. Motherhood was an experience she would never know. It wasn't often she regretted her and Carter's decision not to try to have a child after she lost their first one, but she admitted, times like this were tough. She was glad when her attention was drawn in a different direction as she noticed an unmarked cruiser pull into a parking space across the street. She watched while detective Cecil Vanover got out and walked toward the cafe. "Speaking of the dirty ones," Ashley broke the silence that had lingered longer than Connie realized.

"Him? Vanover? Are you sure?"

"Daddy says so. He went to school with him. Played on the same baseball team. He can tell you all about Cecil Vanover."

"The glass door opened and the tall detective stepped in and removed his sunglasses. He looked at Connie, wrinkled his brow, and sat down at the counter. "What'cha have, detective?" the waitress asked.

"Give me a pepperjack burger, all the way. To go," Vanover replied.

Connie felt Ashley kick her shin, but kept her eye on Vanover. The second kick got Connie's attention. "Watch this," Ashley mouthed.

Connie nodded her acknowledgment, took a sip of her coffee, shifting her gaze out the window while watching Vanover in its reflection. "I'm still amazed how you pull everything off with the kids."

Ashley picked up on Connie's attempt to keep the conversation going to avoid drawing attention. She was smart enough to play along. "It can be hard, but these two are worth it."

"That they are," Connie replied, reaching out and holding Ruthanne's hand, her eyes not leaving the reflection in the window. She watched the cook place the meal in a Styrofoam box, but instead of putting it in a paper bag, he walked to the back and returned with a box twice the size of the food container. He put the burger in the box and struggled to get the flaps to interlock to seal it. Vanover paid for the meal, put on his sunglasses, walked out the door and across the street, got into the police car, sat the bag in the passenger's seat, and drove off.

Connie recognized the drug exchange she had just witnessed. "How did you know that was going down?" she asked.

"Pepperjack burger," Ashley answered. "Before the kids were born, I used to work here. There's no pepperjack burger on the menu."

FIFTEEN

Carter followed Haysi PD's only patrol car until it passed the Haysi Hideout, then he turned into the parking lot. The dilapidated building needed more work than Tim Taylor and a team of tool girls could handle, but inside, it served as the den for Haysi's worst citizens. Walking through the front door, the smell of cigarette smoke choked Carter, causing him to cough in disgust. He continued into the dimly lit room, country music echoing all around, encountering three pool tables with barely enough spacing between them to make a shot. The one on the far right had four men who looked like Billy Jack's counterparts in *The Born Losers* engrossed in a game of eight ball, the stakes of which were slightly higher than the value of the building. Walking past the pool tables, Carter noticed two pinball machines against the wall, along with a couple of arcade games from the early '80s, each game with a grungy looking young man in front of it, cursing every time he lost a life. Carter thought the old arcade games odd for a pool hall in the twenty-first century, but then he remembered he was in Haysi, which always seemed to be at least a quarter century behind the rest of the world. Walking up to the bar, he laid two Washingtons down and asked the weathered bartender for a Bud Light.

After taking a few sips of his beer, both to fit in and to calm his nerves, he approached the *Scorpion* pinball machine, where a kid fresh out of high school was playing. He noted the score, seeing the kid had reach nearly a half million points, telling Carter the young man was more than just a casual player. He pressed the button controlling the left flipper, sending the ball past the bumpers to the top of the machine, and watched as it made its way back through the maze, racking up points each time it made contact with an object in the game. This time the kid nudged the machine with his right hand, but he was too late; the ball exited through the chute behind the flipper. "Son of a fuckin' bitch," the kid screamed at the machine, but no one else in the place seemed to hear him. "Nice game you've got goin' on, man," Carter encouraged him.

"Should have never lost that goddamn ball. Hit the motherfucker too damn hard. I own this fuckin' game; I know better than that."

"That score yours?" Carter asked, nodding his head toward the high score of over two million on the game's display.

"Yeah, Tommy Stidham and me have swapped that high score over the past couple of months now. That son of a bitch will be in here later, trying to beat me. I need to better it before he gets here. I've got to make it tough on his ass."

"Don't let me stop you," Carter said. "I'm just going to watch, if you don't mind."

The kid pulled back the plunger and put his third ball in play. About five minutes later, he began to shake the machine, eventually lifting the right side slightly. Suddenly, the machine went dead, with only the tilt light flashing on the display. "Fuck," he yelled. He looked back at Carter. "I never could do anything with someone watching me."

"Tell you what," Carter spoke up. "I'll play you a game for a beer, how 'bout it? You want to take on the old man?"

The kid sized up Carter. "You got to be kidding, man? You really want to take me on at my game? For a brew? You're damn right I'm in."

"You go first," Carter said. "At least give me a chance to see how this game works." He slid his quarter into the slot.

"Go ahead and get a couple of bucks out of your billfold, too, man. I'm going to enjoy that beer." The kid dropped his own quarter into the game. The first ball popped into place at the bottom of the long runway. The kid pulled the plunger about three-quarters of the way back and let it go, launching the ball through the machine. By the time he finished, he had over 300,000 points on the board.

"Not a bad ball, man. Let's see if I can remember how to play one of these things."

Carter was hoping playing pinball was like riding a bicycle. It had been nearly two decades since he had been between the flippers on a regular basis, but back in college, he was the king of the *Scorpion* machine at the Clinch Valley Student Center. Being a freshman from Haysi, with few friends and even less money, he learned the art of the game. More importantly, he learned how to make a quarter last for hours. He would take on all comers—challenger buys the next game—for hours on end. This went on for most of his freshman year, until he became distracted by a pretty sophomore with auburn hair.

Carter pulled back the plunger and the ball rocketed through the machine, hitting the bumpers and racking up points. In college, he was a master of using the middle flippers to keep the ball away from the bottom of the game, not having to risk the ball going between the flippers. Focused on the ball, he skillfully kept it in play, adding up points, until it finally went behind the left flipper and out of the playing area. For the first time, he looked up at his score... 521,230. Not bad for an old man who hadn't played much since his early thirties. "Beginner's luck," was Carter's only comment as he stepped from the machine.

"Luck, hell. I've been to some pretty big tournaments in Roanoke and seen motherfuckers play like that. That's skill, dude. But this is my game." The kid pulled back the plunger and sent his second ball on its way.

His score added up quicker this time. At one point, he got a rhythm going, pounding the ball against a 500-point pumper over and over, for what seemed like a minute. As the ball finally disappeared through the hole in the front of the machine, his score read 1,582,240 points. "Take that, motherfucker. That's better than the second ball of my high score game."

Carter didn't say a word. He stepped into position and launched his second ball. Ten minutes later, as his ball disappeared, he looked up at his score... 1,618,838. "Last ball," Carter said, as he stepped back and reached for his beer on the table.

"Son of a bitch," the kid said, taking his position. Again, he put his ball into play, this time as skillfully as he ever had. Finally, the ball rolled toward the center, and the kid barely clipped it with the flipper, keeping it in play. The machine lit up like a Christmas tree, indicating a new high score. But the close call caused the kid to lose his rhythm and he soon lost the ball. 3,128,792 points appeared on the display...

"Yeah," the kid yelled. "I guess I needed some motherfucker to push me." He smiled, showing a couple of missing teeth. "That beer is going to taste pretty goddamn good."

"I hope so, because I like it when other people pay," Carter said, as he readied himself for his final ball. For over fifteen minutes, he didn't look up from the game. He never glanced at his score. His entire focus was on keeping the silver ball in play, hitting the double and triple score bumpers, and making sure the ball ricocheted off those with the highest point values. Again the machine lit up, announcing the second high score of the morning, but Carter didn't lose his concentration. As his last ball disappeared, he looked up at his score—4,001,846. Carter stepped back, smiling, admiring his work. "I'll have a Sam Adams this time," he yelled at the bartender.

"You cocksucking son of a bitch, you played me."

"It's been a long time, son," Carter replied. "Carter Sykes," he said, sticking out his hand.

For a moment, the kid didn't say a word, just staring at Carter. "I've heard of you, man. You were pretty damn good back in your day. I'm Brad Compton," the kid introduced himself and shook Carter's hand.

"Come on, you owe me a beer. A Sam Adams, remember?"

"Yeah, I got it. George, a Sam Adams for the old man, a Bud for me," Compton yelled at the barkeep, then looked over at Carter. "If I'm going to get my ass whupped, at least it's by a legend."

"A legend? Really?"

"Yeah, man. When it comes to pinball, the old folks always compare me to Carter Sykes. Now I can take it as a complement."

"Damn. I never knew I was a legend." Carter squeezed his eyes together and shook his head slightly to get out of his moment of self-adoration. "Hey, look, I need a little information. Mind if we talk?"

"After you beat my ass, I'll be honored to talk."

Carter smiled at the young man. He could tell the kid was smarter than he appeared. He knew this could easily have been his fate thirty years ago if his high school government teacher hadn't encouraged him to go to college. "What do you know about Andy Calhoun?" He paused and then added, "And Eric O'Quinn?"

"Ah, shit, man. Don't be asking me about those dudes. I ain't done nothin', man. I don't want no trouble."

"Ain't going to be no trouble, man. I just need some help. I'm trying to find out who killed Andy. It's important to my family. Anything you can tell me will help."

"Dude, there's a turf war going on around here. From what I hear, Andy and his buddy was just starting to deal a little bit, you know, pot, meth, shit like that. They'd be in here most afternoons, selling some shit. Small time stuff, nothing big. Then, a couple of weeks ago, I heard someone say things were changing, that they were ready to expand, if you know what I mean. Word is, The Ace found out about it. I don't care who the fuck you are, you don't want to step on The Ace's turf. That usually gets you a ticket to the hospital the first time."

Carter nodded. "And the second time?"

"Dude, don't even think about it."

"Who's The Ace?" Carter asked.

"I don't know, man. I really don't. But he's big. Bigger than anyone else around here. I reckon he supplies this whole fuckin' area. And not just with meth. Pot, coke, heroin, ecstasy, you name it. It all comes through The Ace. He's connected, man. Got doctors supplying him with Oxy. Knows people, people way up the chain. From what I hear, he's got connections in Florida and Mexico. Anyone fucks with The Ace, he's going to fuck them up real bad."

"Sounds like this Ace is a bad motherfucker."

"I don't mess with him or his men, dude. I stay out of that shit. I drink some liquor, play some pinball and pool, but that's it. I may not be a model citizen, but I know drugs are bad news, and I know The Ace is worse news. I've got eyes, man. I see what goes on around here. The drug scene is bad news, man, but fuckin' with The Ace will get you on the news, if you know what I mean?

"Is that what happened to Andy?"

"He ain't here today, is he? Word is, he was an example, just to remind everyone else that this is Ace's territory."

"Yeah, I think I get your drift. Thanks for talking to me, dude."

"Just don't say nothin' to nobody, man. The Ace has eyes and ears everywhere."

Carter nodded. "I understand, don't worry about me, I'm The Legend, remember? Hey, when you point out that high score, don't say my name. Just tell 'em The Legend put that up, okay?"

"Sure thing, man. At least until I beat it." The kid grinned.

"Somehow, I don't think that'll take long," Carter said, drinking the last of his Sam Adams before getting up. "Just remember, if you can beat my high score, you can get out of this town. I did."

"One day I plan to, man. I really do."

"Good luck. I really mean it. Thanks for the info, and the beer." Carter turned, walked through the bar, past the pool tables, and out the front door of the Haysi Hideout.

SIXTEEN

After missing her previous game, Crystal Calhoun was anxious to get back on the diamond with her little league softball team. The Lady Jaguars of Haysi were poised to take on the Trammell Lady Braves in a Dickenson County showdown. The Lady Braves, led by Priscilla Blevins, were undefeated, while the Jags had only one loss; that loss occurred in their last game, which they were forced to play without their shortstop and three-hole hitter.

Along with a quarter of the Haysi community, the Sykes family was in attendance. Sylvie joined Carter and Connie in lawn chairs along the right field line, just past the bleachers. Tanya paced behind them, too nervous to sit, and Crystal's uncle Ben leaned against the chain-link fence. Brett and Dylan roamed around the field, Dylan talking to friends, while Brett tried to start conversations with good-looking girls from the small Trammell contingent that followed their team.

Blevins was on the mound for the Lady Braves, and after retiring the first two Lady Jags, Crystal stepped to the plate. After a ball outside, she hit the next offering to left center. The well-coached Braves cut the ball off and held her to a double. After the next pitch, a strike, Crystal was standing on third with a stolen base. Unfortunately for the Jags, that was as far as she would get that inning.

By the end of three, both teams showed why they were the best in Dickenson County, and among the best little league teams in southwestern Virginia. Blevins was pitching a brilliant game, having allowed only the one hit to Crystal. Haysi excelled in the field, with Crystal teaming with second baseman Janis Skeen to turn a double play an inning earlier. In the bottom of the fourth, the crowd waited with anticipation as the 2-3-4 hitters of the Jags came to the plate.

Skeen led off the inning with a bunt single. Two pitches later, she stole second when the Trammell catcher missed the low fastball from Blevins. Crystal stepped back into the box, with the count one and one, and took the next pitch inside. The next pitch was a good one, on the outside part of the plate, but Crystal went with it, sending it over the third baseman's head, down the left field line. Skeen scored easily from second, and by the time the ball arrived back in the infield, Crystal was standing on third base with her second extra base hit of the game. The next batter grounded out to second, scoring Crystal, giving the Lady Jags a two-nothing lead.

In the sixth, the Lady Braves scored a run. With a runner on third and two outs, the next batter hit a grounder up the middle. Crystal went to one knee, reached across her body to snag the ball, stood, and threw to first before the Trammel girl crossed the plate. The crowd erupted as if they were in Fenway Park watching the Red Sox cut down Jeter.

Carter was filled with pride watching his niece, but times like this made him wonder what it would be like to have a child of his own—one to work with, teach the finer points of the game. He enjoyed the freedom not having children offered him and Connie, but sometimes, especially times like this, he wished they had tried one more time to have a child. As he watched Crystal celebrating in the team huddle, he shook his head, trying to rid his mind of the thought.

It only took a second for Crystal to run to her uncle, and he opened his left arm, pulling her to his side. "Great game, girl."

"Thanks, Uncle Carter," she beamed. "That was a close one. Those girls are good."

"You know, you're pretty good yourself. I was amazed by some of your plays, especially that last one up the middle. Pretty hard play for a southpaw playing short. If I had half your talent, I'd have played for the Big Red Machine."

Crystal blushed. "I hear you were pretty good too, Uncle Carter."

"Don't believe everything your mama and mamaw tells you, girl. I wasn't good like you. You can play."

"Thanks. I'm going down to The Pizza Parlor for a pop. We won, so we get a large."

"Don't get the suicide," Carter warned.

"Oh, but I always get a suicide," she said with a mischievous smile. "They're the best."

"I'll see you at home. I'm proud of you."

As Crystal ran off to rejoin her teammates, Connie looked at Carter. "You ever wish?"

Carter hung his head, "Yeah, sometimes. But it is what it is. Come on, let's go"

As Connie grabbed her chair, she understood the "let's go" was more Carter wanting to move on emotionally than physically. She had tried to talk about the subject of children several times over the years, even suggesting adoption at one point, but Carter wouldn't hear of it. Losing their unborn baby had been hard on both of them, but Carter seemed to take it extra hard. Connie was never willing to risk putting him through those emotions again, so they eventually agreed not to try anymore. Side by side, they walked back to the Ram, the topic creating an eerie silence between them.

Putting their chairs in the back of the truck, Carter noticed on the adjacent softball field, Mullins Mining was playing Chesapeake Gas in an industrial league softball game. "You know, babe, I've been thinking about playing on one of these teams since I've retired now."

"Carter, I don't want to see you get hurt. These guys are young. Their bones aren't brittle. They still have good reflexes."

Carter had his hand on the door handle but didn't open it. "I may not be young anymore, but I can still hang." He paused, watching the action on the field. "Look, there's Junior Rasnick coming up to the plate. He's as old as I am, and he's still playing. Come on, let's watch his at-bat." Together, the two of them walked toward the field.

"I bet he's the DH," Connie mumbled under her breath.

They watched as Junior, wearing number 28, tapped his bat on the plate, and then raised it to his left shoulder. The pitcher's offering arched into the air, and came down over the outside corner of the plate. "Steeriiikke," the umpire called. Junior dug in again and the pitcher tossed another slow pitch toward home. This one moved toward the inside half of the plate, and everyone watching knew it was a mistake. Junior Rasnick's powerful swing reminded Carter of Joey Votto as he watched the ball sail over the right field fence. Carter looked at Connie, "See, he's been doing that since high school. Surely I can still hit a little."

"Carter, he's six-six, three hundred plus," she told him. "You're five-nine..., umm, we won't mention the weight. He's got power; you've got, uh..."

"Cat-like reflexes? Is that what you meant to say? Thanks, babe."

"I love you anyway, sweetie," she said and gave him a kiss on the cheek as he watched Junior round the bases.

"I still think I got some game left," he mumbled.

After the game, they walked to the dugout as Junior came out, carrying his bat bag. "Nice hit," Carter congratulated him.

"Thanks, man. I got 'hold of that one. I'm slowing down a bit, though. I can't hit 'em like I used to."

Connie nudged Carter with her elbow, but he ignored her. "Looks like you still hit 'em good enough to me."

149

Junior led Carter and Connie across the parking lot. I'm just glad they allow a DH in this league. If I had to play first, I don't know if I'd still play. Those guys with those double and triple walled bats can smoke one down the line. It wouldn't be a matter of whether I could field it; it would be a matter of whether I could get out of the way."

Connie's elbow again nudged Carter, this time eliciting a move of his elbow in reply. "That's the reason Carter doesn't play anymore," Connie laughed.

"Hey, now. I've been threatening to find an over-fifty league. I wouldn't mind stepping out on the field again. Does Cecil Vanover play in a league? I always could hit him."

Junior hit his clicker and the new Mustang in the parking lot chirped. He grabbed the driver's door handle and tossed his bat bag into the passenger's seat. "I don't reckon Cecil's played since his last rehab stint in the mid–'80s. It's a shame; the guys would love to play with a pro."

Carter's mind had already shifted from baseball to cars. "Damn, son, that's a new SVT. I've been wanting to see one of these. Sweet!"

"It's one hell of a car, that's for sure. Son of a bitch will fly down highway 80." He glanced at Connie. "Sorry ma'am," Junior apologized for his language. "It'll out handle that old Dart you used to drive, that's for damn sure," he laughed.

"There isn't much that won't outhandle my old Dodge. But hey, for a poor kid, it wasn't a bad car." Carter nodded his head at the Mustang. "This, this is a sweet ride, man." Carter walked around the sports car, checking out the new body style, every now and then letting an expletive cross his lips.

"I like it," Junior finally said. "It's great for the summer. But you know, come winter, this thing will be parked in dad's shed. I'll be back in that old pickup truck."

"It's hard to beat on old truck," Connie agreed. "Come on, sweetie, let's go find your old truck and get some supper."

****

Carter always drove when they were together, but this time Connie had the keys, and, without hesitation, walked to the driver's door.

"You drivin', babe?" Carter asked.

"Seat's already adjusted for me," she answered.

Carter could sense she was up to something, but decided not to pursue it, walking to the passenger's side of the Ram and hopping in. "Maybe I'll talk on the radio."

"That would be okay, sweetie," she said.

Carter studied her expression and caught the grin on her face. He knew she really didn't like the ham radio on in the truck, more times than not hearing, "Would you turn that thing off?" come from her side of the cab. He could sense she was up to something, but decided to play along. He reached down and pushed the button in the upper left corner of the Icom to turn it on, then turned the knob to change the frequency to the local two-meter repeater. "This is KA4CS monitoring," he announced into the microphone as Connie pulled onto the highway.

"KA4CS, this is K4DCW. I heard you was up." Carter recognized the voice that came from the radio's speaker.

"K4DCW this is KA4CS. Claude, how are you?" Carter asked his cousin.

Claude took a few minutes discussing a laundry list of aches, pains, and health problems that afflicted him. "I guess you're up working on Andy's case?"

Carter let the front of the mic hang toward the floor and lowered his head. There was no way he was getting into a conversation with his cousin Claude about Andy's case on the local ham radio repeater. He was well aware that every scanner listener in the Mountain Empire would be spreading rumors if he said anything. After a quick moment of pontification, he straightened up and pressed the mic. "Just finishing up a couple of things." He sighed, knowing where his next question was going to lead the conversation, but decided it was better than discussing the case. "How's Aunt Helen?"

Again, Claude went into a list of ailments, this time those affecting his mother. Carter glanced at Connie with a smirk on his face, but noticed the grin on hers just before he felt the truck shift into a lower gear. His body was thrown against the passenger door as she took the left-hand curve too quickly. "What was that?" he asked.

"Just having some fun, sweetie," she said as she pushed the gas pedal. The Hemi growled as the transmission once again downshifted. "It's my turn to play, now."

Carter grabbed the armrest as Claude stopped talking and the courtesy tone chimed on the repeater. When Carter keyed the mic, there was urgency in his voice. "Claude, something's come up, I've got to go. I'll catch you later, okay?" After a brief pause, he added his call sign to indicate he was through with the conversation and to stay legal.

Claude responded, but Carter didn't hear what he said. As he hung on with both hands, his gaze found Connie's face. "What the hell are you doing?"

"I told you, just having some fun. Just like you do, sweetie. Buckle up now," she said, as she swung the steering wheel to the right.

Carter's elbow dug into the center console. "Shit, Cons. Slow this damn thing down a little bit."

Connie smiled as she exited the curve and crossed the double yellow centerline making the next left. The tires squalled in pain.

"You're going to get us killed. Slow this truck down."

"Hang on, we'll be home in a couple of minutes," she responded without taking her eyes off the road.

A minute later, Connie caught a coal truck in a right hand curve. Coming out of the curve, she allowed the Ram to drift a little to the left and saw a short straight stretch ahead. She stomped the gas pedal as she let the truck swing to the left. The Ram grabbed first gear and the engine roared as it passed the coal truck. Carter's eyes became fixated on the car coming out of the curve they were approaching. "Connie!" He yelled.

"I got this, sweetie," she said, swinging the Ram in front of the coal truck just as the horn from the approaching car blew. "Wow, that was fun."

"Goddamnit, Connie, slow this thing down. You're going to kill us both."

Connie knew she had reached the limit. She only wanted to give him a little payback for all the years Carter had thrown her around the cab. If she was honest, the last incident had scared her a little; she wasn't quite sure she was going to clear the coal truck. She slowed to a reasonable pace for the next mile before making the left turn into the Breaks. Neither of them said a word until they pulled into the parking spot at the camper.

"Wow, that was fun," Connie said with a laugh. "Now I know why you always drive crazy on that road."

"I don't drive like THAT. You damn near killed us."

"It looks different from the passenger's seat, doesn't it, sweetie?"

Carter knew better than to say anything. He was not going to admit he drove too fast, but Connie had made her point. With a bit of feigned anger, he slammed the door of the Ram as he walked toward the Coachmen's door.

Connie grinned and nodded her head. "That'll teach you," she said under her breath.

Carter walked inside and mixed himself a drink, rationalizing he needed something to settle him down after the hellride he had just been through. He sat down in his recliner and his attention focused on the poster boards as Connie walked in the door.

"Did you make me one?" she asked in an innocent voice.

"Anybody who drives like that can make her own damn drink."

"I'll remember that the next time you drive," she said, walking into the kitchen and reaching into the designated liquor cabinet above the sink.

Carter picked up a marker and walked toward the boards. He drew a line through the question mark after the word "drugs" following the BMW and King Ranch; Connie's recollection of what she and Ashley had seen confirmed that in his mind. Then he wrote the words "The Ace" right in the center of the third board.

"What's The Ace?" Connie asked, settling into her recliner.

"Not what, who," Carter corrected. "From what the pinball kid told me, The Ace is the head of the drug trade in these parts. I put him in the center of the board because if my hunch is correct, everything dealing with Andy's murder will revolve around him."

"Who is he?" she asked. "Some poker player?"

"I'm not a hundred percent sure yet, but I have a pretty good idea. In baseball, a team's best pitcher is called its ace. I saw, after all these years, Cecil still has his number on his license plate. If I were betting, I'd say he would still use the term Ace to refer to himself. After what you saw today, it all makes sense."

"So why not go to the authorities with this information?"

"Babe, all we've got right now is stimulation, pure stimulation. I need some proof, some evidence to tie Cecil to this Ace character. If I can get that, I think I can get the state boys to listen."

"Sounds like we still have work to do, then."

"Yeah, but we made progress today. I do have a pretty good partner, you know?" He walked over and gave Connie a long kiss. "Even if she can't drive."

"Hey, don't blame me. I just didn't want to hear Claude talk about your family's health problems any longer."

Carter rolled his eyes. "Yeah," he said, hanging his head. "Listening to Claude or riding with you. What a choice."

****

After Carter finished with his morning ham radio nets, he turned the Coachmen's built-in stereo system to the local AM radio station, WDIC. As a kid, he rarely listened to the local station with a county music format, but this morning he wanted to gain a better feel for what was going on in the area. During the nine o'clock news broadcast, the story of a body being found at an abandoned strip mine in Buchanan County caught his attention. The name of the deceased hadn't yet been released, pending notification of next-of-kin, but Carter had a pretty good idea who the body had once belonged to. Before the news was over, he had his phone in his hand and the number dialed.

"Haysi PD, Chief Roland."

He didn't waste time on pleasantries. "Roland, Carter Sykes. Is it Eric O'Quinn?"

There was silence on the phone while Haysi's top law enforcement officer considered his response. Finally he spoke. "Yeah, it's O'Quinn."

"Beat to death with a ball bat, right?"

"Not positive on the weapon, but from what I see on the report, a ball bat is a good possibility."

"Is there a pattern to the bruising on the body?"

Carter waited for the answer, assuming Roland was studying the report. Just before Carter was about to ask again, Roland spoke.

"Most of the bruising is on the right side of the body. What's all this about, Sykes? You trying to play Columbo?"

Carter rolled his eyes at another Columbo reference, but pressed on. "All this is consistent with Andy Calhoun's murder. I'll bet dinner whoever killed Andy also killed O'Quinn."

"Holy shit. You mean we got a serial killer here in Haysi?"

"I don't know about a serial killer, but we do have two related murders."

"Wow, first time that's happened around here in at least thirty years."

"If you've got time, I'd love to put some notes together and see if we can crack this case open. I'll even bring someone you'd probably love to meet."

154

"If you're talking about your wife, I'll cancel every meeting I've got; I've got so many."

"See you in about an hour or so, then?"

"I'll be here."

Carter hung up his phone as Connie walked into the rear living area of the camper. "Who was that, sweetie?"

"Cons, we've got a meeting in town. Your presence was specifically requested."

"Oh yeah, with who?"

"I'll tell you when we get there. Let's get a shower and head out. Make sure you put on something nice, okay?"

"Oh, so I'm your trophy wife now, huh?" she said, taking a seductive pose.

"You've always been my trophy wife, babe." He stood up, walked behind her, and put his arms around her waist, gently kissing her on her neck. "And you always will be. But, actually, I think you'll have a lot of input into the meeting."

"And all this time, I was just hoping I was eye candy," Connie laughed, squeezing Carter's arms with her elbows.

"You are eye candy, babe. And a whole lot more."

Connie turned to face him. "Comments like that may get you somewhere," Connie whispered in his ear as she took his ear lobe into her mouth.

"Ahhhh," Carter moaned. "That's what I'm hoping for."

Connie walked away, stopped at the stairway leading to the bedroom, and looked back over her shoulder. "You coming?"

Carter smiled, and then slowly walked toward her. "Not yet, but give me a few minutes." She took his hand and led him into the bedroom.

****

Two hours later, Carter slid the poster board under his arm and opened the door for Connie. They walked into the Haysi Police Department, Carter a half step behind the left shoulder of his wife. "Roland?" Carter called out, when he didn't see the Chief at his desk.

A voice came from the back room. "Is that you, Sykes? I'm back here; be out in a second."

"Yeah, it's me, along with the special guest I promised you." Carter looked at Connie and winked.

A moment later, Chief Roland came out of the back room, stopped, and stared at Connie, "My god, I just stepped back in time thirty-five years. Connie Brown, I'd recognize you anywhere. You haven't changed a bit."

Connie looked at the uniformed cop. "Bill? Wild Bill Roland? Is that you?"

"Pretty much. Less hair and a few extra pounds, but it's still me," he laughed.

"I can't believe Wild Bill Roland is the police chief of Haysi, Virginia? Who would have ever dreamed?"

"Hmm, sounds like I'm in for some stories," Carter chimed in.

"Oh, I've got some about Wild Bill here. Like that night after the football game against Norton. Wild Bill snuck aboard the van carrying their cheerleaders. They were halfway back to Norton before the faculty sponsor caught him."

"Glad that was in the '70s and not today," Roland chuckled. "If a kid did that now, he'd get twenty years."

"How did you get out of it?" Carter asked.

"I told 'em my dad had a van just like it and I thought it was his. Said I got bored with the game and went to sleep. I don't think they really bought it, but, hey, it was the '70s. Giving me a break was easier than dealing with the situation. No harm, no foul, I guess."

"Only question is, did you get any phone numbers?" Carter asked.

"Actually, I got two." he said, reliving the incident in his mind, "And a kiss from the head cheerleader."

"Damn!" Carter said. "Sounds like you did pretty good."

"Damn straight." Roland smiled, the memory becoming clearer. "I got more than a kiss from that girl a week later."

"Um, um, boys," Connie reminded them she was in the room.

"Sorry, Connie. Just getting a little carried away with this walk down memory lane. You ain't changed a bit. Well, except for somehow getting even prettier." He looked up and down her body. "Damn girl, you look great."

"Carter tells me I'm his trophy wife," she replied, grinning at her husband.

"Looks to me like he won first place," Roland smiled at her. "Damn, it's good to see you. I'm glad you finally got rid of that old boyfriend of yours."

"You and me both," Connie said. "Last I heard, he had spent two years in federal prison for tax evasion. His daddy couldn't get him out of trouble with the feds."

"I hate the son of a bitch only got two years," Roland said, almost to himself.

"Somehow I feel a little responsible for your Road Runner," Connie said. "If I hadn't broke up with him…"

"Hey, that old car was a small price to pay to see you get away from that asshole."

"Not to break up this mutual admiration society, but, can we take a moment to focus on these murder cases?" Carter leaned his poster boards up against the wall. "Wild Bill, what have you found out so far?"

"The reports I've seen put the time of death at three or four days ago. I haven't seen a more accurate TOD yet. As I mentioned on the phone, lots of blunt force wounds, consistent with a baseball bat, mostly on the victim's right side."

"What was he wearing?" Connie asked.

Roland looked at the report on his desk. "Red T-shirt and blue jeans."

"Same thing he had on when we left him and Andy at Fred's," she said.

"Unless his wardrobe is like Gilligan's, I expect he was killed the same day then," Carter deducted. "The same day as Andy." Carter uncapped his marker and wrote "Killed same day" under Eric's name.

"Makes sense," Connie and Roland said, simultaneously.

"Same type of murder, same day. Must be the same killer. Question is, why did he leave Andy's body at the scene and haul Eric off to a strip mine? Why not haul Andy off, too?"

"Something startled him," Connie said. "Makes me think they loaded up the stuff in the shed first, then he killed Andy. The killer didn't even finish the job, remember? Andy was alive when Crystal found him."

"Like he saw or heard a school bus coming and knew the kids would be home soon. We can check that theory out this afternoon," Carter said, already planning to be in the Calhouns' back yard before the school bus arrived.

"Anything else Roland?" Carter asked.

157

"Not yet. We'll have more reports later."

Carter looked at his board. "Including the toxicology report, I hope? Roland, let me know when you get that one. We need to see if Eric was clean."

"Will do, Sykes. How can I turn down the man who won the heart of Connie Brown?"

"I don't know, because I can't ever turn him down myself." Connie rotated her head toward Carter and smiled, remembering their lovemaking only a couple of hours earlier.

"More than I need to know," Roland laughed, sensing there was something he didn't wantto know about.

"Let me know if you learn anything new about either case, no matter how insignificant in seems. Most of the time, it's a little thing that breaks a case like this. Something the perpetrator doesn't think is important."

"Will do, Sykes."

"Hey, Roland. Thanks, man. We're going to solve these cases. Together. And you're going to be the cop responsible for it."

"I hear there is a sheriff's election this fall," Connie reminded him. Have you given any thought to that?

"I think the results are already in on that one," Roland said. "I'm just wondering if he'll put a big 45 on the trunk lid of the sheriff's car?"

Carter turned to walk out the door, and then stopped. "One more thing, Roland. Can you get financial reports on Junior Rasnick or Cecil Vanover? There's red flags popping up I'd like to follow up on."

"I'd have to go through the sheriff's office to get those. Somehow, I don't think that's going to happen."

"All right, then. Any judge would probably see it as a phishing expedition at this point, anyway. Thought I'd check. Let me make a call, I do have my sources." Carter walked toward the front door.

"Hey Connie," Roland called out. "Looks like you did a pretty good job in choosing a man after all."

"Yeah, I think I'll keep this one," she said with a smile. "It's only been thirty years now; my free trial period is going to run out soon."

SEVENTEEN

Back in the Ram, Carter pushed the button that activated the connection between his phone and his truck. "Dial Martin," Carter spoke into the air.

"Calling Martin," the truck spoke back.

A couple of seconds later, the phone was ringing over the Ram's speaker system.

"Martin Walker," a man answered.

"Martin, Carter. How are you doing, man?"

"Hey bro, what's up?"

Martin Walker was a thirty-something IT teacher at Dobyns Bennett High School in Kingsport, Tennessee. Carter met him about twenty years earlier, when he was a high school kid who had just earned his first amateur radio license. Even at that early age, the kid had a penchant for technology, and it wasn't long before the teen was working with men four times his age on development teams for amateur digital software. He received offers from big colleges, but decided to stay close to home and attend East Tennessee State University. After graduating, money lured him to a job in Washington, D.C., but within a couple of years he realized he wasn't a big city man, and returned home to take the job at Dobyns Bennett.

"Martin, I need your help." Carter felt a pang of guilt each time he spoke these words, mostly because he felt he spoke them too often. Martin had become a valuable resource for Carter during his last five years with the Kingsport Police Department. While in Washington, Martin dated a girl who, after graduating from Wake Forest, had landed a job with NSA. One night, Jose Cuervo and pillow talk led Martin to discover the Feds had set up a series of portals in their computer system, which, if one knew how to access them, allowed access to just about any information one could imagine, no matter how secure it was. Martin had heard rumors of the existence of such portals, but always thought the stories were just urban legend. Knowing they existed made him obsessed with finding them, which, after years of intense digging, he finally did.

When Carter found out Martin had learned how to get into the secret portals, he began asking the teacher to get information that allowed him to confirm hunches when he didn't have enough evidence to obtain a warrant.

Carter estimated Martin had saved him months of work, and the information he gathered helped put several criminals behind bars.

"I need some info on this case I'm working on."

"Is this your brother-in-law's case? I've been keeping up with it on the news."

"Yeah. I'm being stonewalled everywhere I turn. I can't get any info from the county, the state, nobody. I really need some help."

"You're going to fill me in with all the details so I can include it in the next edition of *Walker, Cyber Ranger*, right?"

In character with his role as a technology teacher, Martin Walker was a bit nerdy. After helping Carter with a couple of cases, he began writing a comic book, *Walker, Cyber Ranger*. After looking at the uphill battle he faced to get it picked up by a major publishing house, Martin decided to self-publish his creation and sell it online. After a year's worth of mediocre sales, the comic went viral among the geek community. He now earned as much money from his comic book as he did from teaching.

"Have I ever let you down?" Carter asked.

"Not once, bro. But new plot ideas have been kind of slow since you retired."

"Well get ready, because the Cyber Ranger is about to catch a killer. Maybe more."

"All right, who are the bad guys?" Martin asked with anticipation in his voice.

Carter nearly laughed. He had always envisioned Martin sitting in his basement, wearing a cowboy hat and boots, surrounded by computers, scouring the Internet for evildoers. "I've got two this time. Vincent Rasnick, Junior, better known simply as Junior, of Haysi, Virginia, and Cecil Vanover, of Clintwood." He paused for a moment, then added, "And while you're at it, see what comes up on Andy Calhoun and Teresa Vanover as well. By the way, Martin, Cecil Vanover is a cop."

Carter could sense the wheels turning in Martin's head, already building the next six-months' plot of *Walker, Cyber Ranger* around the hero catching a dirty cop. "Okay, bro, let me see what I can get."

"Hey, thanks, man. I really appreciate this."

"No, bro, I appreciate it. I need to start a new storyline next month. Just get this case wrapped up so the Cyber Ranger can start his new adventure."

"Wilco."

The phone went dead and the speakers filled with Lynard Skynyrd's "Gimme Three Steps." Connie slowly shook her head and pursed her lips. "Sometimes I wonder if you're not as bad as the bad guys."

"Do you know how many criminals Martin has helped me get off the streets? Trust me, the Feds left those portals open for guys like him to access for a reason. They want us to have the info we need; they just can't legally provide it to us. But if we happen to stumble upon it, hey, it happens. I didn't build the ballpark, babe, I just play in it."

"I guess, but it still seems underhanded to me."

"No one ever said fighting crime was fair. The bad guys do everything they can to stay on the streets. They don't have a rulebook they play by. The lawyers and courts seem to try to help them. Sometimes, we do what we have to do to win one. I'm not saying it's right, it's just the way it is." Carter explained, as he turned the steering wheel and guided the Ram down the dirt road leading to his mother's house.

****

Carter and Connie were surprised to see Tanya's car sitting at Sylvie Sykes' house when they pulled up. They walked to the porch, where Sadie waited for a pat from Carter. "I see you're over being mad at me too, girl," he said, rubbing the Border Collie mix between her ears. Walking up on the porch, he called, "Mom," through the screen door.

"Come on in, we're just looking at some pictures," Sylvie Sykes' voice called back.

Walking into the house, Carter and Connie found his mother and sister on the couch with an old photo album open in their laps, and two more Carter knew contained pictures of his childhood sitting on the floor at the matriarch's feet. They each had a twenty-ounce bottle of diet Mountain Dew sitting on the coffee table in front of them.

"Oh, no. Not picture time," Carter groaned.

Connie's voice lit up. "That means I get to see pictures of little Carter," she giggled, taking a seat beside Tanya.

"Got one right here for you, honey," Sylvie said. She passed the book to Connie and pointed at a picture of a ten-year-old Carter Sykes wearing a cowboy hat and a belt with two holsters, each holding a cap gun, with a badge pinned to his chest.

161

"Oh my god. Look at you, sweetie," Connie squealed. "Marshall Sykes. Ready to catch bad guys even back in those days."

Carter looked at the floor and shook his head. "Oh god, not the cowboy picture," Carter pleaded, without even looking at the album.

"But it's so cute," Connie said. A smile crossed her face. "You know I like men in cowboy hats."

"That's ok. We're going to your mom's in a couple of weeks, remember. I'll make sure she gets out the eight millimeter movies of little Connie. I'm sure there's a little princess in there somewhere."

"That's a couple of weeks from now, this is today," Connie laughed.

For the next hour, the Sykes women sat on the couch, looking at pictures from Carter and Tanya's youth. More often than not, ahs, ooohs, and giggles filled the room, especially when Connie found an especially cute picture of her husband.

For about fifteen minutes, Carter wandered in and out of the room. Part of him wanted to refresh his childhood memories, but at the same time, he didn't want to be there when he became the object of the women's amusement. He finally gave in to his curiosity and sat down beside Connie, putting his arm around her shoulder. She placed a hand on his knee, subconsciously letting him know that she loved him, no matter how silly or childish he looked in the pictures.

"I didn't realize your dad was so tall, sweetie," Connie said when they came to a family picture with Gene and Sylvie Sykes standing behind their children. "In these pictures, it looks like he was well over six feet."

"Six-four," Sylvie chimed in. "We were actually a pretty funny looking couple, Gene being over a foot taller than me. Ben turned out short, like me. Tanya is tall, like her daddy. Carter, well, I've always said he got equal amounts of Sykes and Taylor."

"Well, I think it turned out to be a pretty good combination," Connie said, the rubbing of his knee becoming pats on his thigh.

"I've never had reason to complain with Carter, or Tanya for that matter," Sylvie said. "But Ben, Ben takes more after the Taylors. He's always been short..." she paused, looking for diplomatic words, "...and a handful. If I had to guess, I'd say he's down at that Hideout getting into some kind of trouble right now."

"He hangs out at the Haysi Hideout a lot?" Carter asked. "I didn't see him when I was down there yesterday.".

"What were you doing at the Haysi Hideout?" Sylvie's tone was both confused and accusing.

Carter thought a moment before he spoke. He had never confided to her the dark side of being a detective, the time he had to spend in places she'd rather he never go. He always let her believe the job was full of the glory of saving the world from bad guys. He would never lie to his mother, but he would choose his words carefully. "You know me, Mom. I stopped in to play a game of pinball. They've got the only machine left in this town."

The three women all shook their heads. Connie recognized what Carter was trying to do, and came to his defense. "How long has it been since you played pinball, twenty years?" Connie asked. "I bet you still got the high score, didn't you?"

"I've snuck in a game every now and then over the years," Carter admitted. "There was one guy in there who's pretty good." He quickly, debated whether to brag. "But yes, I got the high score. And I won a beer."

"I didn't have a choice in being his sister, but Connie, you chose to marry him," Tanya picked at her brother.

"I think I did pretty good." Connie resumed patting Carter's thigh again. "All things considered."

Pulling out a group of pictures that were tucked away in the back of the photo album, Tanya opened them and asked, "What's these, mom?"

"Just some old pictures I forgot were in there. They're not important," Sylvie dismissed the question

Tanya had already started thumbing through the old black-and-white photographs. "These are Junior Rasnick and his family. This one looks like Junior when he was about five, although with Junior, he could've only been three, he's so big," she laughed. "I didn't know you had these, Mom."

"I forgot they were there," said Sylvie, leaning over to sneak a glace. "I haven't seen these pictures of Mousey and Evelyn in years. Me and your dad used to hang out with them a long time ago."

"Yeah, I remember playing with Junior when we were young. Probably kept him from beating the crap out of me when we were in high school," Carter said.

Tanya stared at a picture of the Rasnick family. "I guess Junior got his size from his mother. She's four inches taller than Junior's dad. I see Mousey every now and them, but whatever happened to Junior's mother?"

"She died in a car wreck in the early '80s. She enrolled in college in Richlands and was going to school one morning, going over Big A mountain, when the brakes failed on her old Volkswagen Bug. I reckon she lost control and went off a cliff."

"That's so sad," Connie said. "Something like that happening to someone trying to better herself."

"I guess Evelyn's funeral was the last time I talked to Mousey Rasnick," Sylvie said, her mind drifting away in her memory. An eerie silence came over the room.

After what seemed like way too long, Carter finally spoke up to change the topic, "Hey, I'm ready for some lunch."

"Mom, can I make this stomach you raised as a son something to eat?" Connie asked. "I'm afraid if I don't, he'll drive down to Fred's for another batch of chicken and taters."

"Come on, I'll help you," Sylvie said. "You coming, Tanya?"

"Umm, I reckon."

"I guess I'll go out and talk to Sadie; I'll let you gals have your girl time in the kitchen," Carter said, getting off the couch and moving toward the porch.

"Sandwiches in ten minutes, don't be late," his mother warned.

Connie laughed. "He's late for a lot of things, but never food."

****

After lunch, Carter decided he needed a break from the ladies, so he excused himself for a walk in the woods behind his childhood home. Sadie by his side, he strolled, almost instinctively, downhill, through the hardwood forest, made up of a multitude of deciduous trees, dominated by various varieties of poplar and oak. He spotted a squirrel sitting on a branch above him, watching his movements. His mind wandered to the days when he roamed these woods with his .22 caliber rifle, trying to be a man and do what he thought a man should do, put meat on the family table. He stopped and watched the squirrel maneuver to keep the tree between the two of them. He was unable to resist the urge to try an old hunting trick he learned from his grandpa Sykes, so he pulled two coins from his pocket. He leaned against a tree, and began tapping them together, his eyes never leaving the animal in the tree. In less than a minute, the squirrel moved around to his side of the tree, staring at him. "If I had my gun, we'd have squirrel gravy

164

for dinner tonight," he thought, as he extended his arm, pointed his finger at the squirrel, and softly said, "Bang."

He walked another half-mile before coming to the creek that separated the ridges of the Sykes property from those of the Rose family. Being spring, Carter was surprised to find a place he could cross the creek, but he decided it best to stay on the Sykes side. In his childhood, he was always reminded never to go onto the Rose property, and now, even as a retired cop, those admonishments still rang in his head. He looked at Sadie sitting by his side; it seemed even his mother's dog knew better than to cross the creek.

Having Sadie with him brought back memories of his own beloved canine companion, Thor,, who, by all rights, should be walking these woods with him. Carter imagined Thor would not have been so reserved about jumping into the creek and crossing to the other side. He knew his buddy wouldn't have gone far, but the thought of his dog crossing onto Rose property worried him. He really didn't understand why he felt this way; no one in the Rose family ever did or said anything out of the way to him. It was just a feeling that had been ingrained in him since childhood, and he knew he'd never get it out of his psyche.

Over the next hour, Carter sat on a rock beside the stream and got lost in his thoughts. He was quickly becoming aware Haysi wasn't exactly the simple little town his childhood memories lured him into accepting. Its young people were faced with choices he never remembered encountering, especially choices about drugs. When he was a senior in high school, he was approached about trying pot for the first time, but he quickly, without hesitation, turned it down. He heard a couple of kids bragging about smoking weed, but felt they were just trying to act cool. The truth was, he barely even knew the names of any other illegal drugs. Today, there were so many more drugs on the black market in the region. Cocaine, heroin, meth, even prescription drugs are widely available to kids before they even reach high school. As a cop, he was well aware drug abuse knew no economic boundaries, but he had witnessed the vicious cycle and devastation in which they left the poor. Despite many programs designed to help them, most impoverished families had no idea where to turn for assistance with drug problems. Even if they found the programs, nearly all were inadequate, not preparing the addicts for the pressures of the street. Carter was well aware there were far too many kids who simply didn't want help dealing with drug abuse; the drugs provided them with a needed respite from their otherwise miserable reality.

165

Carter also understood the dynamics of the drug trade. He knew many of the area's elite were profiting from the addictions of others. He understood Cecil Vanover didn't get a million dollar mansion on a ridgetop, one hundred thirty grand in cars, a place at the beach, and keep up a high maintenance wife on a minor league baseball career thirty-five years ago. Junior Rasnick didn't afford a brand new Mustang SVT by driving a coal truck three days per week. But just how high up did the region's drug trade go? Where exactly were Cecil and Junior in the food chain? And Andy and Eric, where did they fall? Those were questions to which he still needed to find answers before bringing in the Virginia State Police.

And what about Tanya? She didn't appear to know Andy was dealing. Carter saw no indication of drugs in her life. Her kids were well behaved and well taken care of, she worked every day, and appeared to keep the family together. She had watched Ben go to jail for drugs, she had seen firsthand the consequences of drugs in his life. It just didn't seem to fit her. But was he simply too close to the trees to see the forest? Was this a time he needed to step away and let someone else figure out what was going on?

Suddenly, Carter was startled from his thoughts when the *Hill Street Blues* theme began playing on his phone. Carter didn't have to look at the caller ID; that was the ringtone for his old partner, Tony Ward.

"What's up?" Carter answered.

"I've got some info for you, man. Remember those email addresses you asked me to find out about? The tech guys at TBI did some digging for me during all the spare time they have down in Nashville. Two of them are related to IP addresses the Drug Enforcement Administration has been following in South Florida. One's tied to Texas, one's local, and two are from the Charleston, South Carolina, area. I hate to say it, man, it being your brother-in-law and all, but, if I were a betting man…"

Carter finished the sentence for him, "…you'd put a grand that he was dealing. Sounds like drug suppliers to me, too."

"Sounds like he had a few pretty good connections."

Carter's mind drifted back to his conversation with the pinball kid at the Hideout. "Did the DEA have evidence to show how long ago Andy may have started contacting these addresses?"

"Their tech guys say activity between these IPs and those in Southwest Virginia just started picking up recently. Just over the past couple weeks, maybe."

"Did you find anything else out from DEA?"

"Not really, man," Tony sighed. "Look Carter, just be careful, man. There's something you ain't seeing here. Somehow, your brother-in-law got connected. And somebody knew about it and didn't like it. You thought those swingers were dangerous? You know what we've seen with drug dealers here in Kingsport."

Carter thought back to his days as a detective. Even in that small, working class city, there had been one execution-style murder over drugs. Andy's death appeared to be proof that even Haysi wasn't immune to drug violence, especially if someone like The Ace felt threatened. "Thanks for the info, Tones. Let me dig a little deeper and see what I can find about just how well connected Andy may have become. Holler if you come up with anything else."

"All in a day's work, man. You know ol' Tony always comes through. I'll see you in a couple of weeks."

Carter hung up the phone and dropped it in his pocket. "Florida, Texas, South Carolina," he muttered, looking at the border collie. "Sadie, how deep into this shit was Andy? How deep was he planning to go?" He took a few steps up the hill, away from the creek, and stopped. "And how in the hell did he get so well connected so quickly? And who didn't like it?" He tapped his thigh twice with his left hand. "Let's go, girl. We've got some work to do."

EIGHTEEN

On the ride back to the Breaks, Carter updated Connie on the information he received from Tony regarding the mysterious email address from Andy's contact list. Walking into the Coachmen, he headed directly to the poster boards on the couch, opened a marker, and added, "FL TX SC" to the earlier notes. He stepped back and looked at the boards. Connie handed him a diet Dr Pepper and put an arm around his waist. "Anything?"

"Yeah, way too many drug references," he answered. "Cecil, Junior, Andy, Eric; who around here ain't dealing drugs?"

"Walk me through it," Connie said. She was well aware she was his best sounding board, the devil's advocate to his theories. The last few years of his career, he often bounced his speculations about cases off her, getting her input. Sometimes, just talking aloud, sifting through the evidence in his mind, was all Carter needed to give him a new insight into a case. But many times, it was Connie, looking at the same evidence with a different set of eyes, a non-law enforcement viewpoint, a female perspective, who provided the breakthrough idea that solved a difficult case. Last summer, it was her insight that led to the conviction of Doug Westlake's killer.

"Look at all the drug ties," Carter began. First, there's the meth, albeit a small amount, we found in Eric's house. Then there's the pinball kid, telling me Andy and Eric had recently begun a small-time dealing operation at the Hideout. Then there's the mysterious email addresses, which we find are tied to drug import regions. If Andy was small-time, why would he be contacting drug operators from these areas? He would just get what little he was peddling locally."

"Here's what I don't understand. If Andy didn't like Teresa, why did he recently add her as a Facebook friend? And why does he have two other recent friend additions, a pharmacist and a judge? These guys are definitely outside his local circle of buddies. Do you think Andy could have gotten deeper into the drug business than we think?"

"Hard to say, babe. I never expected him to be in the drug business to start with. But he was, so I guess anything is possible."

Connie thought for a moment. "And if he was getting deeper into the business, somebody would have got pissed."

Carter remembered the pinball kid telling him about The Ace. If Cecil Vanover is The Ace, then we have ourselves a suspect."

169

"And don't forget, there's the rumors about Cecil and Teresa's wild parties. Remember the kind of money we saw in the Carolina Couples in Charlotte? We know firsthand what sex and money can lead to."

"Leave it to you to tie everything to sex," Carter laughed. "But I do agree; we know sex and money are a dangerous concoction. Add in some drugs and you have a potent combination for murder."

"Where can we find out more about drugs, sex, and money here in Dickenson County?" Connie asked.

It didn't take long for the answer to reach Carter's lips. "The Number Nine Club."

"You ready for a night out, sweetie?" she asked.

"Are you sure you want to go out on the town without the TC?" he asked. I mean, the Ram's nice, but it's still a truck. And if the TC ever found out…"

"Well, you can always ask Tanya if we can take Andy's Taurus," she laughed

"That's okay, babe. The Ram will do just fine."

****

"I liked the outfit you wore on our last undercover adventure better, babe," Carter said, looking at his wife sashaying her way down the steps leading from the Coachmen's bedroom into the kitchen. Her outfit for their visit to The Number Nine Club consisted of a calico print long-sleeved top, a pair of moderately tight-fitting jeans, a slim belt, and two-inch-heeled black cowboy boots she borrowed from Tanya. She wore a set of diamond earrings and a small, gold cross necklace on a gold chain.

"You would," she frowned. "I think this will work just fine." She lifted the cross. "I may need to loan you this to keep the lady vampires off of you, though. I hear they may be out tonight."

Carter, ever the frugal one, had just finished getting into the same outfit he wore on their undercover adventure in Charlotte nearly a year earlier—a light blue button-up Tommy Hilfiger shirt, khaki slacks, a pair of dress shoes with a name he refused to learn how to pronounce, and a belt to match. He figured no one at this club had seen him in the Queen City, so, if the outfit worked down there, why change it?

"You look a little, well, familiar, sweetie," Connie said, picking at him. "I bet you've even got those designer underwear on."

170

"Damn right I do. For what I paid for them, I'm going to wear them every chance I get. I just hope you take them off of me tonight," he chuckled.

"I took them off you last time, remember?"

His mind went back to her removing his underwear in the hallway of the fifth floor of the Uptown Suites Hotel. A smile formed on his face. "Yeah, you took them off all right—with a room full of people watching. How 'bout trying to wait until we get back home tonight?"

"I didn't hear you complain about the final result."

Carter replayed the events in Charlotte, his wife riding him like a bucking bronco while a room full of swingers cheered her on. "No, no regrets, babe. You were pretty awesome, no, make that spectacular, in that crowd."

"I'm married to a pervert," she said, feigning disgust.

"Yeah, but admit it, you'd have it no other way."

"I guess not, it keeps me entertained," she said with a chuckle.

Once in the Ram, there was little conversation between them on the ride down highway 80. Both of them knew, just as they did last summer, the night had the potential to break a murder case. They also knew it had the potential to turn deadly. To keep his mind occupied, Carter focused on the job at hand, driving sensibly on the crooked mountain road, partly due to Connie's earlier antics, but mostly just to focus. There was no time left for fun and games. It was time to go to work.

****

Locals often refer to Clinchco, Virginia as "Number Nine" for the coal mine that gave rise to its existence. It was formed over a century earlier to house and support the miners and their families; many of whom were poor immigrants, looking for any work they could find, no matter how hard the work, no matter how dirty or dangerous. Today, many of the town's residents are descendants of those early miners. The town also is home to Dickenson County's only African American residents, whose ancestors had settled there, taking jobs in the mines, trying to escape the cotton fields and sharecropping after Reconstruction.

The still active railroad track that runs through the town hauls ton after ton of black diamonds that power America. The houses are small, similarly built, white, wood framed structures, set on tiny lots, many less than a

171

quarter acre, some right against the hillside. Years ago, the coal company owned all the houses, and as a result, they fell into various states of disrepair. When the house were turned over to private ownership, some of the new homeowners repaired them, and they are relatively nice, with new paint, concrete walkways to the front door, and neatly cut lawns with manicured hedges. Others were transferred to people, who, without the financial means or the willingness to make the needed repairs, allowed the structures to remain in various states of decay—dirt pathways, unpainted plywood walls, calf-high grass, cars on blocks sitting out front, and porches that threatened to fall in on any dogs that might live underneath them.

The centerpiece of the town was the Baptist church: a well-maintained, older, brick building with white trim and steeple. The church served the spiritual needs of the community, but when services were not in session, the building often served as a community center, providing the town's residents a place to gather for both religious and secular events.

At the far end of town, the GPS instructed Carter to turn left, and he drove another three-quarters of a mile past more small, run-down houses, until he and Connie saw a large, new building designed to resemble a barn from Kentucky's wealthy bluegrass region. The paved parking lot was well lit, and was packed with luxury vehicles—Caddies, Lexuses, Infinitis, Yukon Denalis, and Audis. Even a couple of cars and SUVs displaying the Mercedes Benz emblem dotted the pavement. Carter hoped the Ram didn't develop an inferiority complex while parked among such company. While circling the lot looking for an open spot, he spotted a familiar BMW X5 with the license plate "TV45" parked near the front door, almost as if the spot was reserved for it. "Guess who's here." he said.

"Hmm, your old sweetheart," Connie said with displeasure in her voice.

"I wish you wouldn't call her that. You know you're the only girl for me." He glanced at his wife. "You always have been, and you always will be."

"I know, sweetie. But I do get jealous. You are a pretty good catch. Any woman would love to take you away from me. Especially a woman who knows what she lost."

"Trust me, she don't know everything she lost, babe. You are the only woman who knows everything."

Connie knew exactly what he meant. Many times over the years, she had asked and he had always assured her she was the only woman he had ever made love with. Long ago, she came to the conclusion he was telling the truth. Sometimes she thought it was cute, but sometimes, it made her feel guilty, because she couldn't say the same thing. Well, technically she could, she often told herself, because before Carter, all she ever experienced was sex. With Carter, it had always been different. She loved him, even the very first time. Luckily, the subject of her past relationship rarely came up, and when it did, she knew better than to mince words about it. "There's a spot," she said, pointing to a place ahead on the left, happy to change the subject.

Carter pulled the Ram into the parking spot and told Connie to sit still. He got out of the truck, walked to her side, opened the door, and assisted her out of the four-wheel drive. "Wow, a girl could get used to a gentleman like you," she said with a smile.

"I just want to let everybody know that I take care of my trophy wife," he replied.

They both recognized the tune and lyrics of the song "Rock and Roll Ain't Noise Pollution" coming from the inside of the Number Nine Club, but it sounded little like the original AC/DC hit. The band added a twisted, almost psychedelic sound to the heavy metal rhythm, and somehow, the southwestern Virginia accent of the lead singer managed to throw in a little bluegrass twang at the same time. They stopped and stared at the building, listening to the unique sound. "I never thought I'd say this, but I kind of like this version," Carter said.

"It is a different take on our kind of music," Connie replied. "I'm not quite sure I like it, but it makes me want to hear more. I wonder what 'Enter Sandman' is going to sound like?"

"Or 'Fat Bottom Girls,'" laughed Carter. "It'll be interesting." They walked across the pavement toward the front door of the nightclub. Once there, they were greeted by a man in his forties, who looked like he could still play linebacker. He sported a closely trimmed goatee, wore a crimson polo shirt with the club's "9" logo, and had the scent of expensive cologne around him. "I don't think I've seen you guys here before," he said in his unaccented voice. He looked at Carter. "I know you're over twenty-one, but I may need to card the lady."

Connie blushed. "Trust me, he's my boy toy."

The man chuckled, "Twenty-five dollars," he said to Carter.

Carter lifted his eyes as if he was asking the Lord to help him with the cover charge as the band began their rendition of "When I Drink Alone", which now filled the air. "Twenty-five bucks? Geez." He shook his head. "What's the name of this band?" he asked, reaching for his wallet.

"Skynyrd canceled at the last minute," the doorman said sarcastically. "Foddershock was the best we could do on short notice. They're not a traditional classic rock band, but they've adapted for the gig here. Most people enjoy the difference. It gives the place a Mountain Empire feel with a rock beat, if you know what I mean. Now, if you want bluegrass, we can get major stars by the truckload, but most of our crowd prefers something a little harder that Ralph Stanley."

Connie laughed. "Foddershock sounds just fine tonight. If you talk to the Skynyrd boys, tell them we wish them well."

The man nodded. "Will do, ma'am. You folks have a good evening," he said, taking Carter's money as he opened the door.

As they walked in, the smoke-filled air choked Connie, sending her into a coughing fit. Finally regaining her composure, she looked at Carter. "Don't they have anti-smoking laws in Virginia?"

"Sure, but do you really expect them to be enforced here? Look around."

Connie looked around the room and saw well-dressed, well-trimmed people, most in their forties, fifties, or early sixties. Nearly every table had at least one person smoking a cigarette. "Guess not," she said, tugging on his hand. "Let's find a table."

Carter looked around the room. From the few empty tables remaining, he calculated the observance factor of each, wanting to give them the best opportunity to see what was going on. Choosing one along the back wall, he took Connie's elbow and walked her through the table maze, pulled out her chair, then took his own seat with a view of the entire club. A moment later, a young, pretty waitress in a Number Nine Club t-shirt tucked into dressy jeans, asked, "What can I gitcha?"

"A Michelob Ultra," Connie replied.

"I'll have a Bud," Carter said.

"He'll have a Bud Light," Connie corrected, stressing the "Light".

"I'll have a Bud Light," Carter said with a grimace on his face.

At the far end of the room, in front of the band, a dance floor full of inebriated couples attempted to move to the beat of the music, with varying degrees of success. Even on undercover missions, drunken people amused Carter. Most just got stupid drunk. It was the few who got mean drunk who caused trouble, and there always seemed to be a few of those around. Carter noticed a couple of bouncers wearing "Security" Ts who appeared capable of handling most any situation that arose.

"Recognize anyone?" Connie asked.

"Not yet. But I'm sure someone will recognize me. We'll offer to have them join us. Then we'll work to get better acquainted and learn more about this place." The waitress returned with their beers. Carter handed her a ten. "Keep the change."

"Thanks," she said as she sped off to the next table.

"Wow, you actually tipped that girl two whole dollars. I'm proud of you, sweetie," Connie said.

"I'm trying to act more like Marty Calloway," Carter replied.

"I'm glad to see Marty's rubbing off on you," she giggled.

Foddershock began playing their rendition of Tom Petty's "Refugee." "Since we're here, let's hit the dance floor, what do you say, sweetie?"

"I should have known you wouldn't let me sit here and relax." Carter got up, took her hand, and together they walked to the dance floor. From what he had observed, the fact that he wasn't much of a dancer wasn't going to be a problem tonight; he didn't see anyone who looked like Patrick Swayze or Jennifer Gray on the floor. Together, they began moving, trying to find the beat of the music. Carter got a bit too close and accidently stepped on Connie's toes. "Sorry, babe," he yelled into her ear.

"It was obvious it wasn't the first time her husband had trampled her toes on the dance floor.

It's okay. You'll get in the groove," Connie said, without slowing down.

As the song finished, the band's frontman introduced a special guest. A local woman, in her mid-twenties, joined them on stage. The intro to the Pat Benatar hit "Heartbreaker" played, and when the woman began to sing, her powerful voice silenced the hum of the crowd. Except for the sound of the band and the singer, whose voice emulated Benatar's note for note, the nightclub was quiet as a church mouse. Most of the people on the dance floor stopped moving when she began singing, but before the song was half over, couples again began to attempt to dance to the beat. At the end of the song, the young singer was joined by Foddershock's lead singer, and the band transitioned to the classic hit "Stop Dragging My Heart Around."

As the song started, Connie felt a tap on her right shoulder and turned to see who it was. That was all it took for an obviously intoxicated Teresa Vanover to use a hip check to her left side, push Connie out of the way and move in front of Carter. Connie started to retaliate, but Carter raised his hand and a quick shake of his head told her this was the time to keep her jealousy in check and play it cool. As mad as she was, she knew they were

175

there for information, and the business-like look on Carter's face when he shook her off let her know that getting info was the only thing on his mind.

She didn't have to wait long for her chance to stay on the dance floor. A stone sober Cecil Vanover cut her off as she took a step onto the carpet. "I see Tree's finally cornered that husband of yours. Mind if I have this dance?"

Connie's heart raced as she stood face to face with a man she knew was involved in illegal drugs, and suspected might be involved in murdering a member of her family. She focused on keeping her cool and looked him square in the eye. "It might give us an opportunity to watch them a little closer," she said, as she stepped back onto the hardwood and once again began moving to the music's beat.

Cecil Vanover was a good dancer, taking her hands and moving smoothly to the rhythm of the music. Connie found it easy to follow him, even as she tried to keep one eye on Carter and Teresa stumbling around on the other side of the floor, Carter because of his clumsiness and Teresa because of her altered state. As the song ended, Cecil and Connie joined the rest of the crowd in giving the young lady a rousing round of applause. Connie waited as Carter walked toward them, with Teresa hanging all over him, not sure whether it was from drunkenness, lust, or a little of both. She took her husband's hand, and Cecil corralled his wife. "We've got a great table over here, come join us," Cecil invited, as the lights became a bit brighter and The Eagles' recorded version of "Witchy Woman" softly filled the room while Foddershock exited the stage.

Carter acknowledged the invite and said they would join them momentarily. He and Connie walked to their table along the back wall to retrieve their beers. "I almost let her have it," Connie whispered.

"I know, I saw the look in your eye," he laughed. And I wouldn't have blamed you if you had. That was a pretty mean hip check she put on you out there. But," he paused for a second, "we came here to get all the information about these murder cases that we can possibly get. This may be our best chance to interact socially with one of our suspects. We've got to find out how Cecil, and maybe Teresa, fit into this picture. Keep your cool, babe, and keep your eyes and ears open. Let's see where all this leads."

"Easy for you to say," Connie snorted back. "I don't have a gorgeous woman trying to get her claws into me."

"I know," Carter laughed. "I can only dream of that."

Connie punched him in the shoulder. "You pervert. Come on."

Carter and Connie walked into an enclave, closed on three sides by walls, but having a wide opening to the rest of the nightclub on the front, giving it the feel of a VIP room without closing it off completely. There were three long tables in the room, each with seating for twelve. Cecil directed traffic and made room for Carter and Connie at the end of their table. He sat at the head, put Carter to his right, and Connie on his left, facing her husband and the rest of the club. Teresa wasted no time in taking the chair to the right of Carter, leaning up against him, her left hand finding a resting place on his thigh.

"I'm so glad you guys made it down to The Number Nine tonight," Cecil said. He looked at Carter. "All Tree's been talking about since you two had lunch was wanting to get up with you," he said with a wink.

"I guess she got her wish," Connie said, forcing a smile.

"Not yet, but I'm working on it, honey," slurred Teresa, with a giggle in her voice. Carter was a little surprised Cecil knew about his and Teresa's lunch at the Pizza Parlor, but he didn't let it show. "How long has this place been here?" he asked, trying to make conversation while keeping his arms in a defensive position.

"About five years," Cecil answered. "Mousey Rasnick opened it up as a way to keep the local mine operators from taking their entertainment money to the Tri Cities or Pikeville. Mousey's done such a good job with it, he's got some of the most well-connected people of the region driving here on the weekends to let loose and have a good time. Some dancing, some drinking, some good clean fun."

Connie looked around the room and noticed the abundance of silicon and botox sported by the women. "Looks similar to a place we went to last summer," she remarked.

"Oh, yeah, where's that?" Cecil asked.

"Charlotte," Connie said, looking at him for a reaction, but not getting one.

"Did y'all enjoy yourselves?" he asked.

"Very much so. It was a very productive outing."

Cecil moved his left arm to the back of Connie's chair. "How rude of me, I should have introduced you to some of our regulars." He pointed to the couple beside Connie. "This is Jeff and Kim Payne. Jeff runs Black Rock Mining in Norton." Pointing to the couple beside Teresa, he said, "This is Bill and Valerie Williams. Bill is a respected administrative law judge. Guys, this is an old friend of mine and Teresa from high school, Carter Sykes, and his lovely wife, Connie."

177

"Bill Williams," Carter thought. "Where do I know that name?"

Connie noticed Cecil didn't remove his arm from her chair after the introduction. "How do you do?" she asked.

"Good to have you with us, Connie," Bill said, a grin beaming across his face. "Do you need something stronger than that beer?"

"I'm fine, thanks. One of us has to drive." Everyone at the table laughed, though Connie wasn't quite sure why.

"Are they coming back to your place, tonight, Cecil?" Jeff asked.

"Damn straight they're coming back to our place," Teresa stammered. "I'm inviting them and nobody turns me down, do they, Val?"

"I've never seen a man turn you down yet, honey," the bleached blonde, who looked to be in her mid-thirties, replied.

"I have," Teresa said. "But I plan on fixing that tonight." She moved her hand to rub on the inside of Carter's leg.

Carter dropped his right wrist high on his thigh, and used his left hand to finish his beer. "I'm empty," he said, standing up. "I'll make a run to the bar. Anybody else want anything?"

"Don't be silly, Carter. Sit back down there. I'll get a waitress over here to bring you anything you need." He held up his hand and a young brunette in a Number Nine Club t-shirt came to the table.

"What can I get you, Mr. Vanover?"

"Jen, Mr. Sykes here needs a drink. What are you drinking, Carter?"

"A Bud, uh, Light is fine," he said, sitting back down, laying his right forearm across his thigh.

"Connie?"

"I'm fine," she answered, lifting her bottle off the table, shaking it to show it was still half full."

"Bring me a Coke and bring Trees one of those special Cokes."

"Coming right up, Mr. Vanover," the waitress said as she walked away.

"What's the special Coke?" Connie asked, hoping for some drug info.

Cecil leaned over and whispered into her ear. "A diet Coke. I think she's had enough alcohol this evening, but I don't dare tell her that. She'll drink whatever I buy her, and be in much better shape by the time the fun begins at our place."

"Oh, I see," Connie said, visions of what she thought might happen at the Vanover mansion swirling in her head.

The band came back on stage, the lights dropped, and they began the set by playing "T-R-O-U-B-L-E." While it was technically a country song, made even more country by the lead singer's hillbilly twang, Carter used it as an opportunity to get a breather from Teresa's attention. "If you guys will excuse us, I owe my wife a dance, and this song fits her. She is definitely trouble." Carter took Connie by the hand, and she followed his lead to the dance floor.

"Carter, I don't like this," she said once they got on the floor, overlooking his trouble comment.

"Neither do I, babe. But we're this close to getting inside one of their parties. Do we really want to back off now?"

"Just tell me it's all about solving Andy's murder and not about getting inside your old girlfriend's jeans."

"Give me a little more credit than that, Cons."

"I just want to make sure."

Carter almost stopped moving, looking his wife in the eye. "Connie, I'm here to solve a murder case. Nothing more. We need to know how involved Cecil is. And where this drug angle leads. This is our best shot to find out."

"Ok, but promise me you won't let things get out of hand."

"You know better than that, babe. Have a little faith in me, okay? I love you, you know that."

After the song finished, Carter and Connie walked back to the table, finding Cecil and Teresa's seats empty. "Where'd they go?" Carter asked.

"They took off to their place to prepare for the party tonight," Jeff answered.

Valerie gave Carter a seductive grin. "Teresa told me to make sure we got you there in one piece, Carter. She said she was looking forward to having you in her hot tub tonight."

"She enjoys the things you can do in a hot tub," Bill added with a laugh.

Carter took the seat at the head of the table next to Connie and they sipped on their beers as the next song played. When the music ended, Foddershock's frontman grabbed the microphone from the stand and walked to the front of the stage as the band began to play a tune behind him. "We wrote this next song in remembrance of the way things used to be around here. It's about a time when things were good in these parts, when

179

people had jobs, good paying jobs. A time when we thought there was a future for our kids. We're talking about the time 'When Coal Was King.'"

The crowd roared, rising to its feet in honor of the song reminiscing about a past that had left these hills long ago. Most of the club's patrons knew the words by heart and sang along with the band. Connie thought of the story Ashley, the girl from the library, had told her, and Carter considered the economic plight faced by his brother, his brother-in-law, and the pinball kid. Would anything ever bring good economic times to the region the way coal had done forty years ago?, they both wondered. As the band played, they joined everyone in the room in hoping something would come to Central Appalachia and replace coal as king—for both the region and its people.

As the song finished and the band began playing a classic rock hit by ZZ Top, the couples around them finished their drinks. Jeff leaned over to Carter, "It's time to head to the ridge. It's time for the party to begin."

Carter looked at Connie, nodded his head, and they both rose. Jeff and Kim led the way to the front door, with Bill and Valerie falling in behind Carter and Connie. "Follow us," Jeff said, stopping at an Escalade parked close to the door. "Bill and Val will be right behind us. We'll see you at the party."

Connie looked at Carter, a feeling of entrapment filling her gut. Carter had the same feeling, but kept his cool. "See you guys in a few," he yelled across the parking lot, opening the Ram's passenger door for Connie.

"Are we going through with this?" she asked softly.

"Until I can find a way out," he answered, shut her door, and walked to the driver's side.

NINETEEN

A million questions ran through Connie's mind, but she didn't ask a single one on the ride to the Vanover mansion. Her eyes alternated between the taillights of the Cadillac SUV in front of them and the headlights of the BMW convertible shining in the rearview mirror. Carter didn't say a word either, so she knew he was focused on their next move.

Her thoughts turned to analyzing their predicament. She didn't like the way Teresa was coming on to Carter, but, despite her jealousy, she trusted her husband. While she didn't want to go to the party, both she and Carter found themselves literally boxed in. She rationalized that, at this point, going to Caney Ridge was their best course of action. Sure, they could simply not follow the Caddy when it made the left to ascend the ridge, but that would be an obvious escape move, and at this point there was no real reason to do anything that drastic . Besides, going to a party at the Vanovers' just might give them a closer look into Cecil's level of involvement in the drug trade. It might provide more insight into how high up he was on the drug ladder. They might even encounter another person of interest in the case, someone above Cecil. Trying to calm her fears, she glanced at her husband, and decided to put her trust in him and his years of experience to get them out of this situation.

After they made the turn to ascend Caney Ridge, Carter reached out and took his wife's hand. "I just want to make sure we're on the same page here, babe. I have no, let me say it again, *no* interest in Teresa. You are my wife, my love. You always have been, and you always will be. The only reason we're going to this party is to try to find out more about Andy's murder and our prime suspect. We both believe Cecil is involved, and this party is our best chance to find out how. We can't pass this up."

Connie smiled, touched that Carter was thinking of her feelings as they drove to the party. However, she also worried his concern for her might be a distraction to him. She wanted to be his partner, to let him know she could handle herself. "I know, sweetie. If I didn't trust you, I would have thrown a fit on the dance floor when I got shoved to the side. We're a team, we're in this together. I'll follow your lead."

"I just want to make sure we play this thing cool. I don't want it to get messy." He thought for a moment.. "But it might anyway."

"I think you know I'm a pretty cool customer," she reminded him, looking at her husband with a smile. "I'll be fine, let's do this."

Carter's mind flashed to how she avoided the cowboy in Charlotte last summer. He glanced to his right, returned her smile and briefly caught her eye. "Point taken," he said. "Okay, let's do it."

They rode quietly for the final couple of miles until they saw the Vanover house in the distance. The lighting made it hard to miss—bright electric walkway lights, not dim solar lights, ran down both sides of the concrete double drive, giving it the appearance of a short runway at a major airport instead of a residential parking pad. The front entrance was lit, as was the front of the garage, with a LED rope. As they pulled into the drive, one of the garage doors rose, inviting the guests to come inside. As the Caddy parked on the left, Carter pulled the Ram behind it and watched as the Beamer parked on the right, beside the Escalade. "I was counting on that," he said softly. "I want to make sure we can escape if we need to."

Connie looked at Carter, glad his police training always led him to think a step ahead of the bad guys. "Good thinking, sweetie."

The front doors of the Beamer opened and Bill and Valerie jumped out. Carter opened his door, jumped out of the cab, walked between the Escalade and the Ram, and opened Connie's door for her. As she got out, she saw Cecil standing at the entrance to the garage. "Come on in," he called out. "It's time to get the party started."

"Woo hoo!" called out Valerie. "I'm looking forward to this one."

Carter noticed two more cars approaching the house and watched as they pulled into the driveway. His lips formed a frown and his head shook slightly as a compact Lexus CT200h pulled in behind the Ram. "Best laid plans," he mumbled.

"It'll be okay," Connie reassured softly as she took her husband's hand. They walked toward the open garage door and could hear Steve Miller's "The Joker" playing in the backyard, getting louder as they approached. "Glad you guys made it," Cecil said. "Tree's been looking forward to having you here. Come on in and get comfortable."

"Wouldn't have missed this for the world," Connie said, full of apprehension but feigning enthusiasm. Carter looked at her, taking note that, just like last summer, she was now in the zone, playing the part of an eager participant in something he knew scared the living hell out of her. "She would have been one hell of an undercover cop," he thought, as they entered the garage. Cecil directed them straight through and out the door that led to the concrete patio in the backyard, made private by the woods surrounding their ridgetop property.

Carter leaned over, putting his lips to Connie's ear. "He didn't have to build a fence."

Connie giggled, but didn't say a word.

Taking in the expansive, beautifully landscaped backyard, Carter thought about the work required to mow it. "If you can afford this place, I guess you can afford to have someone mow the yard for you," he told himself.

"Wow, this is beautiful," Connie exclaimed. "We've been to some dinners at the houses of some of the best doctors and lawyers in the Tri Cities, and I've not seen anything like this."

"We call it 'Caney Ridge Eden,'" Cecil smiled, moving to her side to join her in admiring the view.

"I can see why. Look at that hot tub, Carter," she exclaimed, looking at the detached building to the right with the glass walls removed. "I told you we need one of those in our backyard." She looked at Cecil. "It looks like it's an in-ground tub?"

"That it is. It's the highlight of every party we have this time of year, Takes the chill off the cool night air." He nodded to the outdoor bar set up next to the house. "Grab a drink. I think you'll find something you like. We'll all be getting in the tub in a few minutes."

"Oh, I didn't bring a bathing suit," Connie remarked.

"Neither did I," Bill said, walking up behind her and putting his arm around her shoulder. Connie looked back to see a mischievous smile across his face.

"We're all friends here, Connie," Cecil explained in a reassuring voice that Connie didn't buy. "Everything that happens on this ridge stays on this ridge. You guys grab a drink while everyone gets settled. Then we'll move to the hot tub."

Carter and Connie walked hand in hand to the bar, where they saw a large, flatscreen TV mounted into the wall, facing the patio. On the screen was an orgy scene from a porno flick, a dozen people engaged in various stages of sexual activity—a woman providing oral pleasures to a man, another with a man taking her from behind while she pleasured the woman on the bed in front of her. Another woman was sitting atop a man, moving up and down in his lap, causing his enormous rod to piston in and out of her backdoor. The camera zoomed in on a couple as the man pulled out of his partner, stroked his member, depositing his juice on her flat belly.

Carter tried to move his eyes away from the action on the screen as he grabbed two glasses and filled them with ice and water. Handing one to

Connie, they turned and watched the other couples enter the yard. All appeared to be wealthy, the men in their fifties, their wives in their thirties or forties, showing signs of multiple visits to their plastic surgeons and personal trainers. Carter watched as each couple grabbed a strong drink before migrating toward the hot tub. One by one, they stopped at the small building to the right of the hot tub's entrance, took off their clothes, left them in the building, grabbed an oversized beach towel, and wrapped it around their body as defense against the cool mountaintop air. "Anyone else want a towel?" Valerie yelled as she grabbed hers.

"Sure," said the man who drove the Lexus hybrid parked behind Carter. He walked over to Valerie, and tried to take the towel from her. She jerked it away at the last minute and laughed. "Not so fast, bucko. I need some help getting out of these things."

"All you had to do was ask, baby," he said.

She laid his towel over the back of a white wicker chair covered by an oversized, dark blue cushion. The man reached for the bottom of her untucked blouse, slowly unbuttoning it to reveal the sexy, black Victoria's Secret bra that covered her large breasts. She raised her arms and assisted as he guided the shirt off her back, tossing it onto the seat of the chair. Without a word, he reached his right arm around her back and expertly used his fingers to unbuckle her bra. She lowered her arms and he caught the lacy garment as it fell into his hands.

"Looks like they're glad to see me," he said with a laugh, reaching up, tweaking a hard nipple between his fingers.

"Could be, Ken. Or it could just be the cool evening air," She teased. "I'm sure we'll find out soon. Right now, I'm getting in the hot tub. Be a dear and help me out of the rest of these things?"

"Of course, ma'am," he said, wrapping his arms around her waist and unzipping her skirt, watching it fall to the concrete. He took the black matching thong by the waistband and slowly lowered it over her hips, rubbing his hands over her globes, sliding his palms over her legs as he descended. He got down on his knees as she stepped out of it, and he helped her remove her three-inch-heeled sandals.

"Something else might be missing you too, honey," she teased.

He looked up to find her shaved womanhood staring him in face. He leaned forward, and methodically ran his tongue along the length of her slit, eliciting a soft moan. "Hmm, you always taste so sweet." He stood up facing her. "Mind if I join you in the tub?"

184

"Only if we remove these," she said, taking his belt buckle in her hand and releasing it. Together they lowered his slacks, then his boxers, stopping when she reached his shoes. She pulled the string on each of them; his toe held the heel in place and, one at a time he pulled his feet from them. Valerie removed his socks, rubbing his feet as she did.

Still squatting in front of him, she looked up into his eyes as she reached for his erection. She stroked it slowly, methodically, before lowering her lips over the tip, tasting his first emissions. Encouraged by his moan, she twirled her tongue around his sensitive head, as his hands began to run through her hair. "Oh my god, baby," he cried out, causing her to pull away.

"Not so fast, honey. We'll finish this later. Come on, let's get in the hot tub."

Ken assisted her to her feet, removed his shirt, wrapped his arms around her, and lowered his mouth to her waiting lips. In an embrace, they walked through the door-less entrance to the hot tub. Valerie removed her towel, hung it on a hook, and held his hand as she took three steps into the bubbling hot water. He hung his own towel, followed her into the steaming water, and they lowered themselves until only their heads remained above the surface. They embraced again, then Valerie swung her leg over his lap, facing him. They began a passionate kiss, their tongues dancing together, their hands exploring the other's naked body under the soothing bubbles.

"Looks like everyone's excited tonight," Cecil told Carter and Connie with a chuckle. "Feel free to join them if you want. Like I said, we're all friends here."

"Really good friends, I'd say," Connie replied. "It's been a really long day. I could use a dip in that hot tub, but I think it's a little, umm, occupied."

"Don't worry, sweetheart, nobody has sex in the hot tub, house rules. They'll settle down … or take it inside. We've got plenty of room in the house."

"That's good, 'cause that hot water will feel soooo good."

"That ain't all that will feel good," Bill, whispered into her ear.

The others began moving toward the hot tub, each getting a towel from the closet, and removing their clothes, some with assistance from a member of the opposite sex. Carter looked at Connie as she removed her top. "You want to help me with this, sweetie?" she whispered. "Somehow, I don't think Bill would pass up the opportunity."

"You sure about this, babe?" he whispered back.

"Yeah, I'm okay. We've done this before. Let's see how much we can learn, then we'll excuse ourselves."

Reaching both hands behind her, Carter fumbled with her bra, finally getting it unhooked, and slipping it over her shoulders. Even though they had been married for more than thirty years, the sight of his wife topless always created a stirring inside of him. He unbuckled his pants, unbuttoned his shirt, and pulled it from his body. One at a time he put his feet on a wicker chair and slipped off his shoes and socks. Slipping out of his slacks, he looked at Connie, who was now standing in front of him wearing only her bikini panties. "Are you glad you bought those designer underwear now, sweetie?" she asked him, rubbing her hand over his rear.

"Yeah," he answered, raising his eyes and nodding his head. "I'd hate to be standing here in my Fruit of the Looms right now."

She laughed. "Those holey white ones? Especially if they had..."

"Don't even go there," Carter warned her.

Connie laughed again. "Don't worry, sweetie, I won't bring up your dirty laundry here."

They each took off their underwear. Carter grabbed two towels from the closet and handed one to his wife. With his arm over her shoulder and hers around his waist, they walked across the concrete path leading to the Jacuzzi. Walking into the hot tub room, they saw the jets were stirring the water in the tub that was several feet wider across than Carter was tall. Couples were sitting boy-girl-boy-girl on a bench along the sides and back of the tub, only their heads above the water. "Water's perfect," Ken, his arm keeping Valerie from falling off his lap, yelled over the sound of the jets. "Hang your towels on a hook and come on in."

Carter looked around, saw an empty hook on the wall, took Connie's towel, and placed them both on it. He reached for her hand and followed her down the steps into the bubbling water. Connie stopped, surveyed the situation once more, and moved toward a space between Ken and the pretty blonde woman on his left, figuring Ken was busy enough with Valerie to leave her alone.

"Is this how all these parties start?" Carter asked.

"Hi, I'm Monica," the blonde introduced herself. "During the winter, we may only have two or three couples over, and since it's cold, we'll stay in the house. Those usually become game nights."

"Game nights?" Connie questioned.

"Yeah, you know, board games like Monopoly, only with a twist. You roll the dice and move your marker to a spot that instructs you what to do, like suck the earlobe of the man on your right." She reached up and touched Carter's earlobe. "Or suck on something else," she giggled. "It's a lot of fun."

"Game night sounds interesting," Carter said, turning toward Connie. "Maybe we should try that sometime, babe." He looked back at Monica. "I'm Carter, and this is my wife, Connie."

"Hi Connie," Monica said. "We know all about you, Carter. You're all Teresa's talked about for the past two days. 'Carter's in town, I hope we can get Carter to the party.' She's been beside herself, wanting to suck your cock, wanting to have sex with you. You're going to be one lucky man tonight."

"Didn't y'all used to date in high school?" the man beside Monica asked, his hand stroking the inside of her thigh.

"Date? Honey, they were hot. Tree says that Carter here was a hunk. Now I see why."

"I think she may have exaggerated a little bit, but yes, we did date in high school. Hi, I'm Carter.", he said to the man.

"Jack," the man replied. "Surely Teresa wouldn't exaggerate."

"I don't know," giggled Monica. "Any man wearing the hot underwear you had on must have something special to put in them. Tree's told me too many stories about you two. Where there's smoke, there must be a hot, burning fire." Her lips formed into a sly grin.

Connie grabbed Carter's lower thigh with her hand. "Sounds to me like Teresa needs to be writing romance novels."

"I guess we'll find out in a minute," Monica nodded toward the back door of the mansion, where Cecil held the door as Teresa, her towel wrapped around her waist, came out carrying a fresh beverage.

"From what Monica's saying, it sounds like you've seen those things before," Connie whispered in Carter's ear.

Carter turned toward his wife and leaned to her ear. "You can rest assured, those things weren't around when I was in high school." They both laughed.

"Everyone, welcome the Mistress of the Ridge," Cecil announced, extending his arm and letting Teresa enter first. All eyes turned to her as she stepped into the room, took a bow, removed her towel, and hung it on what must have been her personal hook. Her dark tanned body at the end of April gave away her use of a tanning bed, and the lack of sag in her fifty-year-old body gave away her use of modern surgical techniques. Connie squeezed Carter's thigh a bit tighter as jealousy swept over her. She knew she was a good-looking woman, but she couldn't keep from thinking about what a couple of procedures could do for her.

Carter's eyes were locked on his old flame. Some primal part of his mind took over his thoughts. "Damn, she looks good. I wonder what it would feel like to feel that body against me, to feel those tits rubbing against my chest, those ass cheeks in my hands. I bet she can use those lips to do wonders to a man," this part of his brain continued to taunt him. "And those legs, those slender, sexy legs. I bet she could wrap them around a man, pull him inside her, hold him tight, and squeeze him, making him moan in pleasure. Carter, you're in for one heck of a night," the evil part of his mind told him.

Then, another part of his psyche took over, the part Carter nearly always listened to. "That's not really Teresa," it said. "It's an image of her that she wants everyone to see, and was willing to pay to get. The Teresa who created her dwells in the core of that woman, a woman who can't be happy with who she really is. Is that the woman you want to be joined with? The woman you want to be one flesh with? Or would you rather have the woman you were given, the woman who is natural and beautiful, who has aged gracefully with you? The woman who has been by your side, for better or worse, for three decades?" Carter placed his hand on Connie's thigh and returned his wife's squeeze with a squeeze of this own, moving his fingers to massage the inner part of her leg.

"Think of how hot Teresa's thigh would feel," screamed the bad part of Carter's brain, but he could hardly hear it now. "Probably weird," said the good side. "Feel what you have, Carter. See how good Connie feels. Is there anything, any amount of silicon, that can equal the feel of your beautiful wife?"

Carter's eyes moved to Connie's face. He noticed each small wrinkle and every year that it represented, every year spent by his side. "This is the woman you love, Carter. Those wrinkles are because she loves you and cares for you. You loved her when you were twenty and you will love her when you are eighty. She is your helpmate. Don't ever forget that."

Carter blinked his eyes and shook his head, as if somehow removing the evil from his thoughts. He watched Teresa lower herself into the tub, move in front of him and motion for Monica and Jack to scoot over and give her room. With the beautiful woman, who was at one time his high school sweetheart, now sitting naked beside him, all he could think of was the love and passion he felt for the lady on his other side, the lady whose thigh he continued to massage under the bubbling water. As Teresa made a scene of settling into her seat, he scooted toward Connie, not so much as to give Teresa more room, but to be closer to the only woman he had ever loved.

Connie sensed something was going on in Carter's mind, and although her female psyche could not understand exactly what he was feeling, she could sense the part of her husband that loved her was taking control. The jealousy which had swept over her disappeared and was replaced by a peace that told her that her man loved her, and only her. Something she didn't understand assured her he cherished their love, and would never do anything to risk losing it, not even with a woman as tempting as Teresa Robinson Vanover. Involuntarily, her arm reached across her husband, around his waist, and pulled him to her. As he looked her way, she placed a small kiss on his lips and whispered into his ear, "I love you, sweetie."

"I love you, too, babe," he said, and lowered his mouth to nip at her neck.

"I know you do," she whispered back, with confidence in her voice.

"I can't believe I'm sitting here in my hot tub, nekkid, with Carter Sykes," Teresa exclaimed, drawing everyone's attention. "I never dreamed this moment would come." She put her hand under the water, finding Carter's knee and running her long fingernails up his thigh. "I'm so glad it finally has."

Carter sat up straight and dropped his arm to stop her hand's progress. "I have to admit, it's a shock for me too, Teresa."

"I hear your retirement has been, well, rather interesting."

"Interesting is a good choice of words," Carter said with a laugh. "There haven't been too many dull moments, have there, babe?" He looked to Connie for support.

"Not many. And somehow, I don't think tonight is going to be one either."

"I've never been accused of throwing a dull party, honey. Especially with a special guest like Carter joining us. Why don't you tell us about Charlotte, sugar?"

Carter felt Teresa scoot closer as Cecil gave her a menacing look from the other side of the tub, reminding her she wasn't supposed to know about Carter and Connie's adventure in the Queen City. "Honey, I'm just trying to get Carter to share some interesting stories with us." She looked at Carter. "You don't mind, do you, sugar?"

Carter wondered where Teresa and Cecil were getting their information. The information about Charlotte wasn't on the police blotter.

189

"It was all just in the line of duty," he said. "Let me tell you, Carter was pretty damn good in Charlotte," Connie defended her husband, then instantly regretted the comment.

"I have no doubt about that," Teresa remarked. "In fact, tonight I plan to find out just how good Carter Sykes really can be." She locked eyes with Connie. "You don't mind, do you, honey?"

If Connie had had powers like Stephen King's Carrie, Teresa Vanover would have immediately erupted into flames. Instead, she somehow managed to hold her composure. "I'll leave that up to him."

"I think I need a drink. You want one, babe?" Carter asked his wife, rising to his feet.

Connie really did need a drink, a strong one, but knew she needed to keep her wits. "Sure, sweetie, I'll take whatever you're having," Connie replied, knowing he would bring her back a glass of water or soda.

"Coming right up," he said, as his hand grabbed the rail and he climbed the steps leading out of the tub.

"Not a bad looking ass on that one, Tree," Monica commented once Carter was out of earshot. "Nice legs, too. I could handle a little of that tonight, if you don't use it all up."

"I've waited over thirty years to feel that man inside me; I'm not planning on there being any seconds left over for anybody," Teresa said with a wink.

"Girl, I don't blame you," Valerie interjected. "Strange dick is always good, but strange that you've waited for is always the best. And that one, well, I can't lay my finger on it, but there's something special about that man."

"You're damn right there is," Connie muttered under her breath. "And y'all will never find out just how special he really is."

The jets on the hot tub shut off and the couples continued their conversations. The ladies talked about Carter, while the men talked about work, sports, and politics. After a few minutes, Carter rejoined the group. He handed Connie a glass filled with ice and a diet Coke, and joined in on the conversation two of the men were having about the Reds and how they looked early in the season. It didn't take long before the women became bored, and one by one, each of them, except Connie and Teresa, began focusing her attention between the legs of one of the men. Some simply stoked their man under the water, while some men sat up on the tub's edge, giving their woman full access to perform her oral magic. Once again, Carter felt Teresa's hand move up his thigh toward her desired destination.

190

He again dropped his arm defensively, but this time it didn't have the desired effect. As she maneuvered around it, he felt her touch his sack with the nail of her forefinger, and he instinctively moved even closer to Connie.

"Anybody else need a drink?" Carter asked, holding up his nearly full plastic glass.

"It don't look like you do, sugar" Teresa answered, her hand getting closer to reaching its desired object. "Sit back, honey. I promise you, you're going to enjoy this."

"Well, I do need to visit the boy's room," Carter said, standing up, forcing Teresa's hand from his leg. "I'll be back in a minute."

"I didn't expect him to be this shy," Teresa said to Connie. "Not after what I heard about your adventure last summer."

"That's Carter," Connie replied as calmly as she could. "He's always been shy at first. It takes him a little while to get going. But once he does, watch out."

"That's what I'm counting on. I think I'll go see if I can speed the process along a little bit." Teresa stood, walked up the hot tub steps, stopped, and looked Connie in the eye. "I've waited a long time to have that man; I'm not waiting any longer." Before Connie could muster a word, Teresa snatched her towel from its hook, and wrapped it around her shoulders for warmth. In seconds, she was inside the house, calling for Carter.

In the bathroom, Carter regrouped. Looking in the mirror, he spoke to the man staring back at him. "Sykes, it's time for you to get your wife and get the hell out of Dodge." He took a deep breath, opened the door, and walked into the hall. He half expected to find Teresa waiting for him and, to his relief, found she wasn't standing right outside the door. Determined to get Connie and get out, he marched down the long hallway, and then stopped as he entered the kitchen. His eyes focused on Teresa Vanover, now with her towel wrapped around her waist, sitting at the breakfast bar, bent over, her left pointer finger against her nose, while she sniffed the line of white powder on the table before her. Carter watched as the cocaine disappeared, fighting an urge to cuff her on the spot. As she raised her head, she caught a glimpse of him out of the corner of her eye, turned her head, and stared at him with a deer in the headlights look, her glazed eyes seemingly lost in the drug. For several seconds, neither of them moved nor spoke.

"Just getting ready for you, sugar," she finally broke the silence. "Let me lay you a line, it will make the experience so much better for both of us."

"Teresa, there's not going to be any experience." Carter's eyes never moved from hers.

"The hell there ain't, Carter, You're going to make love to me tonight. I'm going to let you know what you've missed all these years."

Connie opened the back door of the house, but when she heard Teresa's voice announce her plans for Carter, she stopped, prior to entering the kitchen, Teresa's declaration ringing in her ears.

Carter remained still. He didn't say a word, his attention focused on the woman sitting at the bar.

"Carter. I want you to make love to me like you should have done when we were in high school," Teresa said seductively, a provocative smile crossing her face. "I've waited half my life for it; I don't want to wait any longer."

"But you dumped me, Teresa, remember?"

"You know the reason I left you for Cecil at that festival? I thought his arm was my ticket out of these damn coalfields. He was more than happy to take me that night, to make me feel like a desirable woman. But I never stopped thinking about you, what we might have had. Now, here I am, thirty years later, stuck on Caney Ridge. Like an idiot, I dumped the one man who got out, the one man who could have gotten me out of here. I'll be damned if I'm going to let you get away again, Carter." She stood up, slipped her towel from around her body, walked over to him, and threw her arms over his shoulders, her breasts softly touching his chest. "Make love to me, Carter. Take me away from these goddamn hills, at least for one night."

Carter raised his arms, forcing her to release the grip around his neck. "Listen, Teresa, you're a beautiful, desirable woman. Most men would love to be in my shoes right now. But we were we a long time ago. I'm in love with Connie. I have been since the first day I saw her. And I always will be. As tempting as you are right now, I can't do this to her. I can't do this to you."

"Goddamnit, Carter Sykes," she screamed with flames in her voice. "I'm telling you to make love to me. I'm giving you, no, I'm giving us, another chance. What the hell is wrong with you? Every man in this county would love for me to offer this to them." She stuck her arms straight out, stretching her wingspan, and spun her naked body, giving his eyes access to every inch of it.

"Most men would, Teresa. But I'm not most men. God knows I'm tempted, but I have Connie and I love her. That's the end of the story. I'm sorry."

Teresa backed up two steps, separating herself from Carter. "Then get the hell out of here. Get the hell out of my house. If I never see your sorry ass again, it'll be too soon."

"Teresa, I know how you must feel. I felt the same way at that festival all those years ago, when we were eighteen. You told me then it was over. I'm telling you now, it's still over."

"Get the fuck out of my house," she screamed loud enough for those in the hot tub to hear her.

Hearing the f-word, Connie knew Carter well enough to know the conversation was over. She scampered out the back door before he saw her.

Without saying a word, Carter walked past Teresa and made his way to the patio. Seeing Connie there, he said, "Get your things. Let's get the hell out of here." Without a word, Connie retrieved both her and Carter's clothing from the outdoor closet. Neither of them stopped to get dressed, walking naked through the garage to the front of the house. Seeing the Ram sandwiched between two vehicles, Carter raised his hand. "Get dressed, I'll be right back." He marched back through the garage, across the patio, to the hot tub. Sticking his head in the door, he yelled, "Whoever's driving the Lexus better move it now."

Teresa, with her towel wrapped around her body, stormed out of the house, and stood behind Carter. "Ain't nobody moving nothing until this son of a bitch fucks me," she screamed. The hot tub grew silent and no one moved.

Carter's voice deepened, but he didn't yell this time. "Somebody needs to move that goddamn Lexus. Now"

"Ken, don't you fuckin' move," Teresa said. "Carter Sykes, this is your last chance. Make love to me, and I'll let you go. That's all you've got to do, make love to me one time. Is that too much to ask?"

"What's wrong, Sykes? My wife ain't good enough for you?" Cecil Vanover spoke as he rose from the tub's edge, forcing the woman in front of him to release his erection from her hand. "For years, all I've heard is 'Carter Sykes this, and Carter Sykes that.' Every time Merrill Moore talked about you arresting someone on the channel 5 news, 'Oh, there's Carter.'

Tonight, I'm going to show Teresa that Carter Sykes is a one hit wonder. I'm going to let you prove, once and for all, who the Ace really is."

The word "Ace" rang in Carter's head, but he decided this was not the best time to ponder its meaning. "Somebody move that fuckin' Lexus," Carter calmly warned one more time.

"Not till you fuck me, Carter." Teresa screamed again. "Nobody turns me down." No one in the hot tub moved.

"Have it your way, then," Carter said, as he turned and stormed back toward the garage. He saw Connie, but didn't acknowledge that she was now fully dressed, holding his clothes out for him. "Get in the truck, babe. We're going home." Side by side, they walked to the Ram. Carter went straight to the driver's door, not offering to open Connie's. They both jumped into the cab of the three-quarter ton truck and Carter cranked the HEMI engine.

"Carter, get your fuckin' ass back here," Teresa, standing at the garage door, still wrapped in her towel, yelled.

Carter never heard her. Not because he couldn't, but because his mind had blocked everything out. He moved the shifter of the Ram into reverse, and then moved it to neutral. He reached out, and pushed the four-wheel drive button. engaging 4-Low, a position it had rarely seen. He moved the shifter back to reverse and lifted his foot from the brake, easing the Ram backward until he felt the jar of the bumper hitting the Lexus' hood. The car's owner, who had wrapped a towel around his waist and joined Teresa in front of the garage, screamed at the impact. Carter pressed the accelerator toward the floor, and smoke rose from all four wheels of the truck as they spun on the concrete drive. The hood of the Lexus accordioned, and finally, the car began to move backward without its wheels turning. The Ram's wheels caught and Carter's right foot pushed harder, the engine roaring as he backed the Lexus into the road before he let off the gas. He put the truck in drive, pulled it forward, and made a hard right. With the truck still in four low, the front wheels hopped across the concrete and into the manicured yard. He drove through the dew-soaked lawn, throwing mud and grass into the air. Finally getting the truck turned around, he exited through the driveway. He stopped the truck, put it in neutral, hit the four-wheel drive button, backed up three feet to complete the four-wheel drive's disengagement process, and, in a calm voice, said, "Fuck this, Teresa." He punched the accelerator and the Ram's rear end swung to the left, its rear wheels spinning wildly, the sound of squalling rubber again filling the air. The tires caught traction; Carter straightened the truck and drove down the road, the sound of tire squall filling the night air as he rounded the first curve.

Neither Carter nor Connie spoke a word on the trip back to the Breaks. As they pulled back into their parking spot, Connie handed him the towel that served as her seatcover. "You better wrap up in this before getting out of the truck."

He looked at her, then down at his nakedness, took the towel, and laughed. "I guess that's a good idea."

"And tomorrow, you'd better clean that seat."

For the first time, Carter noticed he didn't have a towel under his rear. "Yeah," he said with a laugh. "Maybe I should buy us some seatcovers after all."

As Carter wrapped himself, Connie reached over and took his hand. "I heard the whole thing," she confessed. "It would have been easy for you to have given in, to have taken advantage of the situation, of the opportunity. I love you, you know."

"Cons, there is no woman, no matter how beautiful, no matter how much silicon or surgery, no matter how enticing, that could ever match you. We might not be as young as we used to be, but I will always love you. Always."

She leaned over the console and her lips found his "What did I do to deserve you?"

"I don't know, but I'm glad you did it. Let's go inside, I could use a drink, a strong drink."

They each opened their door but Connie stopped. "How'd it feel, moving that Lexus?" she asked.

A mischievous smile crept across Carter's face as he recalled the event. "Pretty damn good. I've dreamed of doing that for years. Makes you proud to be an American."

TWENTY

It was nearly nine before Carter got out of bed the next morning. As he put on his robe, he caught a scent of the previous night's lovemaking, bringing a smile to his face. He looked at Connie, who was just beginning to show signs of life, and chill bumps covered his skin. In his wildest dreams, he couldn't imagine having a better lover, or a better life partner. He raised his eyes and mouthed the words "thank you." He wasn't quite sure to whom he was thanking, but something told him there was more to him being blessed with Connie that pure luck explained.

He grabbed a diet Dr Pepper from the fridge and sat down in his recliner. At this hour, all his ham radio nets were over, so he passed up turning on the radio. He hit the power button on his laptop, and turned on his mobile Internet hotspot. While the computer equipment booted up, he learned back in the chair, took a swig of soda, put his hands behind his head, and tried to stretch his body to life. When the computer was ready, Carter clicked on Firefox and his Yahoo! home page appeared. He clicked on "Mail" and found five messages in his inbox—two from Yahoo! Groups, one reminding him of a Tri Cities MOPAR club meeting, one that looked like spam, and one from "Cyber Ranger." "Martin," Carter said, as he opened it.

****

Carter, got the goods you wanted on the bad guys. Dude, this is some deep shit. Big, I mean big, money; money I never imagined existed in Haysi. I didn't see anything that leads directly to murder, but then you're the detective, not me. But there's a shitload of money here, dude, so somebody's guilty of something. And get this … someone else has been looking into Vanover and Calhoun's financials, too, using the same portals. That's odd, because almost no one except the highest levels of the Feds even know they exist. Whoever was in there is good; they encrypted their trail so well, not even the Cyber Ranger can figure out who they are or exactly where they've located. This ain't some local yokel hacking around; it's coming from way up the food chain, someone who knows what they're doing. If I were guessing, with all the money I see here, I'd bet Justice or IRS, but I can't be sure.

Hope you solve this one soon, dude. This is going to make a great story for the Cyber Ranger. Comic book sales will double when I release it.

Walker ... Cyber Ranger
****

Martin Walker wasn't a cop, but Carter had used his hacking skills enough to know he had acquired a pretty good sense for the evidence. There were four different attachments with "Vanover" in the title. As Carter clicked on each one, he quickly realized Cecil had four different bank accounts, in four different banks, that Martin had uncovered. Going back to the first one, it looked like a normal checking account for a detective; direct deposits of paychecks, auto withdrawals for bills, online purchases, including a couple at Adam & Eve, but nothing out of the ordinary.

He closed the file and began examining the next account. In less than a minute, he began to see the amounts of money that caught Martin's attention. Twice each week, Cecil deposited over nine thousand dollars into the account. "Hmm, just below the IRS cash reporting threshold," Carter mumbled. Doing the rough math in his head, he estimated Cecil was depositing around eighty grand each month, or nearly a million dollars per year. The third and fourth accounts, located in different community banks, yielded similar figures. "This son of a bitch is bringing in three million dollars a year, tax free," he muttered under his breath. "And I ain't even looked into accounts in Teresa's name. Looks like ol' number 45 got a little higher than double A in the drug business."

He saved each attachment in a new "Cecil Vanover" folder on his desktop and opened the first of two Calhoun folders. The first account was a joint one with Tanya. Like Vanover's first one, it appeared to be a normal checking account, showing direct deposits every two weeks from Tanya's employer and payments going out to cover bills and purchases. Out of curiosity, Carter scrolled back and noted the date of Andy's last deposit from Lowes. Looking at outlays, he noticed the sporadic nature of the mortgage payment, becoming even more erratic in the months since Andy lost his job. Carter stretched without taking his eyes off the screen. "I thought Jimmy said Andy caught up his house payments," he said to himself. Sitting straight up, he again scrolled through the account. Reaching the current date, he realized that Andy didn't bring the mortgage current with money from this account. Saving it into a new desktop folder labeled

"Calhoun," his attention moved to the second attachment labeled "Calhoun 2."

Upon opening the second account, the first thing he noted was it was just in Andy's name. Carter let out a sigh of relief as he realized his sister did not appear to be involved with this one. The account had only been open three months and already showed all the signs of small-time drug dealing. Frequent ATM and cash withdrawals, soon followed by larger cash deposits. The amounts were relatively small, indicative of small-time street dealing. Without much effort, Carter could match Andy's drug purchases to his deposits from sales, but since it was all done in cash, the statement provided no record as to who Andy's supplier was or who his customers were.

In the month before his death, Andy's withdrawals and deposits began to steadily get larger and more frequent, with the last deposit, only two days before his murder, being over five thousand dollars. The lone check he found written on the account was to First Miner's Bank for what appeared to be three months of mortgage payments and late fees. Carter again glanced at the name on the account to confirm Tanya's wasn't on it, giving him reason to believe she was, as she stated, completely surprised that the mortgage was up to date.

Having seen enough to satisfy himself that he understood the financial situation, he closed the file just as Connie appeared in the kitchen. "No coffee?" she sleepily asked, as she reached in the cabinet for the Maxwell House can.

"I'm sorry, babe. I just received an email from Martin. You know what that means. Work."

"Anything interesting?" she asked while setting up the coffee maker.

"Only if you call three million a year in drug profits interesting."

"I think I would," she stated in a matter of fact tone.

"Looks like Andy had just started dealing. It looks like he was small-time at first, but he was growing. He wasn't big yet, but his operation had become big enough to become a threat to someone. From what the pinball kid said, probably someone known as The Ace. I don't see any signs that Tanya knew what he was up to. He opened up a second account to hide his activities from her."

While the coffee brewed, Connie relaxed in her recliner. Her gaze shifted to the poster boards on the couch. "Have you updated the boards, sweetie?"

"No, I haven't. Good idea, though." Carter stood up, walked over to the boards, and opened a marker. He crossed out the ? following the word "Drugs" beside both Cecil and Andy's names. "Don't think there's a question anymore."

"But there are other questions, sweetie. Who's funding Andy's operation? And who's connecting him with suppliers? I don't think he got an email offering him a job as a drug kingpin."

"Good question, babe." Carter wrote "Drug Funding and Supply" beside on the third board. He recapped the marker, stepped back, and stared at the boards. Connie walked back into the kitchen to pour her coffee, while Carter's full attention moved to the word "Ace" written on the board. "The Ace," he said under his breath.

"What, sweetie?"

"The Ace," he repeated, louder this time. Last night Cecil said he was going to prove to Teresa that he was The Ace. The boy at the Hideout referred to The Ace as the biggest drug dealer in the area. That could be a coincidence. But, in baseball, the ace of a pitching staff is the best pitcher on the team. If I were betting my ass, I'd bet Cecil is The Ace the kid was talking about. The bank statements back that theory up. It explains, a lot of things."

"Yeah, like what Ashley and I saw in the diner," Connie said, carrying her steaming cup back to her chair.

Carter sat in his recliner, not taking his eyes off the word "Ace," playing his conversation with the pinball kid over in his mind. "The kid said no one wanted to mess with The Ace, almost as if giving me a warning."

"You think Cecil could have killed Andy himself?"

"If Andy was moving in on his turf, it's a definite possibility. Andy would have known him, and we're pretty sure Andy knew the killer. Using a ball bat would be a clear sign to those who knew Cecil, knew his baseball background, that he was in charge, and they best stay out of his way. Even though he was a pitcher, Cecil would still know how to use a bat. Best I remember, he was a pretty good hitter back in high school."

"What's next then? You can't just walk in and arrest him. Or can you?"

"Babe, even if I were still a cop, I couldn't just walk in and arrest him. Cecil Vanover's the top cop in this county. He's poised to be the next sheriff. We know what we know, but we still don't even have enough to get a warrant to legally search his bank accounts."

"Well, what's the plan then?"

"Maybe the state boys can do something. But so far, I haven't received any cooperation from them." Carter thought for a moment. "There's only one cop around here I would trust with this information...."

"Wild Bill Roland," Connie said before he could finish his sentence. "If Wild Bill is anything like he was in high school, he's a little crazy, but he's trustworthy. And a pretty good guy."

"Let's get a shower. First, I want to talk to Tanya and confront her about Andy's drug dealing. Then we'll visit Roland, fill him in, and make sure he's on our side."

****

Before leaving the Breaks, Carter examined the damage to the Ram. The rear bumper was pushed against the body, the Reece hitch was damaged, and the tailgate showed the effects of last night's rumble with the Lexus. As Connie walked up, Carter said, "He's had a rough life, Cons. He's been shot, hit in the side, and now this. I had hoped to treat him better."

"He's faring better that that Lexus," Connie giggled. "Somehow, I think he likes being your truck and taking part in all the adventure. I could have swore I heard him laughing as he pushed that little car out of the way last night."

Carter smiled. "Yeah, I think he enjoyed it too. I was thinking. This is going to be a fun one for, what was his name, Ken, to explain to the insurance company. "My wife and I were at a swinger's party and some crazy guy in a Ram pickup backed into my car and pushed it out into the road."

"What are you going to tell our insurance company?" Connie asked.

"That you backed into a retaining wall," Carter replied without hesitation.

"So, you're going to lie, then."

Carter sensed the disappointment in her voice. "No, babe, I won't lie. But, I've been around enough lawyers in my life that I know how to say just what I need to say, and nothing more."

"Oh, that's wonderful. My husband's been taking ethics lessons from lawyers. Next thing you know, you'll be a politician, running for sheriff or something."

"Not on your life. I'm happily retired. The last thing I need is to run for public office. No way."

****

"When are you going back to work, sis? Carter asked Tanya as they sat at her kitchen table, Tanya sipping on a cup of coffee, Carter on a diet Dr Pepper.

"Tomorrow, I guess. I need to do something, Cart. I still have a house payment I'm behind on and three kids to feed. I can't do that sitting here on my butt feeling sorry for myself."

Carter pounced on the opening to ask his question. "Well, I may have some good news for you. Did you know Andy had a second bank account?"

"What? A second account? No, I had no idea. Where did he get money for another bank account? How much is in it?"

"I was hoping you could tell me," Carter said, unwilling to show his hand yet.

"Carter, you know we're broke. The house payment is three months behind. I've got a letter from the bank right over there. Andy wasn't working. When I saw Jimmy Stanley come to the house the other day, I was afraid he was bringing foreclosure papers on top of everything else. What's going on?"

His sister's response convinced Carter that she didn't know anything about the second account. "Andy was doing something. He had a separate account. He had paid the mortgage up to date. It looks like he was trying to take care of his family."

"That's wonderful," she said. She looked at Carter and didn't see a smile on his face. She then recalled that he was a detective, looking for answers, not bringing good news. "It is wonderful, right?"

"Tanya, all indications are that Andy had started dealing."

"Dealing? Dealing what? Drugs? Andy?"

"Everything I'm finding points toward it. The second bank account was opened up three months ago and all the withdrawals and deposits were in cash. Except for the money he transferred to catch up the house payments."

"Of all the lame-brained shit for him to pull. Dealing drugs. He knew better than that. He's seen what's happened to Ben. Even visited him in prison. He knew better."

"It explains a lot. What he did with his days when you were at work and the kids were at school. Why he didn't look any harder for a new job. Why he was so secretive in that shed."

"He was in that shed with Eric...," she paused, connecting the dots. "And Eric's dead, too. Carter?"

"We're convinced his dealing led to his murder. Did he talk much about Cecil Vanover in the last month or so?"

"Only how much he hated that son of a bitch. Most of the time, he hung out with Eric..." She paused. "...and sometimes Ben. Him and Ben had started hanging out more since he lost his job."

"Ben." Come to think of it, I never knew him to hang out with Ben, either."

"I thought it was weird at first, too. But I was glad to see it. It was good to have my brother and husband getting closer. Ben needed someone to hang out with after getting out of prison." She stopped talking, her mind connecting more dots. "Oh shit, Carter. You don't think..."

"That Ben helped him get started in the drug business? I'd almost bet on it. Ben knew he had to give the appearance of being clean or face going back to prison. He still had to meet with his probation officer every month. To get back into the game, he had to have someone to front the operation. Who better than his brother-in-law who was in financial trouble? It's a typical pattern."

For the first time, Connie entered the conversation. "And if they were bypassing Cecil's operation? Bringing drugs into the county from a different source? From Florida, Texas, or South Carolina?"

No one answered Connie's question. They all knew the probable ramifications if her theory was right. After a long half-minute of contemplation, Carter broke the silence. "Y'all stay here. I need to fill Roland in. Tanya, let me take Andy's car. I don't want Cecil, or anyone in the Sheriff's Department to see my Ram parked outside the Haysi PD, not after last night. If they find out we're on to them, this could get hairy. Cons, if anyone suspicious pulls up, especially someone in a sheriff's car, get the gun from the Ram's center console."

"Sure, Carter, you can use Andy's car. What happened last night?" Tanya asked.

"I'll leave that for Connie to fill in. Right now, I need to talk to Roland."

"Carter, be careful," Connie said, anxiety evident in her voice.

"It'll be okay, babe. I'm going to the police station. I'll be back soon."

TWENTY ONE

"Sounds like we need to be talking to Ben," Roland said after Carter laid out what he and Connie had deducted from the evidence they had accumulated. Carter was careful to divulge only the facts, not that they attained them by employing the services of a computer hacker or going to a swingers' party at the suspect's house. "If you're right, it would be in his best interest to talk to us and tell us everything he knows. Until he does, hell, Carter, he's just become a suspect in the murder himself. Don't think Vanover wouldn't try to find a way to pin it on him. A drug deal gone wrong. He'd say Andy took the money for the house payments without Ben's permission and Ben killed him. Really, it'd be an easy case for the DA to prosecute, especially with Ben's record." He grew silent, a new thought crossing his mind. "Worse yet, if Vanover gets word that he's involved, Ben could very well be the next one we find on some strip mine, beat to death with a Louisville Slugger."

"I was afraid you were going to say that."

"Where can we find him?"

"I'd guess he's at mother's house."

"Come on, we'll take the squad car. We need to get to him before Vanover does."

Carter thought about the way he turned his back on Ben the last time he was caught with drugs. "Roland, he's my brother. Let me go talk to him. Alone."

Roland leaned back in his chair and put his hands behind his head. "Sykes, I wouldn't do this for just anybody, not even a fellow law enforcement officer. But you're the man who won Connie Brown's heart. So for you…" he took a deep breath. "…let me know what he has to say, okay?"

"Sure thing, Roland. Just hold what you've got until I get back. If I'm wrong about Ben, I don't want to cause him any trouble. If I'm right, Ben's probably the least of our worries."

"I'm waiting to hear from you, Carter. But I'm not going to wait too long."

****

Carter drove down the dirt road leading to his mother's home with a heavy heart. Ben had always been trouble. In elementary school, he wouldn't do his schoolwork, seemingly preferring to accept the punishment instead of doing what the teachers asked of him. Carter would defend his little brother when other kids picked on him, only to find Ben was the real instigator in the altercation. He had been in and out of trouble with the law—fines, community service, probation, thirty-day county jail sentences. Then, six years ago, the feds busted him on meth charges. Carter hoped five years in the pen would straighten him out. Now, he was afraid Ben's time in jail had only taught him how to keep a low profile, how to get others to do the work, and take the risk for him.

In his visits home over the past few years, Carter saw that having her son imprisoned shook Sylvie Sykes to the core. She made the two-hundred-mile round trip to see him weekly. Something deep inside convinced her she must have failed as a parent to have her son go to jail. Carter tried to talk to her; he explained even the best families and the best parents have kids go astray. He reminded her that he and Ben came out of the same family and he had turned out okay. But his attempts to comfort her made little difference; she still blamed herself for Ben's failures.

As he approached the house, Carter considered taking Ben for a ride, getting him away from the house. He could see a lot of bad things happening by talking to Ben at home—Sylvie overhearing the conversation and defending her younger son or Ben running to hide behind his mother. After weighing his options, Carter decided Ben was less likely to throw a tantrum or cause a scene with his mother in the next room than he was if the two of them were driving alone. He felt the front porch probably provided the best opportunity for a meaningful conversation between the two brothers.

As he parked the Ram, he saw Ben sitting in a rocker on the porch, smoking a cigarette. "What's up, Fart?" the younger Sykes yelled out as Carter came down the walkway. "Mom's inside."

"Actually, I'm here to see you, Ben."

"Oh, shit. What did I do now?"

"Nothing, I hope. But you're going to have to convince me. And after years of interrogating some pretty seasoned criminals, I'm not as easy to convince as I was when we were kids."

"Look, man. Don't come in here stirring up no shit with me. I'm staying here, being good. You can ask my probation officer. Hell, I'm even helping mom; look, I cut the grass. I ain't seen your ass behind a lawnmower around here."

Carter's first instinct was to retaliate to his brother's jab, but, after looking around, noticing the grass was freshly cut, decided he had more important things to discuss than which brother helped his mother the most. "I'm glad to see that, Ben. But I need to ask you a few questions about Andy."

"What about him?"

"I hear you guys were spending quite a bit of time together lately."

"Yeah, so? I mean, he is Tanya's husband. She seemed happy to see the two of us hanging."

"What were y'all doing when you were hanging?"

"Just hanging, man. That's all."

Carter picked up on the avoidance in his answer. "Ben, level with me. I still remember the time when we were kids when you said Beth Miller was picking on you. When I took your side, I found out you had put a garden snake in her book bag, remember? It was always something like that. So don't give me any bullshit answers. I'm not naïve like I was when I was twelve."

"Man, we hung out. You should have been here doing more of that with us, hanging with your family instead of running around the country with that fancy wife of yours and driving those fancy cars."

Carter literally bit his lower lip when Ben tried to bring Connie into this. He slowed his thinking to remind himself of why he was here. He wasn't here to fight with his brother, he was here to get information. He had to keep the conversation focused. "This ain't about me, man. Listen, I know Andy was into drugs. I bet you can fill in the gaps for me."

"Hell, Fart, half this county is using drugs. How else do you think we cope with all the shit around here?"

"Half the county ain't dealing, Ben. Andy was dealing. He had just started, but his business was growing. Somebody had to teach him how. Someone had to show him the ropes." Carter paused, trying to decide how much he wanted to accuse his brother of. It took only a second for him to decide to go all in. "Somebody had to get him connected with the right people. Somebody he started hanging out with about the same time he started dealing."

207

"Hey, I'm fuckin' clean, man. Ask my parole officer. I ain't had any contact with known or suspected dealers since I got out. I've passed all my drug tests."

Carter had heard denials like these before. They weren't necessarily lies, but they weren't really answers to his questions, either. "Ben, I've done this for thirty years. You're smart enough to know you couldn't personally be involved. I'm sure while you were in the big house, you learned that you had to find someone to do the dirty work for you. Andy needed money. He was the perfect stooge for a seasoned veteran con." He took another deep breath. "Someone like yourself."

"Fuck you, Fart. Andy was my brother-in-law. When did it become a crime to hang out with your family?"

Carter thought for a minute, and then decided it was time to lay his cards on the table. "When you decided to set him up in the drug business." Carter waited on that accusation to set in before sliding a hidden card from his sleeve. It was a little cheat he wasn't sure he could get by playing, but if he could, it might make his hand work. "Look, I've seen the email addresses on his computer. I can trace them back to your prison buddies. I can read between the lines, Ben. Don't fuckin' lie to me. For once in your life, be a man, a real man. Help me find the motherfucker who killed our baby sister's husband."

Ben sat back in the chair and stared up the road. Five minutes passed without either brother speaking a word. Carter hated this part of the interrogation process, but he learned long ago the silence was a critical part of the process. To speak first, to say a word, meant he lost. It was Ben's turn to say something, and he had to let him take the time to sort through his thoughts and respond, no matter how long it took. He remained quiet, watching the eyes of the man he had shared a bed with throughout his childhood, watching for anything unspoken he could interpret. "Look, man." The tone of Ben's voice had lost its defensiveness. "I didn't know how much things had changed around here."

"How have things changed?" Carter asked.

Ben took a deep breath and exhaled slowly. "When I went to jail, most everybody was small-time around here. Hell, we all worked together to make sure we had the shit we needed, everybody except Cecil, who made it clear he planned to expand his operation. I guess I should have known I got busted because I refused to join in with his group in the sheriff's department who wanted to control the action. One of the deputies told me I could make a lot of money if I'd play their game. But, hell, man, I didn't want to suck some big wig's dick. I just wanted to sell a little meth, maybe a few pills, and make enough to live on. But no, these motherfuckers wanted to control the whole fuckin' game. So I got busted. I came back and tried to play straight, man, I really did. But hell, there ain't no honest work around here, especially not for an ex-con. One day after Andy lost his job, we were talking and he said he needed some money fast, that he couldn't let his family down. I told him I had some contacts from prison and gave him their emails, told him what to say to get in. He contacted some guys in Florida and Texas and got a small supply. These guys were happy to get their foot back into this area, even small as we were. All Andy had to do was go down to the Hideout and undercut Vanover and Junior. That wasn't hard; they were charging everybody the prices Vanover's high-class friends were paying. All Andy and Eric had to do was stay small and nobody would ever find out."

"But he couldn't stay small?"

"Not small enough. People found out Andy was selling good shit cheap, and they wanted his shit. It's too fuckin' tempting, man. You buy five hundred, you sell a grand. You think, 'If I can buy a thou, I'll sell two.' It's easy, right. The guys in Florida and Texas started pushing us to take more. The buyers wanted more, especially at the cheap prices. All we were doing is providing a service. A needed service."

"Being a real public servant," Carter said sarcastically. "And Cecil and Junior found out?"

"All I can figure, bro. Cecil ran the high-class end of the operation, all the money men. Junior supplied the small dealers who hung out at places like the Hideout. If you wanted to deal, you better go through them. If you didn't, you'd get a visit, if you know what I mean. My guess is, the visit to Andy got a little carried away. Or maybe they just decided to make an example of him, I don't know."

"Why in the hell didn't you tell me all this before now?"

"Man, if anybody finds out I'm involved, it won't be long until my ass is back in the house." Ben thought for a second. "Or worse, Cecil and Junior would come after me, too." Andy's already dead, man. I can't change that. I'd be stupid to admit to anything. Best thing I can do is keep the fuck quiet until it all blows over."

"This shit ain't going to blow over, Ben. Two men are dead. Help me put these guys behind bars. For Andy's sake, man. I can work to get you a deal."

"What, a reduced prison sentence? Five more years in the house? Man, I ain't planning on going back there. Besides, if Cecil and Junior find out I ratted them out, I probably wouldn't make it to jail. They'd make sure I was found on some strip job, somewhere. And if you say I told you any of this, I'll deny it all."

"Think about it, man. I'll get you the best deal I can. But at some point, you need to come clean. If not to help your ass, then for your sister, your family."

"Well, I've never been known for doing what I need to do, have I?"

Carter thought for a moment. "I guess not, Ben. But I keep hoping you'll change."

Both men turned their heads when they heard the screen door swing open. "Carter, I didn't know you were here," his mother said.

"Hi, Mother. I just needed to talk to Ben for a few minutes." Carter stood up, walked to his mother, put his arm around her, and gave her a kiss on the cheek. He squeezed her extra tight, as if to console her for the pain he knew she would sooner or later feel. "I need to be going; I've got some business I need to take care of in town."

"Everything okay?" she asked.

"Everything's fine, Mom. Just some brother stuff. I told Ben I was proud of him for mowing the yard," Carter lied. "Ben, let me know if you change your mind."

"I'm good, bro." Ben's tone turned ominous. "Hey Fart, be careful, okay?"

"Always am." He turned to his mom and hugged her again. "I love you, Mom."

"I've got some lunch ready if you want some."

"That's okay, Mom, I'm not really that hungry. I need to see somebody in town. Connie and I will try to get over this evening, okay?"

"Okay. Love you, son."

Carter gave his brother the same "do the right thing" look he had given him many times in the past. He petted Sadie and walked up the path to the old Taurus. The engine groaned before it finally came to life and he drove back up the dirt road. He decided to see if the radio worked and hit its power button. As the commercial finished, Carter heard a station from Pikeville, Kentucky ID, and begin playing Judas Priest's hit, "Another Thing Coming."

****

Carter wasn't entirely truthful with his mother; he was ready for some lunch, Connie wasn't with him, so he wanted to take the opportunity to enjoy some hillbilly fried chicken and taters without being reminded how bad they were for his cholesterol level. His stomach growled as he caught a whiff of the scent from Fred's. Instinctively, he turned the Ford into the parking lot.

Sitting out front at the picnic table, Carter could hear Connie's voice in his head, telling him he needed to eat better, that the greasy fried chicken and taters were going to clog his arteries. Licking his fingers and lifting a bottle of diet Dr Pepper to his lips, he forced his mind to change the subject, insisting it think of his next move in the case.

Carter realized the information Martin Walker hacked for him would only get him so far. At some point, he would have to have properly obtained documents in order for his investigation to have any teeth, and Roland would have to be the one to convince a judge to grant them the ability to obtain them. He needed to fill Roland in, get the police chief's help in questioning witnesses and conducting raids in an attempt to force some of the smaller dealers to give up Cecil and Junior. At some point, they had to have enough evidence to entice a judge to write a warrant on the man set to become the next sheriff of the county.

Leaving nothing but bone on his thigh and leg, and putting the last crumb of the dozen taters he had for lunch into his mouth, Carter took the final swig of his soda, then picked up his trash. As he turned on the bench, looking for the can, he noticed a faded green, early '90s Ford F150 pull into the parking space immediately in front of his table. Behind the wheel, he saw Junior Rasnick, who was staring straight at him with a look that made him uneasy. "Hello, Junior," Carter called out as the big man slammed the door to the old pickup.

Junior made a beeline to the table, stopping when he reached it. He didn't offer a hand, a greeting, or a smile. As the big man towered over Carter, the tone in his voice was grim and to the point. "Get in the truck," he said, nodding toward the Ford.

"What? Where are we going, Junior?" Carter asked.

"I didn't tell you to ask any fuckin' questions, son, I told you to get in the goddamn truck."

Junior's command let Carter know this wasn't a social visit. He looked at Junior, not wanting to obey. He glanced around and spotted the trash can sitting near the store's front door. Carter was not one to run, but something inside told him getting in that truck was not a good option. Dumping his trash would give him the best opportunity to get a head start on Junior and make a dash for the police station. He tried to remain calm and keep his voice as steady as possible. "Ok, Junior, let me throw this away," he said, nodding at the empty box in his hand.

"Forget the goddamn trash, Sykes; get in the fuckin' truck … now." Junior grabbed Carter's upper arm with a grip that brought a groan from his throat. The trash fell back on the picnic table and Junior guided him to the passenger's door. Without releasing Carter, Junior flung open the door and guarded any escape routes as Carter climbed onto the ripped seat. Carter flinched as Junior slammed the door shut. As the big man stormed around the front of the truck, Carter again thought about trying to escape, but decided it was too risky at this point. The driver's door opened and the left side of the F150 sank as well over three hundred pounds of man climbed behind the wheel. He slammed his door shut, turned the key, and dropped the shifter into gear. The sound of the power door locks reminded Carter of the sound of an officer closing a holding cell at the Kingsport Police Department. Now he knew how those prisoners felt—caught, trapped, at the mercy of the man with the badge. Except Junior had no badge. And Carter had no idea where Junior Rasnick was taking him. He wasn't looking forward to finding out.

TWENTY TWO

"Hi Aunt Connie, where's Uncle Carter?" Crystal asked, as she pushed open the screen door and saw her aunt and mother sitting on the couch, folding and boxing Andy's clothes, preparing to take them to a local church-based charity.

Both ladies looked at each other, then up at the clock on the wall: three-fifteen. They looked at Crystal and Connie said, "I'm not sure, honey. I would have thought he'd be back by now."

"I've got ball practice at four-thirty," the youngest lady announced. "I was hoping he'd take me to practice."

"You always did like your Uncle Carter," Tanya said with a smile. "I bet he'll take you if he gets back."

"Why don't you give him a call?" Connie suggested, handing Crystal her phone. "I'm sure if you ask him, he'd love to take you to practice. It would do him some good to get out on a ball field again. After all that chicken and taters from Fred's, he needs some exercise." She glanced back at the clock. "If I know your uncle, I bet that's where he ate lunch today. I swear, the way he eats, you'd think he'd weigh three hundred pounds."

"He must take after mom's side of the family," Tanya said. "They're all small. Dad's side was all big. Now me, if I get a sniff of good food, I gain weight."

"Yeah, I noticed your dad when we were looking at pictures. I never realized he was such a big man. I bet him and Sylvie were a funny looking couple."

"Older people always mention their size difference. I guess growing up, we never thought anything about it, but they were kind of a funny looking, Dad being over a foot taller than Mom."

"Aunt Connie, he didn't answer." Crystal interjected.

"Hmm, I wonder where he's at."

"Probably in one of those damn hollers where there ain't no cell service around here," Tanya said.

"It's times like this I wish I had my ham radio license; I know I could reach him on his radio. I've seen where his friend in Brazil grew up; it makes Haysi look like New York City, and Carter talked to him every week on that stupid radio." She looked at Crystal. "Did you leave him a message?"

"Yeah."

"Here, I'll text him too. He'll call us when he gets one of them," Connie said, taking the phone from Crystal's hand. She quickly punched the screen and sent the text. "There."

"I hate to mention this, but you don't reckon he met up with that Teresa Vanover again, do you?" Tanya asked.

Connie thought back to their visit to the Vanover mansion the night before. "I don't think so," she chuckled, the vision of the nearly naked Teresa, standing in her driveway with a look of disbelief on her face as Carter pushed the Lexus out of his way fresh in her mind. "I don't think that's happening again."

"Oh, yeah. What makes you so sure? He's my brother, he's a good guy, but he's still a man."

"Just trust me on this one," Connie said, a naughty grin on her face.

"You two went to their place, didn't you?"

Connie didn't say a word.

"You did. Oh, Connie, you've got to tell me about this."

"There really ain't anything to tell." Connie tried to act innocent.

"Bullshit, Connie Sykes. You tell it to me, every single detail."

Connie proceeded to give Tanya the blow by blow of their visit to Caney Ridge. It made her feel good reliving the story of her man rejecting a beautiful woman because he loves her. She stressed the points about overhearing Carter's rejection of Teresa's advances, but downplayed the sexual activity that went on. She figured that was the least she could do to help her husband recover his reputation damaged by his not-so-secret lunch.

As Connie and Tanya loaded the boxes into the bed of the Ram, Crystal came out in her softball practice uniform, her hair in a ponytail falling out the back of her cap, her glove on her right hand. "You guys heard from Uncle Carter?" she asked.

"No, honey, we haven't," Tanya replied. "Come on, Connie and I will run you to the ball field after we drop off these clothes."

The three ladies got in the Ram and Connie drove toward the church. "Before watching you play ball this week, I never realized you were a southpaw," she told Crystal. "I am too, you know."

"Yeah, I guess she gets that from Dad, too," Tanya said. "Carter was always so mad that he turned out right-handed. He even tried to make himself left-handed. I remember when he talked Junior Rasnick into giving him his worn out glove, just so he could try to learn to throw with his left hand. Poor Carter, he couldn't throw a ball twenty feet left-handed, but he tried all summer long."

Connie's eyes opened wide. "Junior Rasnick's left-handed?"

"Yeah. That and him being so tall makes him a great first baseman," Crystal spoke up from the backseat.

Connie pulled the Ram into the church parking lot and they took Andy's things inside. With just minutes to spare, they arrived at the little league ballfield for Crystal's softball practice. Connie noticed the men's softball game was just getting started on the adult field. She spotted the Haysi police car sitting in the parking lot. "Tanya, I'll be right back, there's somebody here I need to talk to."

Tanya saw Connie looking at the police cruiser. "After the story I just heard, I wouldn't miss this for the world," she said, hurrying to catch her sister-in-law. The two ladies walked toward the squad car.

"Bill?" Connie spoke to the officer's back.

The police chief turned around and looked at Connie. He noted there was no smile on her face and an urgency in her voice. Connie seemed to have a purpose now.. "What's up, Connie?" he asked, trying to be cheerful, but keep his tone professional.

"Have you heard from Carter?" she asked. "He was coming to see you this morning."

"Yeah, he came by the office this morning, but I haven't heard from him since. Let me think, he was going to see Ben; he wanted to talk to him about Andy."

Connie thought for a moment. From listening to Carter carry on about cases, she knew her best course of action was to trace Carter's movements, one step at a time, from where she last knew him to be. Since he went to talk to Ben, her next order of business was to talk to her brother-in-law and, see if they ever got together. But first, she had one question on her mind that just wouldn't leave her alone. "Is Junior around the ballpark?"

"Junior Rasnick? No, come to think of it, I ain't seen him. Funny, too, cause his team's playing right now. It's not like him to miss a ball game. You can always spot that big monster on the field. It's funny to watch the first baseman and right fielder back up when he walks to the plate," Roland chuckled. "The man can hit a softball."

215

"Why would the right fielder back up?"

"Because Junior hits left-handed. Hell, the first baseman plays on the grass. I always wondered why no one ever nicknamed him Griffey, after Ken Griffey, Jr. He's got a beautiful swing."

With Carter being a Reds fan, Connie got the reference, but didn't acknowledge it. Her mind was focused on something else. "Bill, give me your cell number." Then she thought about the spotty cell service. "And the frequency of your police radio."

"What's going on, Connie?" Bill asked, his tone matching hers now, as he sensed the seriousness in her demeanor.

"Carter's not come home, and we can't reach him. He's always good to check in and let me know where he is, especially if he's going to be late." She took a deep breath. "I'm getting a little worried, Bill. I'm going to go to his mom's and try to track him down." She pulled her smartphone out and got ready to type his information into it.

"My number's 276-555-8625." He waited for her to type the numbers in. "The town police use 155.250." His eyes drifted across the lot and looked at the Ram, noticing the ham radio antennas on it. "But that is for police use only, Connie."

"Trust me, Bill, if you hear me on that damn radio, it will be police business."

****

"What the hell is going on, Junior?" Carter asked, as the F150 bounced over the rough, crooked mountain road.

Junior drove along without answering, not taking his eyes off the road.

"Junior, where in the hell are we going?"

Finally, Junior's eyes glanced at Carter. "You know, Carter, I always liked you, man. Back in high school, you were all right. A little nerdy at times, but you were all right."

"What the hell are you talking about, Junior? I liked you too, man. It's been good seeing you again. But where in the hell are we going? What's all this about?"

"Look, this ain't my idea, man. None of this was my idea. I didn't want any of this goddamn shit to happen. We tried to warn them, but they forced our hand. They forced us to do it. Now you're forcing us too, Carter."

216

Carter didn't respond, his mind racing, trying to fill in the pieces missing from Junior's rambling. He hung on to the door's armrest as Junior made a hard right, turning the truck up another winding road, this one narrower than the last. His mind clicked to the last time he had been up this road. It was after the first football game of his senior year in high school. Haysi had battled Grundy, then a prep football powerhouse, for nearly four quarters, but trailed by five. With three minutes remaining, they got the ball at midfield, and began to move toward the endzone. The plan was for Seth Jones, the running back, to follow Junior through a tired Grundy line, hopefully getting enough yardage each time for a first down to stop the clock while they moved the chains. Junior, tiring as well from playing on both sides of the ball, somehow willed himself through the Grundy defensive line, with Seth following him, picking up seven or eight yards on each carry. Seven plays later, with the ball resting on the Grundy two, Haysi took its final timeout with only four seconds remaining.

The Haysi coach called the entire offense to the sideline. "One more play," he said. "This time, let's make them sons of bitches stop our big man." The coach looked through Junior's facemask, staring him straight in the eye: "Line up at quarterback." His gaze moved to Matt Bise, the center. "On one, snap the ball and everybody find somebody to push backward. Don't stop until Junior crosses the goal line." The coach looked at Junior again. "Don't you let any of them motherfuckers tackle you, got it?"

A tired Junior Rasnick nodded his head. The offense trotted back onto the field and lined up without a huddle across from the feared Grundy defense stacked to stop the run. The crowd roared as they noticed big number 72 lining up under center. Before the Grundy team captain could ready his troops, Junior yelled, "Hut one," and took the snap. He powered forward, and with three defensive linemen clinging to him, crossed into the end zone.

It was Junior Rasnick's first, and only, touchdown of his high school football career. After the game, his dad, Mousey, invited everyone to his house for a victory party. No one, not even Carter, passed up the chance to celebrate the victory over the hated Golden Wave.

That night would be the last time Carter would drive up this road. His mother took his car from him for a week after finding out he'd gone to Junior's, but the party was worth it. Making his way into the storage building behind the trailer, he found a group of kids partaking in the moonshine Mousey was famous for brewing. Carter noticed that Teresa Robinson, a girl he had a terrible crush on, was among the group. For the next hour, Carter sat in the building, sipping 'shine and moving, one spot at

217

time, toward Teresa. Finally taking the seat beside her, the alcohol gave Carter the boldness to place his hand on her thigh. She, also under the influence of the drink, looked into his eyes and smiled. A couple of kids across the room caught what was happening between them and began needling Carter to kiss her. Carter hesitated, but the 'shine weakened his defenses. He gave in to his classmates' taunts, leaning forward and kissing her on the lips—the first girl he had ever kissed. Not only did she not turn away, she responded to his advance by returning the kiss. The group cheered as they held the kiss a little longer than necessary.

Carter and Teresa would kiss several more times that night as the two of them found a more private spot and snuck off with a Mason jar of white whiskey. At two in the morning, Carter's mother, called by Mousey, showed up to take him home. After he recovered from his hangover, Sylvie forbade Carter from ever going back to Junior's house again. And he never disobeyed his mother's command. Until now.

"Why are we going to your place?" Carter asked.

Junior didn't say a word, staring straight ahead as he drove.

After ten minutes of silent driving, Junior turned the faded Ford onto the dirt drive leading to two single-wide mobile homes, one where he lived, and one where his father still lived. As they approached the trailer on the right, the two junk cars, the unmowed lawn, the debris in the yard, and the lack of any flowers or landscaping, told Carter this was a home without a woman's touch. The new red Mustang SVT sitting in the yard stood out like a sore thumb Almost involuntarily, Carter looked for the building where he had first kissed Teresa, seeing it on the left side behind the trailer. His eye caught Junior reaching between the seat and the door, pulling a .45 from the map pocket. "Go on inside," he ordered.

Carter didn't protest. He opened the door to the truck and slid out. Slowly, he walked toward the older trailer's wooden front porch, the big man falling in line behind him. After walking up the steps, Junior stepped around and opened the door, stepping aside to allow Carter to enter first. "I got him, Dad," Junior yelled into the house.

Seconds later, a small, old, bald man appeared from the hallway. Carter barely recognized the man as Mousey Rasnick; his childhood memory didn't quite jive with what he saw before him. The elder Rasnick was short, slender, and wrinkled, almost fragile looking. His facial features and ears made it easy to see how, as a younger man, he earned the nickname Mousey.

"Carter Sykes, you've grown since I saw you last. Good to have you back here," Mousey spoke in a tenor, hillbilly accent. His open mouth revealed a lack of teeth. "I take it you got over your hangover?"

"It took awhile, but I got over a lot of things from that night," Carter replied, thinking back to his and Teresa's kiss.

"That's too bad, son. It looked like you were enjoying yourself. Care for a beer?"

"No, thanks. I'd just like to know why I was brought here."

"To set a few things straight," Mousey said. "Then to take care of the fuckin' problem you nosing around has created."

"What kind of problem have I caused?" Carter asked innocently.

"In due time, boy. Junior, get Carter a beer. I've got to call The Ace and get him down here. I want him to be part of this."

The son obeyed his father, walked to the kitchen, opened the refrigerator door, and retrieved a can of Budweiser. Mousey took the cordless phone off the hook and dialed. "Ace, I've got Sykes here. Get your ass down here, now." Mousey listened for a second. "I don't give a flyin' fuck what you want. Get your fuckin' ass down here, now. You're going to be part of this shit. I ain't stupid, son; I'm making goddamn sure you're involved, too. Make sure you bring that pretty little slut of a wife with you; she's going to enjoy this." Another few seconds went by and the old man calmly touched the "end" button on the handset and returned it to the base. "Relax, son, take a drink. This will all be over soon."

Carter took the can from Junior, opened it, and sipped. "So Vanover's on his way?"

"Good deduction, Columbo. You're a little late, but it's still a good deduction."

"Want to give me the Paul Harvey version? You know, the rest of the story."

"I know who the fuck Paul Harvey is, college boy." There was indignance in the elder Rasnick's voice. "You'll find out the rest of the fuckin' story as soon as I'm ready to tell you.

Don't worry, I'll tell you everything before you die." He stared at Carter, then grinned a toothless grin. "Drink your beer; you're going to need it."

Carter obeyed, putting the can to his lips and taking another sip.

****

"Mom, have you seen Carter?" Connie yelled out when she opened the screen door of the old house and walked into the living room.

"He left here early this afternoon, Connie," Sylvie called out, walking from the kitchen. "I offered him some lunch, but he said he wasn't hungry."

Connie frowned. "Not hungry? Carter? Your son? My husband? That ain't right."

"Didn't seem right to me, either," Sylvie said. "But he didn't give me a chance to argue. He came by, talked to Ben on the porch for awhile, then took off."

"Do you know what they talked about?"

"No, we'll have to ask Ben." Sylvie turned toward the kitchen. "Ben!"

"What?" Ben's voice replied from the room in the back of the house.

"Come here a minute. I need to ask you a question," Sylvie ordered.

Carter's brother came through the entrance to the living room. "What did you and Carter talk about earlier?" his mother asked him.

"Not much, really. Fart just wanted to ask me a question."

"What kind of question?" Connie ask.

"You know, just a question." Ben's eyes darted toward the television.

Connie sensed he was hiding something with his dismissive answer. But Sylvie, knowing her son better than anyone, beat her to the punch. "What kind of question, Ben?" she demanded.

"You know, brother stuff."

"Ben, we're women; we wouldn't know anything about brother stuff. Why don't you tell us," Connie insisted.

"Nothing really. Just how things are around town, you know, stuff like that."

Connie stared into Ben's eyes, moving toward him until her nose was inches from his. "Goddamnit, Ben." she surprised herself with her choice of words, "I ain't playing games here. If Carter's in trouble, you better damn well tell me. I mean it. I'll kick your ass right here in front of your mama."

"And I'll help her," Sylvie added.

Ben's eyes remained glued on the newscast, but all he heard was Connie's threat. He debated where to lead this conversation. The debate ended when, out of the corner of his eye, he saw Connie's open hand moving toward his head. Milliseconds later, he felt the heel of her palm land just behind his right temple. "I told you to tell me where he's at. Goddamnit, Ben, I mean it."

"Okay, okay, Connie," he stammered, putting his hand on his head where the impact occurred. He took a couple of steps backward, creating room between them. "He was asking me questions about Andy's involvement in drugs. I told him what I knew. I would guess he put two and two together. He is a detective. I figure he was going to talk to Bill Roland about Junior Rasnick."

"What about Junior Rasnick?" Connie asked.

"Everybody in town knows Junior's involved in drugs," Sylvie spoke up. "Ben, are you telling us Andy was involved in drugs, too?

Again, Ben thought for a second before answering, but this time kept his eye on the two women. He began to speak, slowly, deliberately, trying to tell them what they demanded without incriminating himself. "After Andy got fired, he started dealing. He wanted to earn a living for his family, and was willing to do what he had to do. Carter had figured this out, and came asking me about it. I told him I figured Andy was cutting in on Junior and Cecil's turf and they probably weren't too happy about it."

"Unhappy enough to kill?" asked Connie.

"I don't know," replied Ben. "I can't say for sure. But it wouldn't surprise me."

"Did Carter know this?"

"I think he had a pretty good idea. Fart may be a pain in the ass, but he ain't dumb."

For a moment, Connie didn't say a word. Her mind raced with thoughts of her husband approaching the mountain everyone called Junior. Suddenly, things became clear to her. "Oh, shit," was all she said.

"What is it, Connie?" Sylvie asked with concern.

"Andy's killer was left-handed," she spoke slowly arranging her thoughts. " Junior's left-handed. Carter's missing. Junior wasn't at his ball game. Oh, shit. Sylvie?"

The old lady, her face pale and expressionless, sat down in her chair. "Honey, there's something you need to know. Sit down."

"Sylvie, what's going on here?"

"Connie, please sit down. There's some skeletons it's time to remove from my closet."

Connie didn't move, but Carter's mother didn't wait to begin her discourse. The expression on her face was blank. Sylvie's mind had drifted back a half-century. "It all happened a long time ago, before Carter was born. Carter's dad and I liked to drink a little, and the best place to get a little 'shine was from Mousey Rasnick. We became Mousey's regular customers, but Mousey took a likin' to me. There was something about Mousey back then; he wasn't good looking or anything like that, but he had an air about him—an air of importance that attracted a young girl. Gene liked Mousey's wife, Evelyn, too. She was tall, strong, like an Amazon, completely different than I was. We got to playing cards and drinking a lot and one night, well, things went a little farther and…" her voice paused.

"The four of you swapped partners," Connie said, in a matter of fact tone.

The old lady nodded. "It lasted about a year, until first Evelyn, then I, became pregnant. At that point, we stopped. It was the late fifties; there was no DNA tests back then. We were back here in the sticks; none of us had any extra money. There was no way for us to know for sure who was carrying whose child. We decided, together, to go on and raise our families like nothing ever happened. And that's what we did."

Connie took a seat and waited a minute before speaking, but she had to hear the words from Sylvie. "Until…"

"Until the boys, Carter and Junior got to be about ten years old. Gene and I had the two other kids, but Mousey and Evelyn hadn't had any more. Junior, as you know, was the biggest kid in school, and Mousey was small. Gene began wondering whether Junior was his child. He began talking to Evelyn, asking questions."

"And Mousey found out," Connie finished the thought.

"Yeah, Mousey found out. He came over here and told Gene to stop stirring up shit. Told him to let things stay as they were, the way we all agreed. He warned him of the consequences of digging around."

"And Gene?"

"Gene had to know the truth. He had to know whether Junior was his. Gene was working pretty steady in the mines back in those days. He was planning to go to court and ask for a blood test."

"Because he was type B. Carter is too."

"It was the first time I ever saw Gene research anything in his life. He learned that if Junior was type B, or AB, he was probably his kid. I tried to tell him to leave it alone, to let it be, that things were better left the way they were. But he wouldn't. He couldn't. He had to know."

There was a moment of silence as Sylvie debated going on and Connie tried to put all the pieces together. Connie spoke first. "And Mousey wasn't willing to take the chance. Did you tell the police this when Gene was murdered?"

"I couldn't. I was so ashamed of what had happened all those years ago. I couldn't relive it, Connie. I don't reckon anyone knew but the four of us. I haven't told anyone about this, not a living soul. Until tonight. Everyone knows Junior is involved in drugs. But I know Mousey Rasnick. If Junior's involved, I guarantee Mousey is the mastermind of the whole operation. Connie, if Junior takes Carter to Mousey…" her voice trailed.

Connie didn't need her to continue. "We have to stop that from happening, Mom. Where do Junior and Mousey live?"

"You'll never find it," Ben spoke up. His voice, quiet throughout the exchange, startled both women. "And you don't want to go alone. I'll take you there."

Connie thought for a minute. What would Carter do? What did Carter do when he was trying to find her last summer? He came to her rescue, that's what. He turned to his friend, his partner, Tony Ward, for backup. But Tony was two hours away, and she knew Carter might not have two hours to live. Then she took her phone from her pocket. "Not without some backup," she said, dialing Bill Roland's number.

"Bill, Connie Sykes," she spoke into the phone. "Call me the second you get this message. It's an emergency. I need your help. 423-555-6547." She ended the call, placed the phone back in her pocket and turned toward Ben. "Come on. We're going to Junior's."

"I hope he ain't there, Connie," Sylvie said.

"Me, too." She looked at Ben. "You ready?"

"Let's go."

****

For the past two hours, Carter sat on the couch in Mousey Rasnick's trailer, sipping on a Budweiser that had long ago become warm, held captive by the father and son. The big flat-screen TV played a never-ending parade of reality courtroom dramas no one was really watching. Mousey made and received several phone calls to arrange various drug deals, not bothering to leave the room. He didn't try to hide they were part of his— what Carter determined was a rather extensive and lucrative—drug business. Carter could hear the voices on the other end, voices with Latino and eastern European accents, but he was not able to tell which nationalities they were, or whether they came from within or outside the United States. What he could tell was these were big deals, hundreds of kilos of marijuana, cocaine, heroin, even prescription drugs made by illicit Indian pharmaceutical companies, with millions of dollars exchanging hands in each transaction.

"I guess you've graduated from moonshining?" Carter finally asked.

"This is the new 'shine, son. 'Shine on steroids, I guess you could say. And the money is on steroids, too."

"How long?" Carter asked.

"Started with some pot in the '70s. Small time at first. 'Shine was dying around here; hell, it was fuckin' dying everywhere. It was too easy to get legal booze. All I wanted to do was replace the fuckin' income. But goddamn, son, there was big fuckin' money in drugs. And they were easy to transport; a baggie stuck in a half empty can of Maxwell House could net more than a fuckin' trunkload of white whiskey, and there was little chance of getting caught. I was scared shitless the first time I was pulled over in Vansant, but they never even checked the fuckin' coffee can." The old man laughed. "They've never checked the coffee can."

"From the sound of the calls, sounds like you've spread your wings a little bit."

"Who would have thought this hillbilly moonshiner would be working with international drug cartels? Mexicans, Cubans, Jamaicans, Columbians, Italians, even the goddamn Russians are involved. All using me to bring drugs into these hills. Big demand, you know. Lots of people are in pain, both physically and in their head. When they're in pain, they go to the drug store," he said with a chuckle.

"And you're that drug store?"

"Hell no, son. You ever seen a rich pharmacist? They're comfortable, but not filthy ass fuckin' rich. Now the drug companies that sell to the drug stores, they're the rich sons of bitches. That's what I decided I needed to do, become a supplier to the drug stores. Hell, I ain't dealt with an end user in twenty years. There's small guys out there for that. They're the fuckers you arrest on the streets."

"Why bother with Andy then?" Carter asked, letting Mousey know he had made the connection to the murder.

"I had to make an example of him. The son of a bitch was moving in on some of my suppliers, giving them another fuckin' option into this area. That hurt my ability to control the price I paid, kind of the Walmart principle. Then, he turned around and undersold me. He was hurting my

224

clients, my middlemen, like Junior and Cecil. I couldn't let that happen, not even on a small scale. Junior warned him not long after he started, but he didn't pay any fuckin' attention. I didn't want to have to deal with him, I really didn't. But the motherfucker didn't leave me no choice. If I left him alone, everybody would think the old man is weak. I can't have that, can I?"

"Why not just make him part of your organization? From what I understand, all he wanted to do was feed his family."

"That's why Junior went to talk to him the first time. But he wouldn't play ball. He said he felt like he was doing the little man a favor selling cheaper to him. He sounded like that goddamn brother of yours. Hell, we ain't in this fuckin' business to do a bunch of junkies a favor; we're in it to make every fuckin' dime we can. It costs a lot of goddamn money to keep the police, and a couple of judges, paid off. I'll be damn if I was going to keep doing it so that son of a bitch could undercut my business, no matter how fuckin' small time he was."

"And Eric?"

"Just another loose end. You can't leave a loose end dangling, it'll unravel the whole damn operation."

The curiosity was getting the best of Carter. "How big is that operation, Mousey?"

"All the drugs you took off the street in Kingsport came through here," the old man said with a bit of pride in his voice. "So do the drugs in Roanoke, Bluefield, Lexington, most everywhere in the mountains. We have connections in Cincinnati, Charlotte, even down in South Carolina, thanks to Cecil. Hell, we've even got a couple of guys in Atlanta and Nashville in our network. But we can't corner those big markets, so they really ain't worth our fuckin' time. Nobody wants to challenge us here in the hills. They don't think there's any money to be made from us hillbillies. They don't understand how much goddamn money there really is here. And because nobody else wants to bother with it, we can keep our margins higher than anywhere else."

"It's that profitable, huh?"

"People in pain, getting fuckin' gub'mint checks, it's a prime recipe for drug profits. The guys in the city make their money from the fuckin' niggers; they just don't realize we have the same thing going with the goddamn hillbillies. Hell, I smile all the way to the fuckin' bank every time a politician comes up with a new gub'mint program."

Carter sat there silently for a moment, digesting what he was learning. He looked around at the forty-year-old single-wide trailer Mousey Rasnick lived in. "Why do you still live here?" he finally asked. "Why not a nice place? Like Cecil's."

"What, in this fuckin' dump? I ain't stupid, son, that's why. If I lived in a mansion like that dumbass Cecil Vanover, I'd have every fuckin' fed east of the Mississippi looking at me. But as long as I'm sitting here in this goddamn trailer, collecting my fuckin' social security check. I'm just a nobody, not worth messing with. Living here, nobody looks twice at me. But hell, son, don't think I ain't enjoying myself. Every winter, when I go to visit my niece in Florida," the old man laughed, "hell, I ain't got no fuckin' niece in Florida. I'm down in the Caymans, getting twenty-year-old sweethearts to bring me drinks." He struggled to take a deep breath. "And most anything else I want. They all want to keep Uncle Mousey happy," he said with a sadistic chuckle. "Kind of like your mama used to. Besides, the Caymans are a great place to keep your money; the Feds can't track it down there."

Thoughts flew across Carter's mind like symbols on a stock market ticker, but the stream stopped when one name came to mind. "Did you ever use Hartland Trucking?"

"Hartland? Where do you know Jill from? I loved that little bitch. She was one tough broad, that Jill, but I loved working with her. Her husband was a prick, though, a real dumbass. Jill, she had a sweet side, you just had to charm her a little. And I've always been a charmer. Just ask your pretty little mama."

Carter saw Mousey was trying to rile him with the second reference to his mother. "I've got a pretty good idea about you and my mother. Don't think I didn't study dad's murder over the years. I know about y'alls' activities. It's a small town, more people suspected it than you guys thought. I just never could link you to the murder. You guys quit running in the same circles after me and Junior were born."

Mousey's mind went into reflection mode. "I got to know your mama right after high school. She had a beautiful face, sexy little body, just plain, what's the word they use now? Hot, I think it is; she was hot. I never understood what the hell she saw in Gene Sykes, but it appeared I was too late; they were already married, and so were me and Evelyn. Then Gene and Sylvie became customers, pretty good customers. He and Sylvie started coming over and he took a likin' to Evelyn. One night, after some drinks, we all ended up in the sack together. It wouldn't be the last time either."

"Yeah, I figured all that out. But it ended. You had no motive to kill my dad."

"Evelyn and Sylvie got pregnant about the same time. We decided it was best, well, they decided, for us, to stop fuckin' around. It was hard giving up your mama, but I did, for her sake. But Gene was a dumbass. After him and Sylvie had two more kids and me and Evelyn didn't have any more, he got to thinking that maybe Junior was his, too. He couldn't leave it alone. Then he had that car wreck and needed a blood transfusion. He almost died until they found some type B blood."

"And he knew if Junior's blood was typed, it might prove he was his son."

"I wondered why me and Evelyn didn't have any more kids. When we first started in pot and we had little money, we went to the doctor and he suggested I get a sperm test done. Goddamn thing came back negative. I was shooting blanks. For twelve fuckin' years, I'd been raising another man's kid. But Junior was mine. There was no fuckin' way I was giving him up to that goddamn Gene Sykes. No fuckin' way."

Carter continued putting the pieces together. "So you killed him?"

"I went to talk to him, to tell him to drop this fuckin' shit, to leave well enough alone. I told him that it was the way it was and dragging the whole goddamn mess up again wouldn't do anybody any good. He figured out I knew more that I was letting on, and swore he'd find out the truth."

"Dad threatened a blood test."

"He didn't leave me any fuckin' choice. He was going to let the whole goddamn world know I had been raising another man's son. He was going to let everybody know I couldn't have any fuckin' kids, that there was something wrong with me. When he left here, I followed him. Ran him off the road. We started fighting, but he was too goddamn big for me. So I ran to my truck, got a gun, and shot his ass. The first bullet knocked him down, but he laid there, still threatening me. The second one, right in his chest, shut his sorry ass up. I like to never got him in the back of the truck, but I finally did it, and hauled him to the old strip mine. Got home and dropped the gun in the outhouse. Nobody would ever tie me to that murder."

"So why are you telling me all this now?"

"Because you won't ever be telling anybody else. I always knew that one day I'd have to kill me another goddamn Sykes." The old man laughed. "Today's gonna to be that day."

TWENTY THREE

Junior Rasnick heard a car pull up and looked out the front window. "It's Cecil. Looks like Teresa's with him."

"Good, I want her to be part of this, too. We need to make damn sure everybody's got a hand in it," Mousey said as he moved toward the front door. Opening it, he yelled to the couple, "Come on in, I've got a surprise for you."

Cecil and Teresa ascended the steps to the wooden deck, and Mousey stepped aside to let them in the door. They both stopped when they saw Carter sitting on the couch. "What the hell is he doing here?" Cecil asked, looking back at Mousey.

"It's time to take care of a fuckin' problem. And you're going to be a goddamn man and take care of it," Mousey said.

For a moment, Cecil didn't say anything, sorting through the situation in his mind. "Wait a minute, Mousey. Drugs are one thing, Doing a shitty job on an investigation is one thing. I don't mind turning my head from time to time. But being part of a murder? That's another thing entirely. I ain't going to be a part of this. Even if it's Carter Sykes, I ain't going to kill no man."

"Too fuckin' late for that, you're already part of it. You and your little wife, here. Now, we're going to end this problem..." Mousey looked at Carter, "...and get our business, and our lives, back on track. Got it, Ace?"

"Mousey, I ain't never liked this son of a bitch, but I ain't killin' him," Cecil said, shaking his head.

"You don't have to. Junior here will take care of that. But you and your missus are going to have a hand in it. That way I know you'll cover this whole fuckin' thing up. You'll have as much to lose as we do. And me, I'll have the next goddamn sheriff of this county in my back pocket."

Cecil turned to walk out the door but stopped when he saw Junior standing on the front porch. The big man was leaning up against the railing holding an aluminum Louisville Slugger in front of his chest. "Don't be a goddamn fool, Cecil," Mousey called out. "An occasional killin's part of this business. We don't have to do it often, but this is where you earn that fuckin' mansion y'all live in. Tonight, you become the next sheriff of Dickenson County, I'll see to that."

The anchorman's voice from the channel 5 newscast cut through the silence of the room, but no one paid any attention to the latest unemployment figures in the Mountain Empire. Cecil, Mousey, and Junior stared at each other, each waiting for the other to make the next move. After two agonizingly long minutes, Teresa looked at Carter. "Why did you have to come back here, Carter Sykes? Things were good. Most days I didn't think about you or that if I'd stayed with you I could have got the hell out of this county." She exhaled "All you had to do was fuck me last night and join our team. You could have had it all—money, drugs, and me. But no, not Carter Sykes. You're too damn good. You always have been. Remember that Fourth of July at the dam? I tried my best to get you to sneak off to the maintenance building and screw me while you were working. You wouldn't do it. You said it wouldn't be right, that you were on the clock. Well fuck doing right. Cecil was more than happy to screw me that night. I just don't get you, Carter. What the hell is wrong with you?"

Carter stared at his high school girlfriend. "Telling you 'no' at the dam that day was the best move I ever made. It freed me up to find Connie." A smile crossed his face.

He saw her right hand coming toward his face, but his reaction to move was too slow. He felt the left side of his face sting from the impact. "Fuck you, Carter," she screamed. She turned toward the old man. "Where are we doing this, Mousey? I'm in."

"You and Cecil get him to the outbuilding. I think you know the one, sweetheart, the one you two first kissed in." Mousey instructed. "I've got everything set up in there."

****

"Bill, come in Bill," Connie screamed into the microphone. It had taken her a couple of minutes, but she figured out how to get the Haysi police frequency programmed into the ham radio mounted in the Ram. She waited for an answer, but the Icom remained silent.

"Maybe it's programmed in wrong." Ben suggested.

"You know how to fix it?" Connie asked.

Ben shook his head, "No. If it only had channel 19…"

"It does have channel 19. I've seen Carter use it before. I just don't know where it is." She keyed the microphone again. "Bill, come in. Bill, this is an emergency!" she yelled again. They waited but there was still, no response. She dropped the mic into the seat and put both hands on the wheel to take the next two curves, then picked up her phone and hit the last number dialed. After six rings, it went to voicemail, telling her Bill had no service. "Shit," she said, looking at Ben. "Any ideas?"

"I can take you to Mousey's," he offered. "I just ain't sure it's a good idea. We could all end up dead."

Connie's mind raced as she flung the Ram through the next set of curves. He was right. If things were as dire as she feared, going in without backup would be stupid—no, suicide. Not only would it put her in a bad situation, it could further endanger Carter. But Carter made a similar move to save her last summer when she was kidnapped. She knew, as great as the risk was, she couldn't risk doing nothing. She would never be able to live with herself if she didn't try to save her husband and he wound up dead.. As the Ram barreled down highway 80, she grabbed the microphone one last time. "Bill, Bill, are you there? Come in Bill." Another long second with silence. Nothing. "Shit," she said again, dropping the microphone. Another ten seconds passed.

"Connie, is that you?" Bill Roland's voice finally came over the radio's speaker.

She snatched the mic. "Bill? It's me, Connie. Carter's in trouble. Where are you?"

"We're at Lynn's parent's place. There's no cell service up here. You're transmitting on the repeater's output frequency. I couldn't hear you until you got almost to town. What's going on?"

"I think Carter's in trouble. Do you know where Mousey and Junior Rasnick live?

"Yeah, I know where Mousey lives. You don't think Junior and Mousey's involved in all this, do you?" The pause over the radio was short but let everyone know what was going through Roland's head.. "Shit, he's not up at Junior's, is he? Shit."

"Yeah, it looks like it, Bill."

"Wait for me at Fred's. I'll be there in ten minutes."

"We're passing Fred's now…"

"Hey, there's Andy's car," Ben yelled.

"You sure?" Connie asked as she swung the Ram into the parking lot.

231

"Yeah, I'm sure. I'll check it out," Ben said, his door already open as she stopped behind the Taurus. He jumped out and felt the hood. "It's cold," he yelled back to her.

"You know the guy who left that piece of crap parked here?" a fat, middle-aged man yelled from the front door of the store.

"Yeah, you seen him?" asked Ben.

"He left that piece of shit and his trash sitting there hours ago when he left with Junior Rasnick in his truck. If he don't come get it soon, I'm having it towed."

Ben looked at Connie. "Come on," she called, waving her arm. Ben ran back to the truck and jumped in. "Get me to Junior's." Connie commanded.

Backing out of the lot, she picked up the microphone. "Bill, Carter's with Junior. We're heading there now. Meet me up there as fast as you can."

"Wait for me, Connie. Don't go in there alone." Bill pleaded, then calmed his voice. "Connie, don't do anything stupid."

Connie knew Bill was right. A good cop never went in without backup. How many times had Carter stressed that to her when she would tell him how worried she was about him? She looked at Ben. "You got my back?"

In the two seconds it took to answer, a thousand conflicting thoughts ran through Ben's mind. The times Carter had defended him when they were kids. How Carter refused to make a statement at his sentencing, possibly shaving a couple years off his jail time. But the word "brother" kept racing through his mind, and he knew that if he didn't cover his sister-in-law, he'd never live with himself. "I've got your back, Connie," he said calmly.

Connie grabbed the microphone. "Get there as quick as you can, Bill." She dropped the mic back in the cupholder and put both hands on the steering wheel. The Ram's rear wheels screamed as she pulled from the parking lot

"Connie, wait on me, Connie," Bill screamed into his handheld radio, the sound of a screen door slamming behind him.

Connie's mind didn't decode the words. She tapped the brakes, and then turned the wheel hard right, running the stop sign in the process.

****

Cecil led Carter around the trailer and pushed him into the old outbuilding. As Carter caught his balance, he saw the pile of stuff that looked out of place sitting on a table in the corner. He looked at Junior, who had followed them. "Is that the contents of Andy's shed?" he asked.

"Most of it," Junior said with a laugh. "Everything except for the drugs that were in there. There wasn't much, but it was some pretty good shit; a little reefer and a little crank. And best of all, it was free."

"What is all that stuff, then?" Carter asked.

"I was hoping you could tell us," Mousey said, entering the building. "All I know is it's some of the nastiest smelling shit I've ever seen. I put my tongue to it, thinking it might be some crazy ass drug, but it was nasty. Almost tasted like soap, with a hint of bacon added in."

Despite the situation, Carter laughed.

"What the fuck are you laughing at? Don't you know we're about to kill your ass?" Junior asked.

Carter shook his head. "That crazy son of a bitch really was trying to make bacon soap. He really did have a plan besides drugs."

"Bacon soap?" Junior questioned. "That's the dumbest ass thing I've ever heard of."

"Just think, Junior, some big fat lady crawling all over you because you smell like bacon. Doesn't that sound romantic?"

"Fuck you, Carter," Junior said, grabbing him by the upper arm and leading him to the center of the building.

Carter spotted the Dacron rope hanging from an eyescrew placed in the rafter of the old building. Mousey looked at Cecil and nodded at the rope. "Tie his fuckin' hands to the rafter. I want to make sure Junior gets in some good, clean rib shots." The old man laughed. "We don't want a messy job like we had with that goddamn Calhoun boy, do we?" He looked at Carter. "We definitely want you to feel some pain, Sykes. I can't let this be easy for you. We wouldn't want anyone to think we've gone soft."

"Mousey? This is far enough." Cecil said.

"Goddamnit, Cecil, quit being a fuckin' pussy and tie the motherfucker up. I've never seen you have any problem spending the drug money, now it's time to do the dirty work. Or do I have to let your wife do it for you?"

Cecil looked at Teresa. She nodded her head. "Do it, Cecil. I ain't giving it all up. Tie him up."

233

Reluctantly, Cecil put Carter directly underneath the rope. He tried to raise Carter's arms, but Carter resisted. Junior walked behind them, took the knob end of the Louisville Slugger, and placed it between Carter's butt cheeks. "Don't make this hard, Carter. Unless you like it this way."

Again, Cecil tried to raise Carter's arms and again Carter resisted. "If you're going to kill me, you're going to have to work for it," Carter said defiantly.

"Have it your way," Junior said, flipping the bat around in his hands and from his left-handed stance, slamming it into Carter's backside. Carter winced in pain. "That was easy, son. The next one won't be. And it won't be across your ass."

Cecil again tried to raise Carter's arms, this time with less resistance. "Tie him up, Junior," Mousey commanded. The big man handed the bat to Teresa, stepped in front of Carter,, wrapped the rope around his wrists, and tied a simple granny knot. He grabbed his bat and stepped back, admiring his work.

"Is that the best knot you know?" Carter asked.

Junior gave an evil chuckle. "Try getting out of it." He tapped Carter's exposed ribs with the barrel end of the bat. "Anybody want the first swing?"

****

Ben gave Connie turn-by-turn navigation as she propelled the Ram along the steep, crooked roads of Dickenson County. Except for his instructions, neither said a word. "Connie, Connie," Roland's voice came across the radio. Connie kept both hands on the wheel. "Connie, wait on me, goddamnit. I just turned on Deer Lick road."

"Connie, he's only five minutes behind us," Ben pleaded with her.

"Carter didn't wait when he was coming after me," she said.

"Connie, it's only five minutes."

"I'm not going to be five minutes too late," she said, swinging the Ram into the next curve. "Come on, come on," she said with a head nod as she powered into the next straight stretch. "How much farther, Ben?"

"About three more miles," he advised. They both lurched forward as she slammed the brake pedal before the next twist in the road.

234

****

Since no one else volunteered to take the first swing, Junior Rasnick took his position in front of Carter, and looked him in the eye. "I always did like you, Carter. I hate it has to end this way."

"I've got to say, Junior, at least you're man enough to do this face to face," Carter said, trying conversation to expand the moment, trying to buy more time. "Is this how you did Andy?"

"Andy was a mistake," Junior replied. "I just wanted to hurt him a little. I only wanted to scare him enough so he would join our team. The son of a bitch made me mad when he tried to run after the first hit. Even then, if he hadn't ducked, he'd still be alive today." He looked at Cecil. "I'm sure you know, lefties don't like the ball up in the zone, we like it down and in."

Cecil nodded.

"I ain't duckin', Junior. If you kill me, it won't be a mistake. It'll be first degree."

Junior laughed. "Doesn't look like you have much choice." He placed the bat on his left shoulder.

"Wait a minute," Teresa yelled. All eyes in the room focused on her. "Carter, did you mean what you said about being glad I dumped you."

Carter breathed a sigh of relief at the brief stay of execution his former girlfriend was giving him. "Yeah, I meant it, Teresa. I was crazy over you. So crazy, I thought about not going to Clinch Valley, of staying in Haysi with you. If you hadn't dumped me, I may have never gone to college, and would never have met Connie."

"And you love her, right?"

"Yes, I love Connie. I have since I met her. She is everything to me."

"And she loves you?"

"Very much so."

Teresa breathed deeply, and then her tone changed. "Carter, I'm going to be the last woman you're going to make love to before you die. You're little wifey is going to have to live with that for the rest of her life." She looked at Junior. "Get his pants off of him."

Junior backed up three steps. No one else moved.

"Damnit, do I have to do everything myself?" she asked, as she stepped in front of Carter. He turned his head as she tried to kiss his lips,

235

causing her lips to land on his cheek, leaving a lipstick stain. "That's all right, Carter. You'll be calling out my name in a minute." She reached for his belt and unbuckled it.

"Hell, Cecil, your wife has balls. She knows what she wants," Mousey said with a laugh.

Teresa unbuttoned Carter's pants, reached her arms around him, and with her thumb and forefinger, gripped his belt. She tugged them down as far as she could, then slid her hands to his side and wiggled the pants, pushing them over his hips, letting them fall to the floor. She took her right hand and rubbed Carter's manhood through this white briefs. "Umm", she moaned. She noticed the instinctive reaction of his penis to her touch. "I knew you'd like this, sugar. Let me get those things off of you." She pulled the elastic over Carter's hardening erection, circling its tip with her finger. Feeling the wetness oozing out, she moved her finger to her lips. "Umm, my first taste of you, sugar, you taste great." She reached around him with her left hand, hooked her thumb under the waistband, and pulled his underwear over his rear, kneeling as she pulled them down his legs. Kissing his thighs as she stood. She moved behind him and took him in her right hand, slowly beginning to stroke him. Against his will, a moan escaped Carter's throat. "That's it, sugar, let's enjoy this moment," she whispered. "I know how long you've wanted me. I know how long I've wanted you." The speed of her hand increased, causing his body to jerk involuntarily. "I better slow down, I want your whole load inside of me," she whispered. She released her grip on his member and circled around, facing him. She raised both her hands to his cheeks, and kissed him hard on the lips. "Just enjoy this, sugar." Teresa untucked her shirt and seductively removed it, then reached behind her back and unhooked her bra, shaking her shoulders to remove it. She took its cup and held it to Carter's nose. "Smell me, sugar," she pleaded. Dropping the bra on the floor, she again lowered herself, rubbing her enhanced breast against his throbbing manhood on her way to settling on her knees. Teresa reached for him, stroked him a couple more times, then moved her lips so they hovered above the head of his erection, and softly kissed it. "Are you ready for heaven, sugar?" she asked as she opened her mouth.

****

"Here's the driveway," Ben hollered as they approached a one-lane gravel path on the right. Connie's right foot slammed on the brake pedal; only the Ram's anti-lock system kept it from going into a skid. She cranked the wheel hard, sending the truck sideways. As she regained control, she pressed the accelerator and the truck powered up the drive.

"Damn, woman, you're going to kill us before we get there," Ben exclaimed, clutching his chest.

"Connie, I'm only five minutes away," Roland's voice rang out over the radio's speaker. Wait on me. You hear me, wait."

If Connie heard Roland's plea, she didn't respond. With both hands on the wheel, she followed the path to the trailers. Her eyes focused first on the BMW SUV she recognized as Teresa Vanover's, then moved to the trailers and the open front door on Mousey's. "Looks like they're inside," she said, throwing the Ram into park. She killed the engine and opened the door.

Ben opened his door, but stopped as he looked across the cab at Connie, "What now?"

She looked at the center console, reached over, opened it, and reached inside. She pulled out Carter's 9mm handgun and checked the clip. It was full.

"We may need this," she said, holding the piece so Ben could see it. "Come on."

"You know I can't be near that thing. I'm a convicted felon."

"I've got the gun," she said. "Come on."

Connie in front, Ben a half step behind, flanking her on the right, they climbed the deck steps and moved toward the open door. Connie leaned her shoulder into the doorframe, both hands on the gun, and looked inside. Brian Williams greeted her, talking about the latest round of Middle Eastern violence. She stepped in the door, raising the gun to chest level. "Nobody's here," she said. Then they heard the female scream from the outbuilding.

****

As Teresa lowed her lips, Carter's knee came up like a well-placed uppercut, catching her on the jaw just before her mouth engulfed him. She screamed, tumbling onto her back, dazed, but not out. Cecil's right hand found the handle of his police issued weapon and he pulled it from its holster. He stepped forward and aimed its laser sight, putting a red dot right between Carter's eyes. "You fuckin' bastard, I ought to shoot you dead right here and now."

Teresa sat up, regaining some of her senses. "I try to give you the best fuckin' blowjob of your life before you die, and this is the thanks I get? Have it your way then." Her eyes shot to Junior. "Give me that goddamn baseball bat. I'll take care of this piece of shit myself."

Junior handed her the Louisville Slugger. She took it, and faced Carter, standing slightly to his left. She tapped it against his exposed ribcage. "You would have enjoyed the blowjob," she said. "I've never had a man who didn't."

"Sorry, Teresa, you just ain't my type."

With fire in her eyes, Teresa tapped the barrel of the bat on the floor and took her stance. She placed her left foot ahead of her right and rested the bat on her shoulder. She raised her hands and kicked her left leg into the air, shifting her weight backwards. As her front leg began to fall, her weight began transferring forward and the barrel of the bat started to move.

The sound of a gunshot rang throughout the building.

TWENTY FOUR

Teresa Vanover spun and fell to the floor, dropping the bat at Carter's feet. All heads turned toward the door, where Connie Sykes stood with Carter's 9mm focused on Cecil, who instinctively had pointed his weapon at her. "I've killed one man, don't think I won't kill another," Connie warned.

Junior slowly reached in his pocket and pulled out the gun he placed there when he brought Carter into the trailer, pointing it at Connie. She watched him with her peripheral vision, but her focus on Cecil didn't waiver. Mousey's rough laugh was like that of a mob boss at a showdown of crime families. "You won't get us all, darlin'. Drop it, and we'll at least let you live a few minutes longer than your husband."

"Maybe she can't get all of you, but I'll clean up the shit she don't get," Bill Roland said, gun poised on Junior Rasnick as he entered the doorway. "Drop it, Junior; I fuckin' mean it."

Mousey laughed again. "Looks like we have us an old fashioned standoff here, boys. Three against three. And one of you's a girl. Let's see how this plays out."

"I'd count again," a new voice came from behind Roland. Bill stepped forward and to the right as Tom Monroe entered the outbuilding, his gun at chest level. He was followed by Keith Johnson, sporting a Ruger in a similar position. "Looks like the odds just changed, old man. And not in your favor." His laugh was more triumphant than Mousey's had been. "You might take on a girl, but do you really want to take on the Federal Bureau of Investigation?"

"FBI?" Carter mumbled from his compromised position.

"Drop 'em, boys," Roland commanded. Junior looked at Cecil, who lowered his gun and, with an underhanded delivery, sent his pistol scooting toward the door. "Over here." Monroe motioned with his head for Junior to toss his piece toward Cecil's. Junior lobbed his weapon, sliding it beside Cecil's. "Get 'em up high, boys," Roland said, moving toward Cecil and reaching for his cuffs. He laughed. "Get 'em up high. Damn, I've always wanted to say that."

Johnson cautiously walked behind Junior, and the officers began patting down their arrests. In unison, the cops brought a right arm, then a left behind each man's back. After he locked the cuffs, Roland looked at

Johnson. "I hope you boys got something to transport them in. All I've got is Lynn's Jeep Patriot.

"Throw them in the FBI cruiser," Johnson answered. "These three will ride back there just fine."

Connie ran to Carter and threw her arms around him. He lowered his lips to the top of her head and kissed her. "Glad you could make it, babe. McMillan was in a little bit of a jam." He glanced down at Teresa. "You want to help her out?"

Connie looked up at him. "No."

"Cons."

"Okay, okay," she said, releasing her husband and moving to tend to Teresa.

Carter looked up at his hands tied above his head. "Guys, I'm just a little uncomfortable here."

"I got you, Fart," Ben said, walking to his brother. He looked around, retrieved a bucket to stand on, and sat it behind his brother. Glancing at Carter's naked rear end, he said, "You know I'm going to give you hell over this for the rest of your life."

"I'd be disappointed if you didn't. Now, just get my damn hands untied, okay?"

"How is she?" Monroe asked Connie.

"The bullet went clean through. Her shoulder's damaged pretty bad, but I think I can stop the bleeding. I think she'll be okay, but she'll need an ambulance."

"Got one on the way," he replied, already punching numbers on his phone.

Roland, along with the FBI agents, began carefully escorting their charges out of the building and to the waiting federal vehicle. Carter finished buckling his belt and joined his wife at Teresa's side.

"You're one lucky woman," Teresa's weak voice said. "I wish a man loved me the way he loves you."

Connie took a quick glance at her husband. "I know. I'm lucky somebody else gave him up." She focused back on Teresa's shoulder. "Now lay back, the rescue squad is on its way. You're going to be okay."

"I'll never be okay," Teresa said, tears in her eyes. "He loves you. I've wanted Carter Sykes since high school, but he never loved me. He never would touch me like a man touches a woman he loves. He's in love with you." She laid her head back on the ground, crying more from the emotional agony than from the physical pain.

"You never really loved him," Connie spoke into Teresa's ear. "You wanted a way out of these hills. Me, I fell in love with Carter Sykes, no matter where we are. And I'll never let him go."

****

At 10:00 p.m. in Haysi, Virginia, there are only two places open, Fred's and the Haysi Hideout. Since the Hideout doesn't serve food and Fred's doesn't have an on-premise alcoholic beverage license, Carter and Connie picked up chicken and taters and met Ben, Roland, Monroe, and Johnson at the Hideout for a late supper and a couple of beers. As the Haysi police chief, two FBI agents, and a barely retired detective team entered the Hideout, the regular patrons scattered like mice at a cat convention. "Where are y'all going?" Monroe called out, but there was no response from the lowlifes making a beeline for the exit.

"They probably got a whiff of this chicken and are heading to Fred's to get a bite before it closes," said Carter with a laugh as he sat the food on the table and eased himself into a chair. Roland and Ben carried over a round of drafts for the group.

"You better enjoy this, sweetie. I'll give you a mulligan tonight. You know tomorrow, I'm going to be all over you about your diet."

"Keep him in line, Connie," Monroe chimed in. "Dickenson County is going to need a new sheriff."

"Huh-uh," Connie blurted out. "I gave him up to police work for thirty years. Thirty long years. He's all mine now. The next sheriff of Dickenson County should be Wild Bill Roland. Honest, experienced, and dependable."

"Here, here," Carter said, lifting his beer mug in the air.

"Wild Bill for sheriff," the group toasted in unison.

"A couple of things I've got to ask," Carter spoke up, looking at Monroe and Johnson as the cheer subsided. "What is this FBI crap? I thought you boys were with the State Police? And how did you guys get there so quick? I had given up on you two a week ago. I thought you were like the rest of the state police they send to this part of the state."

Monroe looked at Johnson before he spoke. "We've been after Vanover for some time now. We knew he was corrupt; we just needed to prove it. We tried, but we couldn't get a warrant to search his bank accounts, but we knew they were dirty. We just needed him to make a mistake. Thanks to you, he made one. I think we'll get our warrant now."

Carter thought about Martin Walker telling him someone else, someone high up, had used the portals to get a look at Vanover's financials. "That Cyber Ranger is a pretty smart dude," he thought.

"When he assumed the lead on the Calhoun case, we thought we had an avenue to watch him. If he botched the investigation, we had a way to put pressure on him, try to force him into a mistake. We contacted the State Police and posed as investigators, not wanting to alert anyone that the Feds were poking around. Then you showed up and started asking questions. We sensed trouble, thought some local hack was going to mess up our entire operation. So, we called the Kingsport police chief to check on you. Except, the chief was gone on vacation. We spoke to some character named Tony Ward they had put in charge of the department while he was gone. He told us to leave you alone. He said your wife was the best damn detective in Tennessee, maybe the whole country." He looked at Connie and smiled. "He said as long as Connie Sykes was on the case, everything would be okay. Our boss suggested we let you dig around and see what you could dig up, and what kind of reaction Vanover would have to your snooping. So we backed off, let you two do your thing, and monitored you. It actually worked pretty good, put another level between Vanover and us, making it harder for him to see the FBI was on his tail."

"But we didn't go far," Johnson took over. "We were at the Breaks, monitoring all the traffic over police channels, cell phones, and emails, actually sending feeds back to D.C. for them to examine. It was obvious your presence had stirred up a hornet's nest, scared the shit out of the cops who were on the take, and those, like Vanover, who were directly involved in the drug trade itself. We got real interested when we heard Cecil was going to Mousey Rasnick's tonight. The two of them rarely met, but we knew Mousey was a player in the region's drug trade, we just didn't know how big. He was smart,;. It was hard to track him with all his off-shore accounts and his modest lifestyle. We were hoping to hear some info, anything, about their meeting, when we heard Connie's call over the output frequency of the Haysi PD's repeater. We knew something big was going down, and decided it was time to move in. Looks like we arrived at just the right time."

"A couple of hours earlier would have been fine with me," Carter said.

"And miss seeing you tied up with your pants on the floor?" Roland laughed. "No way, man. That was priceless."

"Thanks for the sympathy, guys," Carter said, eliciting another round of laughter from the group.

"One thing I don't understand is how you found out about the money trail?" Monroe asked. "With all the resources of the FBI, it took us six weeks to learn what we did. Vanover had those records locked up tight. We couldn't even get a federal judge to give a warrant for them through Homeland Security."

"Let's just say I have a special cyber superhero at my disposal," Carter said with a smile. "Sometimes, especially when you're on the outside, you have to think outside the box."

"Hey, I'm just glad we've finally got those sons of bitches locked up in the Haysi jail," Roland said. "How long can we keep them there? If I'm going to run for sheriff, I need to get *The Star* over here to take some pics. It sure as hell wouldn't hurt the campaign, seeing the next sheriff bringing down the biggest drug ring in Southwest Virginia."

"I think we can keep them there until mid-morning, anyway. Just make sure the press arrives early."

Roland held up his phone. "I've already sent a text to the editor. Told Rod to be at the station at eight, camera in hand, if he wants to break the story." He looked at the FBI agents. "Hope I can get my picture with you guys."

"Sorry, Wild Bill," Johnson said. "No pics of us. We're FBI; we keep a low profile. Pics of us are out. As far as the world will know, you made this arrest. We'll leave in the morning and a new crew of Federal agents will be in to take them away."

"I've got some contacts at channel 19," Carter interjected. "I can make sure they're here in the morning."

"TV coverage of the Haysi PD, that's a first," laughed Roland. "Go for it."

As Carter sent the text, a young man walked over to their table. "Mr. Sykes, I think I can take you tonight," the kid said, nodding at the pinball machine.

Carter looked up to see the pinball kid looking down at him. He looked around the table, a little embarrassed to let the FBI agents see him playing pinball, but decided it would be more embarrassing for him to turn down a challenge. "I'm pretty lucky tonight, dude," Carter told the kid.

The young man looked back at the pinball machine and Carter's eyes followed, checking out the score of the last game. "Three point eight million, huh. Not far from the record set by The Legend." Carter pushed his

243

seat back and stood up. "Y'all excuse me for a bit. I've got to teach this kid to respect his elders." He patted the young man on the shoulder. "Come on, son, make my day," he said, leading the kid to the pinball game. "You're the challenger, your quarter."

"That guy's pretty good," Roland told the group. "There's only one guy in town who challenges him at that machine."

"Don't worry about Carter," Connie said. "He rarely plays unless he thinks he can win. And when it comes to pinball, I wouldn't bet against him."

Monroe walked to the bar, bought another round of beers, and the group turned their seats to watch the pinball game. Carter had the lead after one ball, but after a great run by the kid and a disappointing round by Carter, the kid led by 100,000 points. "Looks like he's in trouble," Johnson said.

"Oh, I've seen him do this before," Connie's voice emitting confidence in her husband. Her gaze turned to Roland. "You remember that time in college when Donnie thought he could take Carter at pinball?"

"Was Carter the guy who always hustled pinball in college?" Roland laughed. "Yeah, I'll never forget that. Donnie thought he had him. Had a slight lead after each of the first two balls. I didn't think Donnie was ever going to lose that third ball. He must have played fifteen minutes. That kid, Carter, didn't flinch. He looked him straight in the eye, said 'nice ball', and stepped to the machine. Not only did Carter beat him, he went on to shatter his own high score. Suckered him in and played him like a fool. Carter didn't say a word; he just walked back to his table, grabbed his backpack, and walked off. It was so cool. There was nothing he could've said that would have pissed Donnie off more."

"I think that was when I first really noticed Carter," Connie said. "I saw that inside that nerdy boy from Haysi was a pretty cool customer."

They heard the pinball machine erupt, and looked to see it lit up, indicating a new high score had just been set. By the time the kid finished, the display indicating his score read 4,927,218. The boy stepped away and took a drink of his bottled beer. "Who's the legend now?" the boy asked.

"Nice ball," Carter said, stepping in front of the machine and placing his right hand on the plunger, his left over the button controlling the flipper. The four spectators looked at each other. Connie stood and the men followed her to the machine as Carter, more for show and psych than anything, simply hit the plunger with his open hand, sending the ball up the chute, beginning play on his final ball. Time after time, he carefully flipped the ball back to the top of the machine to the bumpers he wanted to hit.

As Carter crossed four million points, the audience alternated their glances between the machine, Carter's concentrated face, and the kid who was watching his new high score be demolished. A few minutes later, the machine lit up again, and a 5 became the first digit in Carter's score. But Carter kept playing, refusing to let the ball roll between or behind the flippers. After another few minutes, Carter looked up at the score and backed away as the ball hit the flipper and rolled down the middle. Seeing the number 6,283,042 displayed, Carter smiled. He looked at the kid and spoke softly. "The Legend leaves you your next goal," then looked at Connie. "Y'all ready, babe?" he asked as he took her elbow in his hand.

"Nice game," Connie told the kid. "He likes you. If he didn't, he wouldn't have said anything." She slid her arm inside her husband's and, arm in arm, they exited through the Hideout's front door.

"Cute couple," Johnson said, tossing a ten on the bar for a tip.

"Wish he'd run for sheriff," Monroe replied. "This county could use a team like them."

****

The Coachmen was in tow behind the Ram when Carter and Connie pulled into the dirt parking lot at the Clintwood Little League ballfield. Still sitting in the cab, Carter saw the Haysi coach hit a sharp grounder toward the hole. With amazement and pride, he watched his niece move to her right, snag the ball with the glove on her right hand, spin, plant, and fire a strike to first base. "Nice play, Crystal," he yelled out the window.

Her warm-ups complete, Crystal Calhoun ran off the field. Carter watched her talk to a dad serving as an assistant coach, then run toward the Ram. "Y'all going to watch the game, Uncle Carter?"

"I wouldn't miss it for the world, honey. Go get 'em girl. Bring another win home for Haysi."

"They've got Molly Sutherland pitching today.. She's tough."

Carter winked at her. "We can handle Clintwood's tough pitchers. Good luck."

She turned and ran back to the bench. Carter and Connie grabbed their folding chairs from the Coachmen's storage compartment, got a cooler from the Ram's backseat, and settled in along the third base line as the umpire called "play ball!" The first pitch was a strike.

"That girl can throw," Connie said.

"Yeah, she's Brenda Vanover and Mike Sutherland's daughter."

"Brenda Vanover? Cecil's sister?"

"Yep."

The second pitch floated a touch high and outside for a ball. The Haysi batter swung at the third pitch and hit a dribbler down the third base line, which refused to go foul.

The next Haysi girl came to the plate and three straight pitches resulted in strikes, the last one swinging, for the first out. Connie leaned over to Carter's ear. "That girl throws hard."

"Yeah, she does." He nodded at Crystal, who was walking to the left-handed batter's box. "This ought to be a good matchup." He clapped his hands together. "Come on, Crystal."

The first pitch was high in the zone, and Crystal got under it and fouled it back against the fence. The next offering was a little too high, and Crystal laid off. "Good eye, girl," Carter yelled. The third pitch was high and outside. "She's being careful with her," Carter leaned over and told Connie. "She's well coached, she knows lefties don't like the ball up in the zone. She'll pitch to her though. It's too early in the game to risk putting two runners on with the cleanup hitter on deck."

On cue, the next pitch was right down the middle of the plate. Crystal swung and drilled the ball over the first baseman's head, down the right field line. Chalk flew as the ball landed on the line and spun to the right.

With the arms of the first base coach waving, Crystal didn't let up. She glanced over her shoulder to see the right fielder moving toward the line to field the ball, then back at the third base coach, who waved her on. She stepped on second without breaking stride and kept her eye on the right arm of the coach, waving in circles. Crystal didn't hesitate, her legs propelling her toward third base.

The Clintwood team was well coached. The right fielder threw to the second baseman, who turned and fired to third. The third base coach turned both hands palm down, got down on his knees, and yelled, "Slide!" at the top of his lung. Crystal slid feet first into the bag just as the ball arrived in the third baseman's glove.

"You're out!" yelled the home plate umpire from halfway down the line, throwing his right hand above his ear, thumb pointing backwards.

Carter jumped to his feet. "No way. She beat that throw," he yelled.

The umpire turned to walk back to the plate.

"Either get in position or get some glasses, blue," Carter continued his tirade. "She was safe."

The umpire stopped and turned back toward Carter, staring at him. Carter was up against the chain link fence, hands on its top rail, and appeared ready to leap it and confront the ump.

Connie quickly grabbed her husband's left arm and yelled in his ear, "Sit down, Carter. It's a ball game."

Carter didn't move, staring at the ump, who continued to stare back.

"Sit down," Connie commanded again. "Don't embarrass Crystal this way."

With the voice of reason in his ear, Carter turned toward Connie to plead his case. "But she was safe. She beat that throw by a mile."

"It was a close play, Carter. The ump made the best call he could. Now calm down and don't get thrown out in the first inning. If you do, you can sit in the camper alone." She patted him on the butt. "Hey, we did get a run."

Carter turned his head back toward home plate to see the umpire walking behind the catcher and Crystal trotting behind the fence to the bench, her coach putting his arm around her shoulder as she hung her batting helmet on the rack on the fence. "Nice hit, Crystal," Carter yelled out. "It's an RBI." She smiled at him, picked up her hat and glove, and watched the next girl ground out to second. Carter tilted his diet Dr Pepper to his lips and sat down with pride as he watched his niece take her position at short.

You said "we," he said, looking at Connie.

"Huh?"

"You said, 'We scored a run.' Are you becoming a Haysi girl?"

There was a twinkle in her eye. "I don't know, sweetie. I did marry a Haysi man, didn't I?"

TWENTY FIVE

One Month Later

Tony Ward put his elbows on the picnic table and stared across at his former partner. "You know, man, maybe you need to run for sheriff." He laughed. "It might keep you and Cons out of trouble.

Carter leaned back and laughed. "Well, let's see, I can knock on car windows and shine my light at teenagers making out behind Food City, or I can solve murder cases in nudist parks by going undercover with my beautiful wife in swingers' clubs. I can spend hours trying to track down some lowlife who robbed a convenience store, or I can be stalked by my sexy high school girlfriend while bringing down one of the biggest drug operations in the U.S." He wiped his mouth with his napkin, stuck it in his now empty Long John Silver's box, and took a sip of his soda through the straw. "The pay ain't that good, but I can eat breakfast at noon. I ain't had to answer to the chief in nearly a year, I ain't had to fill out the first damn report, or beg a judge for a search warrant. I've solved three murders with the sexiest partner I've ever had, no offense, man. Nah, I think I'll stay retired."

"I know it's Cons, but is she really sexier than me, man?" laughed Tony. "But in all seriousness, those folks back there could use you. What was it, half the sheriff's department went down in that sting? I even hear rumors that Hamilton is thinking about running again, saying the county needs some stability in its law enforcement."

"Hamilton? Stability? Hell, they need some real change. Bill Roland is a good man. He saved my ass, you know. He'll do a good job as sheriff." Carter thought for a moment. "I can't imagine Hamilton ever winning another term. But if he does run against Roland, I'll haul Bill's ass to the campaign rallies myself."

"You never know about politics, man. Marion Berry won another term. Mark Sanford is in Congress. You wait. I'll bet Weiner and Spitzer end up back in office at some point. Just wait and see. A lot of people vote for a lot of bad guys."

"I'll campaign for him then, how's that?"

"I'd feel better if you ran for sheriff, Carter. Face facts. Bill may be a great guy, but you are the best man for the job."

"But Tones, if I won, I'd have to leave you," Carter said, feigning homosexuality. "And you know I could never leave you." He laughed. "Besides, my official job now is to give you hell. Says so on my business card. And that I intend to do to the best of my ability."

"And you're damn good at it, man. If I can't talk you into running for sheriff, what's next for you and Cons?"

"I don't know. I thought about something easy, something relaxing, like hiking the Appalachian Trail, riding a bicycle across America, or paddling a canoe to Europe."

The two men stood, picked up their trash, deposited it in the park's can, and walked to the yellow Chrysler TC by Maserati, parked with the top down. "Whatever you do, ol' Tony here wants to hear all the details, okay?"

"You got it, man. But right now, I've got to start my new career as a consultant for self-published comic books."

"Oh, meeting with the Cyber Ranger, huh?"

"Yeah, I promised Martin an exclusive in exchange for his help. He says this thing could be his biggest series yet. You know, the SOB told me he's expecting to make nearly a hundred grand this year self-publishing comic books online? A hundred grand. In his spare time."

"Why does he keep teaching?"

"He says he wants other kids to have the same chances in life he did. He feels if it hadn't been for a high school technology teacher, he would never have got into computers. He owes it to the kids to make sure they have an example to follow, someone to identify with. One day he asked me, 'if not me, who?' I just looked at him. He was right, you know."

Tony looked Carter in the eye. "Remember that, man. If not you, who?"

Carter decided it wasn't time to reopen that conversation. He opened the door and sat down in the convertible. "It's funny. He writes about a Walker, Cyber-Ranger, but he's the real super hero. And he doesn't even know it."

"Kind of reminds me of Carter and Connie Sykes," Tony said. "I don't think you guys know how much you two have done for this town over the last three decades."

"I don't know about that, man. We just do our part, that's all." Carter turned the key and the modified 2.2 liter Maserati engine came to life. "I'll see you later, man." Carter moved the shifter into reverse and backed out of the parking spot. Moving it into first gear, he turned the volume knob on the TC's Infinity stereo and Molly Hatchet's "Flirtin' with Disaster" filled the air as the front wheels of the pseudo-classic emitted a small chirp when he caught second.

****

"Have you got anything to do this evening, babe?" Carter asked Connie when he picked her up from her lunch date with her friend Jenny.

"No, not really. Why?"

"Actually, I thought about running up to Haysi. Thought I might surprise Mother."

"Carter Sykes making an impromptu trip? No planning? What spurred this?"

"I don't know," he fibbed a little. "It's just something I think I ought to do, that's all."

"Hmm, something's up, but, hey, I'm not going to question it. I'm in. It'll be fun to take a ride in the TC with the top down."

Carter ginned. "Yeah, it'll be fun on those winding mountain roads."

Two hours later, they crept down the dirt road leading to Sylvie Sykes' house. Carter cringed each time he hit a pothole or heard a rock fly up against the underside of his prized car. Sadie wagged her tail and greeted them as they walked down the path to the porch. Without knocking, Carter opened the screen door and yelled, "Mom, you in here?"

"Carter?" she called out from the kitchen. "I didn't expect you." She walked into the living room. "Is everything okay?"

"Everything's fine mom," he said, giving his mother a hug. "Connie and I just thought we'd come up for a few minutes and say hello. How are you?"

"I'm fine. Things are settling down after all the uproar last time you were up."

"I'm glad. That was too much excitement for this little town. How's Tanya? And Ben?"

"Tanya's doing pretty good, all things considered. Ben's trying, that's all I'm going to say at this point, he's trying."

"Where is he?"

"He moved out. He found a trailer close to town. Bill Roland helped him get a part time job down at the Pizza Parlor. Can you imagine that, the cops helping your brother out?"

"With Bill I can, Connie said. "I'm glad to hear he's doing better. Has he heard anything about..." she paused.

"Going to jail?" Sylvie finished her sentence. "I don't think he'll have to. They're giving him immunity because he's helping the police put Mousey, Junior, and Cecil away."

"I'm glad," Carter said. "After he helped save me, I'd hate to see him back behind bars."

"Hey, let's call him and Tanya and have them come over for supper this evening. It'll be good to have the whole family over again."

A huge grin crossed Carter's face. "Sounds good to me."

Connie looked at her husband. "Mom, you know he ain't turnin' down food. I'll help you cook."

Everyone, including Connie, who was not able to pass up a second piece of cherry pie, ate too much. After another hour of visiting on the front porch, Ben announced he needed to get going; he had to go to work tomorrow. Since he rode with Tanya and the kids, they all said their goodbyes and drove off in the minivan as dusk settled into the mountains. Clouds from the west darkened the sky, making it seem later than it really was.

"I think I'm going to take a walk in the woods," Carter announced. "I need to do something to walk off all this food."

"Carter, it's going to storm," Sylvie warned him. "And it's almost dark."

"I'm not going to be gone long, mom, I just need to stretch a little bit before the ride back home."

"You can stay here tonight. I've got your old bed made up."

Carter glanced at Connie and thought for a moment. They had been married for over three decades and had never made love in his old bedroom. Was this his chance to check something off his 'dirty things I'd like to do' list? He shook his head, more to talk himself out of it than to respond to his mother's offer. "No, mom, I want to get back home tonight. I just want to take a quick walk in the woods. I'll be back."

"Take Sadie with you, then. It'll do her some good to get out there, too."

"Come on, Sadie," he called to the Border Collie mix and they began their trek. Together, they climbed the hill to the knoll containing the Sykes family cemetery. Carter opened the gate in the chain link fence, walked inside, and stopped at the fresh grave with the tombstone that read "Andy Calhoun." Sadie lay by his left foot as he bowed his head and began to move it slowly from side to side. "It didn't have to be this way, man. Tanya and the kids need you. They are going to miss you, Andy. Hell, I'm going to miss you and the stupid shit you pulled. The whole damn town will miss that." A soft laugh escaped his lips. "Worst of all, the world will never experience the smell of Clean Pig bacon scented soap." It took a long moment for his mind to clear before his thought process continued. "But, if it makes any difference to you now, we got the SOBs who did this, just like I promised. In the end, your death will bring a lot of good to a lot of people in this county, bro. It wasn't all in vain."

Carter took a deep breath and stepped to his left, causing Sadie to scurry under his feet. Stopping first at his grandmother's, and then his grandfather's graves, he bowed his head before each of them, silently paying his respects. A smile crossed his face as memories ran through his mind, a blur of things from his past. Each seemed so real, so eternal in the split second it took to play in his head. He recalled his grandfather taking preschool Carter to the field with him, taking a preteen Carter to town to eat until his heart was content and his stomach was bursting. His grandmother letting a teenage Carter drive her Plymouth station wagon after they turned down the dirt road. A tear ran from his eye as he thanked each of them for the love they showed him during his life.

As he heard thunder rumble over Kentucky in the western sky, he moved further to his left, crossing the empty plot left for Sylvie, and stood before the grave with the stone that read "Eugene Daniel Sykes." He again bowed his head and tears began to flow from his eyes. "I got him, Dad," he sobbed as he spoke. "It took me a long time, but I finally got him." Carter got down on one knee and patted Sadie on her head as she sat beside him. "I was scared, Dad; scared shitless. For a while, I thought I was going to be joining you here in this graveyard. I thought Mousey Rasnick was going to kill us both. But we got him, Dad, Connie and I got him. The motherfucker's behind bars now, where he'll spend the rest of his miserable life." He stood and turned to face the house, looking off into the distance, seeing a flash of lightning. "I've always missed you, Dad. I've always wished you were here. I needed a father, someone to talk to, someone to bounce things off of, a man to help me make decisions." He turned back toward the tombstone. "Why the hell did you have to give a damn about Junior Rasnick? You would still be here if you had just let him go and

253

focused on me, Ben, and Tanya. God knows Ben could have used your guidance."

Carter put his hands over his eyes, hung his head, and tried in vain to wipe the tears. He looked up when he heard another low rumble of thunder, this one louder, moving in from Kentucky. He looked down at the headstone. "Damnit, Dad, why? Why weren't we enough?"

His eye caught a flash of lightning in the air, and he looked back at the grave marker as the next rumble began, closer this time. "Because he was my son," a voice, his father's voice, which Carter assumed was in his mind, replied. "You know I would have done the same thing for you, Carter."

As Carter pondered the words and wondered where they came from, the voice continued. "You've done good, son; better than I ever did. I'm proud of you. But I have it from a good source that your job's not finished yet. You and Connie still have work to do. By the way, you got a good one when you got her."

Carter stood and stepped back as another rumble of thunder rolled across the sky, this one louder still, bringing the first drops of rain with it. "Yeah, Dad, I know. I'm a lucky man to have Connie."

Darkness now engulfed the hilltop until another flash of lightning illuminated the sky, followed a second later by a roar of thunder. Sadie began dancing nearby and Carter heard another voice. This one he recognized as his grandmother's.

"Feel the power," she told him. "Feel the power of this land, Carter." Again the lightning flashed, but Carter didn't hear the thunder. "I felt it. Your mother felt it after Gene died. It's why we never left these mountains, Carter. It's why you couldn't go far, why you couldn't take those big jobs you were offered. You knew the power in these hills. Now it's your turn to feel the power, to know this is where you belong."

The rain began to fall harder, but Carter stood in the hilltop graveyard, getting wetter by the second. But even as the storm cooled the air, he didn't become chilled. Instead, he was filled with warmth. Not just warmth, but heat; a heat he had never felt before. It was hotter than last summer's heat wave in South Carolina.

A chorus of voices filled the air, voices of his departed family. "Feel the power, Carter. This is our land. This is your land."

Carter pulled his shirt over his head, and then removed his shoes and socks, feeling the ground under his feet. Another flash of lightning, this one seemingly over his head, lit up the night sky. The thunder was immediate, and deafening. Carter removed his shorts and underwear, hung them over the chain link fence, and stood there, naked, as the next flash of lightning came from the clouds. "Feel the power of these hills."

"I feel the power," he called out. "I feel the power of this land."

He had no idea how long he stood there in the storm as streak after streak of lightning fell from the clouds to the ground around him, like it was energizing the dirt. Sadie danced through the small graveyard as Carter stood there, staring into the distance. He didn't see the flashlight as Connie approached.

"What in the hell are you doing?" she yelled from outside the fence. "It's storming like crazy."

"Can't you feel it, babe?" he asked calmly. "Can't you feel the power in this storm? In the air? In the ground? In these ancient hills?"

"No, but you're going to get your ass fried by this lightning. Come on. Let's get back to the house."

"You've got to feel this, Cons. You've got to feel this power. Take off your clothes."

Connie gave him a puzzled look. Had her husband gone mad? Another streak of lightning landed mere feet from him, raising the hair on her arms.

"Take off your clothes. Remove all barriers to the elements. Feel the power in these hills, Cons."

Connie shook her head. "What the hell," she said, as she removed Sylvie's raincoat and laid it over the fence. She turned off the flashlight. "We've done some strange things, Carter, but this might just be the strangest. But if you're going to get yourself killed out here, I might as well go with you," she muttered, removing the rest of her now soaked clothing. She walked inside the fence and took her husband's hand. "Oh my God!" she exclaimed, as another bolt of lightning hit beside them, followed by its thunder. "This is awesome."

Time faded as they stood there, holding hands as one, until the storm ended. They turned, faced each other, arms by their sides, hands laced together. Carter looked down into his wife's eyes. "Did you feel it, babe?"

"Yeah, I felt it. What was it?"

"I'm not sure I know," he answered honestly. "All I know is my grandmother told me to feel the power of these hills and I could not pull away. When you showed up, I knew you had to be part of this, because you are part of me." Carter took a long, deep breath. "For the first time in my life, I feel like these old mountains are really our home."

255

"Connie released his hands and took two steps backwards. She scanned her husband from head to toe. A smile broke out across her face. "Sweetie, it looks to me like we're barely home."

About The Author

Adam Lawler was raised in the small town of Clintwood, Virginia, located in the Central Appalachian coalfields. He was both the son and grandson of coal miners, but was fortunate to have a family who valued education and instilled a desire for learning in him at an early age. After graduating from high school, he attended Coastal Carolina Community College, then returned back to the hills himself to earn a bachelors degree in History and a masters degree in Appalachian Studies at Appalachian State University.

At Coastal Carolina, Adam met the most important person in his life, his wife and life partner, Karen. Together, they settled in West Jefferson, North Carolina and raised three children; Cyndi, Wayne, and Rachel. Today, Adam and Karen are empty nesters in West Jefferson, sharing their home with Adam's guide dog, a Doberman Pinscher named Freyja.

Professionally, Adam's love for cars led to him spending over twenty years in the retail automotive business. He also taught classes in History and Southern Culture at the community college level. When type 1 diabetes took most of his vision, Adam refused to sit on the couch and give up his dreams. As the recession began to release its grip on America, he returned to work, first as a Customer Service Representative and later as a Business Development Coordinator at a local auto dealership. He published his first novel, *Barely Retired*, in 2014.

Adam's future plans include writing more novels as he, Karen, and Freyja tour the country in a RV, discovering parts of the country of which they have only read and dreamed. Adam's hobbies include ham radio (he holds the call sign WK4P) bicycling (he and Karen have a tandem), hiking (although the trails have become less rugged), and reading.

Hearing from his readers always brings a smile to Adam's face, and he tries to reply personally to each one who contacts him. See the "Contact" section below to get in touch with him.

Previously Published by Adam Lawler

Barely Retired (Barely #1)

Future Projects

Barely Running (Barely #3)

Snow Day (Penny's Law #1)

Killer Bees (Penny's Law #2)

Riding America

The Women of the Dollar General Store of Fingerville, South Carolina

How to Contact Adam Lawler

If you enjoy his novels, please contact Adam, he loves to hear from his readers.

Email: cqwk4p@yahoo.com
Facebook: https://www.facebook.com/adam.lawler.3382

Please keep in mind that Adam is an independent author, choosing to publish his novels himself, without the support of expensive and time-consuming processes devised by the big publishing houses. Without establishment budgets and backing, he counts on his readers to tell others about his novels, hoping they will like his stories well enough to recommend them to their friends and family. If you have enjoyed one of Adam's novels, please consider taking a few moments reviewing the book on the site where you purchased it, and on other online reader forums, such as Goodreads, in which you may participate. Recommending Adam's novels is the highest compliment you can give him, and it is very much appreciated.

5-6-15

AW

18814125R00158

Made in the USA
Middletown, DE
24 March 2015